I0706082

The Silver Seamripper

The Taiga, Book 2

T.J. Carroll

Cumberstone Press

To C
To G
To R

You are my sunshine

CONTENTS

Chapter 1

Dashi crouched in the shadow of the ruined building. She couldn't see her quarry yet but, with the strange prescience that only exists in dreams, she was certain he was near.

Hunting for her, as she hunted for him.

The thought made her palms clammy in a way that few things did. Moonlight cut through the clouds, sharp and silver, and suddenly Dashi saw him. He was already at the crumbling wall, already within arm's reach of the secret she'd worked so hard to keep hidden. Somehow, she'd missed him moving.

"How did you get past me?" she asked, sliding an arrow back. The smell of charred wood and damp earth filled her nostrils. "Answer me, Sevlin."

Instead of answering, Sevlin knelt in front of the gnarled tree and reached into the exposed roots. The bow felt like a branding iron in her hand. Dashi knew what was needed: a killing shot. If Sevlin found the golden needle then he was a danger to Idree, yet she couldn't bring her fingers to let the arrow go.

"*Stop it*." Dashi took a step sideways, trying to see how far he'd dug. He kept his face averted, though she could see the edge of the scar that carved into the meat of his left cheek. He kept digging, pulling out the rocks that she'd wedged into the roots and thumping them onto the ground, one after another.

"If you don't stop, I'll—"

The arrow was flying before she'd finished speaking, though she was certain she hadn't released it. Sevlin pitched forward into the tree, crane feathers protruding from between his shoulder blades. His cheek rasped against the bark as he slid slowly down the trunk.

"*Sevlin.*" Dashi squatted next to him. Her hand hovered over the arrow. "I didn't want to...I didn't mean..."

"Didn't you?"

The voice should have startled Dashi. For one thing, it came from behind her, where there had been no one moments ago. For another, it belonged to a dead man.

Baris curled a heavy arm around Dashi's shoulders, pulling her upright and against his side. She barely came up to his chest. That part was accurate, dream or not.

"Best shot on Ejen's guard force. Don't think I haven't noticed." Baris' grin was sly. "*You* never miss. If you hit him, it's because you meant to." He looked at someone over Dashi's head and raised an eyebrow in question.

"Acts first, thinks second," a second voice said. The tone was affectionate, the phrase worn from fond repetition. "Even after all this time."

Dashi spun out from under Baris' arm so she could stare at Altan. The moonlight made his hair look white and ancient, but his smile was undimmed.

"I never did cure you of that," Altan said, "but plunging forward recklessly seems to work for you."

"Why shouldn't she plunge? There's no challenge in walking when you were born to gallop, eh Dashi?" Baris ruffled her hair. His touch was lighter than it should have been, more like the breeze than solid flesh and bone.

Zayaa stepped out of the shadows. Unlike the men, who were shaded in silvers and grays, Zayaa's face was vivid, full of the luscious beauty that Dashi always associated with her. She smiled at Dashi, an expression so dazzling that Dashi couldn't help but beam back. *All of them. Together again.*

Altan's demeanor changed abruptly, from indulgent to grimly omniscient. "Don't trust it," he said.

"Don't trust what?" Dashi asked.

"This." He gestured around them and Dashi wasn't sure if he meant the place she'd chosen to hide the needle or the dream itself. "Anything."

"He's coming," said Baris. Like Altan, his expression had become heavy. "Be on your guard, fighter."

But he's already here, Dashi thought. *I shot him.* She glanced involuntarily at the tree and started.

Sevlin's body was gone.

A dark hole gaped at her from between the twisted tree roots. The golden needle was gone too.

Dashi jerked awake, chest heaving, face slick. She was up and moving a few seconds later, her boots and a sheathed knife in one hand and her bow in the other. Idree didn't stir, but Dashi wasn't worried about leaving her sister unprotected. Ejen's walls would keep out raiders, and the real threat to Idree couldn't be stopped with a few arrows and a barred gate anyway.

It was easy enough to leave Ejen, the town in Thracedon where she and Idree had been living for the past year. The walls were made for keeping people out, not in, and the guards' eyes were trained on the rocky hills, searching for raiders. Dashi dropped from the wall and rolled into her landing, slithering through the tall grass until she got to a rock formation she could hide behind. She was good at sneaking; no one would see her in the night.

The desire to check on the golden needle—to touch the statuette that housed it and reassure herself that it was safe, that *Idree* was safe—was a tangible thing. Dashi could feel it in her fingers, tight on her bow, and in the way she kept rewetting her lips. She'd tried to destroy the needle on more than one occasion. Gold was a soft metal, after all, and through a combination of heat and force, she *should* have been able to beat it into a new shape. No matter how long she labored, the dents left by the hammer evaporated between one blow and the next, leaving the needle whole and smirking up at her. Dashi sometimes wondered if she should have left the thing in the taiga, buried in an unmarked grave. But she couldn't stand the idea of not knowing where it was, of not being able to reassure herself that the threat to her sister lay slumbering and untouched.

She'd chosen a middle course: a hiding place near enough to visit when she was feeling insecure, but not so close that it burdened her every thought. Hiding the needle outside of town had other strategic benefits as well. Since Dashi and Idree were foreigners, Ejen's residents could evict them without notice. If that happened, or if the town walls ever fell and they were forced to flee, Dashi could collect the golden needle on her way out.

After a brisk walk, Dashi reached the dilapidated hut. It had been partially burned during Thracedon's civil war and a nearby pine had been quick to take advantage, sending its gnarled roots to conquer the southern wall. Yet the hut still stood. That appealed to Dashi. So did its resemblance to the Purek ruins she'd once explored with her friends. A branch creaked behind her and she froze, bristling with all the fear and possessiveness of a wolf guarding a kill, before finally deeming it safe to ease inside.

As always when she awoke obsessive and terrified, Dashi went straight to the tree roots that ate into the southern wall, just as Sevlin had in her dream. Reaching between layers of roots, she pulled out smooth river rocks, making a neat stack that reached calf height. Dashi never brought the statuette out. She had an almost superstitious aversion to the cursed thing and no desire to see its hawkish visage. The face of Khagan Nuray haunted her dreams enough as it was. Instead, she stuck her arm into the hole, fingers questing through the dirt and root hairs until they brushed cool metal. The statuette buzzed dully, as the golden needle, agitated by Idree's relative proximity, vibrated inside. Dashi's shoulders sagged in relief.

That was the real value of the statuette: not its golden exterior, but the magical needle it concealed. It was the reason Dashi could never breathe a word of the statuette's existence to anyone, even her sister.

Especially her sister.

The golden needle was an artifact, a powerful holdover from the ancient Pureks, from a time when veins of magic coursed through the land. Using the needle, magic could be stitched to a person, delivering either a painful death or, if the person was lucky enough to survive, incredible powers. Only one person could wield the golden needle at a time: the seamstress. *Idree*.

The problem lay not so much in Idree's exceptionality but in the people who would want to use her. Seamstresses had no real power of their own, only the ability to confer it to others, and they'd been manipulated and abused for centuries by whoever happened to be ruling. As Dashi saw it, being the seamstress was more curse than blessing, and she had no intention of allowing it to befall her sister. Although Dashi had survived the khan's race and recovered the golden needle, she'd decided to forego the hefty reward in favor of keeping her prize hidden. She'd told Idree and Sevlin, her erstwhile ally in the race, that the needle had been lost during the fight with Negan, the khan's consul. Had Idree known the truth, she would only have fretted over the danger. Sevlin would have wanted to bring the golden needle back to the Tyvalan queen and Dashi couldn't bring herself to trust anyone else with Idree's future.

Satisfied that everything was as it should be, Dashi wedged the rocks back into place. *Just another dream*, she told herself. *Everything is fine.*

She was still chanting those words when she pulled herself back over Ejen's wall. Reentry required substantially more skill than leaving, but she'd been careful. She thought.

"Another midnight excursion?"

The voice spoke in Thracedonian, but it sounded more amused than irritated, which was a good sign. Sener was the most popular of the shift captains, always ready with a quick smile or joke, but when it came to Ejen's security, there was little room for levity.

Dashi finished coiling her grappling hook before turning around. Sener leaned against the base of the watchtower, the shadows making him look bulkier than he was. One hand rested casually on his sword.

"*You* know I have nightmares," she said in Thracedonian. "Sometimes I need to move around after." Referencing the nights they'd spent together in his barracks room was a cheap trick, but Dashi had never been above those.

"And *you* know I'm supposed to report curfew breakers. Especially guards who are leaving the city without authorization. Such a person might be suspected of being in league with raiders."

Dashi rolled her eyes. "You Ejeners think every foreigner is trying to sack your town."

"You probably would have tried to sack Ejen if we hadn't invited you to stay instead."

"All the more reason not to report me now." Dashi leaned one hip against the wall, close enough to feel the heat from his body, and surreptitiously dried her palms on her pants. "Ejen still needs my bow, just like it did then."

Sener huffed and she knew he was rolling his eyes. "Your invitation was based on the novelty of your companions. We'd never seen a horse as ugly as Spit or a girl as sweet as Idree. A rude older sister was just an afterthought."

Dashi snorted. Sener's teeth flashed as he grinned, pleased at her reaction.

"At least you're not bloody this time," he said.

Dashi heard the question he was carefully not asking. "What are you doing on duty now?" she asked, changing the subject. Sener's regular shift had ended hours ago.

"Uzbruk's wife went into labor early so I was called back for a double." Sener stifled a yawn. "Stay and talk to me, Dashi, or I'll fall asleep and let the whole place be overrun by bandits." It was part truth and part lie. Sener would never fall asleep on duty—his dependability was one of the reasons he'd been made shift captain at such a young age—but Dashi could tell he wanted her to stay anyway.

She hesitated, not wanting Idree to wake up and find her gone. "Only for a little while," she said, deciding she was too keyed up to sleep anyway. "Then you're on your own with the bandits."

Sener hung his arm around her shoulders. It wasn't as heavy as Baris' had once been and his smile wasn't as familiar as Altan's, but he chased away the remnants of the cold panic nonetheless.

Chapter 2

Idree had chosen their cottage because of the summer roses, which clung to the whitewashed walls, perfuming the evening air. *Dashi* had chosen it because the yard had scalable fruit trees abutting the city walls. After a stint in Karak City's prison, she didn't like the idea of walls around her unless she could easily visualize a way out.

She didn't miss Karakal. It was difficult to romanticize a place where she'd either be dead or in jail, and Dashi's thoughts usually faced forward anyway. Her sister, however, was prone to lingering glances over her shoulder, metaphorically speaking. Idree'd had a harder time adjusting to their new home. The customs were different. The language was foreign. The people were at once too wary and too curious. Still, Idree had survived. *They'd* survived. Now, a year later, Ejen was their home. If they didn't speak Thracedonian like the natives did, they were passable, and if they made the occasional cultural misstep, their new neighbors swept it aside with a laugh and a head shake.

Dashi stepped into their small yard, singing a Thracedonian song under her breath.

"I met a girl, wild and strong...said she was the daughter of a bandit band..."

A black and white goat appeared beside the cottage, straining against its tether. Whistling, Dashi pulled up the stake and moved the goat to an uneaten portion of the yard.

Idree's dark head poked out of the cottage's door, her face lit up with a smile. "I thought you might have to work late."

Dashi grinned and shook her head. "I'm off until tomorrow night."

"You can come to the harvest festival then!"

Dashi followed her sister back into the cottage, raising her eyebrows when she saw what Idree was doing. "You're making cheese? Tonight?"

Idree shrugged one shoulder. "The festival doesn't start until moonrise and we had the extra goat milk."

Dashi flopped into a chair, immediately rocking back to balance on two wooden legs. "I'm glad you talked me into getting that goat. She's been useful."

Idree frowned slightly, her concentration on arranging the cheesecloth evenly over the bowl. "I still don't see why we had to name her Clod."

"It's—"

"Mori tradition. I know. But just because we're half Mori doesn't mean we need to go around saddling things with awful names. Look at poor Spit."

"Spit likes his name."

"Pfff."

"Bat isn't any better," Dashi said, referring to Idree's mare.

"*I* didn't name her. That reminds me, her foreleg is healed. She was dying to get out today."

Dashi smiled. A year ago Idree would have hesitated to even approach a horse. Now she rode for pleasure. "Busy day making boots?"

Idree nodded enthusiastically. "Four customers before noon, all merchants here for the festival. I worked until my fingers cramped, but Onsmit said I did well. Actually," she looked up, dark eyes shining, "he said he's never had an apprentice who can fasten a sole so well. He said I can stitch the uppers soon."

Dashi smiled, covering the inward wince she felt when Idree said the word *stitch*. Idree had just started her apprenticeship with Ejen's bootmaker and she came home singing its praises every day.

"How's Sener?" Idree asked.

"Fine, I guess." He hadn't been pleased with her foray outside of Ejen's walls, but Sener was easygoing by nature and quickly mollified. "He had to work a double shift last night, but he has tonight off."

"You'll be seeing him at the festival?"

Dashi thought back to Sener's suggestively raised eyebrow when he'd asked if she was going. "Probably."

"It's getting around about the two of you. I heard Marah saying Ejen had one less eligible bachelor since we'd arrived. She seemed to think Sener would be taking himself off the market for good soon."

Dashi drew back slightly. "Not with me, he won't."

Idree's eyebrows lowered. "What's wrong with Sener? I like him."

"Nothing's wrong with him. He's fine."

"He's attractive and friendly and has a good job." Idree dropped a dirty dish into a basin of water. "And he doesn't make you mad."

"He doesn't make me mad," Dashi conceded. "So what?"

"So you should think about settling down."

"Settling down? Ancestors above, Idree, are you my sister or my grandmother?"

"I don't mean having a litter of babies but—"

"*Babies?*" Dashi's chair rocked forward, the front two legs slamming down hard.

"—you should think about where you'd like to be—"

"I'd like to be right here." Dashi tried for a patient voice. "Or wherever," she waved her hand to indicate the world on the other side of the cottage walls, "we decide to go."

Idree clamped her lips shut, spooning curds from the cheesecloth. A few years ago, Dashi might have left it at that, but she knew Idree a little better now.

"What's this about?"

Silence. Finally, Idree said, "Just let me know if you're planning to leave."

"Planning to leave for *where*? You were just talking about me settling down, not leaving."

Splat. Another spoonful of curds dropped into the bowl. "Planning to leave *me*, Dashi."

"I'm not leaving you for Sener."

"Not just for Sener." Idree's hands stilled, but she didn't raise her eyes. "Him or someone else. Some*thing* else. I woke up last night and you were gone and I started thinking—"

"I couldn't sleep." The answer came out a little too quickly, but Idree didn't seem to notice.

"I just don't want to be the last to know."

"Idree." Dashi laid her palms flat on the table, right in front of Idree, so that her sister couldn't help but see them. "No one is going anywhere unless we both agree. I promise."

"Alright." Idree's hands were moving again, meticulously scraping the cheesecloth.

Dashi leaned back cautiously, still watching Idree. "I like it here. I know you don't believe me, but I do."

"It must be boring for you. There aren't any ruins to explore, no adventures to go on."

"Raiders attack regularly. That's always exciting." Dashi narrowed her eyes at a sudden thought. "Is this why you were so upset about the Yassari boots? You thought I was getting bored here?"

"Well, you did go back to stealing things. It seemed like the logical reason."

"I stole *one* thing. Anyway, I told you: I had a score to settle with the Yassaris. *Have.* I don't think a pair of boots makes up for being forced to wear an explosive belt."

"They didn't make you wear it."

"They invented it. They knew it would be worn by someone."

Idree shrugged. "Call it even. They were crawling all over Ejen for days looking for the thief. The only reason you didn't get caught is because Sener kept his mouth shut." She gave Dashi a pointed look, as if to say she was mentally adding that to his list of attributes.

When Dashi'd heard that a Yassari caravan was approaching Ejen, she knew she would do *something*. They were the inventors of pyrothrite, the highly explosive granules that had been locked around Dashi's waist as a means of forcing her to retrieve the golden needle. Technically, it was a Karak noble who'd put the explosive belt on her, but practicality beat culpability: the Yassaris were nearby and the Karak noble wasn't. It was easier to make them pay.

Truth be told, Dashi *had* been a little bored. Stealing from the secretive inventors had been more difficult than anticipated, however, and she'd arrived to her shift an hour late and injured. Sener had covered for her tardiness and refrained from mentioning her wound, even though there was no way he'd missed the blood. When the Yassaris arrived the next day, making threats and waving reward money around like an incense offering, Dashi had waited for Sener to step forward. He hadn't moved.

"Let's look at them again," Idree said, startling Dashi.

"For someone who was so angry about me taking the cursed things, you're the one who always wants to drag them out."

"I'm a bootmaker's apprentice," Idree said primly. "It's professional curiosity."

Laughing, Dashi pushed her chair against the wall and swung up to the rafters. She shimmied along one of the beams before reaching a loose spot in the thatched roof. The boots dropped into Idree's waiting arms.

"You'll never be able to recreate them," Dashi said, landing lightly beside her sister. "Not without Yassari help. And I've heard they never share information."

"*I* heard they can always tell who stole from them and that their inventions catch fire if someone tries to copy them."

"Well, we know the first isn't true; they didn't find me when they came through. And if you think the boots are going to self-destruct, then stop looking at them like that." Dashi flicked Idree's finger away from the soft calf leather.

"I'm not trying to figure them out," Idree protested. "I'm just appreciating them." She flipped the boot upside down so that the sole faced the light.

The bottoms appeared innocuous enough: sturdy brown soles with even stitches lining the perimeter. *You'd never know they were anything special,* Dashi thought, like she did every time they examined the boots. But as Idree dragged her fingertips over the sole, the surface rippled, cupping Idree's fingers in an effort to hold onto them. Idree pulled her fingers back and the tiny bowl-shaped ridges froze, alert, waiting to see what else touched them. When nothing did, they slowly relaxed, smoothing back into unremarkable, flat leather.

Idree shivered. "I never get used to that."

Dashi nodded wordlessly.

"They're handsome boots," Idree remarked, turning the boot. Decorative red stitching swooped across the leather uppers, each swirl creating a picture of a fantastical bird, one with horns, another with two sets of eyes. "Do you think these birds are real? On their island, I mean."

"Who knows?" Dashi said, focused less on Yassari fauna and more on the practical implications of boots that could alter their traction. They would try to grip a slippery surface—ice, for instance—but what if the wearer *wanted* to slide?

"Look," Idree said, pointing. "This one's beak looks like a trumpet."

"We need to experiment with them," Dashi said at the same time. "Maybe I should wear them tonight." She wondered what they'd feel like, gripping the ground while she leapt and spun at the festival. Probably she should climb something in them. The watchtower, or—

"What? No! Someone will notice them."

"It's a special occasion! What's the point of having boots I can't wear?"

"You should have thought of that before you stole them," Idree said firmly, taking both boots. "The Yassaris have only been gone a month and they made it clear their reward stands. If we traveled somewhere, that would be one thing—it's not like that caravan could have alerted the whole continent—but people *here* will notice."

Scowling a little, Dashi took the boots from her sister and pulled herself back into the rafters.

"That red sash I made last month would look good with your blue deel," Idree called from below. When Dashi didn't answer, she added, "Sener will like it."

"We're not talking about Sener again," Dashi grumbled, dropping to the cottage floor.

"Fine," Idree agreed. "Let's talk about the harvest festival. It's almost time and you smell like horse."

Dashi sniffed at her guard uniform experimentally. "I always smell like horse."

"Change."

Festivals in Thracedon were much like festivals in Karakal: whirling and stomping dances, wild fiddle reels, and free-flowing mead and wine. The songs were in Thracedonian, not Karakalese, and there were no goathead matches, a vicious horseback sport that Dashi loved. Otherwise, the atmosphere was similar.

Lanterns, covered in bright, filmy cloth, glowed like strange moons. The beat of the goblet drums thrummed against Dashi's skin. She pulled Idree past laden tables and rows of idling elders, to the dancers parading in concentric circles. Idree pointed to an opening in the outer ring and then they were in: arms linked, palms touching, stomping and spinning along with scores of other feet. Idree and Dashi wove in and out of the other pairs, alternately clapping and kicking their feet together.

The song ended on a twanging note a few minutes later and Dashi leaned over, her breath stolen by laughter. When she straightened Idree was watching her, a crooked grin on her face. Neither girl held a drink, but Idree raised an imaginary glass in a toast.

"To Thracedon," she said in Karakalese.

"To Thracedon," Dashi echoed, smiling.

Another song began, the first notes promising something even faster and more breathless than the last, just as someone grabbed Dashi's hand. She looked up to see Sener, his easy smile directed first toward Idree, then at her.

"Dance?" he asked.

"Next one." Dashi tilted her head toward Idree. "I've already been claimed."

"Ah, you're a popular one." Sener's eyes drifted toward the crowd.

"No, it's fine," Idree said quickly, giving Dashi a conspiratorial look. "You two, dance. Marah was beckoning to me anyway."

Dashi frowned at her sister's transparent attempts at matchmaking, but Idree was already turning away. Dashi stood for a moment, watching her sister's head, a flash of black in a sea of color, before turning back to Sener's waiting arms.

Chapter 3

Sunlight streamed through the barracks window, pushing past the tatty curtains and through Dashi's eyelids. She groaned and slung her arm over her face, trying to return to the peaceful darkness. Usually, she was up at dawn, some impulse or another making it impossible to sleep late, but the previous night—fast and raucous and full of laughter—had stretched well into the morning and it felt like she'd closed her eyes only minutes ago. Her head pounded. Her mouth felt cracked from thirst.

Sener slumbered beside her, oblivious. Slowly, so as not to aggravate her head, Dashi eased into a sitting position. She dressed, fingers stumbling, and closed the door softly behind her without bothering to say goodbye. Stepping outside of the barracks building, she stifled another groan at the light and managed to raise a hand in greeting to Ejen's bootmaker, who was standing outside his shop, brushing off some leather.

"Fair day, Onsmit," she called, squinting in his general direction.

"Fair day?" His voice was gruff. "Your sister have a thick head like everyone else this morning?"

"Not that I know of."

"She didn't show up today and we have three orders due by the end of the week," Onsmit growled. "Idree might be young, but I thought she seemed different than my last apprentice. *He* ran away after he got the tanner's daughter with child." He shot Dashi a withering look, apparently blaming Idree for that too.

"I heard the miller's boy came down sick." The lie unspooled smoothly. "Probably Idree is the same. I'll check on her."

"You do that." Onsmit turned back to his work, a curt dismissal.

Dashi's mouth settled into a frown as she strode away from Onsmit. She and Idree had danced countless rounds together at the festival. She'd deposited a visibly drooping Idree at their cottage a few hours before sunrise and, ignoring her sister's knowing look, stumbled off to find Sener.

The cottage looked snug and clean in the hazeless morning, everything just as they'd left it. Her sister's pallet lay unmade, a rolled deel beneath her pillow propping it at the angle she liked. The table was clean. Idree's porridge dish was still unused, neatly stowed in the cabinet. Dashi turned slowly, searching for any signs of her sister's morning routine.

A low groan from outside had her scrambling to the backyard, but it was only Clod, the goat, rubbing her bony forehead against the shed door and nagging to be let out. Mechanically, Dashi looped the tether around Clod's neck before staking her near some tall grass. The goat took a mouthful, eying Dashi dolefully.

"Yes, yes, I know you like Idree better," Dashi muttered.

Clod bleated again, more insistently this time. Her udder hung heavy and full beneath her, an additional oddity to add to the pile. Idree always milked Clod first thing. Unease prickled Dashi's skin. She shook it off. Her old friend, Baris, had called that ominous feeling 'breath of the ancestors,' but she didn't have time for superstition right now.

Think, she told herself sternly. Idree had been laughing with her friend Marah just before she'd gone home. Maybe her sister had decided to go back out after Dashi had dropped her off. There was certainly no indication that anything worse had come to pass.

"I'll be back to milk you in a few minutes," she told the goat as she left. "With Idree."

Marah, the farmer's daughter, hadn't seen Idree since the previous night.

"Sure haven't," the girl said, propping her lanky frame against the henhouse she was cleaning. The smell of chicken dung and musty straw assailed Dashi while she waited for the rest of the answer.

"Did she mention any plans for today or where she might be going?"

Marah thought about this. "She talked about the shop, about how busy they were. I assumed she meant to work today.

"Did she seem at ease? Worried about anything?" Dashi's leg began to jiggle. The slower Marah talked, the more impatient she became.

"Well, she did mention how busy the shop was—"

"And you're *sure* you didn't see her again after we left? The two of you didn't make plans to sneak out later for a few cups?"

Marah considered this question carefully too and Dashi had the urge to shove her into the henhouse. "No," she said. "Idree doesn't care for wine or mead."

"Who danced with her? Who talked to her?"

"Mostly me and the other girls. My father danced with both of us and so did my younger brother."

"What about—"

"—I thought that man was going to ask her," Marah continued placidly, oblivious to Dashi's agitation, "and then I could tease Idree about dancing with a bald man, but he never did."

"What bald man?"

"He came up to her as I was going to get a drink. I'd never seen him before. When I looked again, he was gone and Idree was dancing with my brother."

Dashi's fidgeting stilled. "Anything else stand out about him?"

"He was bald, like I said, and broad. Lots of muscle. He looked friendly enough when he was talking to Idree though. He seemed to recognize her. I remember thinking maybe he'd seen her at the shop."

"Did you hear what he said to her?"

"He asked her about the festival. He talked funny." Marsh pronounced the Thracedonian word for festival, drawing out the vowels in an exaggeration of Idree and Dashi's Karakalese accent. "Like Idree but worse."

Dashi's heart stuttered in her chest.

Marah kept talking. "You could try Jerna. Idree danced with him a few times before she talked to that man."

"Thanks," Dashi muttered, but her mind was far away, roving the streets of Karak City, as she tried to place the stranger who'd been talking to Idree.

Dashi tried every one of Idree's acquaintances. No one had seen her sister after she'd left the festival. No one but Marah remembered her speaking to a bald, muscular man from Karakal. Dashi wanted to punch something. How could he have been at Ejen's harvest festival—among scores of suspicious townsfolk, no less—without being remembered?

She had better luck once she broadened her search. The ostler confirmed that he'd talked to the man, who'd inquired about buying a horse, but spent most of his time inspecting the guards' mounts. Remembering that Idree had mentioned selling boots to men from the merchant convoy, Dashi went to where their wagons were parked. The bald, muscular man wasn't lounging with the convoy guards, but one of them remembered meeting him two days ago when he'd asked about buying baked goods in Ejen. Another merchant reported that the man had been interested in acquiring antiquities and rare artwork.

Dashi raised a hand to her forehead and squeezed. In Karak City, she'd trafficked in ancient Purek artwork. Idree had worked at a bakery. Yesterday morning, when the stranger had visited the ostler, Spit had been stabled with the other guards' horses. She could no longer suppress her unease: these were all inquiries designed to find her and Idree. Someone had come for them, and she could only think of one reason why.

Her feet took her out of Ejen. She'd forgotten about her headache, though it still throbbed in the background of her consciousness. Her thoughts were fixed on Idree and the stranger and the enormity of her own stupidity. Why hadn't she stayed by Idree's side all night? Mead and dancing and a roll with Sener: that's what she'd traded her sister's safety for.

Dry-mouthed, Dashi slid down the slope to the derelict hut, not caring if anyone was watching from Ejen's walls. She'd thought she'd been prepared for what she would find, but the sight still hit her like a physical blow: carelessly discarded rocks and a gaping hole between the tree's roots.

Like Idree, the statuette that held the golden needle had vanished.

Chapter 4

Dashi was on the road, galloping toward Karakal, within the hour. She'd wanted to go immediately—to fly off on Spit without a second thought or a backward glance—but she made herself wait. She needed supplies. She needed weapons. She'd even dug up the money they kept buried beneath the goat shed, reasoning that once she found Idree they wouldn't be returning. Ejen was no longer safe. Upon this realization, Dashi climbed into the rafters to retrieve the stolen Yassari boots. She might as well wear them now.

She left the goat tethered to a neighbor's doorpost and then she was gone. No goodbyes. No ties. A year of her life, done. *Funny*, she thought. She'd started to think of Ejen as home and its residents as her neighbors and friends. When it came down to it, however, they were nothing. Only Idree mattered, and Dashi had already failed her.

The road out of Ejen was too busy to discern individual tracks, but Dashi pointed Spit toward Karakal without hesitation. That was where the stranger was from and that was where he would return. She could still salvage the situation, she told herself; she would intercept him before he reached Karak City and kill him. She and Idree would disappear again. The whereabouts of the needle and the knowledge that Idree was the seamstress need never reach Karak City.

The Karak-Thracedon border was riddled with bandits, but Dashi pushed forward, heedless. The deluge of tracks started to thin the farther north she went until there were only a few sets of recent tracks before her. She passed through a small town, whose single ramshackle street she remembered from the first time she and Idree had ridden through, on their way to Ejen. Encouraged by a few coins, the town's innkeeper admitted to seeing a bald man and a girl pass by.

"He was in a hurry. Wanted a second horse for the girl, but we don't have spares. Was about two hours ago. His horse won't be carrying them much farther at that speed, I wouldn't think," the innkeeper drawled. "Girl didn't talk much. Seemed scared. He kept a hold of her the whole time."

There was no point in asking why the innkeeper hadn't tried to help Idree. People in this part of the country survived by keeping their heads down, not by sticking them into others' business.

"No one else was with him?" she asked.

"Not unless they skirted town and met him on the other side." The innkeeper shrugged unconcernedly.

"Weapons?"

"Crossbow and sword, from what I saw."

Dashi flipped another coin to the innkeeper and remounted. Spit shook his head in protest, sending flecks of foam flying. Dashi kneed him forward anyway. Idree's mare followed gamely behind.

"C'mon, old man," she muttered to Spit. "Idree needs us. We'll rest later."

It was a lie. There would be no rest—for any of them—for a long time to come.

She switched mounts shortly after the town to give Spit a break. *A two-hour lead*, Dashi thought, smoothing the curve of her bow with

satisfaction. With only a single, tired horse, the stranger's lead would continue to dwindle.

The stranger had taken the needle along with her sister, which meant he'd somehow recognized their significance to each other. That meant he would keep Idree alive, Dashi reassured herself. The seamstress was simply too valuable to do otherwise. Living could come in many forms, however. What *condition* would her sister be in, that was the real question. She wondered if the man had told Idree why she'd been taken.

The road continued, threading between the hills that peppered the border. She spotted dark shapes blotting the horizon, weaving and dipping toward the earth. *Vultures.* Frowning, Dashi veered off the road, keeping a line of hills between her and the location of the scavengers. Her bow stayed ready. Her eyes searched for bandits. A breeze bounced between the hills, carrying with it the smell of heat-scorched grass and something sharper.

On a hill that overlooked the road, Dashi saw what had attracted the vultures: a body—much too large to be Idree's—its arms splayed wide. A horse swayed nearby, head pointed to the ground. It had been run nearly to the point of death.

Dashi let her breath out slowly. There was no ambush waiting; it had already taken place. A vulture hopped gracelessly away from the body as she approached, its feathered cowl rocking with each movement. It retreated to the top of one of the granite steles used to mark distances along the road. Dashi glanced at the stele, absently noting the chiseled lettering written in Karakalese instead of Thracedonian.

Karak City, 10 days ride.

She dismounted, growing more certain with each step: this was Idree's kidnapper. Not only did he fit the description of the stranger in Ejen, but she recognized his face, rendered stark beneath the recently shaved head and the even more recent pallor of death. *Osol.* He worked for the Karak noble who'd broken her out of prison and fitted her with an explosive belt, using it to force her to compete in the khan's race. Dashi stared, stupified. In her paranoid dreams, it had always been Sevlin who figured out the truth of the needle, who tracked her to Ejen. *Osol* should have assumed she was dead when she didn't return from the taiga, either killed by one of the hazards of the race or blown up by the pyrothrite belt. How had he found her? Where had she misstepped?

Prints from a dozen horses mottled the ground. Blood marred the dust in irregular constellations. Osol had inflicted violence as well as received it. Dashi thought of the bandits who roamed the area but discarded the idea. Bandits would have taken Osol's saddle, or at least his supplies. Instead, his saddlebags had been turned inside out, the contents strewn over the ground: food, clothes, bedroll, all abandoned.

Dashi kicked through the supplies and ran her hand over the saddle, searching for hidden compartments like the one in her saddle. Finding nothing, she turned to Osol's body. It was warm, the limbs still flaccid. *A two-hour lead, the innkeeper had said.*

He'd been shot once, a crossbow bolt to the back that had pushed through his chest when he'd fallen on it. His throat had also been cut, though Dashi assumed that had been done afterward, just to make sure. She tilted his chin from side to side, examining the wound: a single, neat slice. A knife, not a sword. She ran her hands along the body, first over his deel and then beneath, searching for anything the killers had missed. Her fingers came away tacky with blood but empty.

Still squatting next to the body, Dashi tried to make her aching brain work. Osol had somehow tracked her to Ejen, figured out her secrets—both Idree and the golden needle—and then stolen them both. Now, it appeared that someone had done the same to him. But who? And where were they taking Idree now?

The vulture lurched into motion, the heavy beat of its wings startling Dashi to her feet. It thumped to the ground a short distance away and began to pace in front of a dusty screen of bushes, the stringy cords of its neck bobbing in time to its uneven gait. When Dashi approached, it croaked a protest but hopped backward. She grabbed the booted foot that protruded from beneath the bushes and, after a few minutes of struggle, dragged a second body into the open. It was another man, similar to Osol in both sturdiness of build and the violent manner of death. Even without his uniform, she would have known he was a soldier from the scars on his face and the backs of his hands.

She stared at the unmistakable green and gold braid that adorned the dead man's chest, her denial morphing slowly into dread. The toe of her boot scuffed over a small, silver disc, partially concealed by a coating of dust. Her own saddle was adorned with similar ornaments, each engraved with a different symbol. Hers beseeched the ancestors for various gifts—luck, prosperity, health. *This* ornament was a brand, denoting the owner: of the saddle, of the horse, of the person who rode it. Dashi picked it up, rubbing it against her deel until there could be no denying what she was seeing: an upturned wolf's head, set against a backdrop of rolling hills.

The symbol of Karakal. Of the khan.

Chapter 5

Dashi could picture the lush gardens that had wrapped the house like a mantle. Now ash covered the ground where a house had once stood. The shrubbery had been uprooted and the fruit trees felled, leaving behind blackened stumps and empty sockets in the soft earth, like a mouth of decaying teeth. Only the altar remained intact, though it too had been changed by circumstances. Its offering recesses were empty and the white marble was smudged gray where smoke had engulfed it.

This was where the Karak noble had lived, the man who'd employed Osol, Idree's kidnapper. This was where Dashi had been fitted with a Yassari explosive belt and forced into the khan's race to find the golden needle. Judging by the green stalks poking through the charred crust, the fire had raged months ago. Yet the noble—*Captain Ese*, according to a servant of one of the neighbors—hadn't rebuilt. No one else had either. The damaged area had been left untouched and unimproved, a monument to destruction. Dashi's eyes moved to the neighboring residences, their green tile roofs bright in Karak City's dawn. How fortunate for their owners that the fire hadn't spread but had taken only a single house belonging to a single noble.

Even if Captain Ese was still alive—and, judging by the state of his house, that was an open question—Dashi had no time to look for him. It was dangerous to show interest in someone who had been so obviously damned anyway. She slipped away before anyone saw her, the Yassari boots silent and sure despite the slick cobblestones.

She'd come to Karak City hoping for answers: about how Osol and, by extension, Captain Ese, had tracked her to Thracedon; about why the khan's men had followed Osol and where they'd taken Idree. Thus far, her questions remained unresolved, and her search remained fruitless.

Mostly *fruitless*, she amended. The single nugget of information that Dashi *had* uncovered concerned where the khan *wasn't*—Karak City—and where he was instead—New Osb, a new royal residence reportedly being constructed in the far east of Karakal. Although Dashi assumed the khan would want the needle and seamstress delivered to him directly, there was nothing solid to substantiate Idree's presence in New Osb. Even so, Dashi had already begun her preparations for the days-long journey. She could only hope that Idree would be waiting at the end of it.

Chapter 6

Dashi shifted in her saddle, her eyes on New Osb. A few years ago, none of this had existed. She knew because she'd traveled here with her friends, only to abort their exploration when they discovered a contingent of the Karakalese army camped at the ruins. There had been nothing but tumbled stones then. Now, a city rose from the same foundation, a tender shoot springing from a decayed log.

Around her, the other members of the New Osb convoy gawked at the height of its walls and exclaimed over the end of their journey. Even the prison laborers shuffling along at the rear craned their necks to see past their guards. Hardly anyone in Karakal had seen the khan's new residence and no one—not the newly hired servants or craftsman, not the jaded merchants—was immune to its mystery. Dashi's gaze flicked to the ridge of close, black trees that rose behind New Osb. *The taiga.* The mere sight of it made her twitch with unease, her mind conjuring animals of gigantic proportions and mist that gave the impression of sentience.

"Isn't it grand?" A young woman riding beside Dashi asked in a breathless voice. "My mother will never believe I'm working in the khan's new palace."

Dashi forced her gaze back to New Osb. *The taiga can keep itself*, she thought firmly. *My business is within the khan's walls.*

"It's amazing," Dashi said. "That's why I was so excited to serve the khan here."

"It's the opportunity of a lifetime," the other woman agreed.

Indeed. No one knew why the khan had moved to the eastern reaches of Karakal, but a new palace, especially one so far from everything else, needed staff: people to do everything from carrying messages to carrying meals. Dashi had applied to be in the latter group. It had taken weeks of painful waiting while she had the necessary documentation forged and then lied and bribed her way through rounds of interviews, but now she was here. Positioning herself close to the khan was her best shot at discovering where he was keeping Idree and the needle.

The convoy drew closer to New Osb, passing teams of yaks pulling sledges and beleaguered men and women coaxing stone blocks into place with pulleys and levers and sometimes their bare hands. Guards were sprinkled liberally throughout, their bright deels unmistakable in the ocean of browned, sweating prisoners. Shabby tents stretched to the river, enclosed by a tall fence: the prison laborers' quarters. Dashi didn't look back at the line of prisoners trudging behind her, but she could imagine their despair as they surveyed what awaited them.

Like Karak City, New Osb had been built as a series of concentric circles, with walls separating each section. Much of the space between the walls was still unclaimed, though a few shops and homes had been erected: merchants selling food, craftsmen working leather and metal. There was even, Dashi noted with a pang, a bootmaker's shop. That's where Idree *should* be: bent over boot soles and chatting with customers. Instead, Dashi remembered the room she and Sevlin had seen in the Purek temple last year, full of shackles and altars and bones.

Dashi kept her body loose as the convoy approached the first gate, smiling and nodding at whatever the other new hires said. *Give them what they want to see,* Zayaa murmured in her mind. *It's the best disguise there is.* Zayaa had been talking about being stopped by a customs official, but it was the same principle. In Zayaa's recounting, the official had been searching for untaxed contraband and Zayaa was on her way to a behind-closed-doors sale to a Karak noble. Without missing a beat, she had transformed herself into a high-priced prostitute, pulling her neckline down and rubbing herself all over the customs official, before finally being waved through, her pockets still stuffed with undeclared Purek jewelry.

At the next gate, the convoy stopped again. Dashi sat quietly as the line crept forward, studiously ignoring the itch to move as it built beneath her skin. The wall towered over her, even taller than the ones surrounding Karak City. The golden paint on the gate was so shiny that it looked wet. A naked pole stuck straight out from the wall above it, waiting for some sort of ornamentation. Cold sweat slid down Dashi's neck and tunneled under her deel.

A soldier took the letter of hire from her hand and began his litany of questions.

"Where did you work before?"

"Why do you want to serve the khan?"

In Karak City, everything was for sale. Her savings not only bought her a recommendation from a noble household—obscure enough that the chance of running into someone who was *actually* from said household remained low—but also purchased the bones of a backstory. Now she recited the facts she knew about the noble household from which she supposedly hailed, smoothing it all over with an awestruck tone and a few shy smiles. She wasn't sure if her answers really mattered, or if the guard was only watching for the ease with which she delivered them. Whatever the test, she passed it. He motioned her forward, telling her to report to a woman named Marzhan.

Dashi crossed through the cool innards of the stone wall and out the other side, blinking at the sheer size of the place. The New Osb courtyard was in a state of productive disarray. A pair of workers knelt nearby, installing one row of pavers after another. Piles of wood and stone waited to be used. In the distance, she saw a new stable building rising, workers scrambling to slide beams into place. One day, swarms of caretakers would tame the place. Bushes would be coddled and gravel paths raked until they shone whiter than the moon. At the moment, however, everything was stark and unrefined.

Towering above the bustle, the khan's palace gave the impression of severity and strength, built directly atop the Purek ruins. The original foundation was charcoal in color but, part way up, the walls changed to light gray, cutting a jagged line across the side of the palace where the present deviated from the past. There was a main building and several attached wings. Gold ornamentation surrounded each window, capturing light and hurling it at unsuspecting passersby.

"Palace servants are expected to possess the utmost loyalty and discretion," a strident voice announced to the crowd of new hires. "Nothing less will be tolerated."

Dashi stood on her toes, gaining a glimpse of the speaker: a thin, birdlike woman whose hands and feet moved incessantly.

"Grounds servants, go with Terbish." The woman indicated a silent, grizzled man beside her. "House servants, come with me. Deposit your belongings in your rooms and let the ostler know if your mount is your own or if it was provided for you at the time of your hire."

The new servants began dispersing and Dashi gave Spit a regretful pat as she walked him over to the ostler, pausing to gather her weapons and sling her saddle over one shoulder.

The thin woman motioned Dashi to a halt before she could go any further. "Saddles and weapons go here," she said tersely, indicating the neat rows behind her. "You can do what you want in your spare time, but all weapons must be checked out and checked back in with the weapons master."

Dashi's hands clutched tighter. As the pile of weapons attested, everyone in the convoy except the prisoners had been armed. They'd been traveling through open country on an unguarded road and, while Karakal was safer than Thracedon, there were still dangers. Arming oneself was both common practice and common sense. Even in Karak City, most people kept some sort of weapon on their person. Divesting herself of her bow and sword had never been asked of Dashi. Then again, she'd never been inside the khan's residence before.

"Saddles to the left. Weapons to the right," the woman repeated as more servants approached.

They began sorting their weapons into the established piles: swords, daggers, metal-tipped staffs, crossbows and bolts, longbows and quivers. There was even an ax. It was all given up with the perfect alacrity of established custom. Dashi placed her saddle beside the others, stalling. Had her bow always felt so light? It really was the perfect weapon, custom-made for her.

I'll keep the knife in my boot, she told herself. *I won't be completely unarmed.*

The woman's eyes had narrowed. Dashi massaged her expression into pleasant acceptance. Then, she forced her fingers to unfold and dropped her bow and sword.

Chapter 7

Dashi's plans fell apart almost immediately. Marzhan, the birdlike lady with the rapid instructions, assigned her to the kitchen.

"I thought I was going to be working on the main floors," Dashi said before she could stop herself.

"Cook needs help. That's you."

The rest of the newly hired servants were already moving off to their assignments, leaving Dashi to drag her feet in front of the servant's entrance. Marzhan glanced at a list handed to her by a bedraggled young man. Dashi watched him slip back into the kitchen, the door closing hungrily after his pasty, sweating skin. He looked like he hadn't been outside in months.

"I was a household servant at my last position," Dashi tried. "That's why I came to New Osb." How could she find Idree if she was stuck in the kitchen?

Marzhan raised her head slowly, her dark eyes traveling from Dashi's face down to the green and gold servant's deel. "You came to New Osb," she said in an even voice, "to serve the khan. It is for me to decide the how and where. While that pitiful backwater estate you came from may think you're fit to work on the main floors, you have the least experience of any of the new hires. You will work in the kitchen. If you don't know something, you will ask Cook. If you complain, you will find yourself on a horse back to Karak City."

Dashi's hands balled into fists. *Go now*, she told herself, *before you do something stupid. Before she labels you a troublemaker.* Somehow she made her mouth form an apology and forced her feet to walk down the gloomy kitchen stairs, but Marzhan's gaze stayed on her the whole time.

The head cook was a big-boned, cheerful woman who, fortunately, didn't hold Dashi's lack of enthusiasm against her.

"Marzhan says you have ambitions," she said with a conspiratorial wink later that afternoon. "Don't we all?"

The pasty man Dashi had noticed before was in one corner, kneading dough.

"Tadrik is a prime example," Cook said, following her gaze. "He was my first scrub boy. He's been promoted now that you're here." Cook grinned bracingly. It was clear she intended her comment as encouragement, though as far as Dashi could see, it only meant she would be working in the kitchen in perpetuity.

"The Founding Day Feast is closing in on me, so I'm thankful for the help, whatever way the ancestors chose to deliver it. You can start with the potatoes." Cook motioned to a tub overflowing with tubers. "Oh and stay out of the workrooms. The guards are carrying the wine from there to the wine cellar and you don't want to be under *their* feet, I'd warrant." This statement was accompanied by another wink.

Dashi nodded, though she didn't know the location of the workrooms or the wine cellar. She didn't know the location of anything. The other servants had been given assignments throughout the palace: cleaning floors, hanging tapestries, and polishing silver. Boring things, to be sure, but things that would enable them to observe the activities and inhabitants of New Osb. Dashi, on the other hand, would be observing muddy potatoes.

She thought about saying something—Cook seemed agreeable enough—but Marzhan's words still rang in her head. *You will find yourself on a horse back to Karak City.*

Dashi picked up the scrub brush and attacked the potatoes.

At the end of that first day, she rose from her stool and stretched, ready to fill her stomach. Cook was laying out steaming bowls of stew for the servants, each piled high with the potatoes and turnips that Dashi had prepared. None of the servants had arrived yet, but Marzhan was there, eating standing up, her toe tapping. Before Dashi could plop herself down at the table, Cook held up a hand.

"Sorry, my girl, but I need you to fetch some thyme so I can get the breakfast dough rising. After that, I promise you can quit for the night."

Between Cook's sympathetic expression and Marzhan standing there, watching her every move, Dashi could only nod. *At least I get a chance to look around*, she thought, as she crossed the courtyard to the wing of the palace Cook had mentioned. Four guards flanked the small door set into the stone wall, which seemed like an excessive amount of security for an herb garden, but they let her in after a glance into her basket.

The door brushed closed behind her, cutting off the bustle of the courtyard. Though she'd expected it, the small atrium garden wrapped within the walls of the palace still came as a surprise. After days of guarded small talk with the other travelers, followed by an afternoon in the palace kitchen—the bright snap of fire, Cook cackling loudly at her own jokes, the muted *thump, thump* of a knife on a cutting board—the quiet made Dashi sag in relief.

There was still plenty of life here, but it was diffident and unobtrusive, allowing her the space to think: leaves, green and gauzy against the stone walls; a flowerhead, yellow as a moon, bowing to the ground; a moth, flexing its wings. Leaves huffed against each other at the breeze she'd let in, then fell silent again. The effect was vertiginous, like stepping into another world by accident.

Windows circled above her, looking down from each floor of the palace so that anyone in this wing could catch a taste of paradise, but there was no one looking through the glass right now. A door, flanked by stained glass, led into the palace itself. Dashi automatically noted the lock before turning to follow the path to the corner of the garden. Humming a Thracedonian tune under her breath, she knelt to pluck tender shoots of thyme.

"There's more at the opposite corner."

Dashi spun around so quickly that she upset the basket, sending thyme skidding over the path.

"I'm sorry." The man behind her was at least a decade her senior. He smiled apologetically and pushed a floppy mass of dark hair away from his face.

"I was over there when you came in, but you didn't see me," he continued, motioning toward a chest-high row of bushes. A stone bench peeked through the branches. "This garden is usually empty. Even *my* guards are too bored to bother coming inside," he added, almost jovially. "They'd rather wait out there and look at the bustling courtyard than watch me pruning herbs. It's the only place I'm allowed a little freedom."

Dashi started to reply, then changed her mind, warned off by the mention of guards and the fine weave of the man's deel. She didn't know enough about who populated the halls of Karak power to recognize him. Something about him put her in mind of the khan. An advisor, perhaps? Either way, Marzhan had been very clear in her instructions to the new servants: they were not to speak unless required to, and they were not to make eye contact with anyone but other servants.

Dashi dropped her gaze to the herbs. The last thing she needed was for someone to complain about her demeanor to Marzhan. She'd never be let out of the kitchen then.

"I just planted more thyme in the opposite corner," the man said, seeming not to notice Dashi's bowed head. "You'll have to be gentle because the roots won't be set, but if you need more, it's there. What's it for?"

He seemed genuinely curious, though that was almost as improbable as the idea of one of the khan's advisors kneeling in the dirt to plant herbs.

"Breakfast pastries," Dashi said.

"Ahh, the cook does do an excellent job on those. Probably the entire reason she was hired. They are favorites of Temur's from childhood, did you know? Have you tasted one yet?"

"I—It's my first day here."

He tilted his head, appraising. "You do seem tired. Here." Before she could think of what to say, he knelt and began gathering up the thyme she'd dropped.

"You don't have to—"

The floppy-haired advisor dropped the herbs into her basket and straightened. "Do you—"

"Honored One." A stern-voiced guard leaned through the door that led inside the khan's palace.

"Looks like my time is up." The advisor gave Dashi a half-smile before he turned away. "Another day, perhaps."

Dashi finished cutting the thyme and let herself out of the little oasis. The guards on the outside of the garden were gone, presumably having left with the khan's advisor. He must be someone important, to be so carefully protected. The atrium garden, on the other hand, did not appear to be well guarded at all, despite its inner door into the palace.

Dashi smiled as the hum of the courtyard drew closer. It would be a good place to start her search, or at least familiarize herself with the layout of the palace—

Her feet stopped moving. Her heart almost did too. Rounding the corner in the opposite direction was Captain Ese, the noble from Karak City.

Chapter 8

The basket bounced over the ground, sprigs of thyme scattering for the second time. Before it stopped moving, Dashi's hand was at her boot, glinting with metal as she drew it back.

Captain Ese reacted just as quickly, ducking her first swing and coming back up with a punch that whistled by her ear, just a hair too far to the left. He grunted when Dashi's elbow hit his stomach but caught her arm, pulling her to him. With his other hand, he deflected her knife, pushing the blade past his shoulder as he swung her bodily into the palace wall. Pain crashed through Dashi's side. Her fingers tangled in his hair and she jerked his head forward, smacking his forehead into the stone over her shoulder.

"What," she panted, "are you doing here?" Her knife was in place now, pressed against the base of his throat.

He blinked twice, a thin rivulet of blood running down his forehead. He should have been worried about the knife, but he was staring at Dashi's face like she was a nightmare come to fruition.

"Get off me," he hissed, and Dashi felt the jab of something sharp at her armpit. She wasn't the only one who was armed. "Before we're both found out."

That got her attention. She hadn't been thinking about the courtyard of people around the corner or how anyone looking out the palace windows could see her, a supposedly unarmed servant, with a knife to someone's throat. She'd only been thinking of the satisfaction of hurting this man, who had so much to answer for. She let go of him but kept her knife out, tucked down at her side where it was less visible.

He was thinner than she remembered. His face, which had been strong and full of masculine vigor, now jutted sharply at the cheekbones and chin, and his nose skewed to the left where it had been broken since she last saw him. *Thinner...and shabbier.* She noticed now that he wore the same green and gold servant's deel that she did, the cuffs smudged with dirt. His hair was no longer tied at his nape but hung disheveled around his face. He'd grown a beard, which wasn't in itself out of fashion, but it was unkempt and bristly and made him look like a boar on two feet. He plucked a small pair of spectacles, another new addition, out of the dirt and perched them on his nose.

"Back from the grave, little Dashi?" he asked in a soft voice. "Or exile, more accurately."

"What are you doing here?" she asked again.

"The same as you: proudly serving the khan." His lips pulled into a sneer, even as his eyes searched her face, her uniform, the door to the herb garden behind her. The smugness was familiar; he was a man with money and power and all the answers.

"No," Dashi said. "You have a plan for everything. Too afraid to go into the taiga? Get some girl out of prison. Don't think she'll cooperate? Lock Yassari explosives to her. So what plan is this?" She motioned to his servant's uniform. "Because I don't think you'd be wearing a servant's deel and getting your hands dirty without a good reason, *Captain Ese.*" It was a great pleasure to finally name him aloud.

His expression went from indolent to aggressive in the span of a heartbeat. "Stay out of my way, little Dashi." He took a step back, then another, putting distance between them before he turned his back on her. "And beseech your ancestors that I stay out of yours."

Dashi waited a long time before she bent to pick up the thyme, now dusty and broken. Her heart was strumming like a wild instrument and she couldn't seem to order her thoughts. Did Captain Ese know that the khan already had the golden needle? Did he know that Idree was the seamstress? She wanted to believe that the answer to both of those questions was no—Osol had died before he could report his kidnapping success to his master—but she could think of no other reason why Captain Ese would be here, in disguise, no less.

"What took you so long?" Cook asked when Dashi got back to the kitchen. She squinted at the broken sprigs of thyme, then looked back at Dashi.

"I got lost," Dashi said with an apologetic grimace, "and I dropped the basket."

Too late, she saw Marzhan hovering nearby. The woman pursed her lips, Dashi's admission only confirming what she already thought: that Dashi was unfit for anything but the basest kitchen labor.

"It'll wash." Cook pawed at Dashi's shoulder comfortingly. "Now get yourself a bowl. A little thing like you must be starving and you'll need your strength: we'll be putting in longer hours the closer we get to Founding Day."

Many of the other servants had eaten and gone already, leaving behind a stack of dirty bowls waiting to be washed. Dashi ladled some soup into her bowl and, when she turned around, there he was again: Captain Ese, seated with a few of the grounds servants at the long table.

That's what he must be masquerading as, Dashi realized, remembering the dirt on his sleeve. She couldn't wrap her head around seeing him like this: everything different, everything a lie, and no one else reacting to it. He even wore a vial of incense oil around his neck now, as the truly pious did. *What a charade.* The other grounds servants seemed to regard him with genuine camaraderie, which only made Dashi suspicious of them all.

Cook plopped onto the bench beside her, the sudden weight making Dashi bounce.

"Oh to be young and energetic enough for courting," Cook said, though she was neither old nor particularly lacking in energy.

It took Dashi a moment to realize Cook was referring to the way she was looking at the grounds servants.

Dashi shrugged, forcing herself to stop staring at Captain Ese. "Some of them are handsome enough."

"Don't let Marzhan catch you."

"Is that not allowed?"

"She says it's a distraction." Cook gave Dashi her customary wink. "I say life needs some distraction, even if you have *ambitions*."

"You say ambitions like it's a bad thing," Dashi said, chewing slowly, "but I came here because I wanted to serve the khan."

"And so you are. Some of those potatoes you cut found their way up to him." Cook laughed at the expression on Dashi's face, which was halfway between obstinate and incredulous. "There's nothing wrong with ambitions, but think twice lest you get what you want. That lot," she aimed her chin at a small knot of servants cloistered at a table, "doesn't strike me as particularly happy."

Dashi turned, studying the men and women. They hovered over their bowls, lips nearly touching the broth, as they shoveled food into their mouths. Their uniforms were similar to hers, although, even from across the room, Dashi could see the material was of better quality. They were also painstakingly clean. After a day in the kitchen, hers was blotched with food. Gold pins flashed on the breast of their deels with every movement: a wolf's head raised to howl.

"Who are they?" Dashi asked.

"The khan's personal servants. They're the ones who attend to his every need: clothes, food, rooms, messages, everything. No one else."

"That is a great honor. Is that why they get their own table?" Dashi asked, her mind whirling. That's where she needed to be: at the khan's table, at his bedside, hovering in the background every time he made a decision, catching every word he spoke. That was the only sure way to find out where Idree was being kept and what he intended for her.

"They get their own table," Cook said, "because they only have a few moments to eat before they have to hustle back to the top floor. They cannot wait for a seat to free up."

"Yet they don't seek other positions," Dashi said thoughtfully. "They must be satisfied." That would complicate things.

"Perhaps. Perhaps not. Seeking another position would have to be done carefully, so as not to show dissatisfaction with serving the khan. There was an opening last year when the khan gave one of his servants to the Zalikal house, but it doesn't happen often." Cook shrugged. "Better to leave that way than the other way though."

Dashi raised her eyebrows. She'd never heard of the khan executing his servants.

"The last time was years ago," Cook said, reading her mind. "In Karak City."

"Why?"

Cook's lips pulled together, suddenly reluctant. "His Most High is very wise. I'm sure he had a good reason."

Just then, Marzhan appeared at Cook's elbow and the two of them launched into a heated discussion about the Founding Day celebration. It was the biggest holiday in Karakal, meant to honor the country's birth centuries ago, when the survivors of the magical cataclysm stumbled out of the taiga to start a new life. Dashi tried to listen, in case they said anything useful, but they were mired in a discussion about which foods the international delegations would prefer, and the details washed over Dashi without lodging in her consciousness.

"—wants a lamb pie and the other delegations prefer fish—"

"—three days from now. I can't do it!"

"The princes from both countries will need—"

Would Idree get a feast this year? Like a mouse sniffing its way back home, Dashi's thoughts had gone to the same place they always did when she had an idle moment: her sister. It had been nearly a month since Idree had been kidnapped and so far all Dashi had accomplished was buying forged documents, joining a convoy that traveled at a slug's pace, and scrubbing potatoes. When she'd left Karak City, Dashi had thought a servant's disguise would greatly expedite her efforts in rescuing Idree. *And stealing back the golden needle*, she added mentally. If the golden needle was left behind, it could be used to track Idree down again, no matter where they fled. Unfortunately, by Cook's estimate, it could take months to be promoted out of the kitchen and *years* to crack the khan's bubble of personal servants.

Dashi's foot, propped on an empty chair, flexed involuntarily, and she felt the soles of the Yassari boots grab hold of the worn wood. *We're ready*, they seemed to say. *Just tell us where to climb.*

Cook and Marzhan droned on, certain that a banquet full of pompous guests was the most important thing in the world. Each word grated against Dashi's skin. The khan's personal servants finished eating and hurried off, one by one. Even befriending them to ask about Idree looked improbable, as they seemed to have neither the time nor the inclination for small talk.

Across the room, Captain Ese also stood up, his eyes sliding to hers as he tipped his bowl, sluicing brown broth onto the table. He turned to the door, leaving her to clean up the mess. The glide was still in his walk, like a dancer or a snake. Dashi had forgotten that. It was that gait—that, and the breadth of his shoulders—that had told her he'd be a good fighter. She thought about rushing after him, but she didn't know what she wanted to say and she didn't want to draw attention to herself. Instead, she rose and began clearing the dishes from the table, half-listening to Marzhan and Cook.

"—That'll all change when the consul gets back—"

"—Any day now—"

A bowl clattered out of Dashi's hand. She saw the dark water closing over Negan's lifeless body, the fletching of the arrow that poked from his back. The consul was dead. He had to be. *But* you *managed to survive,* mused the dark voice of her mind, the one that still sent her nightmares about the race and Negan and the taiga.

"I thought N—the khan's consul was dead," Dashi said.

Marzhan was looking at her like she was daft, but the thought of Negan, alive and stalking the halls of New Osb, was so pressing that Dashi didn't care.

Cook cleared her throat delicately. "The *previous* consul joined the ancestors about a year ago, but the khan named a new consul almost immediately. Stunning woman, brilliantly smart. She hasn't been around much though. Traveling for the khan."

I'll be stuck in the kitchen, so I doubt I'd see her even if she was *here,* Dashi thought, but she nodded, relieved.

She ignored their conversation after that, focusing instead on the two tasks before her: tackling the mountain of dishes and locating her sister. Her hands swept through the warm dishwater, washing and stacking mechanically, while her mind turned over her options. She couldn't wait for a spot to open among the khan's personal servants or until she was promoted out of the kitchen. In a few short weeks, autumn would turn to winter. Fleeing across the near-taiga and the steppe would become nearly impossible then. She couldn't leave Idree as a prisoner until *spring.*

Dashi stacked the last bowl in the drying rack and, through a jaw-cracking yawn, bid Cook goodnight. She yawned again—a real one this time—but she ignored the door to her quarters, instead striding out of the courtyard to begin her search for Idree.

Chapter 9

Dashi didn't venture inside the palace that night. Inside her head, Baris' voice was deep and slow: *Observe first, then engage. A second's pause can write your strategy for you.* So she circled the perimeter, counting the guards, learning who was stationed where, who liked to stay for a chat even when their shift was over, who looked alert, and whose attention drifted. The shift change happened seamlessly, the off-duty sentries filtering from their posts to their quarters. There were even guards posted inside the wine cellar. If the khan defended his wine that zealously, how many guards would be posted around Idree?

Her eyes marked the exterior of the palace, noting the places where an entry—or exit—might be made. There weren't as many as she'd hoped. Although the foundations were old, the bulk of the palace had been built recently, which meant there were no vines or crumbling stones to use as handholds. Every angle was sharp. Every plane was smooth and clean. Even the wing of the palace that was still under construction, a room so massive that Dashi could think of no use for it—stabling all the horses in New Osb? hosting an indoor market?—wasn't an ideal entry point. It bristled with guards to make up for its incomplete walls and there were tools and piles of cut stone strewn everywhere, waiting to trip someone in the darkness.

Deep down, Dashi nursed the hope that she might see Idree. Maybe her sister would peer out a window, backlit by cozy candlelight. Or maybe whoever was in charge of Idree would allow her a moment of fresh air after the sun sank. But the only people Dashi saw were guards, focused and regimented, and a lone servant, who scoured the courtyard with a stout push broom.

Her second and third days in New Osb passed in the same manner. She rose before dawn to help Cook prepare breakfast—a salty grain mash for the servants and guards, pastries for New Osb's more important inhabitants—then spent the day gathering and preparing various foods at Cook's direction. She rarely saw anything outside of the kitchen walls, unless she was sent to gather something from one of the cold cellars or the herb garden.

Although she conducted a covert staring war with Captain Ese at mealtimes, she still had no idea why he was there. When she tried to inquire about him, Cook waved away her question: "The grounds servants aren't my concern, thank the ancestors. I have enough to manage in here."

Cook was slightly more forthcoming when Dashi worked the conversation around to women in the khan's orbit. There were some female advisors, though none who fit Idree's description, and a revolving door of young women in Karak City, though none since the khan relocated to New Osb.

"This place is too bleak for beautiful young women. Well, except for the consul," Cook said. "But she's a different bird altogether. I don't think it'll be long before the khan decides to move back to Karak City."

At night, Dashi stalked the palace grounds, monitoring the guards' movements for any changes. It should have given her whiplash: a year spent in guard ranks, fending off attacks, and now she was on the other side, testing defenses for a chance to invade. But, in truth, it felt more natural this way. Years of exploring Purek ruins had taught her to think of buildings as puzzles, with right moves and wrong moves and, always, a goal in mind. The khan's palace was the same, only with guards instead of traps and Idree as the prize instead of a dusty scroll.

On her fourth night, Dashi called a cheery goodnight to Cook's back. With loud footsteps, she opened the kitchen door and closed it again. When she doubled back to hide in a little-used closet, however, she was silent. Through the crack in the door, she watched Cook knead the dough for the breakfast pastries. *Slide, turn, push, repeat.* A knock at the kitchen door startled them both, but it was only a guard.

He raised his shaggy head to give a theatrical sniff. "Smells good. Are you making the salted pork ones again?"

"No, just currants and cloves tomorrow. I'll be making plenty of the salted pork ones for Founding Day though. I'll set one aside for you," Cook said with a wink. "What with the palace overflowing with complaining nobles and sneaking foreigners, you'll need your strength."

"Better put two aside then." The guard grinned. Firelight glinted off the rank insignia on his chest. He jingled a key ring meaningfully. "Do you need anything from the wine cellar?"

"You mean, besides a bottle for myself?" Cook quipped, and they both laughed. "Let me tally for tomorrow. This whole thing would be easier if I could send someone whenever it was warranted like I did back in Karak City. You lot keep that door locked up like it houses gold bars, not wine." Cook jabbed a wooden spoon in his direction as she said the last part, but her words were frayed at the edges, a practiced complaint. The guard didn't even bother to respond.

There was a moment of silence while Cook bent over, using her finger to scratch figures into the flour that covered the table.

"Seventy bottles for tomorrow," she said after a moment. "A Thracedonian delegation will arrive tomorrow, and Marzhan says a convoy of our nobles sent a runner to say they're arriving early. I had all the meals planned out, and now I'm supposed to feed fifty extra people! Not that anyone asked me..."

A sympathetic grimace from the guard. "I'll make sure they're delivered in the morning so you're not waiting."

Cook pointed a flour-white finger in his direction. "*That's* why you get pork pastries."

The guard retreated into the night, leaving Cook to slap the pastry dough into a firm puddle, before placing it near the banked fire for the night. She locked the kitchen door from the inside, then went into the small room where she slept, taking the oil lamp with her.

The kitchen was shrouded and silent when, a half hour later, Dashi crossed to the narrow servant's staircase. She had no reason to climb those stairs during the day, but she knew they led to an alcove off the great hall, used for staging food during large feasts. *Right into the center of the palace.* She liked that, the idea of striking at the heart of her enemy. Her steps were slow and cautious, testing each stair. Behind her, Cook's snores echoed through the dark kitchen. Dashi eased the door at the top of the stairs open, her breath stuffed in her throat.

The great hall soared overhead. The window facets, outlined in lead came, refracted the moonlight, winking like a thousand octagonal eyes. The effect was magnified by the silver plating that covered the ceiling. There were guards at the far end of the hall: two on either side of a dais that held a throne fashioned from carved wood and granite. She wondered if Idree had ever been in this room.

Despite their positions near the throne, the guards were relaxed: arms crossed, mouths moving, voices too soft to hear. Dashi stole into the empty great hall, sliding through the shadows that clung to its edges, her

Yassari boots as light as goose down. She slipped out almost as quickly as she'd entered, stepping into a high-ceilinged corridor lined with doors. She slid into one room after another. There were sculptures and plush seats, ornate tables and rolling carts waiting for refreshments. There was even a Niryak board, its legions of soldiers covered in gold leaf and topped with chunks of lapis, nothing like the worn wooden nubs Dashi was used to seeing. Even now, she could picture Altan and Zayaa bent over a battered board: Altan, struggling mightily against defeat, cursing under his breath; Zayaa, wearing that serene smile that said she'd already outsmarted everyone in the room. Shaking her head, Dashi let herself out. There was nothing here she needed.

On the next floor, at the top of a wide, ostentatious staircase, she found locked offices belonging to the khan's advisors. Her lock picks were in her pocket, but Dashi hesitated. According to the titles on the doors, the khan had an advisor for everything from agriculture to roads, but nothing seemed to pertain to Idree or magic or Purek antiquities. Whose job was it to supervise the seamstress or search for the veins of magic she would need in order to stitch? *The consul,* she thought, but there was no office for her. Either it was located on the khan's floor, or the consul traveled too much to warrant one.

She crept back down the double staircase. Night was fading and she had neither the time nor the method for getting into the khan's personal rooms tonight. Maybe via the servants' staircase, she mused. It might not be as well-guarded as the main one.

A man's voice, low and indistinguishable, brought her thoughts to a halt. Unable to tell where it was coming from, she ducked behind one of the gaudy statues that adorned the first-floor hallway. She was next to the interior entrance to the atrium garden. The door clicked open, sending a wave of cool air crashing into her side and offering a glimpse of moonlit greenery. Dashi crouched, frozen, as someone came through the door. If she was caught, even *seen*, it would all be over: the chance to get Idree back, her position—

"I am not aware of any, Honored One," a man said quietly.

"And you couldn't tell me even if you were," someone responded. "I know the situation you're in, and I appreciate your discretion. Perhaps one day, when my brother trusts me again, I'll have a chance to thank you properly."

Dashi braced herself for discovery, but the two men turned in the opposite direction. One was a guard. The other was the same advisor Dashi had encountered in the garden a few days ago. She didn't have long to wonder what he was doing in the garden, and this time at night. Brisk footsteps from the opposite direction announced the arrival of two more guards. The advisor and his guard shot each other a panicked look, then darted out of sight through a doorway. Dashi grabbed for the door on the other side of the statue. She had a fleeting fear that she'd find it locked, but it opened on the garden on silent hinges.

The smell hit her at once: an autumnal crispness, verdant despite the season. She could hear the wind whipping over the rest of New Osb, but inside the garden's high walls, everything was still. Dashi dropped behind a row of bushes, out of sight in case the guards happened to glance through one of the windows overlooking the atrium. She waited, ears straining, but heard nothing. After a few minutes, she began to relax.

The sky was a deep, fathomless black, lit only by the sliver of moon balanced on the wall. It was later than she'd thought. Her shoulders drooped. *I'll find her*, she told herself. But the Founding Day guests would start arriving tomorrow—she'd heard it straight from Cook's lips—and the palace would be swarming for days. Searching for Idree was about to become exponentially more difficult.

Moonlight snagged on a familiar flower, its dusky pink blossoms tracing up the garden wall. Dashi plucked a bud, her eyebrows rising in surprise. *Summer roses.* The cold nights should've killed them this late in the year; the blooms must have been protected by the tall garden walls.

She thought of Idree clasping her hands together as she surveyed the small white cottage. Pink roses climbed around the door. *"It's beautiful, Dashi, like a dream! Can't you just picture us living here?"*

Yes, Dashi thought. It *had* been like a dream: a beautiful dream that had come to an end.

She put the bud in her pocket and started for the door. She didn't see the hand that snaked out from behind the shrub next to her, but the feeling of it closing around her throat and jerking her upward was impossible to miss.

Chapter 10

The hand released her as quickly as it had grabbed hold and Dashi's feet thumped back to the ground. Captain Ese stood there, glaring. Keeping one hand wrapped firmly around Dashi's bicep, he propelled her out of the garden and through the palace shadows, past the stone terrace at the back of the great hall, until they reached the yew hedge that served as a border between the palace and the grounds.

"Down," Captain Ese ordered, his hand burrowing into her arm. "Crawl."

"Get off me," she hissed. "I—"

"Shh."

For a second, there was nothing. Then, faintly, the sound of footsteps. Dashi stayed perfectly still, the yew so close it tickled her nose. As soon as the guard had gone, Captain Ese shoved her through the hedge. Dashi was aching for a fight. She hated being manhandled and she'd hated Captain Ese even before this encounter, but the fear of more guards kept her silent. Finally, after they'd passed both stables and reached the smaller outbuildings, Captain Ese stopped.

He wheeled her around, bringing them nose to nose. "What do you think you're doing?"

"You tell me. You're the one who brought me out here." She grabbed his index finger and twisted it, forcing him to let go. She took a step back, studying him. "Were you meeting with that advisor in the garden? Or spying on him?"

He leaned toward her. "*Why*," he asked, grinding the word like it was made from stone, "were you sneaking around the atrium garden?"

Dashi had never seen him angry before. In her memories, he had a cool, satisfied air, something that, she assumed, came from having the answer before the question was even asked. He was practically vibrating with rage now: hands twitching, head jutting forward, the vial of incense oil around his neck swaying dangerously.

"Serving the khan," she said. "Isn't that what you told me the other day?"

"People who *serve* blend in. They're unremarkable, like the paving stones in the street. You only really notice them when one sticks up." His eyes were jumping, aggressive. "You," he jabbed a finger at her chest, "are the stone that is amiss."

"Oh, come off it. You're no better at being a servant than I am."

"I am not here on some lark. An innocent person—" He cut himself off. "Your presence here is dangerous."

She wanted to retort that an innocent person was the entire reason she'd come to New Osb, but she didn't want to give away anything about Idree.

"Osol is dead," she said, deciding on a different tack.

Something shifted in Captain Ese's face. It was difficult to tell in the uncertain light, but she thought it might have been grief. When he spoke again the anger had leached from his voice, leaving behind a tone closer to the one Dashi remembered: mocking and insouciant.

"I warned him not to underestimate you."

Dashi shrugged one shoulder. "As far as I'm concerned, he didn't get half of what he deserved." She couldn't think of a punishment bad enough for her sister's kidnapper. "But it wasn't me."

A beat of silence that said Captain Ese wasn't sure he believed her. "Who, then?"

"Would you believe bandits?"

His lip curled.

"I didn't either." She reached into the inner pocket of her deel, her fingers brushing over the summer rosebud, before producing the saddle ornament she'd found near Osol's body.

Captain Ese's hand shot out, but he stopped just shy of the ornament, fingertips hovering over silver. Dashi, who was watching him carefully in the moonlight, saw the fury on his face, not quite concealed. She thought of a different time, a different conversation: Captain Ese drawing Altan's blood-stained pendant from his pocket like a trump card and showily tossing it to her.

"After I found Osol, I went looking for you in Karak City," she said. "Your estate was burned. Your trees felled. Your gardens uprooted. All that was left was the altar because no one, no matter how much they were paid, would be willing to tempt the ancestors. No one has taken over the land either, despite its value. That's not an accident. It's a proclamation, and only the khan could have made it."

"I hope you didn't come all the way to New Osb to tell me something I already know." His hand dropped back to his side, away from the saddle ornament.

She took a deep breath, not sure if what she was about to say was smart but feeling desperate enough to plunge forward anyway. "You once told me that we could work together if we had a common goal."

"And now you think we have one?"

"Wrecking the khan, everything he wants, everything he's *thought* of wanting. Negan wouldn't have killed my friends without his say-so, nor would his men have killed Osol on a whim."

She couldn't tell how her pitch was landing. Captain Ese's face was a mask. She didn't know what was between him and the khan, or if it would be enough to make him help her—a few minutes ago he'd looked like he hated *her* too. What she *did* know was that Captain Ese almost certainly understood more than she did about the khan and New Osb and everything else that was happening. After seeing what was left of his estate, she also knew he was a hunted man. Someone she could trust would be an ideal ally. Someone with exploitable vulnerabilities was the best she could do under the circumstances.

"Do you know why Osol was searching for you?" Captain Ese asked, interrupting her thoughts.

"No." The question had burned inside her since finding Osol's body.

Captain Ese smiled. Genuinely, or so Dashi thought. It was hard to tell with him.

"Your pride is your weakness, Dashi. You cannot resist the chance to show off, to poke a finger in someone's eye." He paused, savoring the reveal. "The Chertai vase."

Dashi tried not to let her emotions play out on her face, but Captain Ese chuckled anyway. Long before she and Idree had settled in Ejen, Dashi had stolen a valuable vase from this man. At first, she'd hoped to pay a blacksmith to remove the explosive belt locked around her waist. Then, when that proved infeasible, she'd hidden the vase as a nest egg for Idree. She'd eventually retrieved it and sold it to an art dealer in southern Karakal. She and Idree had used the proceeds to finance their escape to Thracedon and to purchase their cottage in Ejen.

"The art dealer remembered you," he said. "A desperate young woman selling an original Chertai vase? He could hardly have seen that very often."

Dashi winced. It had been a risk, but she'd had no other options. She didn't know anyone in Southern Karakal who could've gone in her place, and she wasn't about to trust some local errand boy with a valuable piece of art. She'd tried to mitigate it as best she could: a confident air, cleanish clothes, arriving on foot so the dealer didn't glimpse her exhausted horse. Anything to look less like a bedraggled fugitive. Less like a thief.

"The art dealer was the starting point, the proof that you'd made it out of the taiga alive." Captain Ese said. "Osol—" His voice dipped slightly. "Osol began canvasing the southern part of the country, searching for any mention of someone like you."

"That's *how* you found me," Dashi said. "Not why you were searching in the first place." They couldn't have known she had the golden needle.

He nodded, almost approvingly. "At first, it seemed like no one would return from the khan's race, that everyone had been killed in the taiga, but one of Consul Negan's people limped back eventually. She reported that a female racer had found the statuette but that it had been lost when the racer was killed. To assuage the khan's anger, she was also quick to report that Negan suspected the female had been hired—"

Dashi snorted. *Hired*? She hadn't seen a single cent. Well, not unless you counted the Chertai vase, but she'd stolen that beforehand, fair and square.

"—by me, to steal the needle out from under the khan. That's why my estate was burned, because of what she told the khan, and because you never returned with my bargaining chip."

"I didn't tell anyone you sent me if that's what you're asking. Negan figured it out when he saw me." Dashi thought of Negan's face contorted with anger, his fist flying. *"How?"* he'd screamed at her. "No one escapes that prison." She remembered the taste of her blood and the sight of torchlight flickering over a deep crack in the earth.

"Like everyone else, I believed you'd died," Ese said, ignoring her. "Then an art dealer contacted me with a deal on a Chertai vase, one that I supposedly already owned. We realized you must've escaped the belt if you made it to Southern Karakal. We also knew you'd had the golden needle at some point. Osol was sure you *still* had it, that everything could be turned around if he could just get it from you." There was a trace of sadness in his voice. "Maybe the khan was somehow on to you too, or maybe it was Osol who was being followed. Either way, it's obvious the needle is no longer in your possession, or you wouldn't be here. Without the needle, you have no value to me." He flapped his hand dismissively, shooing her away. "If Temur has it, it will be impossible to get back."

"You don't know that," she retorted.

"I know he had a safe box installed and that there's a small army of guards and servants on his floor at all times."

He didn't mention Idree, Dashi noticed. He thought Dashi was here solely for the needle, that she was motivated by greed, or maybe damaged pride. *Good. The fewer people who knew about Idree, the better.* If even wily Captain Ese didn't know about her, maybe Dashi could contain this.

Still, her heart sank at Captain Ese's words. She *needed* the golden needle. If it stayed in the khan's possession, he could track the seamstress wherever she went. Idree would never be free unless Dashi could steal it back.

"So instead of helping me get the needle from the khan," Dashi said, "you'll keep playing servant—hiding in plain sight—so that he can't punish you."

"No one is *playing* and he doesn't want to punish me. He wants to kill me." Captain Ese's voice was hard. "If you'd brought me the needle after the race, things would be different now."

For you, *maybe*, Dashi thought. *She* would always be in this position: trying to save Idree. Trying to protect the seamstress.

Captain Ese's face twisted, his eyes narrowing. It reminded Dashi that they were in the remotest part of the palace grounds and that the khan might not be the *only* person Captain Ese blamed for his situation. She shifted back a step, the Yassari boots finding traction even in the dewy grass.

His next words were reflective, however, not threatening. "A year ago, I would have jumped at what you're proposing: an epic revenge, something to be sung about a hundred years from now. That's why I put you in the race. That's why I wanted the needle in the first place. It wasn't enough that I succeeded, that the person I loved was alive, and that we were happy together. I also needed to deny my enemy everything *he* wanted. I needed to scorch the ground he walked on and salt his dreams with failure. But *I* was the one who failed. I reached too far and, when I fell, I pulled everyone down with me."

His hand strayed to his throat, playing with the vial of offering oil that hung there. The stuff was expensive and only the devout—or desperate—carried it, using it to flavor the smoke of altar candles as they beseeched the ancestors for favors.

"No," he murmured, "these days my goals are simpler."

Dashi's lip curled. "Not the master of plans you used to be, Captain Ese, if you're relying on offering oil."

"An adequate guess, little Dashi, but no. Though I'll make an offering tonight and beg the ancestors to give you the brains not to keep wandering around."

Dashi cast about for some biting retort, but Captain Ese turned on his heel and disappeared into the thick night, leaving Dashi where she'd started: no leads, no allies, no information.

"Stay out of my way, little Dashi." His voice floated back in the darkness. "And it's Ese." He leaned heavily on the first part of the word in the traditional Karak pronunciation. "Just Ese. I'm not a captain of anything anymore."

Dashi stayed behind the outbuildings long after he left, thinking about how to find her sister and wondering why, if Ese found her nightly wanderings so foolish, he was doing the same thing.

Chapter 11

Despite Ese's warning about sneaking around, and despite the arrival of dozens of guests for Founding Day, Dashi made her move the following night. She'd already checked most of the lower floors and what remained would soon be filled with guests. The khan resided on the top floor with his bevy of servants and guards. That, Dashi felt sure, was where he would keep both seamstress and needle.

When she slipped out that night, she headed straight for the small overhang that sheltered the entrance to the wine cellar. It was narrow, with a steep pitch that would make the footing precarious, but it was the only exterior route she'd been able to map to the top floor. Elsewhere, the palace was too rawboned and slick, with no places to cling.

Dashi pulled herself onto the overhang and, from there, to the ledge of the nearest window. The Yassari boots prickled against the soles of her feet, a static-like crackle. She took another step, flexing her foot against a ridge of brick outlining the window, and felt the boots fidget again, greedy for the climb.

I should have tried these out sooner.

She didn't look at the receding ground. That was the first trick to doing anything dangerous: never focus on the fall, only on the next step. Within minutes, she was braced outside a window on the khan's floor. Light glowed from within. There were always lamps burning somewhere on this floor, even late at night.

Dashi peeked around the window's edge. The room she looked into was an office, larger and grander than anything she'd seen on the first floor. Which made sense, because it was the khan himself seated at the carved wooden desk, not some lowly advisor. He looked much as he had before the start of the race, the only other time Dashi had seen him up close: narrow-faced and supercilious, his black hair tied neatly. His desk sat on a carpeted platform—*Does he need to be on a dais at all times?*—and there were a dozen men and women arrayed in front of him. *Odd*, Dashi thought, noticing that the man she'd met in the garden was not present.

The khan's voice rose, barely audible through the window. His face was alight with frustration.

"—want our imports increased!" He lunged, slapping one of his advisors, hard, in the face.

The advisor's head turned with the impact, but he displayed no other reaction. No one else did either. The khan settled himself back into his chair, pointing at someone else and continuing at a lower volume. Dashi watched for a while longer but, with the conversation continuing at a normal level, she couldn't hear anything.

She crossed below the window to avoid being seen, gripping the sill with just her hands, the ground swaying perilously below. Breathing hard, she peered into the next room, which was empty, save for two guards. There were plush lounges and tables covered in game boards and sparkling decanters. A painting over the fireplace captured her attention for a moment. It showed an ancient khagan in full royal headdress, kissing a woman as she reclined on a couch. The frame was showier than the original one had been, but Dashi recognized the art anyway.

She crossed below the next two windows, which looked into the same room, before finally reaching the last window on this side of the palace. The small room was empty of people and, before she could talk herself out of it, Dashi pulled herself up to perch on the sill. Sweat materialized on her palms. She had to wipe them before she could grip her lock picks properly. The first two tumblers turned over easily, but the third one resisted her efforts. Her wrist arched, increasing the pressure until her tension wrench skidded sideways. Dashi blew out a frustrated breath. *A woman can't afford to let anything outsmart her*, Zayaa chided, *least of all a lock.* Dashi wiped her palms and tried again. This time, the third tumbler was more amenable, and the lock flipped over with a barely audible click.

Dashi dropped into the room, pulling the window nearly closed so that it wouldn't be noticed from outside. She went to the table in one corner and, taking a chair, wedged it beneath the door handle. The handle locked from the outside, not the inside; it was the first thing she'd noticed through the window. As for the chair, it wouldn't hold anyone for long, but it would be enough to give her a warning. Dashi turned in a slow circle, breathing shallowly.

The room was so clean as to be impersonal: a bed, meaty pillows, embroidered blankets, everything neatly arranged. A few paintings hung on the walls, all modern Karak pieces. A plush pair of chairs sat in front of an unlit fireplace. A door opened somewhere on the khan's floor then closed again. It was a quick sound, but it made the back of Dashi's neck twitch, a reminder that she needed to be quick.

Idree's deel and boots weren't in the wardrobe, but perhaps she hadn't been allowed to keep any of her things. Or perhaps she was wearing them at this very moment. The deels that *were* in the wardrobe were Idree's size, as were the dainty slippers stacked beneath. *Plenty of women wear that size*, the practical part of her mind countered. *This might not even be her room.*

Dashi let out a frustrated breath. Maybe a lover stayed here, or a friend or sister. *No, not a sister;* she seemed to remember some gossip about the khan not getting along with his sibling and she thought it was a brother anyway, not a sister. What about the consul? The woman had no office on the first floor and it would make sense for both her bedroom and office to be on the khan's floor so that she was always at his beck and call. Except...this room didn't seem pretentious enough to belong to Karakal's top official. It was boring, nearly uninhabited. And she didn't think the door to the consul's room would only lock from the outside.

There was a faint footprint on the rug in front of the wardrobe, too smudged to draw any other conclusions. She touched it wonderingly, surprised that dirt would have the audacity to appear under Marzhan's roof.

The sound of a door opening came again and this time it was accompanied by voices. Many voices. The khan had dismissed his advisors for the evening. If people were on the move, it was time to go. Hurriedly, Dashi put everything the way she'd found it, backing toward the window as she scanned the room once more, desperate to justify the risk of coming inside.

Just as she brushed the window pane, she darted forward again, this time going to the bed. Her hand skimmed the thick blankets, stopping to rest on the pillow. Its angle was different from the one next to it, identical to the way Idree always propped her pillow in Ejen. Sliding her hand between the pillow and the mattress, Dashi pulled out a deel, meticulously rolled and positioned to make the pillow a little higher on one end. It had been washed. There was no mud splatter from the days she'd spent on the road, no smell of horses or fresh air. But it was Idree's, the one she'd worn their last night in Ejen. The night Dashi had lost her.

Dashi shoved her hand into the pockets of Idree's deel, but they were empty. She wasn't sure what she'd been hoping to find. A note addressed to her? Step-by-step directions on what to do next?

More footsteps outside the door. Idree might be nearby—maybe only across the hall—but Dashi made herself move. She put the deel under the pillow at the wrong angle, so that Idree would reach to adjust it. Then, she pulled out the pink bud she'd plucked from the atrium garden the previous night and placed it beneath the pillow for her sister to find. The petals had wilted, but their color was unfaded, almost identical to the blooms that had grown outside the cottage in Ejen.

Dashi's dreams were kaleidoscopic and fitful. Zayaa, Altan and Baris filtered in and out, bickering and scheming and laughing, as if they had the gall to believe themselves still alive. Finally, her mind rested on something else: a memory, not a fanciful rendering. It was the painting of the khagan and his lover, only this time it wasn't hanging on the khan's wall. It hung from a pillar, passing judgment as she stood below it.

The ruined building was an unusual one. Its single room was taken up by a giant, built-in tub, now dusty and dry. Bathhouses weren't uncommon among the Purek ruins. What made this one unusual was its isolation from any other buildings. Its opulence suggested the construction had been undertaken with care. The walls were rose-colored marble, with golden seams joining each slab. The benches in the bath were silver. Ornate pillars split the main room. Some were tall, bearing the load of the domed ceiling through a complicated network of buttresses. Others only reached halfway, existing solely to display the artwork and jewels at the top. A large amethyst necklace dangled from one. A string of pearls looped around another like a vine. There was even a khagan's headdress: a wide circlet mounted with a mass of golden snakes pointing in all directions.

"This place is unreal," Zayaa breathed. "Ancestors above, *look* at that amethyst. What I wouldn't give for that."

"Why so many benches?" Dashi wanted to know. "We're in the middle of nowhere. Who's going to sit on them?"

Altan pointed at a painting of a trysting man and a woman, the movement making his golden hair flutter and resplend in the lantern light. "This could be where the khagan retreated with his mistresses."

"A bath with a mistress? I'd retreat there, and never leave." Baris was a hulking presence on the other side of Altan: wide where Altan was streamlined, dark against his light. He raised one club-like arm to point at the painting. "That's the one?"

Altan was already consulting the small leather journal in which he took notes. "Looks it, yes. According to this, there might be a scroll concealed behind it, so we'll have to inspect it carefully before we sell it." His teeth flashed in the dim light. "Wouldn't want to give away two things for the price of one."

Baris ran his hands over the bottom of the pillar, checking for traps. Taking out a leather climbing harness, he looped it around the pillar, then hooked it over his shoulders and waist.

"Why don't you let Dashi do it?" Altan asked.

"Worrying is your job, Boss. The hard stuff is mine." Baris had already begun shimmying up the column, leaning back into the climbing harness. The exertion turned his voice harsh.

There was a flash of silver as a blade slid out of the pillar, fast and smooth as an eel, right into Baris' shin. He grunted and adjusted his grip in time to avoid the next one, which would have gotten him in the stomach. With a quick twist of his fingers, he pulled the release on the climbing harness and dropped to the floor, muttering curses.

"You were saying?" Altan unhooked the climbing harness for him.

Zayaa handed Baris a cloth for his leg.

Altan looked at Dashi. "Can you go fast enough?"

"Let me handle the hard stuff, Boss." She said it to make them laugh, but Baris' smile was strained.

Dashi wiped tar on the bottom of her boots and adjusted her climbing harness, several sizes smaller than the one Baris used. On the ground, Baris could beat her at almost everything. But on horseback and in the air, lightness mattered as much as strength, if not more so. Dashi zoomed upward, almost sprinting up the vertical surface, her boots only touching the pillar for a split second before pushing off again. Blades flashed in her wake, too slow to catch her. She grabbed the painting from its hook, pausing only to sling it over one shoulder, then began her descent, dropping in great bounds. She handed the painting to Altan seconds later, panting but triumphant. Baris clapped her on the shoulder.

They celebrated that night. The painting was in fantastic condition and would command a good price on Karak City's black market. A hidden scroll had indeed been found, pressed between painting and frame. Altan and Zayaa dropped everything to pour over it, their sides pressed together from shoulder to hip, the frail parchment nearly touching their noses.

"Oh, just the rank structure of the Purek military," Altan said with a careless wave when Dashi asked what it contained. "Boring stuff."

Baris slung one heavy arm over Zayaa's shoulder and another over Altan's, wedging his head between theirs. "Are you going to pretend you're ninety years old tonight, or can we celebrate finding what we came for?" He pulled out a dark bottle, dangling it with a wicked grin. "Go clean off the ancient dust and get ready for a good time."

Dashi snatched Baris' cup from his hand and downed it in one gulp. His laugh boomed, echoing between the hills of the near-taiga. He refilled the cup for her and got himself another, ruffling her hair as he reclined beside her.

Zayaa came back to the fire in new clothes: a purple deel with strange purple birds stitched onto the silk. They had sharp cheekbones and rounded, human eyes, and beaks that resembled noses. The birds peaked from behind stitched leaves and flowers, as if they were in the middle of some clandestine activity and didn't wish to be caught.

Baris laughed when he saw it. "Apropos."

"Altan said I shouldn't wear it in Karak City," Zayaa said, beaming at his regard, "but I had to have it."

"A little too close to the bone," Altan agreed, "if anyone's looking."

"Why?" Dashi wanted to know.

The other three shared a glance.

"The bird is a character from old mythology," Altan said after a beat. "A devious sort. It might attract attention." He tilted a saddlebag toward Dashi. "I brought your favorite pastries from Auntie Nima's."

"Ah." Dashi took a bite. "You're the best."

By the end of the night, she was sprawled against a log, listening to the night birds and Zayaa, who was telling them a story about some exchange she'd had in the city market. Altan gazed at Zayaa like he'd forgotten other people existed. It was Baris, however, who woke Dashi in the middle of the night.

"Wake up, cricket. I have a challenge for you."

"What is it?" Dashi sat up. Baris' challenges usually involved carrying a pack of sand up and down the stairs for hours or seeing how long she could hold her sword extended, but she loved him all the more for them.

"We're retrieving something from the ruin."

She rubbed her eyes. "Altan said we'd get the rest in the morning."

"This isn't for resale. This is a gift for Zayaa's naming day."

"I don't think she'd wear the snake headdress," Dashi mumbled, because that was the only thing her sleepy brain could remember.

Baris pushed her shoulder, grinning. "Not the headdress, you dolt. The necklace. The one with the huge amethyst pendant."

Dashi hesitated. A necklace like that would be worth a lot of money in Karak City. They didn't usually gift themselves with such expensive relics.

"Please," said Baris.

They went into the domed bathhouse together, Baris holding the lantern, while Dashi bounced lightly on her toes, readying herself for the climb. The amethyst gleamed down at them: an unblinking purple eye.

She gave Baris a sideways glance. "Why are we doing this again?"

"Because a beautiful necklace deserves to be worn," he said with customary glibness. "You saw how happy the new deel made her. This will match it."

"Are you sure she wouldn't rather have the snake headdress? It's an easier climb." But she started up the column anyway, because Baris had asked nicely.

When Altan woke her at dawn, she'd been dreaming about wolves and forgotten all about the necklace.

"Psst. Dashi."

Dashi rose to one elbow, looking around wildly. "What's wrong?"

"There's an amethyst neck—"

"Baris already beat you to it," Dashi said, flopping back down.

"What?" Altan had a strange look on his face, but Dashi was too sleepy to figure out what it meant.

"Maybe you can both give it to her," she mumbled, closing her eyes.

She never did find out how the necklace came to Zayaa—if Baris gave it to her, or if they decided to jointly gift it, as Dashi had suggested. For her part, Dashi gave Zayaa a fine set of map-making tools, which Dashi thought was eminently more practical and which Zayaa used often, though not as often as she wore the amethyst necklace in front of Altan and Baris.

Chapter 12

As Cook had predicted, guests for the Founding Day celebrations began arriving the next morning, one day before the first feast. Riders and horse-drawn carts trickled through New Osb's gates. Heavy wagons, piled high with the goods of opportunistic merchants, crept up the incline into the city, lugged by teams of yaks. Once, when Dashi was running across the courtyard from one of the cellars, she caught a glimpse of the road through the open gates. A line of travelers stretched over the hill and out of sight.

"I can't believe so many people made the journey from Karak City," she remarked to Cook, thumping an onion down on the block to be chopped.

"There'll be more coming," Cook said, her cheery demeanor turned dark by lack of sleep and the strain of near-constant activity. "The khan decreed that each noble house send representatives."

"From the whole *country?*"

"Nobles coming out of our ears," Cook grumbled, madly stirring a pot of sauce to prevent it from sticking. "This one grouching about the journey. That one complaining about the food. Do your best, Marzhan says. The people must be here to witness history, the khan says. But if the feast is a disaster, no one will care that I wasn't given any notice. I'll be out on my rear, without a job. And that's the *best-case* scenario!" She pointed a dripping wooden spoon at Dashi.

"Wait," Dashi said before Cook could continue. "No one let you know that this many people were coming?"

"Not soon enough that I could do something about it! The international delegations have been arranged for a while, so I'd already planned for them. But that many of our own nobles? It takes *weeks* to get food all the way out here and—"

"How long ago did you find out?"

"Marzhan swears she gave me as much notice as she could, but she only told me two weeks ago, so I don't see how that could be true." Cook continued grousing, taking her anger out on the sauce.

Two weeks would have been shortly after Idree arrived. *The people must be here to witness history, the khan had said.* The timing couldn't be coincidental. Dashi wondered if the khan planned to unveil the golden needle, then promptly discarded the idea. For one thing, the needle was small and relatively unimpressive. The khan, Dashi knew, appreciated pomp. Secondly, announcing the existence of a tiny, easily concealed object of incalculable value seemed like a poor strategic move, practically an invitation to thieves.

No, she thought, if the khan planned to unveil something at Founding Day, it was more likely to be the seamstress. If that happened, freeing Idree would move from *difficult* to *nearly impossible*. Everyone, in Karakal and beyond, would know about her sister. Even those who hadn't made the journey to New Osb for Founding Day would hear about her. *Do something*, her mind screamed, but she couldn't think of what. She hadn't managed to catch even a glimpse of her sister yet, let alone the golden needle.

The day wore on. Dashi chopped garlic and sluiced dishes through soapy water and wiped the sweat from her forehead. All the while, she was trying to figure out how to help her sister. By midmorning, the kitchen was bustling. By afternoon, the ovens had made it oppressive.

Dashi would have done almost anything for a breath of fresh air, but there were no opportunities. Even the house and grounds servants, no strangers to hard work and discomfort, grabbed their bowls and backed out of the kitchen like scared dogs, disappearing in search of some place cooler to eat.

Cook didn't dismiss the kitchen servants until after midnight, with a warning that they would be back to work before dawn. The courtyard was still bustling when Dashi dragged herself through it, her eyes lingering on the wall she'd climbed the previous night. Undeterred by the late hour, guests were everywhere: gossiping in small groups, gawking at the torchlit palace, and moving so much luggage that it looked like they planned to stay for months. Grounds servants, looking as tired as Dashi felt, tugged draft animals behind them. Guards, called in to work extra shifts, stalked back and forth, telling guests to go inside and warning a man not to let his horse eat the ornamental plants. The shaggy-haired guard who was Cook's friend scolded a pair of children for trying to peek into the wine cellar as he emerged.

A plan—or as much of a plan as she usually made—began to coalesce in Dashi's mind. *The feasts.* With the khan, his advisors and the guests all attending the nightly feasts, most of the guards would be assigned to the great hall. The khan's floor would be the emptiest it would ever be. Even Idree would probably be at the feast. There would be no better time to search for the golden needle.

The Founding Day celebrations began at night and continued for three full days of feasting, dancing and, for those wealthy enough to bring their own birds and dogs, hunting. For the kitchen servants, this translated to more heat, more bustle, and more barked orders from an increasingly cranky Cook.

"I said one hundred potatoes, not seventy!"

"Someone get that great oaf to unlock the wine cellar. We're short thirteen bottles!"

"Go ask Marzhan if the dumplings are supposed to be served to the lesser nobles or if they're only getting six courses. And get these," Cook waved a list over her shoulder without looking, "on your way back."

This last command was barked through a haze of steam so Dashi couldn't be sure it was meant for her, but she snatched the list from Cook's hand anyway, desperate to be outside.

"Where's Marzhan?" she asked, sidling up to a servant directing the waves of guests through the courtyard. The pin on his chest marked him as one of the khan's servants. His name floated up from the depths of her subconscious: *Jagun.*

"How should I know?" Jagun snapped.

"Well, have you seen her? She was right here an hour ago."

Jagun gave Dashi a once-over, taking in the grease spots on her sleeve and the splash of dark sauce that marred her golden sash. "You shouldn't be out here in that. Founding Day is for celebrating Karakal's might, not its filth."

A fanfare of horns split the air before Dashi could respond, heralding the arrival of an esteemed guest at New Osb's outer gate. Someone important enough to be announced had likely also garnered Marzhan's attention, Dashi decided and she turned her back on Jagun and slipped through the flow of incoming bodies.

The atmosphere was festive, bouncing with energy. Gauzy streamers swayed against walls. Feathers danced atop hats. Metal sparkled at throats and fingers. Most people in the crowd were Karak nobles, though Dashi did see a few people wearing Thracedon's black and gold. It made her think of Ejen, of that same flag, whipping proudly overhead while she and Sener and the other guards repelled attack after attack. She wondered which of the Thracedonian princes was currently ahead in the civil war and which had sent a delegation.

Marzhan was easy to spot, the only person looking sour-faced amidst the revelry. She stood behind two of the khan's advisors, listening as they conversed with a tall man who radiated importance. A gold circlet flashed against his dark hair. Heavily armed soldiers in Tyvalaran colors flanked him. A pair of women to Dashi's left gaped openly at the sight of the Tyvalaran prince, and Dashi remembered the conversation she'd overheard among the servants that morning.

"Good looking...A notorious womanizer."

"Tyvalarans have no standards. Steer clear...unless you want to be handsomely *rewarded. Ha!"*

The Tyvalaran soldiers fanned out in front of their prince as he started toward New Osb's inner circle. Dashi pressed back against the wall, searching through a gap in the crowd for someone with a light tread and broad shoulders, for unnervingly pale eyes and a scar that cut from ear to mouth. The servants had been gabbing about the holiday for days, but she hadn't ever considered the possibility that Sevlin might be in the foreign delegation. The sight of the Tyvalaran prince brought the idea rushing straight at her, however, in all its horrifying permutations. But as each unfamiliar Tyvalaran soldier passed, a small part of her relaxed. Perhaps Sevlin no longer had the queen's trust, Dashi mused, as the last of the soldiers marched up the hill. He had failed to retrieve the golden needle. Maybe he'd been demoted. Pushing aside the guilt that twined with her relief, Dashi turned away.

Marzhan had fallen into step with one of the Tyvalarans, her hands moving in time to her words. Behind her, more Karak nobles filed through the gates, their faces dusty. Other guests were arriving by water.

Dashi could see dozens of small riverboats pulled up beside the bridge she'd crossed to enter New Osb. The river continued to the east, fishtailing back and forth, before plunging irretrievably between the dark ridges of the taiga.

"Reminiscing on your time in my lovely prison?"

Ese's voice made her start, but she didn't turn.

"*Your* prison?" Her eyes moved to the other side of the gate, where New Osb's third wall slowly unfolded from the earth, a seedling raising itself toward the sun. Ragged laborers scrambled over it like ants, setting block after block under the watchful eye of guards. *Prisoners*. Probably some who'd arrived in the same convoy as she had.

Ese moved into her field of vision, adjusting the delicate spectacles that perched on the broken hump of his nose.

"I was the commanding officer at the prison," he said, low-voiced in the hubbub. "How do you think Osol was able to get you out so easily?"

Dashi had a fleeting memory of Negan, the previous consul, inches from her face. *"I sent a summons to the captain in charge of the prison, requesting that you be turned over to my custody. Do you know what I received instead? A body! He said you were already dead."*

"Whose body did you send to Negan in my place?" she asked.

Ese's shoulders rose once, unconcerned. "There are plenty of people with no one to miss them in the dirt circle. Plenty of bodies too."

"So you made a show of rescuing me when you were responsible for that cesspit all along?" Dashi scoffed. *Fitting*.

"To the contrary, that 'cesspit' was much improved by my tenure. The previous captain let the guards entertain themselves any way they liked. Poor rations and a little dirt were nothing compared to the festering ulcer it once was. That you were intact enough to ride in the khan's race is a testament to how good your treatment was."

"It's a little self-serving to keep the prisoners in good shape so they can better do your bidding."

"You would have preferred it the way it was before, with daily privation and nightly depravity?"

"No." She felt the scowl on her face. "But I don't have any tolerance for your self-righteousness either."

"I hear it's much easier to wind up in prison these days, now that the khan needs laborers. You might have been one of their number," he nodded toward the prison laborers, "if your feud with Negan's brother hadn't come to my attention. Still destined to arrive in New Osb, only as a prisoner instead of as a...*rescuer*."

Rescuer. Dashi stiffened. *Idree.*

"A message from Osol found its way to me this morning. Post mortem, of course." He flicked a piece of dust from his sleeve, seemingly uninterested in their conversation. "He confirmed that you'd been hiding the golden needle."

"You knew that."

His eyes strayed to the parade of nobles streaming through the gate. "He also reported that your sister is the seamstress."

Dashi huffed a laugh. "I should've guessed you were only speaking to me because I might be of use now."

"Oh, you're of no use to me, not when the khan already has the golden needle." Ese's voice was flat. "I suppose I'm just curious. It's not every day you find out a magic wielder has reemerged."

"She's not a magic wielder," Dashi said firmly. *She won't be. I'll get her out before the khan can locate a vein of magic.*

"She will be," Ese said. "I give credit for what you've done"—a nod to her servant's uniform, to the idea of sneaking into the khan's stronghold—"but you won't be able to rescue her. Temur will never let her out of his grasp."

He will.

"How old is your sister?" he asked.

"Thirteen."

"Thirteen," he repeated, thoughtful. "Your sister is the seamstress and *you* were chosen to enter the khan's race to find the golden needle."

"*Chosen*? You make it sound like I won a prize."

"Didn't you? You escaped a death sentence—for a crime you *did* commit—and were given a chance at your freedom, which you ultimately gained."

"I—I—" She was nearly speechless. "You expect me to be *grateful* because you strapped pyrothrite to me?"

"I expect you to move on. When soldiers fail at an assignment, they do not stand and rail at the enemy. They move. They adapt."

"I'm not one of your soldiers."

"If you were one of my soldiers we could have omitted this exchange entirely," Ese said. "I was only noting the roles you and your sister are playing, not plumbing the reaches of your gratitude, though it is clear such an expedition would not take long."

Dashi rubbed her temple. She needed to return to the inner circle. Marzhan had long since disappeared.

"What are you saying?" she asked. "That Idree and I are involved in this mess by one big coincidence?"

"I'm saying that if you have not thought about your sister's historical importance—of your own—it might behoove you to start." He turned to leave. "I do not believe in coincidences, only connections."

Dashi snorted as she watched him go. She wouldn't have pegged Ese as the type to put stock in some cosmic destiny. Then again, she hadn't thought he'd wear offering oil. She let her eyes drift, over the khan's crowd, over the khan's walls, but her gaze was inward, sifting Ese's words for truth.

Chapter 13

That evening, Dashi lugged plate after plate up the kitchen steps to the staging alcove off of the great hall. Food flowed out of the kitchen like a river, each dish carefully crafted by Cook: braised lamb flanks still radiating heat; *Khuushuur* dumplings filled with goat cheese and garlic; yak shanks, roasted with beets and tarragon; a thick rice mixture served with onions and mare's milk curds. Tureens of sauces, stacks of plates, piles of bread. Dashi had never seen so much food in her life.

She could see a small sliver of the great hall—the dais and the area immediately around it—but only if she peered through the joints in the tall screens that had been erected to hide the staging area. A handful of musicians coaxed notes from square fiddles, the music careening around the large space. At the front of the hall, an entertainer exhaled a plume of fire, then produced a perfect flower, seemingly out of the smoke. The crowd of nobles and foreign dignitaries applauded.

The khan was there too, clapping primly. Idree was not.

Dashi returned to the kitchen and hefted another platter upstairs. She peeked through the screen again. Still no Idree. A crash made Dashi wheel around, her hand reaching for one of the serving knives. She drew a shaky breath and straightened slowly. One of the servants had turned too quickly, sending a wave of gravy sluicing over himself and another woman. The woman peered down at her front in dismay, then at the goblet of wine she'd been about to serve, where a chunk of meat now bobbed.

"Don't just stand there," Marzhan snapped. "Get it cleaned up before someone slips. Then get yourselves cleaned up. A fresh deel for both of you." Her eyes darted across the alcove, alighting on Dashi. "You have serving experience. Until Barga gets back, you'll take her place."

Dashi opened her mouth, then shut it again. Being a house servant was the position she'd wanted all along, but tonight was not the night for a promotion. Her lowly kitchen position was what would let her steal away, once all the food had been brought up.

"I'll let Cook know you're with me," Marzhan said. "Don't mess up and remember to flourish as you place your tray." She demonstrated a bow and an artful twist of her hands as she set down an imaginary tray.

"Yes, Marzhan." She could do that. *Probably.*

"Follow Erdene." Marzhan pointed to a servant slightly older than Dashi. "She knows which tables to serve."

"Yes, Marzhan." She could no longer see the dais through the crack in the screen. Had Idree come?

At Marzhan's signal, the servants hefted their trays and began the march into the great hall. Erdene headed for a table near the dais and Dashi's stomach dropped. Her sister still hadn't arrived. Was the khan planning to unveil the seamstress at tomorrow's feast instead?

The foreign delegations were allowed weapons, Dashi noted enviously as she passed. It was only a token nod to self-defense, however. The Tyvalaran and the Thracedonian soldiers standing discreetly behind their respective dignitaries could never hope to defeat the Karak forces, if that's what it came to. Still, Dashi respected the impulse. It was always better to go down fighting than to be slaughtered like a calf.

Erdene peeled off, angling for one end of the table while Dashi went to the other. Doing her best attempt at an elaborate flourish, Dashi set her trays down. The Karak nobles kept up their chatter, not acknowledging the servants but exclaiming over the food as if it had materialized by magic.

Dashi glanced down the length of the table, making sure that Erdene had also finished; they were supposed to arrive and leave in unison. Erdene nodded her readiness, but as she stepped away, Dashi caught a glimpse of the Tyvalaran table behind her. The man seated at the prince's right hand was flawless from this angle: a straight nose and strong jaw in profile; hair and skin in shades of brown; a naturally serious mouth, though at the moment it was tipped up in levity. Dashi couldn't see the scar that cut the opposite side of his face, tracing from ear to mouth, but she knew him just the same. *Sevlin.*

The recognition took only a fraction of a second. Dashi looked away.

"What are you waiting for?" Erdene hissed from beside her. "Move!"

Move. That seemed like a good idea. As in, away from Sevlin. Away from the threat of being recognized.

Dashi started back toward the curtained area, placing one foot carefully in front of the other. *Don't stumble. Don't speak. Don't do anything to attract attention.* Even her breaths were measured, the same as when she was hunting. *Except I'm the prey this time.* She fought the urge to look over her shoulder to see if Sevlin had noticed her. *He didn't. Servants are invisible.*

"These next," Erdene said, indicating a second set of trays.

Numbly, Dashi picked them up. At least these were supposed to go to the back of the hall, far away from the Tyvalaran table. She caught glimpses of Sevlin over the heads of the seated guests as she followed Erdene. Where had he been when the Tyvalaran delegation arrived? And why was he seated with them now—at the prince's side, no less—instead of standing at attention with the other Tyvalaran soldiers? Perhaps she'd been wrong. Perhaps he hadn't been punished for his performance in the khan's race but *promoted*...to the prince's personal guard. That would explain the obvious closeness she saw as the prince laughed at something Sevlin said. She glanced at the dais, where the khan had elected to eat alone. She couldn't imagine *him* ever dining with his bodyguards as equals, but Tyvalar was more egalitarian than Karakal in many respects.

Dashi stopped where Erdene did. This table held a hodgepodge of people: lower-ranking Karak nobles, and a few Tyvalarans and Thracedonians who hadn't made it into the seating arrangements with the rest of their delegations. The conversation was stilted and segregated.

Tension gripped Dashi's shoulders, trying to trick her into rushing, but she shook it off, forcing herself to move fluidly. *Sometimes being slow is faster and being fast will slow you,* Baris murmured. *Focus.*

She was about to set her tray down and make her exit, when one of the guests leaned back in her seat, bumping Dashi's elbow. The tray teetered, sloshing broth onto the floor before Dashi righted it. The woman glared over her shoulder as if was *Dashi's* fault.

"My apologies, honored guest," Dashi said. She bowed her head in a show of contrition, noticing as she did that some of the broth had splashed onto the woman's sleeve, changing the fabric from gold to brown.

Ancestors protect me, I need to get out of here before she notices. Dashi snuck a look at the guest from beneath her lashes. Slightly older than Dashi, her curly hair was set in complicated rows of knots on top of her head. Her clothing, too, looked different from everyone else's. The woman stared, first at the broth in front of Dashi's boots, then at Dashi's face.

"You are no servant," the woman said, her voice an angry hiss. "You are an abomination."

"Er, apologies again," Dashi said, laying her tray on the table and stepping away before the woman had a chance to say more. From the corner of her eye, Dashi saw the woman's head turn as she passed, her eyes narrowed.

Dashi ducked inside the staging area, peeking back at the hall through a seam in the screen. The woman was talking to the man beside her and no longer staring after Dashi. Sevlin was still deep in conversation with the Tyvalaran prince. He hadn't noticed her either. Dashi exhaled. The food was served. Barga would be back soon. The ordeal was over. What's more, it had given her a golden chance to slip away. Cook would think she was still serving. Marzhan would think she'd gone back to Cook.

"Wait," Marzhan said, palming a wine bottle. "Refill Prince Zevi before you go back to the kitchen."

Dashi's fingers accepted the bottle before she realized her error. *Prince Zevi...the Tyvalaran prince? The one seated right next to Sevlin?*

"But, I—" Her mind churned, looking for an unshakable excuse.

"Now's not the time for hysteria. Barga is already busy and you did fine just now. Prince Zevi is just like any other guest. Only more important. And he's been waiting for his wine for far too long. Go." She gave Dashi a helpful push past the edge of the screen.

The Tyvalaran prince was indeed peering around for a server. He looked up, caught Dashi's eye, and raised one finger in a subtle summons. Dashi briefly contemplated spilling the wine on herself. Marzhan would send her to get a clean deel and Dashi would be spared the ordeal of going near Sevlin. But then Marzhan would know exactly when Dashi left and, when Dashi went searching for the golden needle instead of returning, it would be noticed.

Better to get this over with and make her exit when no one was watching. She swallowed and started for the Tyvalaran table, smoothing out her stride in a conscious imitation of Ese's so as not to slosh any wine. She stopped just behind the prince. He was deep in conversation, his expansive gestures denying Dashi access to his empty goblet. Sevlin, mercifully, was turned away, conversing with the woman on his other side.

Dashi tore her eyes away from Sevlin and fixed them on the prince instead, willing him to stop moving his arms so she could pour his wine and be gone. When the moment presented itself, she took a steadying breath and reached between the prince's right shoulder and Sevlin's left one. Thank the ancestors for small wonders, she thought, withdrawing the bottle a moment later. Not a drop spilled. She glanced at the other goblets on the table—she certainly didn't want to be summoned a second time—but they were full. *Good.*

She took a step backward just as the khan rose from his dais. Along with the other Karakalese in the room, Dashi bowed her head and fell still. She was stuck, an arm's length from Sevlin, until the khan released his subjects. The foreign visitors, who did not adhere to Karak customs, only dipped their heads respectfully.

"Esteemed guests—Tyvalaran, Thracedonian, Yassari, and Karak—welcome." The khan's voice echoed against the high ceilings, easily reaching the back of the hall. "It is an honor to gather here on our Founding Day."

"The Karakalese celebrate this day each year as the birth of our nation: the day when our ancestors gathered at Wolf's Head Rock and laid out the plans for a new nation. Founding Day also reminds us that, before there was a Karakal, before we were Karakalese, we were something else. We did not spring forth into the world on this day. Our ancestors already existed. They already ruled. The entire continent was their dominion. The taiga was their garden. The steppe was their lawn. On Founding Day, we honor the legacy of our ancestors, the Pureks, even as we weave it into our future."

As the khan droned on, Dashi was acutely aware of the Tyvalaran guards arrayed along the wall at her back. It would take one word from

Sevlin, *one glance*, and she would be outed as an imposter. He wouldn't know exactly why she was here, but he knew her well enough to guess that it wasn't to serve rich nobles their wine. She watched the khan from the corner of her eye, her hands clenched around the wine bottle to keep from fidgeting.

The khan raised his hand and then dropped it. Hundreds of Karak heads rose in unison, released from their obeisance. Dashi lifted hers cautiously, first checking to see where Sevlin's attention was focused. His expression, when she glimpsed it, was frighteningly intense: his jaw tight, his mouth a narrow slash. She caught sight of the piercing eyes that sometimes hunted her in dreams, but they were focused on the khan, not her.

Dashi followed his gaze, wondering what had made Sevlin react so strongly. The khan's voice, which had been building to a crescendo in the background, broke through her thoughts.

"—Let this Founding Day mark the birth of a new age. Today, I usher Karakal into an era of prosperity and power, like the khagans of old. No longer will our people, proud descendants of the Pureks, fight over the scraps of an empire. Our destiny is to unite the continent in peace, to wade in the same powerful streams as our forefathers."

The khan paused, nodding to a nearby guard. The guard flicked a cord and a curtain behind the dais fell in a crush of blue velvet. Dashi's mind grappled with the sight in front of her: a pair of arms covered in iridescent scales; antlers protruding from a head; an owl's head atop a woman's body. A fourth creature floated into the air above the others, its wings, milky and translucent like a moth's, batting the air lazily. They weren't people, precisely. Nor were they animals, though the requisite parts of several different species were on display.

The khan swung his arms wide, gesturing to the monstrosities beside him. "Honored guests, I give you the Heralds of Karakal."

Chapter 14

There was a smattering of applause from the Karakalese nobles. Mostly because the khan seemed to expect it, Dashi guessed. No one in the foreign delegations applauded. The Tyvalaran soldiers rippled with movement—stances squaring, hands moving to weapons—but when the prince flicked a glance at them, they stilled.

Sevlin's face looked like it had been carved from wood. The prince bent to whisper something to him and he shook his head slightly, his eyes never leaving the monsters standing beside the khan. The crowd was buzzing. More than one person had jumped to their feet, ready to flee.

The khan raised a hand. "Rest easy, honored guests, whether you are from Karakal or from far away. My heralds are not here to harm anyone today."

Dashi's fingers twitched uneasily around the neck of the wine bottle. Was it her imagination, or had he paused before the word *today*?

"The heralds' presence announces that Karakal is ready to take its place among history's greats: those who mastered not only the land but also," he paused dramatically, "its magic."

The mention of magic brought a collective gasp. Dashi couldn't seem to look away from the heralds. Her eyes were drawn to their peculiarities, like lightning to earth. For a moment, she forgot the great hall and the wine bottle in her hands. She even forgot that Sevlin sat an arm's length away, able to recognize her at any moment. When she did finally manage to reclaim her gaze, Dashi saw her feelings mirrored everywhere: guests with eyes and mouths wide, their expressions a mixture of fascination and revulsion. Even the servants were not immune. Marzhan herself stood motionless—a sight every bit as incongruous as a man with antlers—with her mouth open in wonderment instead of a barked order.

There were four heralds altogether, but they seemed to take up more room than they should, as if the very laws of light and space had been altered in their making. The herald with the silver scales on his arms looked around the room with bulbous eyes. He shifted from side to side, unable to decide where, or maybe how, to stand. When he opened his mouth, Dashi saw rows of teeth. The herald hovering on translucent moth wings bared her teeth and Dashi, along with everyone else, gaped. The khan glanced up at the moth-woman, a faint, satisfied smile on his lips.

The other heralds, Dashi decided, just seemed uncomfortable. What little Dashi knew about the stitching process came from Sevlin, who'd described the recovery as arduous and uncertain. The owl-woman was shaking in great, full-body shudders that rippled the midnight blue cape she wore. Every few seconds, she would turn her head in a circle and bend her knees, on the edge of launching herself off the dais. Were there wings beneath her cape? The man with the antlers held himself perfectly still. Everything about him, from the shallow rise and fall of his chest to the stiff angle of his arms, looked painful.

"The ancestors have given us this," a woman at a nearby table murmured in Karakalese.

"I was always told this is what *caused* the cataclysm," a man replied. "Nothing green will grow here."

Idree made these creatures. Her sister's absence surprised Dashi. *She* would have kept Idree a secret—the more people who knew about a prize, the more who would become thieves—but the khan's penchant for grandiosity was well known. Dashi had assumed his desire to brag about his seamstress would trump all else. She edged away from the Tyvalaran table, thinking. She'd planned to search for the golden needle tonight, but what if she could find Idree too?

Although she was the only person moving, no one noticed her slip through the arched doorway that led from the great hall to the rest of the palace. Dashi paused for a moment to look back. Her timing was perfect. The prince was whispering to Sevlin again. Marzhan was still immobile, staring at the creatures. The khan's voice rang out, unwittingly providing the perfect distraction as he invited his guests to step closer to the heralds. *Who would want to get* closer *to those things?* Yet, a handful of guests rose from their seats, propelled either by curiosity or a desire to impress. One young man pushed his way to the front and bowed deeply to the khan. Whatever the khan said was inaudible to Dashi, but the man pointed to the moth woman in response.

The khan said something to the woman, beckoning with one finger. She hesitated, then jerked forward, an errant dog brought to heel. When she was nearly level with the young man, he reached out and ran a hand down her hip and leg, ignoring the snarling expression on her face. Several more men pressed forward, eager for a turn. Dashi suppressed a snort. With this kind of pageantry, no one would note her absence for a long time.

Recalling the layout of the palace's first floor, she started for the atrium garden, letting her polite mask slip now that she was alone. It seemed a strange coincidence that Sevlin should be here, in the khan's new city, at the exact moment that the heralds were unveiled. She knew how badly he wanted the golden needle—and, by extension, the seamstress—for Tyvalar. The other guests might not understand the mechanics of making a herald, but Sevlin would. He would know that the khan had found both the needle and the seamstress. *And, apparently, a vein of magic.*

I have to get Idree out of here before Sevlin gets involved, she thought, peeking through one of the windows that overlooked the atrium garden. Seeing only moonlit greenery, Dashi eased the door open. There were hundreds of people in the palace tonight, but here they seemed a world away. Every sound stood out against the quiet: her breath, the rustle of her clothing, the soft tread of her boots. Nearby, the needles of a shrub shivered, listening.

"A fellow wanderer in the night." The voice was soft and unfamiliar.

Dashi froze. Whoever had spoken was on her right, but she didn't see anyone until a dark head emerged from behind a screen of branches. The moonlight cut across his face, revealing the advisor who'd told her about the herbs.

"Ancestors above," she blurted, "are you *always* here?" This was the third time she'd seen him in or near the garden and whatever circumspection she should have possessed was gone, shaken away by the events of the past hour.

"Very nearly." He sounded amused, not offended, by her candor. "It's one of the few places I can go that is relatively unobserved."

She glanced pointedly at the dark windows that surrounded the atrium. "Very private."

"Not many people come here on a good day and, in the dark, I'm practically invisible. It's a good place to meet, ah, visitors."

Did he mean a tryst? She couldn't figure out why he wouldn't just bring someone to his bedroom, but her musings were cut short by another, more pressing, concern: his guards. He had traveled with a herd of them before, nearly as many as the khan.

He caught her nervous glance at the bushes and smiled knowingly. "Don't worry. I only have one overseer tonight and he's loyal to me."

"I'm on my way back to the kitchen," she said uncertainly, struck by the strangeness of that statement and by the darkness cloaking the guard's whereabouts. "I was only passing through."

He cocked his head, throwing his thick hair askew. "The kitchen is on the other side of the palace. I'm not allowed to roam much, but even *I* know that."

Not allowed? "There are too many guests the other way. I'm...not supposed to be seen with my deel a mess," she said, glad that the shadows hid her clean uniform.

He shrugged, too courteous to pry. "Ese said not to talk to you if I saw you again, but you seem fairly innocuous to me."

"You know Ese?"

"Since he was an awkward thirteen-year-old. You just missed him."

She nodded to cover her surprise. Was Ese one of his...visitors? There was a warmth in the man's voice that was impossible to mistake. He didn't just know Ese but knew him *well*. What's more, he sounded like he *liked* him. It was a reckless thing for one of the khan's advisors to admit, considering the death notice on Ese's head.

"I take it you've developed a callous against his manipulation," Dashi said, "since you seem to think highly of him."

The floppy-haired man laughed, still quiet. "He's always been a, ah, planner, though not always this bad."

"I'll take your word for it." Despite her curiosity, Dashi stepped toward the door. The advisor seemed to be in the garden all the time; she could find out about Ese later.

"Goodnight," the man said softly, as Dashi stepped outside.

She knew there were still guards patrolling, but after days of being inundated with people and carts and animals, the palace grounds seemed empty. Dashi relaxed fractionally as she pulled herself up onto the overhang above the wine cellar door. The Yassari boots tingled pleasantly as she climbed to the khan's floor, their strange soles catching and then releasing with perfect timing. They weren't enough to let her make truly impossible climbs, but they could make a difficult one easier.

When Dashi peeked into the window of the khan's office, she couldn't help the grin that spread over her face. *Empty.* She perched precariously on the sill, working at the lock. It opened with a click of approval, but as she stowed her tools, her gaze shifted rightward, toward Idree's window. At the beginning of the night, Dashi had only hoped to locate the golden needle, but now greed took hold. She wanted the needle *and* her sister. After the disappointment of not seeing Idree in the great hall, worry throbbed in her chest.

She drew the office window nearly closed, careful not to reengage the lock. Then, she hopped to the next sill, working her way across the palace wall to the far window. Idree's room was exactly as it had been before. Impersonal. Empty. *No. Idree should be here.* Dashi wanted to pound her fists against the stone. *If she wasn't in the great hall and she wasn't in her bedroom...*

Dashi exhaled slowly, thinking. There were more rooms on the khan's floor where her sister—and the needle—might be. She couldn't access them from this side of the building, but maybe she could go in through the khan's office after she'd searched it. She slunk back across the sills, her mind spinning uneasily, assessing the plan like it was a ruin and there were traps hidden throughout.

She was soundless as she slid through the office window. Flexing her aching fingers, she turned to survey the room. The shadowed shelves at the perimeter drew her first, but there was no sign of the lock box Ese had mentioned, or any other likely hiding spot for the golden needle. She went next to the khan's desk. It was a massive block, half as long as the room itself, with rows upon rows of small, cubby-style drawers. Ignoring the lower ones, which were unlocked, she went straight for the top row, where the drawers were wide and adorned with filigreed brass keyholes.

The minutes ticked by as she worked each lock, the time broken only by her muttered curses and her need to stop and stretch her fingers. *Zayaa would've been finished and gone by now,* she thought. On the other side of the office door, she heard the susurrus of conversation: servants, always quiet, even when their master was away.

The first drawer had papers in it—some sort of trade agreements, by the look of them. The second drawer contained more papers and this time Dashi didn't even stop to glance through them. The third drawer was full of gold bars, stacked in neat, even rows from front to back. The sight made her fingers twitch, but she shut the drawer resolutely without taking anything.

Maybe this one, she thought, as she started on the final drawer. The sound of footsteps passing the office door made her freeze. She rethawed only after the danger had passed. The mild sweetness of sealing wax greeted her when the final lock popped. She looked down upon more paper: letters, this time, pressed flat by the weight of the khan's signet.

Blowing out a frustrated breath, Dashi closed the drawer and gathered her tools. She went around the room, peeking behind tapestries and paintings and silently shifting furniture, but the lock box was not set into the walls. She stopped before a large table in one corner, her eyes drawn to what lay on top: a map so large that it had been laid out in sections, side by side, spread over the tabletop like a carpet.

Maps had dictated much of her former life, deciding when and how much she ate, where she slept, and which ruins she explored with Altan, Baris and Zayaa. If they weren't following a particular map, they were creating one: Altan's golden head against Zayaa's dark one; the scratch of handwriting; Baris and Dashi sprawled nearby, offering input.

This map showed Karakal's eastern border, where the known world—New Osb being its easternmost outpost—bumped into the taiga. Graceful handwriting covered the papers, describing topography, river depths, and the location of Purek ruins. Dashi hovered alongside the table, her gaze leapfrogging between notations as she mentally overlaid this map with her own knowledge of the eastern region. She'd only been to two of these ruins. Her finger found them and, yes, the map acknowledged that both had been raided previously. Other ruins, unfamiliar to Dashi, appeared to have been more fruitful, yielding a number of scrolls and antiquities. Altan would have gnashed his teeth in frustration if he'd known he'd overlooked such bounty. But then, he'd been hunting for the golden needle so he'd focused his—*their*—attention on the northern border region, not the eastern one.

The brief descriptions jotted beneath each ruin reminded her of the copious notes Altan and Zayaa used to take, now that she thought about it. Some makers filled in their maps, trying to disguise their lack of knowledge by adding drawings of fantastical places and beasts. Altan and Zayaa had despised that. *"Ignorance isn't bliss, it's an abscess,"* Zayaa had always said, in a tone of dark amusement. *"Refusing to acknowledge something doesn't make it go away. It just festers."*

This mapmaker seemed to share the sentiment; much of the taiga had been left blank. To one side of the map—two days northeast of New Osb, Dashi estimated—she found a point that made her eyebrows rise.

"Foundation and walls located. 1 killed and 2 injured. 2 scrolls point to the area south of the river."

Her eyes tracked back to the Temuli River, which curled in front of New Osb before plunging into the taiga and cleaving itself into two branches. The northern branch of the Temuli was a dark, truncated line, unknown and unmapped. The southern branch, by contrast, trailed deep into the taiga. Someone had walked its contours, meticulously documenting as they went.

"Temple complex for the training of acolytes," read a notation along its southern shore. *"Tapestry points to the 'Finger of the Mother' itself, not the southern reaches."* The word *not* was underlined four times, frustration evident in every stroke of ink.

A notation at a nearby site read: *"Earthen ruin. 17 scrolls. Murals confirm artifact is on Mother's Finger."* This time, the mapmaker had included the Purek character for 'river.'

17 scrolls! What a haul, Dashi thought, though she frowned at the word *artifact.* The dates on each notation were recent ones. Whatever artifact the map referred to, it wasn't the golden needle. The second part of the notation was a little easier to parse. The Pureks tended to anthropomorphize geographical features. Judging from the notations, 'Mother' looked like it was the Purek name for the Temuli River. Mother's Finger, then, might refer to the peninsula that lay between the two branches of the river. She glanced at the corresponding strip of land on the map, but it was blank.

Staring down at the dogged notes and the unmapped reaches, Dashi felt a wash of familiarity...and a begrudging admiration. This must be the work of the new consul, dispatched to add to the khan's collection of Purek antiquities. The map, and the exploration efforts it represented, were nothing short of extraordinary. The ruins it showed were inside the taiga. *Deep* inside. Not only had the new consul braved the taiga multiple times, but, perhaps more notably, she'd made it back. Even Negan hadn't accomplished that.

The scrape of metal on metal jerked her attention away from the map, riveting her on the door to the office. Someone was unlocking it. Dashi flung herself at the window, banging her shin against the frame as she ducked outside and shut it behind her. The door to the office opened, spilling a shaft of light onto the center of the sill, a finger's width from the tips of her boots. She let go of a relieved breath, settling in to wait. After several minutes of steady light, however, Dashi chanced a look. Two guards stood with their backs to the window. A pair of the khan's advisors were at one of the shelves, bent over a book. Their animated discussion showed no signs of waning. As she watched, one of them flopped into a chair, his posture unhurried.

Cursed ancestors. Tonight had been a perfect chance to move around New Osb with impunity, yet she had nothing to show for it. *No needle and no Idree.* Dashi slumped for a moment, awash in frustration, before she forcibly straightened her shoulders and began her descent.

She had just stepped onto the small roof that overhung the wine cellar when she heard the jingle of keys and the woosh of a door closing. Crouched on the slick roof tiles, Dashi stilled, one hand against the wall. A guard appeared from below the roof's edge, striding away from the cellar and across the courtyard. He carried no wine bottles, just a massive key ring in one hand.

The guard disappeared, but Dashi stayed where she was, turning over the idea that had blossomed amid her disappointment. She thought of Cook complaining about the locked wine cellar and about how the wine in the Karak City palace hadn't been locked up at all. She thought about how Idree was missing from both the great hall and her room on the khan's floor.

Gently, Zayaa admonished in her head, following her turn of thoughts. *Patiently. Locks are like most things; it's best if you go at them from an angle, instead of trying to plow straight through, the way you usually do.*

Dashi nodded—to herself, to the Zayaa who lived on in her mind—and dropped to the ground beside the wine cellar door, her hand already on the leather wallet that held her lock picks.

Chapter 15

Dashi slid the lock picks back into the wallet with one hand, casting a final glance behind her. The moon had risen and, though the palace cast a long shadow over the wine cellar door, she was in plain sight. Every sound, from the scuff of her own feet to the calls of the night birds, was drowned by the noise coming from the great hall: fiddles and a deep bass drum, clapping hands and stamping feet, occasional shouts of laughter. Even small actions, like picking the lock, had seemed muffled and alien. Dashi kept turning around, expecting to find someone sneaking up on her, the telltale sounds of their approach hidden.

Without warning, the door to the wine cellar started to open on its own. "Captain?" A head of lank hair leaned out, looking left.

Dashi struck fast, lifting the knife from her boot and bringing the handle against his ear like a hammer. He hit the ground hard, his slumped body preventing the door from closing. Dashi stepped over him and into the wine cellar, swiveling to assess the next threat. Inside, casks of ale and pallets of wine bottles stood sentry, stacked higher than her head. The cellar was deeper than she'd expected, much larger than the food cellars with which she'd become familiar.

Grabbing the downed guard by the ankles, Dashi maneuvered him behind a stack of casks. She crouched beside him, keeping an eye on the rest of the wine cellar while she tied his hands with some rope that was wrapped around a pallet. His pockets bore only a few coins. His sword belt was much too big for her, so she drew the sword and left the scabbard on the ground.

Her pulse thundered in her ears. She'd played a careful game as a servant: skulking, listening, spying, but always staying well behind the line of official attention. Somehow, without entirely meaning to, she'd just galloped across it. An unconscious guard meant someone would be searching for the perpetrator. The worst part was, she didn't even know if her transgression would be worth the cost.

A few minutes spent examining the rows of pallets gave Dashi a sinking feeling. Yes, she could see that the dirt floor had been trampled by many feet, but that *would* be the case, wouldn't it? And yes, there had been a guard *inside* the locked cellar, but that didn't mean he was protecting anything she wanted. Dashi began walking down each row, searching for something—*anything*—interesting. All she found were bottles collecting dust and the pulse of music, feverish and incessant, coming from the great hall overhead. As she turned down another row, frustration bubbling in her chest, a rectangle of light appeared on the wall opposite her, a man's shadow looming in the center. Both the light and the shadow disappeared as, somewhere in the cellar, a door shut.

She couldn't hear anything over the music. She couldn't see anything because the rows of pallets and ale casks crowded around her. But she knew someone was there and, with a start, she realized there was a second door, in the back wall of the wine cellar. Her pulse doubled.

Dashi pulled herself up onto the nearest stack of pallets. She lay flat on top, dust tickling her nose and music throbbing through the ceiling just above her head. A man appeared from behind a row of casks.

"Vitraish said everything is fine," he said, shouting to be heard over the music. "Just fever moaning, though how he could hear anything over this, I'll never know." He raised his lantern, turning as he tried to pinpoint his companion in the dim cellar. "Where'd you go?"

Dashi waited until he'd reached the row where his companion lay. Muttering a curse, he knelt to feel the man's pulse, at first not noticing his bound hands.

"What—"

Without warning, Dashi launched herself from her perch, landing squarely on the man's back. He'd been squatting over his friend and, though Dashi was small, she still sent him sprawling onto the ground. She was up instantly, her left arm crooking around the front of his neck, her right hand locking it in place so that he couldn't dislodge it. He threw himself back into the cellar wall in a brief, violent effort to force her off. Pain exploded up Dashi's shoulder, but she kept her head down, tucked in tight against his. He fell forward, first to his knees and then onto his face, as his brain shut down from the lack of blood.

Dashi allowed herself a flare of elation—her friend Baris would have been proud; he'd been the one to teach her that move—and then she was hustling for more rope. The second guard wouldn't be unconscious for long. Thankfully, he'd fallen next to one of the poles that supported the ceiling so there was no need to move him. She tied his hands to the pole and then, for good measure, she tied his feet to a pallet so that he was stretched out, a trussed pig ready for the spit. He could probably kick until he pulled the stack of pallets over onto himself, but she didn't think he would. She sliced wide strips of cloth from the first guard's uniform and tied them over both guards' eyes. If she came out this way again, she didn't want them to be able to describe her.

He smelled strongly, though not unpleasantly, of spice and smoke. Sure enough, she found a pipe and pouch in his deel. She tossed them aside and resumed her search, her hand finally coming to rest on the cool hardness of keys in his breast pocket. She held the key ring up triumphantly. There were dozens of them. One of them *must* be useful.

Holding his lantern in one hand and the first guard's sword in the other, Dashi headed in the direction of the second door.

The door wasn't at the end of the first row she checked, nor of the second. The music above her increased in tempo and she wondered if the khan had sent his monstrous heralds away, like toys he'd tired of, or if they had to stand next to his dais and watch the dancing. Dashi thought of how he'd reeled the moth toward himself and shuddered.

A breath of air greeted her when she started down the fifth row of casks. It was damp and earthy, not fresh, but it was moving, and that in itself was significant. The pallets nearest to the wall had scuff marks in front of them and, when Dashi bent to inspect, she saw that they'd been placed on rollers, allowing them to slide to one side. She gave the pallets a shove, biting back a cry of elation as the stack shifted to reveal a doorway. Like the wine cellar, the passageway had an earthen floor and inlaid stone walls, which met in an arched ceiling overhead. The ground sloped sharply and the air that touched her face was noticeably cool. The thought that Idree could be so close, perhaps at the end of this passageway, was an intoxicant, sudden and heady, in her bloodstream. She had to force herself to move slowly.

Suddenly Dashi whirled, the sword raised. There was no one there.

She squinted at the gray outline of the wine cellar. She'd been sure she heard someone behind her. She paused, listening again. There was a faint *drip, drip, drip* of water. A scratching sound, oddly familiar. A rodent, maybe, or perhaps wood being sanded down. Beyond that…someone talking. No, *singing*. Dashi could hear snatches of it interspersed with the music from the great hall, which was growing fainter as she went deeper.

"I met a girl, wild and strong
Said she was the daughter of a bandit band
Her touch was a mercy, her kisses honey

While I slept, she took all my money
No bed, no home, now I roam
Looking for the daughter of a bandit band."

Dashi's heart quickened. The song was Thracedonian; the same one she'd been whistling the night before Idree disappeared. And *that voice.* It was a little high-pitched and nearly tuneless, but it was beautiful to Dashi. She passed a door on her left—stout wooden planks set into the side of the passageway—but she didn't bother with it. Whatever it contained was secondary to that song. Her steps followed her heart, faster and faster until she was almost running. The passageway turned left, then right, then left again, but the singing grew louder. She stumbled to a halt as the passage split to either side.

Idree, Idree, her heart pounded. Dashi took a deep breath, trying to keep her sister's name inside. There would probably be more guards. Idree's singing had devolved into humming and—Dashi shut her eyes for a moment—it seemed to be coming from the right. Someone moaned and Idree made a soothing sound before resuming her humming.

The light grew brighter as Dashi pressed forward. It glinted off the metal bars that abruptly replaced the wall to her left, stretching from floor to ceiling. It illuminated the rows of beds and their sickly inhabitants. Dashi's eyes skipped over these things and moved on, cataloging it all but only seeking two things: threats and Idree.

There were no threats that she could see. Many other people, but no threats. Each person was confined to a bed, kept there by chains that snaked under the blankets to their arms and legs. Even without the chains, Dashi didn't think they would have been dangerous. They were all sickly and pale and their raspy breathing filled the room. *That* was the familiar sound she'd heard: not a rat scratching, not wood being abraded, but lungs, struggling to fill with oxygen. Dashi had a fleeting image of her mother's plague-ridden body, chest shuddering with each breath. She recognized the smell too: rot and vomit and blood. That's how her mother had smelled, near the end.

Dashi pursed her lips and pushed those thoughts away. Sick people weren't her problem and, in any case, she doubted the ones in front of her were contagious. She remembered Sevlin's stories about the first seamstress: *these* people had a sickness caused by the golden needle, by having their bodies stitched with magic.

Her sister was at the opposite end of the room, bent over one of the beds so that at first Dashi hadn't noticed her. Her hair swayed as she moved, looking inky and wet in the lantern light.

"Idree!" The whisper bounced against the walls. Dashi glanced reflexively over her shoulder.

Her sister looked up. Shock, then joy registered on her face in quick succession, before being replaced by a thin-lipped fear.

"Dashi!" She stood quickly, nearly upsetting the lantern at her feet. "You have to get out of here!"

"Are you alright?" Dashi had her hands on the bars, her knuckles squeezed white. The practical side of her brain noted the locked cuff around Idree's right ankle and wondered if the room housed any weapons superior to the sword she'd picked up from the guard. Some other part of her, deeper and more primal, was checking Idree's face and bare arms, analyzing her expressions and the way she moved.

"Did they hurt you?" she asked.

Idree made an impatient noise, crossing the room so that she stood in front of Dashi, with only the bars separating them. The chain on her ankle scraped the floor with each step. "Listen to me, Dashi. You need to leave." Behind Idree, heads raised from pillows. Pairs of bleary eyes watched Idree's back.

Dashi reached through and took Idree's hand. "I'm sorry," she said, weeks of apologies tripping over her tongue. "I'm so sorry. I should have known someone would come for you. I should never have let my guard down. Or I should have left the needle in the taiga. But I was afraid it would show up again somehow. The stories made it seem like it had a mind of its own and I thought it better to keep it close so I could—" She cut herself off. "I'll tell you everything later. How many guards are there?"

"You *knew*?" Idree's expression returned to shock.

"I'm sorry. I should have protected you better." The words which had so often been reluctant to roll off her tongue came easily now. She wanted to say 'I'm sorry' over and over, until her voice cracked under the strain of repetition. She deserved that. She deserved worse.

"You knew since the *taiga*?" Idree pushed her hair away from her forehead, then let it fall back again. "And you never told me?"

"I—"

"How could you not tell me I was the seamstress?" There was genuine hurt in Idree's voice.

"I'm sorry, Idree. I didn't want you to have to worry about it. I thought I could handle it for both of us. I thought about telling you a few times in Ejen, but you were having a hard time when we first got there. And then all of a sudden you were settled and happy and I didn't want..." She shook her head. "I'm here now. I'll make it right."

One section of bars was on hinges and Dashi went to it, distractedly rifling the pockets of her deel in search of the keys she'd taken from the guard. "How many guards?"

"Six. They don't usually come here though. They don't like," Idree lowered her voice, her eyes darting to the beds, "the ones who've been stitched."

"Good." Dashi inserted a key into the lock on the door. It didn't turn. "And no wonder. I saw some of them upstairs." She nodded to the beds, as she shoved a second key in, only to have it stick halfway. "Will those chains hold them if they decide to grow horns or something?"

"It doesn't happen all at once. It takes days. And most of these won't make it anyway."

Idree's voice was calm. *Too calm.* Dashi glanced up sharply. "How many have you stitched?"

"Sixty-four."

"And only the four upstairs survived?"

"Yes."

Dashi opened her mouth, then closed it again. During the khan's race, Sevlin had told her the stitching process was arduous. The results were either fantastical, like the half-animal creations she'd seen upstairs, or they were fatal. There was no in-between. But...her thirteen-year-old sister had watched *sixty* people die?

Dashi shoved the third key in, then the fourth. Why would one stupid guard have so many keys...*ah*. For the shackles on all the stitched patients. There were twenty beds. Dashi slid the first twenty keys to the bottom of the ring and started on key number twenty-one. It didn't fit either.

"What happens when one survives?" she asked.

"They're...in awe," Idree whispered. "Grateful. At least at first."

Remembering how the khan had displayed the heralds upstairs, Dashi grimaced. "Did they at least volunteer?"

Idree shook her head. "They were all prisoners. But not all of them are bad. Just everyday people, really."

"I hear it's a lot easier to get jailed in Karak City than it used to be. *Some* of us had to work at it." She glanced at Idree but her sister didn't laugh.

"There was a boy who reminded me of you, but he didn't make it. I thought he would because he'd started to make the change. He grew a beetle's shell and four legs, but he died anyway."

Idree didn't look good, Dashi decided. Yes, all her limbs seemed to be working and there were no visible injuries, but something didn't seem right. Dark circles rimmed her eyes and her skin was paler than normal. Her initial reaction at seeing Dashi had seemed authentic enough but, now that they were talking about the stitching, her voice had gone dreamlike and emotionless.

"Where is the needle? Do you have it?" Dashi asked. That was too much to hope for, really, but she had to know for sure.

"No, the khan keeps it. I only get it when it's time to stitch."

"*Where*, Idree?"

"In his rooms," her sister said vaguely. "I can hear it at night, trying to get to me."

That's what Dashi had been afraid of. The needle would always pull toward the seamstress. If she took Idree now, the khan could use the needle to track them. But what was the alternative? Leaving Idree to watch more people die while Dashi searched for something so small it could be hidden nearly anywhere?

No. Now that Idree was in front of her, Dashi couldn't let them be separated again. *I'll figure out a plan once we're gone from this place.* Maybe she could circle back on their pursuers and take the needle from them in an ambush.

"Where does this corridor go? The wine cellar and where else?" Dashi asked, trying to focus on the immediate problem. "Rotting *bullocks*, why won't any of these keys work?"

"There are more cells, like this one, but smaller. For the survivors. Past that, it's just the lift box."

"Lift box?"

"It takes me to my room. But I stay here, mostly. They get upset when I leave and...I can still feel them. Even up there. They're calmer when I'm nearby."

"All the way up to the khan's floor?" Dashi pressed. She didn't need to look at the chained patients, immobile except for their raised heads and eyes tracking Idree's every movement, to know who '*they*' were.

Idree nodded. One of the stitched patients groaned and she turned toward him. The movement was involuntary, the way a mother rushes to comfort her crying child before she even realizes what has hurt him.

"And it comes out in his office? Or in another room?" Dashi asked.

"The hall. Through a section of paneling." Idree's voice sounded a little more solid.

"How does it work? Would we be able to use it?" Dashi asked. She needed her sister focused on the present, not on magic or guilt or whatever was making her sound strange. Plus, it was useful information. She didn't think going to the khan's floor would be preferable to exiting through the wine cellar, but it was always good to have a second escape route in mind.

"You need a key." Idree nodded to the giant ring of them in Dashi's hand. The less she talked about the stitching, the more she sounded like herself. "Probably one of those, assuming you took them from a guard. Once it's unlocked, you pull the lever, wait a minute and the lift box starts to go up. Anyone could use it."

Anyone, that is, who could *get* to the lift box. Right now, Dashi couldn't even unlock Idree's cell, let alone get them out of New Osb.

"But, Dashi—"

"You don't happen to know about any other secret exits, do you?"

"No. But, Dashi—"

Click.

The lock turned over. Of course it would be one of the last ones she tried, Dashi thought. She probably could have done it quicker with her lock picks. She pushed the door open. Instantly, the stitched patients began moaning loudly and thrashing in their beds, their movements made louder by their clanking chains.

"What's wrong with them?" Dashi asked, alarmed. None of them seemed to see her. They only had eyes for Idree.

"They don't want me to leave. It's the fever. They're calmer when I stay close." Idree's dreamy voice was back.

"Well, they're going to have to get over that. Let me see your ankle." Dashi looked down the hall. The noise didn't appear to have triggered any alarm among the guards. She thought of the second guard grumbling about moaning as he walked into the cellar. Maybe the stitched patients raised this sort of ruckus all the time.

"I need to stay close to them," Idree murmured.

Dashi stepped into Idree's cell and shut the door, not enough to reengage the lock but enough to make it look like she had. The howling lost its intensity immediately, fading away into whimpers.

Dashi grabbed Idree's arms, shaking them lightly. "Idree. I need you to focus. We don't have much time."

Her sister blinked, looking at the beds and then back at Dashi. "I'm sorry. It's hard to concentrate. I've stitched so many. I can feel them in my skin, especially when they're upset."

"Alright." It was anything *but* all right. Dashi took a breath, trying to think. They'd need to make a quick exit. No lingering at the doorway while things yowled in the background. Maybe she could carry Idree on her back if Idree was too befuddled.

"Alright," she said again, kneeling in front of her sister to better access the ankle cuff. Her fingers flew through the keys. Most were too big so she didn't bother trying them. "Here's what—"

"Dashi, I can't go with you."

Dashi's head snapped up. Idree *looked* clear-eyed. Although she wasn't, obviously, because that statement made no sense.

"We'll be hunted," Idree continued. "I don't want you to be killed. And if you're captured alive, they'll keep you here in case I refuse to stitch. You'll be what they threaten me with every time."

"Is that what happens?" Dashi asked sharply. "They threaten you if you don't stitch?"

Idree looked away and Dashi took a steadying breath. Ancestors above, the khan better hope their paths never crossed.

"I'll be the seamstress as long as I'm alive, Dashi. The khan has nearly located the seamripper and when he does, he'll be unstoppable. There's no running."

"What's a seamripper? The small hooked thing that tailors use?"

Idree shrugged. "Something old and magic, like the needle. I don't know exactly but, whatever it is, the khan wants it badly. I heard him say so."

Dashi's thoughts flashed to the map she'd seen in the khan's office. *An artifact*, it had said. She didn't want to make Idree go all dreamlike again, but she needed to know as much as she could. "The vein of magic that you use to stitch, where is it?"

Idree blinked twice, clearly revisiting something in her mind.

Dashi shook her arm. "*Idree.* You have to talk to me. Where is the vein?"

"Right under the palace." Idree paused, focusing on Dashi with an effort. "It's why he built it here."

"How do you get to it?" *Three more keys down.*

"There's a door in the passage. The one you came from, through the wine cellar. Didn't you see it?"

"I saw a door, but I heard you singing so I didn't bother with it."

There was so much Dashi wanted to know: how Osol had managed to whisk Idree away in the middle of Ejen's harvest festival; how she'd been treated since; what it was like to handle magic. But there wasn't time for any of it. Her skin felt like things were crawling over it. *Breath of the ancestors.* They needed to leave.

None of the small manacle keys had opened Idree's cuff. The rest were too big. Dashi pulled out the leather wallet of lock picks and flipped it open.

"Idree, put your foot on my knee. I need better light."

When Idree didn't move, Dashi grabbed her ankle and lifted it. Still, Idree wouldn't budge, wouldn't even shift her weight.

"Idree, come *on.*"

"Dashi." Idree's voice was breathy and forlorn. "I told you to leave."

Dashi stiffened, as sharp metal pricked her spine.

"Drop whatever is in your hand," a man's voice commanded, "and get to your feet."

Chapter 16

Dashi rose slowly, releasing the lock picks in a clatter of metal. *Stupid, stupid,* to turn her back on the door. The sword she'd taken from the guard lay on the ground. She'd dropped it so she could have both hands free to work on Idree's shackle.

"How did you get in here?" the guard asked. He sounded more curious than alarmed. He must not have seen his fallen comrades yet.

"I...walked." She could hear him fumbling for something in his pocket, although the sword point stayed where it was, sharp even through the fabric of her deel. He was looking for something to tie her hands, she realized, the same way she'd bound the guards in the wine cellar.

"Don't be smart. The wine cellar is locked. Did someone help you?"

Dashi was silent, thinking. Escape would become infinitely harder after he'd tied her up. Right now, her odds were the best they'd ever be.

The stitched patients had resumed their clamor now that the guard had opened the door, and Idree kept looking between Dashi and the beds, her hands ripping at each other agitatedly. Her eyes looked huge and dark in her face.

"Stop yammering!" the guard yelled, close enough to Dashi's ear that she winced. The patients paid no attention. To Dashi, he said, "You'll talk to someone before this is through. Put your hands behind your back."

As he looked down to take her hands, the pressure from his blade slackened momentarily. Dashi dove right, her hand reaching for the sword she'd abandoned. Steel hissed through the air behind her and she ducked, still moving but knowing that she was too slow, that his blade would fall before she could defend herself. Metal crashed behind her. Dashi swept up the sword, rolling over to block the blow that must certainly be falling.

She panted up at the stone ceiling, surprised to find no guard looming above her, no blade waiting to fall. Cautiously, she sat up. Both guard and sword lay, motionless, on the ground. The guard was facedown in a pool of blood. The sword, flung by some unknown momentum, had wedged itself between the metal bars of the door. In front of everything, stood Sevlin.

He had a sword in one hand and no expression on his face and while Dashi stared, still dumbfounded, he leaned over and wiped his blade clean on the guard's back. He straightened, locking eyes with her for a long moment. She couldn't tell exactly what was in those fathomless depths. Anger? Disappointment? Something negative, she was sure. He turned away from her and knelt in front of Idree.

"Hello, Idree."

"Sevlin," Idree said in a calm voice, and that, more than anything else she'd seen from Idree so far, concerned Dashi.

The Idree from their previous journey into the taiga would have giggled or played with her hair or done something else that made her infatuation with Sevlin immediately obvious. In Ejen, Idree had grown both a little older and a little more secure with herself, but she still would have blushed and looked away from Sevlin's scrutiny. But *this* Idree—Seamstress Idree—had detached herself in a way that Dashi had never seen. It was frightening. Dashi wanted to shake her, to yell at her, to do *something* to force her to come back to herself. She couldn't stand seeing her sister like this, as a dreamy shadow of herself.

"Tell me more about this seamripper you heard the khan talking about," Sevlin said.

Idree's eyes drifted to the left.

"Idree," he persisted. "Tell me."

"It's old and magic," she said, repeating her earlier words. Dashi could barely hear her over the wailing patients.

"What does it look like?"

"I haven't seen it."

"No one said? The khan? The consul?"

Idree pulled away from him, reaching toward a stitched woman with wild hair, and Sevlin let her go. She made soothing noises as she knelt beside the woman, and began stroking her hair, patting down a stray curl only to have it pop up again. Dashi got to her feet and went to the door, pushing it nearly closed. The din lessened instantly.

Sevlin stood too. "Do you know where it is?" he asked Idree.

"The taiga, of course."

"Can you...feel it?" Dashi asked. "Like you can with the stitched patients?"

Idree closed her eyes, and for a moment Dashi thought she wouldn't answer. "No," she said in a distant voice. "The needle calls to my heart and the stitched scratch at my skin. I can feel the vein too. It becomes hot right before I dip the needle. But nothing else. The seamripper is my opposite. A counterbalance for the needle."

"The khan said that?" Sevlin asked in a sharp voice.

A counterbalance for the needle. Could such a thing undo the needle's hold on Idree?

Idree stood up and went to another patient, her chain pulling out behind her like a clanking tail. This man was older than Dashi, with a scarred face. Not a dramatic scar like Sevlin's, but a spattering of little ones, from many fights over many years. His lips were swollen and bruised looking, but when he saw Idree he smiled sleepily, his mouth parting to reveal two enormous tusks, protruding from either side of his bottom jaw in twin crescents. Idree patted his head fondly.

"Did the khan say that? Idree?"

"Hmmm?"

"The part about counterbalance." Sevlin went to stand in front of Idree again. He put a hand on her arm, but his voice was gentle.

Dashi caught a snatch of voices from the passageway and turned her head, listening. Whatever she'd heard was gone now, but that hardly mattered; she'd lingered much too long. Dashi shouldered Sevlin aside and grabbed Idree's hand, leading her sister to where they'd been standing before the guard came.

She knelt on the ground and tugged her sister's cuffed ankle forward. This time Idree complied. Dashi scraped the scattered lock picks into her lap. The torsion wrench was missing. She looked around, spotting it half-hidden beneath one of the beds.

"I don't know," Idree said to Sevlin, as Dashi returned with the wrench. "In the taiga. A temple—no." She looked confused. "I went to a temple with *you*. I can't remember it though."

Dashi reflexively looked over her shoulder. There were definitely voices now. They came closer, then began to recede. The guards must be walking down the passageway, going from the lift box to the wine cellar. When they arrived and discovered the two guards she'd tied up...

One of the lock picks tumbled from her lap. *Concentrate*, she told herself sternly. *Idree is depending on you.*

"Look at me, Idree," Sevlin said in a grave voice. "You're strong. Keep doing what the khan wants. Do you understand? You have to bide your time for a little longer. But remember you're not alone. We'll come back for you."

"We will *not* come back for her," Dashi snapped. "We will take her with us right now."

Sevlin shook his head. "The guards you tied up will be discovered any second. Then they'll come looking for who did it. Idree isn't even free yet. Besides, she's right: if you take her without the needle, they'll hunt you until you're dead. You won't even have a head start. You'll be run down on the open steppe."

"So we'll go…" *Where? Into the taiga?* She narrowed her eyes at the ankle cuff. How many tumblers were *in* this thing?

Sevlin raised an eyebrow. "With no shelter and no supplies? On the cusp of winter? At least here she won't freeze or have a leg torn off by a giant rat."

Dashi shot Sevlin a glare. She hated that he was doing this: bringing up shared experiences, insinuating himself into her decision-making, telling Idree that *they'd* be back for her. As if he had any right to voice his opinion. As if they were friends.

A shout went up from the direction of the wine cellar, bouncing off walls until only the tone was discernable: surprise, outrage. The bound guards had been discovered.

"If we—"

"There *is* no 'we,' Sevlin." She angled the torsion wrench and pick carefully, probing the keyhole. Suddenly they were yanked from her hand.

Dashi exploded to her feet, so close to him that she had to stare straight up. "What is *wrong* with you—"

"I know you hear the guards. We're leaving now before they get here."

"I'm not leaving Idree," she said, snatching at his wrist. He didn't struggle, but neither did he open his fist to give her the lock picks. "And you don't get a say."

"I do when it's my country that will be jeopardized."

She gave him a hard look. *Always the line about duty to country.*

"If we're caught," he continued, "the khan will say it's a Tyvalaran plot. He's been wanting a war for some time now. He won't have it because of me."

"So leave."

"If *you* are caught, they'll torture you and find out about me that way."

"Find out what? That you exist? That I know your name? There's nothing to find out, Sevlin."

Sevlin opened his mouth to say something and then cut himself off with a shake of his head. "Don't do this, Dashi. *Look* at her. Do you think you'd be able to escape with her like this?"

Idree stood motionless in front of them. Now that the stitched patients had calmed, so had she, but the expression of mild interest on her face did nothing to reassure Dashi. No, she couldn't escape. Not with Idree like this. Not with pursuit already so close. Not without supplies. Sevlin was right.

He must have seen the realization on her face. His hand opened and she snatched the lock picks from his palm, shoving them into the leather wallet and turning to her sister in the same motion.

"Idree," she said, taking both of her hands. Idree's dark eyes regarded her solemnly, but she said nothing. "I have to go. I'm sorry. I'm so sorry." The second time she said it she could feel her eyes start to burn. *No tears. Not right now.* She blinked hard and said, a little briskly, "I'll be back and then we'll get you out of here. Just...stay safe, alright? And try—" Her throat was tight, making it hard to get any more words out. "Try, um, to get a little break from this bunch." She nodded at the beds.

"They become—"

"I know: they become upset when you leave. But *try*, alright? It's not good for you to be down here all the time."

Sevlin tugged her arm. "We have to go."

Dashi turned away from her sister and walked to the door. Goodbyes were like burrs; best to pull them off quickly. The stitched patients started moaning when she opened the door but quieted again when Sevlin pulled it closed. The click was unbearably loud. Dashi flinched without meaning to. She took one last look at her sister through the bars.

Idree looked sad but only vaguely so. Her brow furrowed slightly. "You're wearing the boots."

Dashi smiled tightly. "Only for special occasions, remember?"

Then Sevlin had her arm, propelling her away from Idree. She shook him off before they reached the turn that would have taken them back to the wine cellar. Voices came from that direction, growing louder by the moment.

"Straight," Dashi whispered, indicating the way to the lift box. Idree had said it could get them out.

They encountered no one else as they passed the cells reserved for the stitched survivors. The cells were empty, their inhabitants still entertaining the khan's guests. Nor were there any guards. They must have all gone to the wine cellar.

"Where does this lead?" Sevlin asked. The low timbre of his voice made the hair on the back of Dashi's neck rise.

"Didn't get to eavesdrop on that part of the conversation?"

"You shouldn't expect privacy in a cell."

Dashi glared up at him. She'd forgotten how tall he was. Thracedonians tended to be shorter and stockier. She'd gotten used to people not towering over her.

"Idree called it a lift box. It comes out near her room. Well, the room the khan has for her," she amended. It wasn't Idree's room. That was back in Karak City, over Auntie Nima's bakery. Or in their cottage in Ejen, with a thatched roof overhead and a goat nibbling the grass outside.

"Where is it?" Sevlin asked.

"The room?"

"What floor? What's it near?"

Dashi grimaced. "It's on the khan's floor. Idree's room only has one window that's any good for climbing through, but it'll be tough for you. I didn't get a look at the hall, but any windows off the other side of the palace are a straight drop."

Sevlin looked at her.

"*What?* I had about three seconds and there were people outside. I didn't make it to the hall."

He gave his head one slow shake. "I didn't say anything."

"Good. Don't."

The lift box appeared at the end of the dim corridor. It sat on a wooden platform, reminding Dashi of the khan on his dais. The lift box was, as its name implied, just a box, slightly shorter than Sevlin and only a little wider. Dashi's frown deepened. It would be a tight fit for both of them. Half a dozen ropes sprouted from the top of the box and ascended into the darkness above. Other ropes plunged through a hole in the platform to the gears below.

Dashi pulled out the key ring with its damnable legion of keys and started plugging them into the locked door of the lift, one by one. Her luck seemed to have changed, however. The second key opened the door. Inside, there were two levers and nothing else. Sevlin charged in, obviously familiar with such a contraption, but Dashi was more hesitant.

She glanced up again. She hadn't given much thought to how the lift box worked when Idree first told her about it. Now that she *was* thinking about it, she found that she didn't want to get inside. Trapped inside a wooden box, she could neither fight nor run. All it would take was someone—a retributive-minded guard, say—sawing through the ropes and the thing would plunge to the ground. Even if that didn't happen, and they reached the khan's floor, escape from there would be nearly impossible. She stepped back onto the earthen floor.

Sevlin shifted impatiently inside the lift box, making the planks creak. Above it, the ropes swayed in response. "Coming or not, Dashi: pick one."

Behind them, the sounds had changed, ratcheting up in intensity. The echoes of shouted commands and running footsteps tumbled down the passageway, foreshadowing what was to come.

There had to be a better option than pressing against Sevlin in a coffin-sized box and dangling five stories in the air. She would rather climb the ropes herself than be blind to the world around her. Dashi's eyes darted over her surroundings but the end of the passageway offered few options: up, with Sevlin, or back, in a futile attempt to fight through what sounded like a hundred guards, though she knew the number couldn't possibly be that high.

Unless...

Dashi eyed the low platform on which the lift box rested. It was wide enough that it nearly touched both walls of the corridor and Dashi had to lean over to catch a glimpse of the sides. The ends were open. She could see the glint of the gears and wheels that allowed the lift box to work.

There was a narrow space between the platform and the wall, just enough that she would be able to wiggle between the wall and slide in next to the gears below the platform. She glanced at Sevlin speculatively, unsure if he would fit. *So what if he doesn't,* her mind demanded. *He's not your problem.*

Sevlin's eyes narrowed. "What?"

"Pull the lever and get out."

Sevlin tipped his head back, peering upward as if he might glimpse the khan's floor.

"Stop looking for things you can't see," Dashi said, exasperated. "Come on."

Without answering, he pulled the lever and stepped out of the lift box, closing the door behind him. The box began rising slowly, swaying gently from the movement of his exit. The gears whined, sliding the ropes downward through the holes in the platform.

"Now what?" Sevlin asked. His hand played with the hilt of his sword. It was the only sign that he was nervous.

"Slide down next to the wall and get under the platform."

He motioned for her to go first.

She shook her head. "I can get in and out easier than you can. Besides," she added, casually, "if I go first and then you end up not fitting, I might not come back out and help you fight."

Sevlin gave her a sharp look, but he stepped into the space between the wall and the platform. It was a large crack, really, tight where it pressed against Sevlin's boots. From there, his maneuvering took a comical turn. He shimmied one way, then the other, forcing his too-large body to squeeze between the platform and the wall. The whole process took less than a minute, but to Dashi, standing there with nothing to do but watch Sevlin and listen to the approaching guards, it seemed like an eternity. The lift box was ascending so slowly that, had she actually been going to the khan's floor, Dashi would have preferred to climb the stairs rather than wait for it to carry her.

The wooden edge of the platform cut into Sevlin's chest, pinning his back against the wall. He exhaled in a long burst, forcing all the air from his lungs, and then shoved himself beneath the planks. There was an audible—and painful-sounding—scrape of skin and fabric. Then he was out of sight.

As soon as Sevlin's head disappeared, Dashi jumped into the narrow space after him. There were a few twists and uncomfortable moments as the edge of the platform pressed against the wider parts of her, but then she was through, hidden just beneath the wooden edge.

Chapter 17

Somewhere to Dashi's left, the gears whirred, pulling the lift box upward. They sounded close; Sevlin must be nearly on top of them. She had a sudden fear that the hem of his deel would tangle in the gears. The guards would rip up the planking to investigate why the lift box had stalled and—*Stop it*, she told herself, forcing a slow exhale. *Sevlin is nothing if not careful.*

The guards' voices were loud enough to be heard over the gears by now. Someone swore. Lantern light, spliced into thin lines by the planking's seams, moved over Dashi's face, followed by a shadow when someone stepped onto the platform. The planks bounced with each step the guard took, a mere hand's breadth from Dashi's nose. Sevlin's body exerted a line of pressure along the left side of her body, warm but rigid with tension.

A man's voice: "The khan will have our heads."

A woman: "No. We've still got them." From the sound of her voice, she was staring upward, watching the lift box retreat. She pivoted, grinding out a shower of fine dust onto Dashi's upturned face. Dashi pressed her lips tightly together and closed her eyes.

"Athak, wait here," the woman said crisply. "The rest of us will go up to the khan's rooms in case the guards there need backup. We don't know how many intruders there are. This could be the second time the lift has gone up, or it could be part of something more coordinated to get to the khan. Athak, if the lift starts to come back down before someone has come to relieve you, it means they're doubling back. Cut the lift ropes."

The woman's boots were replaced by another pair, which stayed resolutely immobile as the remaining guard watched the lift box float upward. Sevlin's hand moved incrementally beside Dashi, his fingertips pressing briefly against her thigh, which was the only part of her he could reach without serious movement.

Well? What does your plan call for now?

Dashi gave an answering nudge of her shoulder against his. *I have it under control.*

Another press, more insistent, against her thigh. *What are you going to do?*

She could feel all his consternation in that small movement. She worked her right hand over to his bicep and pinched. *Stop pestering me. I told you I have it under control.*

He fell still after that. She turned her head cautiously, wary of any unnecessary movement. His face was already turned toward her.

The light fell in bars across him, highlighting random bits: the indentation where his neck and collarbone met, just visible where his deel had fallen open; his chin and the cleft above it; the bridge of his nose, his scar a faint shadow just out of the light's grasp. His eyes were shadowed too, but she knew he was looking at her and it made her restless and annoyed at the same time. She thought, somewhat inexplicably, of the golden needle, buzzing against the sides of its statuette, not knowing exactly who it was trying to get to but angry that it wasn't there yet.

She made herself turn away. It was time to go.

Willing her movements to be silent, or at least quieter than the whining gears, Dashi shifted sideways, sliding the sword ahead of her. Without the space to use her arms and legs, her progress was awkward, an injured beetle on its back. At the edge of the platform, Dashi took a steadying breath. She hoped the guard was facing the other way. She rose from her position, slipping slowly up through the crack between the wall and the platform like an apparition rising from its grave. The ancestors smiled upon her: the guard was indeed facing the other way.

Dashi stepped onto the platform, carefully shifting her weight to keep the planks from vibrating. Her final two strides were quick and, as the guard started to turn, she cracked the hilt of the sword down against his head. She drove her shoulder into him, sending him toppling onto the platform, head bouncing. Sevlin appeared a moment later, having extricated himself from beneath the platform much quicker than he'd hidden. He sliced two strips from the man's deel and used them to blindfold and gag him, while Dashi tied his hands and ankles with two more.

She took a step back, surveying their work. The lift box was still winding its way upward.

"Did he get a look at you?" Sevlin asked, quiet and intent.

"I don't think so. His eyes were still open when I knocked him over, but they were unfocused."

"Good."

The harshness of that single syllable made Dashi look up sharply.

"I meant what I said before," he said, sheathing his sword. Only then did she notice that he'd had it out. "If the khan had any reason to suspect that I was down here he would use my involvement as an excuse for war. Tens of thousands would die, not just one guard."

"You think the khan would go to war over a Tyvalaran bodyguard straying into a wine cellar?"

"It's more than just a wine cellar, and the khan can go to war over anything he wants."

Dashi turned toward the wine cellar, her strides lengthening into a jog. They didn't have much time before the lift box reached its destination and the guards realized it was empty. Sevlin fell into step beside her.

She wondered if he'd followed her into the wine cellar, or if he'd been snooping on his own and merely wound up at the same place. Another thought struck her: he was so worried about someone identifying him, but there was one person who still could. Well, two actually, though she wasn't sure how much sense Idree would make if questioned.

Dashi dipped her chin at his sword. "Is that what you would have done to me if I'd refused to leave Idree? Eliminated a witness?"

Sevlin gave her an incredulous look and kept jogging.

They reached the empty cells, then the split in the passageway. She knew there was no time to free her sister, but her feet still faltered at the junction. Sevlin glanced sideways, his giant strides eating up the ground as he continued without her.

Dashi took one last look in Idree's direction. "I'll come back," she whispered, before breaking into a run.

Sevlin didn't acknowledge her presence—or her absence, for that matter—when she caught up to him. They passed the door that Idree said led to the vein of magic. Sevlin didn't acknowledge that either, apparently possessed by a single-minded desire to get out undetected so he could report to his prince.

Dashi's thoughts jumped ahead of her feet, searching for her next move. She should still be able to blend in among the servants, at least for a few days. It would be risky. The guards might decide to search among the staff for a culprit but, with so many guests, Dashi had a feeling suspicion would fall elsewhere. Perhaps the presence of so many foreigners could work in her favor. She gave Sevlin a sideways glance. He was already paranoid about the Tyvalarans getting blamed but, if they *were* blamed, it might give her another chance to get Idree and the needle out of New Osb.

The guards she'd tied up were gone. Sevlin returned from the far row of casks, sword drawn but looking more at ease.

"No one," he confirmed.

Face pressed against the crack in the wine cellar door, Dashi nodded. She'd spent several minutes watching servants and guests walk across the courtyard. It was finally empty again. Music seeped from the great hall, flooding the courtyard with a fervent, joyful tide that was at odds with her mood.

Despite the music, she could hear a rhythmic pounding and it wasn't a drum. It was the beat of boots. The guards had discovered the lift box was empty. Now they would be doubling back, spreading methodically over the grounds to find their quarry. She'd seen wolves hunt in the same manner, encroaching bit by bit, provoking their prey into panicking, into a race where the wolves held all the advantages. The guards would be looking for someone running. She had to make sure she didn't fit that description

"It's clear," she said over her shoulder and darted into the night. The farther she was from the wine cellar when the guards returned, the better.

Dashi pressed against the palace wall, mindful that someone could be watching from an upstairs window. She ditched the sword the first chance she had, wedging it in some fancy bush that had been planted near the door to the atrium garden. It hung vertically, suspended in the branches like a strange ornament, hidden by the spiky foliage. Although Dashi had savored the feeling of a weapon in her hand again—of power—she was safer without it. A servant holding a weapon only invited attention.

The sheer volume of the music seemed to suppress all of her senses and she kept looking over her shoulder to make sure the presence at her back wasn't a guard. It was always Sevlin dogging her steps, though she wasn't sure why. As a guest, he could have gone in through the main doors of the great hall. Maybe he preferred a more covert reentrance.

Dashi led him along one side of the great hall, stopping at the shrubs near the corner. Light spilled from the windows, making her skin prickle. She ducked deeper into the shadows. A moment later, Sevlin slid in next to her. His deel had looked dark blue earlier, but now she saw there was a pattern woven into the fabric: leaves and raindrops, understated, almost invisible except in a certain light. Dashi didn't know enough to price the material, but she'd never seen anything that fine at the market stalls.

Sevlin followed her gaze and shifted once on his feet. Practically an admission of embarrassment from him.

"Why did you stop?" he asked.

"If you go around the corner, there's another set of doors that connects the terrace to the great hall."

Dashi could hear the ebb and flow of voices, indecipherable over the music, as guests spilled outside. She glanced up at the moon. It was nearly midnight. She'd been gone for over an hour. She hoped Marzhan and Cook hadn't noticed. Maybe she could say she'd spilled something on her deel and had gone to change. That wouldn't justify an hour's absence, but it might divert scrutiny.

"Where will you go?" Sevlin asked, following her thoughts.

"Back to the kitchen." She gave him a narrow look. "How did you end up in the wine cellar when you were supposed to be dining with the Tyvalaran delegation?"

"Are we doing this now?" He crossed his arms. "How did *you* end up in the wine cellar when you were supposed to have left the country?"

"I—" She shook her head. "It's a long story. Too long to get into here."

"Then when?"

Dashi hesitated. "I don't know," she said finally, settling on a strategy of evasion. "I have to be careful. Maybe in a day or two."

Or never. Never was also a possibility. She tried to remember how long the foreign delegations were staying. A week, maybe? Could she avoid him for that long? Meeting another person, especially a Tyvalaran, would only increase her chances of being caught. She suspected the only reason Sevlin had been able to slip away from the great hall tonight was the same reason she'd been able to: the khan's monsters had provided an enormous distraction.

There was a second reason she didn't want to meet him. Sevlin might act like he shared her desire to free Idree, but Dashi knew better. Now that he knew Idree was the seamstress, Sevlin would want her—and the needle—for his own purposes. Accepting his help would allow him to set his claws into her sister. Dashi wasn't about to spring Idree from one prison only to have her land in another.

Sevlin shook his head. "Sooner. I need answers. And we need to talk about what Idree said."

Dashi raised an eyebrow in question.

"About the seamripper. If the khan thinks it's the needle's counterbalance, he will be aiming to get it before anyone else."

She shrugged. "So let him." *I know where Idree is now*, she told herself, *and Idree said the needle is on the khan's floor. All I need to do is find it—and some supplies—and then Idree and I can be long gone.*

Sevlin's scar twitched with disapproval. "If we can find the seamripper, we have a chance to stop this for good."

"I'm not worrying about some relic, which may or may not be powerful, and which the khan may or may not ever find. My sister is *right here*, Sevlin."

"What if the seamripper can undo the needle's hold on Idree? Maybe that's what *counterbalance* means."

"'Maybes' and 'what ifs' aren't a good enough reason for me to leave her here."

"Then at least answer my other questions," Sevlin pressed, "Tonight, after the feast." The corner of his mouth pulled down in a grimace. "I would suggest meeting in the room I was assigned, but I'm fairly certain we'll be overheard." He cocked his head, eyeing her consideringly. "How long have you been a servant here? Where do the other servants go for privacy?"

She knew what he meant: where did the servants go for their trysts? "I have no idea. As far as I know, no one has time for that."

"How about the mews? Behind the stables."

Where Ese had taken her. "I don't know," she hedged. "I don't know if I can get away."

"You can," he said firmly. "Like you did tonight. Two hours before dawn."

Dashi hesitated, then nodded. "I'll be there."

She wouldn't. She'd say she slept through their meeting time or that someone had been watching her. And she'd do the same thing the next time he cornered her too. After tonight, it would probably be difficult for him to get her alone.

There was a heavy pause, though Dashi was unsure what, exactly, lay unsaid. Did he suspect that she didn't trust him with Idree? Or was he merely searching for the appropriate pleasantry for someone with whom he'd battled taiga rats but hadn't seen in a year?

Finally, Sevlin gave a curt nod and turned toward the corner of the palace wall, where he could slip in among the guests once more. Dashi turned away. Now all she had to do was—

She froze, reaching blindly backward and snagging Sevlin's deel before he could step out of the bushes.

"What is it?" Sevlin's voice was low.

"I..." *I don't know.* The great hall dumped its music into the night, oblivious to any drama outside its walls. The wind whispered across Dashi's cheek, bringing with it the smell of spices and smoke.

A guard.

She saw him a heartbeat later: a dark shadow with a gleam of metal, carefully checking the bushes that girded the periphery of the palace. It was the guard from the wine cellar, the second man she'd subdued. He pushed the branches aside, leaning forward for a better look.

"Are there more?" Sevlin whispered, his mouth nearly against her ear.

"Not yet." She'd known the guards would come searching, but she'd hoped they would waste time rechecking the wine cellar and its passageway. Unfortunately, they seemed to have concluded rather quickly that the intruder had escaped.

That's it. The guard was looking for an *intruder*. He'd started to rouse when she'd blindfolded him and gagged him but, as far as he knew, she was alone. The guard took another stride toward them and thoughts began to coalesce in Dashi's mind: rumors about another Tyvalaran, the prince; servants, giggling behind their hands.

She whipped around, grabbing a handful of Sevlin's deel with one hand and the back of his neck with the other, and pulled his mouth down to hers. His back went rigid. Then, abruptly, he loosened, returning her kiss, winding one arm around her to pull her against him. His hand slid slowly up her spine, then trailed back down to clasp the swell of her buttocks. The fingers of his other hand were splayed across her hip—tight with tension, not straying far from his sword. He pressed her back against the palace wall, kissing her harder.

"Sorry," he murmured against her startled intake of breath when the cold stone seeped through her deel.

Through one slitted eye, Dashi watched the guard poke at the bushes, closer and closer. She saw the moment he caught sight of them. The guard raised his sword and Dashi's fingers dug into Sevlin's shoulder. But the sword lowered immediately, as the guard realized what he was seeing. Dashi tilted her head back a little more, deepening their kiss, making sure she acted her part.

The guard cleared his throat, loud enough that it was audible even over the music. "You two: step out here."

Chapter 18

Sevlin jumped, pretending to notice the guard for the first time.

"Into the light," the guard prodded.

They stepped forward, into the shaft of light that fell from the windows. The guard regarded them for a moment. He was smirking, and Dashi saw the way his eyes lingered on her servant's deel and then on Sevlin's face.

"For an honored guest, you sure have...strayed," he said to Sevlin.

"Am I being detained by your country?" Sevlin demanded. The note of haughtiness in his voice caught Dashi off guard.

"You're from the Tyvalaran delegation?" the guard asked.

"Well, it should be clear I'm not Thracedonian," Sevlin said sneeringly. "I demand to be released."

"There's been a disturbance," the guard said.

"What kind of a disturbance?"

The guard ignored his question. "I'm to stop anyone suspicious."

"Suspicious? I am a *guest* of the khan!" Though Dashi had always thought of Sevlin's expressions as stiff, his face had become suddenly mobile, pinching together in obvious exasperation. "This is a...personal matter. I would like to see it resolved quietly."

"The khan has many guests, *most* of whom are in the great hall." The guard glanced behind them and waved someone over. "*You're* out here.

You can see why that might seem strange." The guard turned to Dashi. "What about you? Marzhan didn't keep you busy enough?"

Dashi made a noncommittal noise.

"Don't feel like talking?" He tilted his head toward Sevlin. "You must have been chatty enough earlier."

Dashi was saved from responding by the appearance of the shaggy-headed guard who'd joked with Cook.

"What is it?"

"Captain," the first guard said. "I found these two, er, *occupied* in the bushes."

The guard captain squinted, sizing them up. "You're a member of the Tyvalaran delegation?" he asked Sevlin.

"I am," Sevlin said in that same cavalier tone.

"Then return to your delegation and don't tarry in the bushes. We're investigating a crime and the safest place for guests is where they belong."

He motioned for the first guard to accompany him. Sevlin left without a backward glance. The guard captain watched them go, only turning back to Dashi once they'd disappeared.

"Cook has said good things about you," he said in a thoughtful voice, "so I'm surprised to find you skipping out on her on such a busy night."

Dashi wound her hands into her deel, trying to look embarrassed and contrite. "I was pulled from the kitchen to serve. The cooking was mostly done anyhow."

The guard captain looked in the direction Sevlin had gone. "I'll have to let the consul know about this when she returns. I'm obligated to report all interactions with foreigners, no matter who the parties are or how...unequally yoked." He turned his gaze back to Dashi, his expression regretful. "We're done here. But next time one of Tyvalar's princes promises you all kinds of things, don't believe him."

Dashi's head jerked up. *One of Tyvalar's princes?*

Not trusting herself to speak, she nodded and headed for the kitchen.

By the following morning, guards oozed from the pores of New Osb. They paced at every exterior door to the palace and stood in evenly-spaced pairs around the building's perimeter. They kept watch in the kitchen and outside the atrium garden. They had, according to the gossip at the servants' breakfast table, checked every room in the servants' quarters, before moving on to the rooms of the main building.

Dashi could tell, from the wide eyes and the small, nervous twitches as the servants spooned their morning gruel, that no one knew why. If Idree's presence was a secret, then the attempt to steal her was just as well-kept. Only Cook seemed privy to the previous night's events, though her knowledge extended only to Dashi's purported romantic escapades.

"You know what happens when you play with fire," Cook asked. She plunked a bowl down next to Dashi for emphasis but kept her voice low, sending a hooded glance at the guard who stood at the bottom of the narrow kitchen stairs. "You burn something down. And believe me, it's not going to be the Tyvalaran prince who goes up in flames."

Tyvalaran prince. Dashi had been turning those words over all night and she still didn't know what to think.

To Cook, she said, "Couldn't we have met last night and then gone our separate ways without anyone getting set on fire?"

"You won't go your separate ways once the consul catches the scent of this."

"The guard captain said he'd have to tell her. I know there will probably be some punishment for shirking my kitchen duties but—"

"A reward, more like it," Cook snorted, turning to the oven. "*She's* not a servant; she won't care that you left me short-handed. She'll just want you to climb into bed with him."

"Cook, I'm very sorry about—*what?*"

"Whatever the khan wants done, the consul makes it happens," Cook said, a touch impatiently.

"I know that." Dashi thought of the starting line at the khan's race. Of the previous consul, Negan, pulling a scarf over his nose and mouth to keep the dust at bay as he prepared to ride to his death.

Cook glanced over her shoulder. "Think, girl," she hissed. "When the khan wants someone punished, it's the consul who figures out how. When the khan wants information about something, it's the consul who makes sure he gets it. *Especially* information about foreign princes."

When the khan wants information about something...*like the seamripper.* Dashi would wager her weight in offering oil *that's* where the new consul was now: out searching for the seamripper. As Sevlin had said, if it could somehow counter the needle's power, the khan wouldn't want anyone else to have it. What new notations would be added to the map upon her return, Dashi wondered.

"The consul is on her way back now—a messenger arrived at dawn," Cook continued. "She'll be here for the end of the Founding Day celebrations and there won't be any turning her down when she pushes you back into the arms of the Tyvalaran prince."

Slowly, Dashi's thoughts caught up to Cook's words. *Into the arms...of Sevlin?*

"You might not think that sounds so bad, climbing onto a man like that, but he won't be yours, and neither he nor the consul will shed a tear if you cease to be useful." Cook jabbed a wooden spoon at Dashi's face. "Someone always ends up in ashes.

An authoritative voice broke through their conversation. "His Most High has ordered everyone to the courtyard." It was one of the khan's personal servants. He held the kitchen door open invitingly.

Cook opened her mouth to protest.

"Everyone. Advisors. Guests. Servants. Even you, Cook."

Cook set her spoon down and rinsed her hands. Everyone else was already filing outside, exchanging anxious glances. The courtyard was packed with bodies. It did indeed look like every single person in New Osb was waiting there.

"What—" Cook began, but she was silenced by the sight of the khan emerging onto his balcony, flanked by advisors.

The heralds were there too, blinking in the sunlight, like nightmares that had somehow survived the dawn. The owl woman shivered, hunching her shoulders so that her head was nearly buried in the folds of her cape. The moth woman hovered just above the balcony, a barely contained flag surging over gusts of wind.

Even though it was full of people, the courtyard was silent, waiting for the khan to announce why he'd gathered them there. But the khan, who had always seemed to revel in public speech and spectacle, never moved. He stared straight ahead, neither acknowledging the advisors, guards and heralds who flanked him, nor the crowd below.

A uniformed crier stepped to the front of the balcony. "Citizens of Karakal. Honored guests and esteemed colleagues," he intoned. "We are gathered this morning to address an insult to Karakal's sovereignty. A threat to our might. A reproach against the established order of our society."

Though the khan wasn't speaking, his pompous speech from the previous night was still fresh in Dashi's mind; the crier's words sounded like they'd been pulled verbatim from his lips.

"Last night, loyal guards discovered an enemy within, who, in defiance of all decency, attempted to move against his Most High, the Great Khan of Karakal, on the sacred anniversary of our founding."

This drew a murmur from the crowd.

"Testimony was given: a guest who observed this traitor's movements last night. Evidence was assembled: a hidden weapon where there should have been none. And of course, the evidence of the crime itself: a plot to acquire means of power, foiled by a loyal contingent of guards, one of whom was slain. His Most High, with the advice and counsel of his closest advisors, delivered a verdict both judicious and fair: *guilty*."

Dashi's breath slowed. *A hidden weapon. A slain guard.*

"While this crime might normally be dealt with privately," the crier continued, "today we celebrate Karakal's might: the strength and power that elevates us from the rest."

Two guards stepped forward, holding the arms of a man between them. He'd been there all along, off to the khan's left, and no one on the balcony had seemed to pay him much attention. Dashi hadn't either.

It took her a moment to recognize him. He looked slenderer in the light somehow, but his dark mop of hair was the same, and so was the way he twisted his hands in front of him. It was the advisor from the atrium garden: the one who'd shown her where the herbs were grown, the one who wasn't afraid to admit he knew Ese. Gold-plated chains hung from his wrists. Each slide of his fingers made them wink.

Stone-faced and silent, the khan flicked his hand toward the man without looking at him. The moth woman fluttered downward, landing gently on the balcony. The crowd was silent, pressed together in the courtyard, and Dashi had a fleeting recollection of the way Ejen's herds would huddle flank-to-flank, stiff-legged and quiet, when something alarmed them.

In one deft movement, the moth woman flipped the man over her shoulder. That, in itself, made the crowd gasp in surprise; she was not a big woman but seemed to manage the task with ease. The man struggled mightily, kicking his legs and crying out in fear, but it seemed to make no difference to the herald's efforts.

The moth woman's flight back into the air was unhurried and swirling, just the way a real moth floats on unseen currents. She passed over the khan and her fellow monsters, up the side of the palace, until she was well above its roofline. The crowd's murmurs increased in volume, rising with the moth. Finally, she halted her ascent, circling with languid wingbeats.

The khan's voice rang out. "Drop him."

The herald dipped forward at the waist, tossing the man carelessly from her shoulder. He fell silent and fast, his body barely twisting in midair. There were screams as the man hit with a crack, landing on the shiny, barely-trod cobblestones of New Osb's courtyard.

The khan slowly opened his arms, taking in everything gathered before him. Perhaps beyond.

His voice settled over the silent crowd. "Thus fall the enemies of Karakal."

Chapter 19

After the death of the advisor, the courtyard emptied quickly. The servants returned to their work at a near sprint, the normal complaints and discomforts of drudgery forgotten amid shaky glances at the herald who still floated above the courtyard. Dashi wondered if the khan's other advisors felt the same nerves, if they feared the cudgel might someday fall on them.

"Those *things* give me the shivers," Cook offered when Dashi brought it up later. "But at the end of the day, it's got naught to do with me. The khan does what he pleases, even with his own." Then she dispatched Dashi to find Terbish, the head of the grounds servants, to ask when the khan would return from his hunt.

The courtyard bristled with eyes now, a stiff gale of attention that left Dashi with her muscles braced, plowing forward. She kept her gaze fixed on the ground, except for one darting glance at the wine cellar door as she passed. The guards stood six deep there, blocking both the door itself and the overhang she'd used to get up the palace wall. She swallowed, dry-mouthed at the sudden impossibility of climbing up the exterior of the palace.

The guards were sparser on the outskirts of the grounds and she delivered her message to Terbish with only half her attention. Her real focus was Idree. *Always Idree.* She knew where her sister was, but the way was now barred. She had a fair idea of the location of the needle—in a lock box somewhere on the unexplored half of the khan's floor—but no way to get there either.

As Dashi passed one of the partially constructed stables, a wave of movement in the shadowy interior drew her eyes. She halted, immediately on edge, only to realize that the moving thing was a leg, rocking restlessly. Its owner lay slumped against a pile of unused trusses in the corner.

Dashi stepped inside, moving cautiously until her eyes adjusted and she could see the man's face.

"*Ese?*"

He rolled away, swatting a hand in her direction even though she hadn't reached for him. The movement sent a wave of odor in her direction: sawdust, fresh and wet; mead, sharp and sweet.

"Go away, little Dashi."

"Get up!" she hissed, suddenly conscious of the activity outside the unfinished building. "What are you doing?"

"Before your interruption, I was trying to sleep." The slur in his voice was slight, but it was there.

"And before *that*?"

He squinted at her, still not raising his head from where it rested on the trusses. "Filched a bottle off a merchant's wagon. Keep your voice down. I can't see Jochi if other people are around."

"My voice *is* down. Who's Jochi?"

At first, there was no response and Dashi wondered if he'd fallen asleep.

Then, softly: "*No.* No, no, no." The tone was unlike any she'd heard him use before, a crushed, bruised, hopeless version of his normal voice. He slung an arm over his eyes and turned onto his side.

The idea of Ese being a morose drunk had never occurred to Dashi and, at another time, when there wasn't any chance of him being discovered, she might have found it amusing. Right now, she wanted him to snap out of it.

"You can't stay here, Ese. Go sleep it off in your quarters."

Again, there was no answer. She nudged him with her boot.

"Of all the people I have known in my life," he said, voice muffled against his arm, "it is strange that I would have no one left but you with whom to share this."

"You're the one who puts so much stock in fate; chalk it up to that. And we're not sharing anything, Ese. You're drunk. I want you to get out of sight so you don't get fired. That's it."

"Why wouldn't you want me to get fired?"

"Because you're vindictive enough to tell someone about me on your way out."

Ese raised his head to look at her. To her shock, she saw that his eyes were glassy with unshed tears.

"That man who was executed," she said slowly. "You knew him."

Ese stared past her without responding. When Dashi glanced over her shoulder, she saw the domed top of the cage that the guards had carried into the courtyard after the execution. They'd stuffed the body of the khan's advisor inside and hung it over the inner gate.

"Jochi."

The familiar, immediate way in which he formed the word made it sound like Ese was addressing someone behind her. Dashi's neck prickled, but she resisted the urge to turn around.

Ese was still staring, not really talking to her. "He was the reason for—"

A pair of servants passed the stable, their voices jovial and clear. Too clear. Too close. All it would take was someone stepping into the doorway and Ese and Dashi would be perfectly visible. Standing in a half-built stable might not be incriminating in itself, but it was memorable: the paving stone that was amiss.

Still, Dashi didn't move. "The reason for what?"

"For everything. You being in the khan's race. Osol tracking you down in Thracedon. *This.*" He plucked at his servant's deel. "I thought if I could get the leverage, I could free him…"

Dashi's brows rose. *"Don't worry,"* the advisor had said, *"I only have one overseer tonight and he's loyal to me."*

"He wasn't one of the khan's advisors," she said. "He was a prisoner?"

"He was the khan's brother."

"*What?*"

"Jochi was a threat," Ese said, his eyes never leaving the top of the cage. It swayed slightly, pushed by a wind coming from the taiga. "As innocent as he was, he was the only person who could reasonably challenge Temur for the khanate."

"*Did* he challenge him?"

"No. Temur didn't have anything Jochi wanted. The guards reportedly found a sword stashed by the garden where he was allowed to take his walks," Ese continued, "but I know that was fabricated. Temur has hated Jochi for years, even before the race, even before he found out about my involvement in it."

The crier's words, still fresh from that morning, rang in her mind. *"A hidden weapon…a plot foiled by a loyal contingent of guards, one of whom was slain… a verdict both judicious and fair: guilty."*

Dashi felt a pinch in her gut. *She* had hidden the weapon. *Sevlin* had slain the guard.

She cleared her throat. "That's why you wanted the needle? It was to be a bargaining chip to free Jochi?"

Ese's mouth gave a bitter twitch. "Oh, I had plans, little Dashi, such great plans. I was going to find the needle and make the seamstress stitch for me. Once I had a small magical army, I would depose Temur and set Jochi up as khan. He's—he would have been a much better ruler. I had already been planning this when the prefects arrested you. I didn't know who you were, just that Negan had requested that you be turned over for execution in a rather personal way. Imagine my delight when I discovered you were exactly what my plans were lacking."

He smiled faintly. "When a month passed and you didn't return with the needle, I should have fled with Jochi. I should've done that in the beginning. But hiding from someone as powerful as Temur is a difficult thing and before I could complete the arrangements, that woman returned from the race. It was *my* name she mentioned, but Temur blamed Jochi. He'd already been wary of his brother—Jochi was always under guard—but afterward, Temur became...stringent. Paranoid. He put a death notice on me and sent Jochi to New Osb before it was even finished. Away from me, away from any Karak nobles who might support him."

Dashi could hear the emotion in his words, held at arm's length by the alcohol in which he was drowning. Ese's insistence that she return the needle to him and not to the khan made sense now. So did his anger at finding her near the atrium garden, which they must have used as a meeting place. He'd been trying to cover a vulnerability: not his death warrant but the fact that he was secretly meeting the man he loved, right under the khan's nose.

"So you came to New Osb to be with Jochi," she guessed, "and sent Osol to search for the needle when you realized I was still alive."

"Osol hasn't been in my employ since my estate was burned. No money means no servants." Ese laughed, louder than he should have, and Dashi winced. "Osol went to the leather circle and hired out as a guard for merchant convoys. But he's—he *was*—my loyal friend. When

I told him you were still alive and were the last person to be seen with the needle, he went searching for you on his own."

An image of Osol, belongings trampled, throat laid bare beneath the endless blue sky, floated into Dashi's mind. He'd died trying to help his friend. *Don't feel a kinship for him*, she told herself sternly. *Idree wouldn't be in this mess if Osol hadn't kidnapped her.*

To Ese, she said, "You have to go back to your room. Say you're sick. Rinse your mouth and change your clothes so you don't reek of mead."

When he didn't move, she hauled his arm over her shoulders, bracing her legs to lift him to his feet. He lurched forward, swaying the vial of incense oil that hung around his neck. A shaft of sunlight caught the glass, turning it translucent. Dashi's hand darted out, breaking the cord with a snap.

She held up the vial. "This isn't offering oil. It's a powder."

"Give me that." His hand swung at the vial, but it was a clumsy movement and she jumped back easily, leaving him wavering on his feet.

"What is it?" she asked, though a suspicion had already taken root.

"You don't demand answers from me. Not today."

"I'm not demanding, just asking," she said, trying to soothe the belligerence from his voice. She took another step backward. "He has food tasters and guards. How will you administer it when I can't even get close enough to search for the needle?"

"Is your pride smarting, little Dashi?" He leaned heavily against the wall.

How could Ese, a grounds servant who wouldn't want to be recognized, get close to the khan? The khan kept to his floor, never walking the grounds unless he was visiting his birds or dogs—

Dashi sucked in a breath. "His hunt provisions?"

"Temur has tasters even on a hunt, but this particular poison doesn't work well when ingested anyway. It makes you violently ill after only a few bites and, after that, you're unlikely to eat enough to finish the job." He held up a finger, but the professorial gesture was undercut when he began to slide down the wall. "Absorbed *tactilely*, Adder's Dust will circumvent even the most careful food tasters."

"So you'll put it on—" Dashi broke off, stumped. *Something Ese had access to. Something the khan would touch directly.* "His reins?"

"The royal gauntlet," Ese said, with a trace of his normal smugness, "is embroidered in golden thread and lined with calf leather soft enough for the bare hand of the Most High. And it's coated in poison."

Dashi inhaled sharply. "You've *already* given it to him?"

"It takes repeated exposures in quick succession. Temur hasn't hunted in weeks. Too preoccupied with your sister, maybe. But today...I guess he was feeling *celebratory*." Ese ran a hand over his face. When he dropped it, he was finally looking at Dashi. "I couldn't pass up the chance. Not when Jochi—not when I was holding his murderer's gauntlet in my hands."

She held his gaze, willing his attention to stay on her face and not her fingers. "How long will it take?"

"Faster than he deserves. Three or four more hunts, if they happen in quick succession." Ese's chuckle was brittle. "I took an arrow for his father once. They gave me a title and a promotion for saving that khan's life, but *this* khan will be dead by my hand."

Given his current state, Dashi had no doubt she could outmaneuver Ese if she wanted to keep the vial. She also did not doubt that he'd come for her later. The Adder's Dust was his revenge; Ese wouldn't let it walk away. She dropped the vial, still warm from Ese's body, into his palm and turned to go.

"You'll stay out of trouble?" She glanced over her shoulder. Ese's head tipped back against the unfinished wall, a sardonic smile creeping onto his face.

"Don't worry, little Dashi. Don't botch my plan and I won't botch yours."

I already did. Even if the khan had always wanted Jochi gone, it was her actions—the failed attempt to free Idree, the sword inadvertently left in an incriminating location—that had provided the impetus.

Dashi nodded once, telling herself that Ese's words weren't laced with warning, that he couldn't possibly know what she'd done, both last night and a few minutes ago. She told herself that it wasn't wrong to take advantage of his distraction and grief, not if it gave her the means to free her sister.

Then she stepped out into the sunlight, her arm held against her side to contain the small pile of Adder's Dust that she'd poured into the folded corner of her sash.

Chapter 20

Administering the Adder's Dust turned out to be easy. Dashi timed her arrival the next morning so that she entered the kitchen after most of the other servants but before the khan's personal attendants, who slept on the top floor so they could be near the khan both day and night. With so many stairs to descend, they usually arrived late to meals.

Feigning sleepiness, Dashi shuffled to the pot of barley porridge that Cook kept simmering over the fire. She ladled a generous helping into her bowl, surreptitiously unfurling the end of her sash over the pot as she did so. Three quick stirs and the Adder's Dust was indistinguishable from the rest. After that, it was a game of patience.

A few hours later, Dashi was beginning to despair. Maybe she hadn't gotten enough Adder's Dust from Ese. Maybe he was misinformed about its gastronomical effects. Maybe he'd lied.

She'd just retrieved a load of vegetables from the cold cellar when the sound of retching reached her. Peeking past the door, she saw Jagun, the same servant who'd been so unhelpful in finding Marzhan, vomiting spectacularly onto the cobblestones of the courtyard.

"Ugh!" A squat advisor took a step back. "It splattered on my boots."

The khan and the rest of his entourage, on their way across the courtyard, were, fortunately, too far away to have been hit. That was something Dashi hadn't considered when she'd spiked the morning's porridge: what would happen to a servant unlucky enough to vomit onto the khan's shoes?

"Don't just stand there," someone barked. "Clean up this mess!"

A second servant snapped into action, leading the heaving Jagun away.

Within the hour, the contagion—for that's what everyone but Dashi believed it to be—had taken all of the khan's personal servants, a dozen of the regular servants, and nearly as many guards, who'd come to the kitchen later that morning looking for leftovers. It had, in short, worked even better than Dashi had hoped.

"It started with one of the grounds servants," Marzhan said to Cook. "Terbish said one of his men was very sick."

So she'd provided some cover for the aftereffects of Ese's binge, Dashi thought, keeping her face averted. Somehow she doubted he'd be grateful when he found out how she'd managed it.

"Ancestors protect me, what a disaster," Cook exclaimed, pushing strands of graying hair away from her face. "What if the guests catch it? And the feast! How am I supposed to finish preparations like this?"

Dashi lurked nearby, pretending to be focused on the carrots she was chopping. Her chance was at hand. She could feel it.

Marzhan cast about the room, her eyes settling on Dashi in an appraising squint. "You filled in as a server, didn't you?"

Dashi nodded.

"And you did fine."

It was more of a statement than a question, but Dashi nodded anyway. *If you don't count spilling broth on a guest and kissing a member of the Tyvalaran delegation. And,* the dark part of her mind supplied, unasked, *giving the khan an excuse to execute his brother.*

Cook, doubtlessly thinking of Dashi being pulled out of the bushes with Sevlin, gave a derisive snort.

Marzhan glanced at her. "I'll need her for the rest of the day, plus anyone else you can spare."

"Not a soul," Cook said immediately. "Not if you want to serve more than empty plates tonight."

"I'll need at least one more person," Marzhan said firmly, holding up a hand to forestall any more threats from Cook. "You choose who." As she stalked off, she called back to Dashi, "Get a clean deel and take the khan's food up immediately."

"Well, I'm in a real fix now," Cook muttered. "But you..." She wiped the sweat from her forehead and gave Dashi a tired wink. "*Ambitions*, see? I told you to be careful which ones you held."

Cook arranged and rearranged the food until everything looked so perfect that Dashi wanted to scream. Eventually, however, everything was deemed satisfactory and Dashi began the laborious process of ferrying the trays up to the khan's floor. When she reached the top of the servants' stairs, there was an immediate click, as someone slid the door bolt back.

The door swung open, revealing a pair of guards. As she stepped inside, Dashi counted at least two dozen more, stationed throughout the room. Her eyes darted, plucking as much information as she could. It was the art, however, which really commanded her attention: tapestries, relief sculptures, paintings. Each piece was Purek. Each piece had been procured by Dashi, Altan, Baris and Zayaa. She told herself that was expected. Since Dashi and her friends were the only ones who explored the ruins, every piece of Purek art had touched their hands at some point. Still, there was something different about knowing that this art belonged to the man who'd commissioned her friends to hunt it...and then commissioned their murders.

"That way," one of the guards said, nodding toward an enormous door decorated in gold and ebony. He gave Dashi an encouraging smile. "It opens into another waiting room. The khan is in the room on the right. Knock first."

He held the door for Dashi and, as soon as she'd sidled through, balancing the trays of food, he closed it again. She glanced around at the plush waiting room. There was enough seating for a dozen people, but today, with so many sick and abed, it was deserted.

The rise and fall of voices came from the door to her immediate right, just as the guard had said. Dashi slid her trays onto a low table in the waiting room, her eyes straying to Idree's door. She wondered if Idree had found the rosebud she'd left under the pillow. Caught between the relief of finally seeing her sister and the panic of nearly being caught, Dashi had forgotten to ask. Altan's voice was in her ear, insisting that she move—*"Assess your goals. Don't conflate them with the desired outcome s."*—so she forced herself to turn away. *Find the needle*, she told herself, *then you can see Idree as much as you'd like.*

The two doors opposite Idree's were unlocked and led to the same room. It overflowed with books and scrolls, reminding Dashi of the ruined Purek library she used to visit with her friends. Small desks were scattered throughout, the kind used by scribes in the message offices of Karak City. Weights were stacked neatly at the corners of each desk, meant to hold scrolls open for perusal or copying. Though no dust marred the work surfaces, Dashi was unsurprised to find that the whole room had an unused feeling. With the consul away, it seemed unlikely the khan would be laboring over any ancient scrolls. Even so, Dashi made a cursory, albeit vain, search for a place where the golden needle might be secured.

The murmur of voices from the khan's meeting swelled as Dashi returned to the hall, and she felt a corresponding spike in her pulse. *Three more doors.* The first led to a bedroom, clearly unused and, therefore, a waste of her time. Dashi pressed her ear against the next door and, hearing nothing, opened it. It was also a bedchamber, though more feminine and inviting than the last. The consul's, she guessed. She silently rifled drawers and stuffed her hands under the bed. In the wardrobe, she found enough shiny baubles to make a crow jealous but no golden needle.

An adjoining door led from the consul's room to the final room Dashi had yet to search. When Dashi eased it open, she knew immediately that she was looking at the khan's bedchamber. The appointments were more luxurious than anything she'd ever seen. The ornaments on the bed were made from gold and studded with jewels. She measured the mattress with her eyes; it was almost half her height. She hesitated on the threshold, suddenly dry-mouthed at the enormity of trespassing in the bedroom of the most powerful man in Karakal.

It was curiosity that drew her forward, impelling her to break the plane of the khan's room at last. There was a table near the doorway. On it, just out of arm's reach, lay a scrap of paper, the ends still curling from its recent confinement in a courier tube. Dashi nudged it open, scanning quickly. *"Location of the seamripper is definitive: the Mother's Finger. Will need the heralds to ensure access,"* the consul had scrawled. *"Returning now. This courier will precede me by three days."* It was dated yesterday.

The recent date was jarring and Dashi jerked away from the message, suddenly impatient. Despite the room's opulence, there were no obvious hiding places. The small tables seemed to exist solely for the sake of the artwork they displayed and did not contain any drawers or concealed spaces. A second, smaller room was dedicated to the khan's clothing, but each wooden wardrobe was full to bursting. Dashi prowled back into the main room, unsatisfied. The golden needle would be kept somewhere accessible—Idree must be using it with some frequency to have stitched sixty-four people already—not hidden beneath piles of fabric.

Her eyes moved to the wall hangings. These, she noted, were modern imitations of Purek art. They contained the requisite coloration patterns, but the artist seemed unaware of Purek sacred numbers. Each one showed the khan in some impossibly grand scenario: standing atop a snow-capped mountain; felling a great stag; surrounded by beautiful women who pawed at his bare chest. Dashi snorted at that last tapestry, but as she lifted it, her derision transformed into vindication. The safe box Ese had told her about was nestled into the wall, a metal egg in a stone nest.

Her lock picks trembled as she took them out, mirroring her nerves. There were two locks, their elliptical faces set flush in the metal door. They would undoubtedly be stubborn ones too; only the best for the khan. Suddenly, and with a ferocity she hadn't felt in months, she wished for her friends, for someone to help her bear this burden. *I got this far on my own. I can do this too.* Shoving the tapestry to one side with her shoulder, Dashi let her tools feel the contours of the lock. A minute ticked past, then another. Her picks sidled up to the tumblers, coaxing them into shifting, one by one. *Please. Idree is counting on me.*

The top lock gave in with a sullen *pop*, but she felt no sense of victory. She was only halfway there and it had taken her much too long. *Steady,* Baris warned, as she delved into the second lock. She tried to conjure every relevant experience, every lesson Zayaa had ever given her, but her hands were shaking. How much time did she have until someone noticed her absence or, more likely, the absence of the food she was supposed to deliver? The pick slid out of her sweaty hand, bouncing onto the rug at her feet.

"Cursed ancestors." Scooping it up, she wrestled her focus back into place. She forced the needle out of her mind. Idree, too. The lock was the only thing that existed and she half-closed her eyes, imagining its interior passages.

Finally, it clicked open. Holding her breath, Dashi eased the door open and stared at the khan's treasures. Disappointment began curdling her stomach right away, but she forced herself to be thorough as she searched the box. *Maybe it was here. Maybe it had just been pushed to the back.*

Golden coins, golden bars, golden necklaces.

The elaborate headdress the khan had worn on the night he unveiled the heralds.

Several dozen jeweled rings, neatly seated in a velvet display cushion. One fell out when she moved it, rattling against the interior of the lock box, but she didn't care.

Neither the needle nor the statuette was there.

Mechanically, Dashi returned the door and the tapestry to the position in which she'd found them. Idree must be stitching someone right now. *What catastrophically bad timing.* Dashi forced herself to take steady breaths. Blood roared in her ears. There wouldn't be another chance like this one and she was about to piss it away.

She slipped back into the hall and picked up the now-cold trays of food just as one of the khan's advisors poked his head out of their meeting room.

"You're late," he said flatly.

Dashi tensed for further condemnation, but he merely motioned for her to follow.

"It's the Tyvalarans who are key," someone said as she entered. "Concessions from them—a formal alliance, even—"

"We have already broached it with the queen's representative."

Dashi inched forward, trays on each arm, head bowed. There were five people in the room: the khan, seated at the raised desk, plus four advisors, arranged in a semi-circle before him. Guards stood at attention all around.

Dashi's eyes darted to the khan's slippered feet as she lowered her trays. He leaned back in his seat, listening to his advisors with an air of heavy-handed benevolence. The ease with which he presented himself, the utter lack of concern for his brother, whose body was, at this very moment, swaying over the front gate, set her teeth on edge. His left hand drummed against the arm of his chair. His right hand—

Dashi's feet faltered.

His right hand caressed a chain that draped his neck. On it, hung the statuette that held the golden needle.

Chapter 21

Somehow, Dashi ignored the panic thrumming inside her. Somehow, she backed out of the room without incident, then put one foot in front of the other, until she found herself back in the palace kitchen. Cook pointed her at a pile of potatoes and she attacked them obediently, too despondent to care as the hot, soapy water turned her hands raw. The khan must wear the needle during the day, she thought, recalling the familiar way he'd smoothed his fingers over the golden statuette. *Stealing it isn't going to be difficult; it's going to be impossible.* She longed to turn to someone, to lament this turn of events, but she was an island in the busy kitchen.

"You've been summoned by one of the khan's guests," Marzhan announced, leaning over the countertop where Dashi was working. "To deliver extra writing materials, ostensibly, but given the late hour and the fact that you were requested specifically, I'd guess it's more than that."

Requested specifically? What—?

"No need to play at being surprised," Marzhan said, catching sight of Dashi's expression. "I know all about you and the Tyvalaran prince."

Behind Marzhan's back, Cook grimaced and held up her hands in a gesture of helplessness.

Marzhan stared at Dashi's face as if seeing it for the first time. "You're half nomad."

"Mori," Dashi said, wondering if she was imagining the trace of suspicion in Marzhan's voice. "But I was raised Karakalese."

"Go now—you cannot keep the Tyvalaran prince waiting—but remember where your allegiance lies."

"To my khan. To Karakal," Dashi said. *To my sister. To myself,* she thought.

"Foreign intrigue falls beneath the consul's purview," Marzhan said, and now suspicion had been replaced by a note of warning. "She's due back tonight or early tomorrow. Were I you, I would have something to report to her."

Dashi took the basket of writing materials while Marzhan rattled off directions to the rooms which held the Tyvalaran delegation. Inside, she was seething.

"What is *wrong* with you?" she hissed when the door to Sevlin's room opened.

The Tyvalaran soldier holding the door looked at her blankly.

"I, ah, I'm here to see Sev—Prince Sevlin," she said.

The soldier took a step back, revealing a second soldier...and Sevlin leaning against the frame of an interior door, his arms crossed over his chest.

Dashi took a step toward him, but the soldier's arm shot out, blocking her way.

"It's alright," Sevlin said, in an overloud voice. "She's my guest." To Dashi, he inclined her head, inviting her to step inside. His eyes swept over her, taking in her servant's deel and ancestors-only-knew what else. The second soldier was also looking at her, but he had his hand on his sword.

The room she'd entered was an antechamber, though it was still twice the size of the room she shared with five other servants. It was, of course, much nicer as well: plush rugs; shiny furniture; a wide fireplace set invitingly with kindling.

Dashi opened her mouth, but a subtle flick of Sevlin's hand stopped her from speaking. He nodded to the soldier—another silent command, though for what, Dashi couldn't tell—and motioned for her to precede him into the other room. She saw the corner of a bed and heard a fire crackling invitingly from within, but something made her hesitate on the threshold. A rustle of cloth. An exhale, slight, but still audible. Someone else was inside.

Sevlin sighed and reached past her to swing the door wider, revealing two Tyvalaran soldiers playing a game of cards. They stood up when they caught sight of Sevlin.

"I was being courteous," he murmured, brushing by, "not leading you into an ambush, unarmed."

Dashi smiled, wide enough to show teeth. "I'm never unarmed."

One of the soldiers held up a fiddle, a smaller and more delicate instrument than its Karakalese cousin. "Background music, my prince?" she asked, smiling mischievously.

"Please." Sevlin walked to the middle of the room, where two dressing screens had been maneuvered side by side, creating a small, sheltered space between them. Inside, two chairs sat facing each other. The soldier struck up a tune on the fiddle, simple and easy, not at all in keeping with Dashi's mood.

"There are holes in the walls," Sevlin said in a soft voice, answering Dashi's unspoken question, as he stepped between the screens. "Spaces for someone to stand between the walls and see and hear what goes on in here. Inside the screens, with the music playing, we'll be protected from spying."

Dashi's eyebrows rose. Was every room in the palace like that, or only the ones assigned to visiting dignitaries? And, more importantly, how did she access these observation points?

"When you said you could be overheard in your room, I thought you meant you were sharing it with other soldiers," she said.

He glanced meaningfully at the screen, where the shadow of the fiddle-playing soldier could be seen.

"You know what I mean, *Prince* Sevlin. Sharing it with your *fellow* soldiers, not a royal protection detail."

He shrugged, unconcerned by the misunderstanding.

"Why, in the name of the ancestors, would you summon me to your room? In case you didn't notice," she paused to pluck at the hem of her servant's uniform, "I'm trying to blend in."

"I'm sorry to have compromised your reputation," he said in a dry voice. "If not for me, your well-known humility and obedience would have made you a model servant, I'm sure."

"This isn't a joke, Sevlin. Everyone will remember this—Marzhan, Cook, the guard captain—*everyone*! I won't be anonymous anymore. I'll be the servant who was invited to your bedroom."

"I was counting on people noticing," he said coolly. "It seemed like the only way to force you into a conversation. You might not care what I think, but you care what your supervisor thinks, at least in the short term. And this is far less risky than sneaking around a foreign palace, only to be left waiting for someone who never shows."

"There were guards all over last night after what happened." *Probably true.* "I couldn't get away." *I didn't try.*

"Don't lie to me."

"Like you didn't lie to me, *Prince* Sevlin?"

"I never lied."

"You said you were a soldier!" She hissed, struggling to keep her voice down.

"I *am* a soldier."

"You're right, I should be commending you, Prince Sevlin, for being so honest and forthcoming." Dashi rubbed distractedly at her forehead. "I feel like we've had this argument before. Oh, wait. That's because *we have*."

Sevlin's anger was a difficult thing to spot. His voice stayed low and controlled, his pronunciation precise as always. But his mouth drew a little narrower and his eyes snapped back at her.

"*You're* going to lecture *me* on being honest?" He leaned toward her. "You were lying the entire time we were in the taiga."

"*So. Were. You.*" Dashi stood up, sending her chair scraping backward. "I'm going back to the kitchen. We're done here."

Sevlin didn't move. "We're not done until I say we are."

"Going to have your royal bodyguards detain me?" She said it sarcastically, but the flicker of the guards' shadows on the dressing screen suddenly seemed a little more ominous. They were armed—*fully* armed—and all she had was a knife in her boot.

"No. But if you leave now, you won't have anything to report to whoever is debriefing you."

"So I'll make something up." The idea of Sevlin ever divulging something by accident was absurd anyway.

"Lies are sticky things. You don't know what information the khan's people already have. You don't know what they want to hear."

"And you do?"

"I have a fair idea, yes."

"How do you know I won't run straight to the guard captain—or to the consul, whenever she returns—and report everything we discuss?

That's what they're going to expect from me: a new piece of information every time I'm finished with you."

The right side of Sevlin's mouth quirked upward, abruptly lightening the mood. "Every time you're finished with me."

"What?"

"Trust you to say it so baldly."

"You made it a bald proposition," she said, "requesting me by name."

"Indeed." His lips remained amused.

"Someone's trying to get servants to jump into bed with you and you think it's funny?"

"I've planned for this."

"How could you possibly have planned for it? It *just* happened."

"It's been done before. I'm not concerned that it's the case with you."

"Why not?"

He unbuckled his sword belt and slid it from his waist, stretching his long legs out in front of him. The sword belt, she noticed, stayed within easy reach. "You're not in my bed, for one thing."

The word 'bed' on Sevlin's lips was like a compulsion; Dashi's eyes darted in that direction before she could stop herself. She couldn't see it—it was hidden by the dressing screen—but she shifted anyway, turning her body away from it and crossing her arms. *People will tell you exactly what they want,* Zayaa whispered, laughing at her. *All you have to do is pay attention.*

Sevlin's gaze tracked her movements, but he continued smoothly. "Secondly, you," he said, gesturing at her with the hilt of his sword, "do things for yourself, not for country."

She didn't like the way he'd said that, like doing things for herself was a character flaw. Why *should* she do anything for the khan or Karakal?

"Third, even if you *have* agreed to be the khan's spy, it still depends on me being stupid enough to fall for it, and I'm not."

"What about your brother, the other prince?" she asked. "I gather he's popular with women."

"Half brother," he corrected. "And Zevi isn't simple, no matter how he sometimes acts. Don't worry, the Tyvalaran delegation came prepared on multiple fronts. I'm sure the other delegations did too."

"I'll sleep well now," she said in a sarcastic voice. "Why would you come at all, knowing you'd be spied upon?"

He leaned back in the chair, eyelids closing partially. "Careful, Dashi. More questions like that, I'll start to think you *are* after information."

"Fine, but if someone *is* watching through your walls, won't they think it's strange that we're inside a makeshift dressing room while your soldiers serenade us?"

Sevlin shrugged. "You can say that I'm scared to have my soldiers too far away. Or that I like to lie on the floor. It makes no difference to me."

Frowning, Dashi shoved away the picture of Sevlin lowering himself to the floor and forced herself to think through the implications of what had been asked of her, of what would continue to be asked of her. She didn't want to pass information, real or otherwise. She didn't want to see Sevlin again and again. It felt...dangerous, somehow.

Sevlin was watching her. She wondered if he could see her exhaustion, the low-grade tension that pervaded everything she'd done since Idree had been taken. The fear that dragged at her like a millstone.

"Will you sit?" he asked.

The door opened and a third guard came into the room, his shadow joining the other two.

"I'd rather stand."

"You can flip upside down and walk on your hands if you'd rather." He leaned forward, resting his elbows on his knees.

"Get on with it, Sevlin. You didn't bring me here for a cozy chat."

Unbidden, Dashi recalled a story Sevlin had told her soon after they'd met: as a boy, his home had been attacked and, at his mother's urging, he'd left her to die in order to protect his sister.

"Your *sister* is the queen of Tyvalar?" she blurted.

"How long has Idree been acting as seamstress?" Sevlin asked at the same time. He paused. "Lyazzat is my half sister."

"I mean, the sister you told me about. The one you saved. That was the queen?"

He brushed a hand over his scarred cheekbone, touching the memory. "Yes."

When he'd told her the story, Dashi had assumed that the attackers were bandits. They must have been assassins, she realized.

"Do you share a father or a mother?" she asked.

"A father. The Tyvalaran royal line is matriarchal. It's the mother's blood that counts toward whether someone rules or not."

"Prince Zevi?"

"Is in line to rule if something were to happen to Lyazzat but only because there are no other female heirs. Someday, when Lyazzat has children, he will fall after them."

Dashi was silent, rearranging what she knew about him. His mother had urged him to save Lyazzat at her own expense, even though Lyazzat was not her daughter. No wonder Sevlin waxed eloquent about duty and love of country. That was his experience, watching his mother ruthlessly sacrifice herself not for a blood relation but for a monarch. A symbol. A nation.

"Is this how it's always going to be?" he asked, breaking into her reverie.

"What?"

"You answer a question with a question. You get information but don't give any."

"Says the master of deception, himself."

Sevlin gave her a sharp, uninterpretable look. "Idree," he prompted.

"The khan has had her for about a month."

"But you've known she was the seamstress for longer than that." His voice was soft, almost lost beneath the fiddle music.

Dashi kept her face immobile.

"Because you had the needle all along." When she still didn't answer, he added, "I wondered, at first, if you'd actually lost it and doubled back to search for it after we parted ways. But I can't imagine you lingering there with Idree and the odds of finding a needle in the middle of the taiga...I'm not sure I believe in coincidences that big.

"Only connections for you too, eh?" she muttered, thinking of Ese. "I don't have the time or energy to dredge up the past, Sevlin. If there's something you want to talk about that has to do with *the present*, then let's hear it."

"What else did Idree tell you about the seamripper?"

"Nothing. That was the first I'd heard of it, when she mentioned it in front of you."

Sevlin had gone still, eyelids sliding down so that his pale irises were nearly hidden. "You didn't discuss it before I got there?"

"No."

"And you didn't hear the khan discussing it while you were serving him just now?"

"I—how do you know about that?"

"The first messenger I sent was told you were occupied and couldn't come right away. If you'd been waiting on someone of a lower rank, you would have been relieved immediately, since I'd requested you by name. The only people in New Osb who have higher rank than I do, are Zevi and the khan, and you weren't serving Zevi."

"I didn't overhear anything useful," she said slowly, stalling.

If she described the map she'd seen and how much effort the khan had invested in finding the seamripper, Sevlin would want it even more. Would he leave New Osb? That could be both good and bad. If Sevlin stayed, he could be useful in helping Idree escape. On the other hand, he would almost certainly try to bring Idree under Tyvalaran control. Grief hit her suddenly, mixed with a sinking certainty. She and Idree would never be able to disappear. They would never find a place like Ejen, where they could set up a normal life. Not when Sevlin knew about Idree. Not when the khan held the golden needle.

A pounding on the outer door made both their heads turn. It was loud enough to be heard over the fiddle music. The soldier in the antechamber called something and there was a muffled response.

A few seconds later, he appeared in the bed chamber. "Prince Sevlin, I think you need to hear this. There are soldiers at the door."

Sevlin got to his feet, his lips pinched with annoyance. "What? Why?"

"A custody claim. They said that—" The soldier snuck a look at Dashi.

Sevlin's expression morphed to wariness. "*What* did they say?" His voice had gone soft again.

The soldier shifted on his feet. "Well...ah, your Yassari is better than mine, sir. I may have made a mistake in translating."

Sevlin strode into the adjoining room. "Let her come," he said without looking.

Dashi glared at the soldier who'd moved to block her path. Sevlin was already leaning against the door, engaged in a rapid volley of words with the person on the other side. It was a woman's voice, one Dashi thought she recognized: the angry guest from the feast.

Sevlin said something in Yassari, his eyes roving over Dashi all the way down to her feet. "She says you are not a servant," he informed Dashi in an undertone.

Dashi shrugged. *Well, I'm not.* "I spilled broth on a lady at the feast. She said I was..." Dashi paused, trying to remember the exact wording. It seemed ages ago. "She said I was an abomination. I think she wanted me fired."

Sevlin said something else in Yassari and the woman replied. There was a snuffling from the other side of the door, rapid and hollow, like paper being shaken.

"She didn't mean abomination," Sevlin said. "Bad translation on her part. She meant *imposter*. A thief lying in wait."

He was still leaning against the door, but Dashi saw the tightness in the lines of his shoulders and neck. He was angry, or perhaps worried, though his tone was unfailingly polite. Then again, he could be saying awful things in Yassari and Dashi wouldn't know the difference.

"She said she spoke to you in Thracedonian and you answered." His voice was flat.

"I...I can't remember. I might have, I suppose."

Dashi could see Sevlin cataloging that information, drawing his own conclusions. The sound of snuffling came again, more insistent this time, moving back and forth at the gap below the door.

"Why does it matter if I answered in Thracedonian?" she asked.

"Because it was in Thracedon that someone stole a pair of custom-made boots from a Yassari caravan. Boots that, according to her, were designed as a gift for the Queen of Tyvalar and were set to be delivered there in a month's time. Boots that sound an awful lot like the ones you're wearing."

"Hmmm," Dashi said, mentally replaying that moment at the banquet: the woman's anger, the way she'd looked down at the spilled broth—or maybe Dashi's boots. "Coincidence?"

The right side of Sevlin's mouth dropped incrementally, unamused. "*She* doesn't seem to think so. And neither does the thiefmark."

"Thiefmark?"

"A beast the Yassaris breed to track stolen property. Right now it is alerting to something behind this door."

One thin claw appeared below the door, dragging along the floor. The beast keened, frantic and shrill. The woman let out a burst of staccato words.

"She says she was waiting for the rest of the Yassari delegation to arrive before she made her move," Sevlin said, eyes closing briefly, "but that they arrived a few minutes ago. If you're not willing to go with them peacefully—or if I'm not willing to give you up—she's also alerted the guard commander of New Osb. They'll be here momentarily to remand you into Yassari custody."

Chapter 22

The pounding on the door resumed and Dashi took an involuntary step backward.

"What happens if I'm in Yassari custody?"

Sevlin closed his eyes briefly. "The punishment for stealing a Yassari invention is death. It is the worst crime in Yassar, to steal someone's ideas."

"Well, I'm not in Yassar, am I?"

"It doesn't *matter*, Dashi." He turned fully toward her, hands rising to grasp her shoulders. His fingers dug into her like he wanted to shake her, but his voice was calm. It was, her mind informed her distantly, the first time he'd touched her since the bushes. "They're given special dispensation on the continent to pursue thieves—no matter who, no matter where. It's one of the concessions they demand in exchange for trading their inventions with us, the right to execute the citizens of other countries. You could request a chance to appeal, but…"

Dashi glanced down at her boots. That's how she thought of them now: *hers*. They were by far the best boots she'd ever owned. She thought of how they'd clung to the wall while she climbed to Idree's room. Nice or not, however, they weren't worth *this* much trouble.

"I could give them back?" Even as she said it, she understood that it didn't matter. If the Yassari woman had already notified New Osb's commander—and there was no reason to doubt her—then Dashi's careful masquerade was at an end. There would be no more pretending to be a servant. There would be no quick rescue for Idree.

"You actually stole from them." Sevlin's voice was incredulous, as if, until her admission, he'd thought this whole thing might be a misunderstanding. "Returning the boots won't make a difference. The real point is to deter future thieves. Recovering the stolen goods is secondary."

"Why, in the name of all my crooked ancestors, would I come peacefully then?" Dashi spun away from his grasp, her eyes roaming over the wide chimney and the door to the bed chamber before finding the only window.

"I can't believe this," Sevlin muttered behind her.

The Yassari woman yelled something else.

Dashi crossed the room, pausing to examine the cold fireplace, before continuing to the window and peering out. "I didn't know they would be so angry about it. Well, I mean, I *did*, but..." *I didn't know they'd try to kill me over it.* She'd heard lots of things about the Yassaris over the year; she'd just thought most of it was made up.

The window option didn't look great. The wall was sheer on this side of the palace, unadorned by any architectural frippery that might ease her descent. Dashi glanced upward, trying to recall the roofline.

"Do you have—"

"Here." Sevlin handed her a coil of rope.

It wouldn't reach the ground, but that was beside the point. Dashi took it, unlatching the window with her other hand.

"What are you planning?" he asked, voice low.

"The opposite of what we did with the lift box: they go down, I go up." Dashi wedged a chair below the window and tied one end of the rope around the back. She tossed the other end outside without looking.

"I meant afterward," Sevlin said.

She stopped next to the fireplace, one hand on the marble facade. Regret was choking her. If only she'd figured out a way to get the golden needle, to free Idree. But both her anonymity and the element of surprise had evaporated at the Yassari's accusation. Which left her with only one choice: searching for another advantage. "What if the seamripper can undo the needle's hold on your sister?" Sevlin had said. "Maybe that's what *counterbalance* means." She'd told him, then, that it wasn't a good enough reason to leave Idree in New Osb. Now, she had no choice.

The sound of boots reached her before she could decide what she wanted to tell him. *The khan's guards.* Her eyes met Sevlin's. He'd put his sword belt back on at some point and stood with his feet wide, his soldiers gathered next to him, awaiting orders. The soldier who'd been playing the fiddle glared at her and Dashi suddenly wondered if Sevlin would order them to detain her.

When he opened his mouth, however, all he said was, "Good luck."

"Goodbye, Sevlin. Sorry for, " she motioned to the door, where the Yassari woman was still yelling, "*this.*"

Dashi ducked into the fireplace cavity, pulled herself through the large, open damper, and began to climb. There was only one way to do it: wedging her back against one side of the chimney while working for a grip with her hands and feet. Not many fires had burned in this fireplace; the brick lacked the patina of creosote that would one day slicken the mortared joints, making the climb even more difficult.

Below her, someone set a flame to the waiting pile of kindling, sending up a crackle of sparks. The chimney would heat quickly, but hopefully the smell of smoke would confuse the thiefmark. A few seconds later, Sevlin's door opened and the sound of dozens of footsteps bounced up the chimney cavity. Cursing silently, Dashi redoubled her efforts, sliding her back higher up the stack with each push of her legs. Her boots gripped the rough surface, trying to convince Dashi that they were worth the trouble they'd just caused. They weren't. She could almost hear Idree: *you should have thought of that before you stole them.*

She'd left Sevlin in a very difficult position: not only convincing their Karak hosts that the Tyvalarans had nothing to do with Dashi's servant charade, which would undoubtedly be read as a failed spying attempt but also deciding how much to aid the Yassaris. She listened for the shout of discovery, waited for the shadow of someone peering into the fireplace. Voices still reached her, but they were rendered hollow and strange by the chimney. Once or twice she heard Sevlin's voice, carrying with it a note of concern, but she couldn't discern what he was saying. The fire was heating the chimney fast, masking her exit but sending up enough smoke that she could feel a cough building in her lungs. She climbed faster.

Her hand scraped the top of the chimney and she swallowed a curse. The opening was covered by a cowl of hammered metal. Dashi pried at it, wiggling it from side to side and pushing upward, while also keeping herself wedged in place. Metal scraped agonizingly against brick and she froze, listening hard.

Scraaaape. More dust. The chimney cowl slid up incrementally. The light from below darkened briefly, but when she looked she saw nothing.

The heat and smoke had grown unbearable. She shoved the cowl off with one final push and slithered through the opening, landing in an ungainly heap. Despite the commotion in Sevlin's room, the courtyard below her was silent. *Good.* She still had time. Heaving herself to her feet, she picked her way across the tile roof, legs wobbling from the climb. The roof descended in a series of steps, and Dashi hung from the edge of each, dropping lower and lower until she was perched above the side of the palace that was still under construction. An easterly wind careened over her, bringing with it the smell of the taiga's evergreens and the rattle of dry leaves.

Someday the exposed joists would hold an arched roof between them, but right now they supported only moonlight, looking like the iced-over ribs of a winter carcass. Most important to Dashi, however, was the wooden scaffolding that had been erected along one of the walls. A block and tackle hung from one end, ready to lift the next load of tile. She only had to balance along the top of the unfinished wall until she reached the scaffolding, then she'd be able to swing down on the rope.

Testing the footing, Dashi started forward, stepping carefully over the first joist. Shadows draped the palace grounds below, pooling in layers along the walls and hedges like trains of dark fabric. Dashi paused to listen, but she heard only the breeze shaking the dead leaves and none of the telltale clamor of guards mobilizing. Had the Yassari woman been bluffing?

She stepped over the next joist, absorbed by the careful dance of placing her feet along the top of the wall. Something—either the persistent low-level rattling, which seemed to be drawing closer, or an instinct too inchoate to name—made Dashi turn. She had a fleeting glimpse of a narrow, whiskered snout and a dun coat over piled muscle. Then the thiefmark threw itself at her. Its claws raked the back of her thighs before she leaped away, teetering on the edge of the wall. Her hand went for the knife in her boot but before she could get there, the beast snarled, its needle-like teeth stark against black gums, and lunged again. Dashi threw her hands up in front of her face and throat, but the beast went for her feet, catching her ankles and upending her into the courtyard below.

Her hand shot out as she fell, somehow grabbing the scaffolding when she was halfway to the ground, but the momentum of her fall was too great. Pain exploded in her shoulder and the scaffold was yanked from her grasp. She landed in one of the ornamental bushes that lined the base of the wall, its branches grabbing at her skin and snapping beneath her weight. It shook her loose, tumbling her gently onto the cobblestones where she lay, bruised and panting.

Groaning, she rolled over, gripping her dislocated shoulder. Her vision was still spinning from the fall, making the ground and the pair of boots in front of her coalesce, then fracture again: one pair of boots, then seven; two pairs, replaced by six. Panic obscured her pain and Dashi tried to push herself to her feet, but hands were all over her: gripping the back of her neck, biting into her injured shoulder, pulling the knife from her boot. Someone shoved a cloth into her mouth to cut off her scream.

The Yassaris wore yellow hoods that covered everything except for their eyes. They put the thiefmark back on its leash, though it still snarled and spit in her direction. Someone lit a lantern and the flare of light was so sudden that Dashi had to shut her eyes. It was like being surrounded by seven suns: faceless and gleaming yellow, looming above her.

For a moment, no one said anything. Dashi's gaze darted between the hoods, but their eyes, when she found them through the slits in the fabric, were flat and devoid of sympathy.

One of the hoods spoke. "You are charged with theft from the United Yassari Merchantry."

Chapter 23

The Yassaris bound her hands, yanking horribly on her shoulder, and checked her for weapons, immediately removing the knife from her boot. *Their boot. Whatever.* They didn't take the boots themselves, however, which Dashi found strange. Instead, they marched her to the edge of New Osb's inner circle, where the wall rose high above them like a stone cudgel, waiting to fall. More Yassaris were waiting there, each wearing the full yellow hood over their faces.

Must keep the hoods packed away for special occasions, Dashi thought, but her attempt at flippancy landed flat. She was scared. Snippets of information about the Yassaris, things she'd leached from years of rumors and gossip but thought she'd forgotten, bubbled up in her thoughts.

An angry store clerk, leaning over her. "*Mind your manners, or the Yassaris'll take you. You'd learn respect on that island, I'd warrant.*"

Baris, uncharacteristically serious, as one of the infamous metallic wagons trundled past. "*Strange folk, the Yassaris. Like a bunch of hornets in a gilt hive.*"

Idree's face, marred by a faint frown. "*I heard they can always tell who stole from them and that their inventions catch fire if someone tries to copy them.*"

The thiefmark lunged in her direction, snapping viciously. Both its whiskers and its sharp face and canines put Dashi in mind of a weasel, though it was the size of a large dog. Three more Yassaris appeared from the darkness, dragging a wooden feeding trough between them. Without a word, they placed it next to the wall, then joined the others in a loose semicircle around it. Hands shoved Dashi forward, insistent when she reared back. Yellow hoods bent and lifted her, still kicking and making muffled exclamations through her gag, toward the trough. They secured her legs to one post and tied her arms to the other, so that she was suspended uncomfortably over the center, with nothing supporting her torso or hips.

This position proved agonizing for her shoulder, splintering any coherent thoughts. She pushed against the corner of the trough, attempting to force her shoulder back into place, but the angle wasn't right. She tried to rock the trough; without being able to brace her feet against the ground, she couldn't seem to get enough momentum to tip it. She stopped, panting around her gag.

The Yassaris had spoken to one another in Yassari when they first apprehended her. To her surprise, Dashi realized they'd switched to accented Karakalese.

"—theft of goods. Who will testify against the accused?" a deep voice intoned.

"I will testify." A woman's voice from beneath a yellow hood. She was shorter than the rest. "I recognized the craftsmanship of the boots and alerted my—" A pause as the woman searched for the right word in Karakalese. "My master?" The other Yassaris gave no indication if this was the correct word choice or not.

"Who will testify against the accused?" The first voice asked again.

"The thiefmark will testify." Another voice: male, young. "He alerted to stolen property as we entered New Osb and again, just now, when he climbed the wall after the thief."

"Based on evidence and testimony, I find the accused guilty of the theft of goods from the United Yassari Merchantry."

There was a pause, and Dashi had the sense that it was a practiced one, a silent cadence being counted out. The next words were spoken in unison, all the Yassaris joining in.

"The debt is final. Owed in red, if not gold."

Dirt crunched underfoot as one of the yellow hoods stepped forward, towering over Dashi's prostrate form. She thought of the skeleton that she and Sevlin had found in the Purek temple. It had been spread over an altar, shackles knocking into wrist and ankle bones, its naked spine arched at some remembered agony.

The Yassari fumbled at his throat, pulling out a cloth bag hanging from a cord. From the bag, he extracted a large thorn, finger-length and strangely serrated along one edge. Without warning, he leaned forward and plunged the thorn into Dashi's left forearm, dragging it toward her hand. Blood welled instantly. He meticulously wiped the thorn on Dashi's sleeve, before moving to her feet, where he drew the thorn along each boot, scoring the beautifully stitched designs. The implication was clear: the boots' perfection had been tainted by her theft.

"The debt is fertile. Paid in red, if not gold." Again, the Yassaris spoke in unison.

Blood was dripping frantically from Dashi's arm, splatting the dirt in a regular rhythm. Squatting next to the trough, the Yassari man tipped a small envelope over the fallen blood, then scurried backward.

Green bloomed instantly: a plant, growing before Dashi's eyes. Its stem was abnormally thick, its leaves waxy and red-veined. Strangest of all, it seemed to be consuming her blood. As Dashi watched, the plant doubled, then tripled in size, obscuring the muddy patch where she was watering the earth.

The unfurling tendrils moved with an eerie sense of purpose, hovering over errant droplets and sliding around the leg of the trough, where more blood had dripped. In moments, the plant had climbed, serpent-like, all the way up the side of the trough, its leaves so thick that in some places the wood was hidden entirely. Dashi yanked against the ropes as the plant moved closer. Its leaves whispered restlessly, a sound not unlike the thiefmark's raspy breath. Her mind conjured an image of herself, wrapped in fast-growing vines, the breath squeezed from her lungs. One of the tendrils rose above the others, its leaf trembling rhythmically, like it too had a pulse throbbing within. The tendril paused for a moment, a weathervane sensing the wind, before plunging into the cut on Dashi's arm.

Dashi gasped around the gag. It felt like an ember had embedded itself in her. Worse, she could see it growing beneath her skin, marching up her arm, writhing from within. The pain from her dislocated shoulder retreated into the background. She threw herself wildly from side to side, arching her back, her bound legs beating the trough in muffled thumps. It was an instinctual reaction, born of fear, not hope or a well-articulated plan, so Dashi was caught by surprise when she managed to flip the trough onto its side.

A cry went up from the Yassaris, who had drawn well away from the plant. A cry went up from Dashi too, as her shoulder jammed back into place. Her legs remained securely fastened, but her arms—she tugged experimentally—were looser. She wiggled her hands, trying to slip free before the Yassaris could grab her. Each movement sent blood flicking onto the ground. The plant pounced, plunging green runners into each droplet. A second tendril crawled into her wound, working its way toward her inner elbow, making her skin stretch and slither. With the trough now on its side, Dashi's face was level with the puddle of her blood. She swallowed a scream as the leaves rushed past her cheek, searching for her arm.

One of the Yassaris approached, edging closer until his yellow hood blocked out all else. It was the same man who'd cut her; she could see the bag that held the huge thorn swinging from his neck. He knelt, careful not to touch the plant or her blood, and began to retie the ropes on her wrists. Dashi tried to jerk away, but her efforts only exacerbated the blood flow. It rushed down her arm, gloving her hand and leaking between her fingers. A groan slipped from her mouth as the plant forced another tendril into her wound. The Yassari's eyes flicked to hers for a moment, emotionless and remote through the slits in his hood. In that pause, Dashi attacked.

It was a small movement—just a flick of her wrist, really—but her palm was spilling over with blood by that point. *Splat, splat.* Drops peppered the yellow fabric covering the Yassari's face. The plant's tendrils pivoted in mid-air, following with unseen eyes. The man flinched, leaning forward to swipe at his eyes, and the plant launched one of its runners at his face. He screamed as it punched through the slitted opening and speared his eye.

He fell forward onto Dashi, grappling with the plant, and for a moment the bag that held the thorn dangled in front of her face. She lunged for it, teeth snapping closed on the cord, her head rearing back to break it. The Yassari man flailed. Another tendril shot into his face.

Dashi spat the cord onto her chest, rolling her body so that the cloth bag dropped next to her. She twisted her wrist, managing to paw it open and then, through another contortion, maneuver the thorn into her waiting hand. The thorn sliced through the ropes as easily as any knife. The plant had grown a terrifying amount in just a few minutes. Her forearm was pulsing and so distended that it looked like it had been transplanted from someone twice her size. She hacked at the branches where they dove under her skin, severing them in a puff of moisture. Tendrils still writhed inside her arm, but she'd have to remove those later.

Someone tackled her before she could cut her legs free. Dashi hit the ground hard, crushed beneath yellow fabric. Hands encircled her neck.

She punched blindly, the thorn tucked between her fingers to add impact to every punch. The Yassari rolled off her, backpedaling like she held a real weapon.

Heat and pain exploded inside her forearm and, glancing down, she saw that the plant had found her again. It seemed to be everywhere: scurrying up her arm; diving into her cut; sinking green fingers into her deel and her pant leg, every place her blood had dripped. Dashi slashed wildly, cutting the remaining rope, hacking vines from her clothes and her wound, only to have more spring up a moment later. She stumbled away from the trough, hastily checking the backs of her legs and arms to make sure she hadn't missed anything.

A shout made her spin around, brandishing the thorn like a ward against a coming evil. One of the Yassaris sprinted toward her, a wickedly curved dagger in each hand. The others were mere steps behind. A crumpled yellow form lay next to the trough: the man who'd gotten the plant tendril in his eye. Vines protruded from his hood, waving their fiendish arms at her as she turned to run.

Chapter 24

Dashi dipped from shadow to shadow, moving as unobtrusively as her ragged breathing would allow. She'd crisscrossed the inner circle several times to avoid the Yassaris and their thiefmark, but now she'd reached her destination: the stables. This was her best guess for where she would find her confiscated weapons. The guards' arms were stored in the palace armory, but Dashi doubted a servant's belongings would be accorded such an honor.

She left the stable door cracked, letting in a beam of moonlight to guide her steps past the stalls and their slow-breathing occupants. There were rooms at the back for storing tack and assorted tools. She hoped her weapons were there as well.

She'd just stepped into the room when she heard someone enter the stable behind her. Dashi slipped behind the door, positioning the thorn between her knuckles. The footsteps paused before each stall but never stopped, moving inexorably closer. The doorway glowed brighter as someone held a lantern aloft to look inside the storage room.

"Ese!"

His arm jerked up, flooding his face with harsh light. The lines beside his mouth and eyes transformed into deep crevices.

"Little Dashi," he murmured. "You're popular tonight. Everyone is requesting your presence."

Dashi wet her lips. "How many are searching for me?"

"How many people are in New Osb? Whatever the number, they're all searching for you."

"Well, I appreciate you finding me with such alacrity," Dashi said dryly.

Ese bowed mockingly. "Anything for an ally. Although," he straightened, holding her with a slit-eyed gaze, "as far as I know, *allies* don't steal from one another."

Dashi took a wary step backward. She'd been so relieved to see Ese instead of the Yassaris, that she'd forgotten what she'd done the last time she'd seen him.

"Did you think I wouldn't notice that the vial is half empty?" he asked softly. "Or did you think that, in my grief, I wouldn't mind sharing the Adder's Dust?"

"It was the only way I could—"

"Get what you wanted? No. It was the most *expedient* way but not the only one. Tell me, did you manage to free your sister?" When Dashi didn't answer, he smiled grimly. "I thought not. If you'd stolen my revenge but freed your sister, that would be one thing. Jochi would have liked that, at least. But you took half the Adder's Dust and you have nothing to show for it."

"Not nothing. I found what the khan wants next. I can't free Idree directly, but I can do it indirectly." *If the seamripper can sever the needle's connection to Idree. If I can even find it.*

"Ah, the machinations of conceit," Ese said to the ceiling, setting down the lantern. "Your search for a bargaining chip will fail, just like mine did."

The words were too closely aligned with her doubts. "It was never *your* search because *you* never went," she snapped. "I'm not sending someone else in my place, I'm going myself. *I* won't fail."

Ese was on her quicker than she could move, grabbing the front of her deel and slamming her against the wall. The tools rattled ominously on their hooks, a warning that they could be overheard.

"You don't know *anything* about what I tried or what I've been through." Ese's voice was a harsh whisper, rank with stale wine.

He released her suddenly, his anger gone and his face ashen. Dashi loosed a breath, dropping her hand—and the Yassari's thorn—back to her side. She stared at him, trying to read his expression.

"Where are you going?" he asked. "You're known to the guards. Worse: for some reason, you're also known to the Yassaris."

"It's a long story," she said cautiously, still unsure of him.

There was a twinge of movement in her forearm: the plant tendrils, somehow still alive though they'd been severed half an hour ago. It was the reminder she needed. Dashi rolled up her sleeve, struggling to peel it back from her swollen forearm, and picked up Ese's lantern. He didn't say anything when she pulled the glass off and angled the flame toward the skin of her inner arm.

The flame kissed her skin, nipping initially, then biting down hard the longer she held it in place. The plant didn't react at first, but as her skin reddened, it began to writhe in earnest, driven to a frenzy by the heat. Dashi ground her teeth, her breath coming in harsh gasps. The tendrils slithered back toward her wrist, trying to escape the same way they'd entered, roiling her skin like liquid. They emerged with a squelch: four in all, flip-flopping over the wooden floor. Using a pair of shears from one of the shelves, Dashi held them in the flame one at a time, watching with sick satisfaction as the stems blackened and steam sputtered from the severed ends. Finally, they lay still.

Dashi straightened unsteadily and set the shears down. Bright blotches swam before her eyes from staring at the flame for so long.

"I have to go back into the taiga," she said, pulling her sleeve carefully over the burnt skin. She kept her eyes locked on Ese's face. Anywhere but her arm. "I need my bow. Any other supplies would be good too."

"Wearing another pyrothrite belt?" he asked in a light voice, but he was staring at her arm.

"The bow, Ese."

He motioned to a shelf above her head. "There are some supplies there. Rope, medical, tins of dried meat for hunts. The bow, though..." He shook his head.

"Where?"

"There's a second armory. Next to the guards' barracks," he added before she could get too excited.

"Are you sure?" Ancestors above, how could she get her bow back from *there*?

"You don't have long," Ese said, a trace of impatience in his voice. "A few minutes. Maybe less. Whatever you're planning, you'll have to do it without your bow."

No. Bad enough she was venturing back into the taiga. Bad enough that Sevlin had been right about the impossibility of escaping with Idree. To go without her bow was...she might as well go without her hands.

A lantern appeared briefly through the cracked stable door, moving across the courtyard. Her window of escape was closing.

She swallowed hard. Ese was right. The bow was a lost cause. Dashi turned to the shelf he'd indicated, rifling through the contents while he watched impassively.

"A little help would be nice," she snapped.

"I thought not sounding the alarm was helpful enough."

"What alarm?" Dashi thought of the torches atop Karak City's walls, signaling the gates to close.

"It was a figure of speech."

"Oh." She turned back to her meager supplies. "It's in your interest for me to escape. If I'm caught and tortured the khan might find out about you."

"It's the Yassaris you have to worry about tonight, little Dashi, and information extraction isn't what they have in mind. Though you're right: to be absolutely safe, I should kill you myself. I understand there is a reward."

Dashi glanced up sharply, but Ese hadn't moved.

"Unfortunately, what I want more than reward money is to remain anonymous enough to administer the Adder's Dust—what's left of it."

Despite the assurance that he wouldn't stop her, Dashi wasn't sure she believed him. There was too much anger threading his voice.

When he didn't say anything else, she asked, "Will there be enough?"

"To kill him, no. Not anymore." He raised his hand in a mock salute, laying the blame at her feet. "But it will weaken him. Severely and noticeably. Weakness invites its own dangers. Perhaps, like Jochi, the khan will be killed off by someone close to him. Or perhaps I'll find a way to do it myself."

Ese paused, clearly savoring the thought, but when Dashi stood and slung the saddlebag over her shoulder, he stepped in front of her.

"Make no mistake, I won't forget what you did," he said in a quiet voice. "But I believe in repayment, not absolution, and when our paths cross again, I'll get it."

"And if I refuse?"

Ese stepped away from the door. "Believe me, little Dashi, you don't want me arrayed against you."

Dashi dropped to the ground beside the outer wall and surveyed the scene in front of her. Clouds had come rolling in while she'd stolen out of New Osb. Now and then, the moon found a window to peak through, but the night had a heavy cast to it that had not been there earlier.

Tents, dusky silver by night, covered the land between Dashi and the river. This was the prisoner labor camp, a halo of slums surrounding the jewel of the khan's palace. Although she could see no guards, she knew they were there, either huddled in their tents or pacing their route if they were on duty. She worked her way south, skirting the edge of the slum without veering too close, careful to stay low. Ese's words—that she was destined to come here, either as a prisoner or as her sister's rescuer—hung in the air.

Behind her, New Osb's gates remained closed. *They think I'm still inside,* she thought as she crept to the edge of the river. Riverboats nosed at the shore, tied to pilings that had been sunk into the mud. Dashi eyed them warily, the way one might watch a half-wild horse for signs of mood and temperament before mounting. She'd forded a river on horseback before, even jumped off and swam when the mood struck, but a boat was not something with which she had experience.

The Temuli River was a lazy ribbon connecting New Osb to Karak City, which was where most of the boats had originated. Once they unloaded in New Osb, the boats began the laborious process of returning to Karak City, either being poled along the sides of the river where the current was weakest, or when topography allowed, being towed by teams of yaks from the shore. None of the boats went east from New Osb. There was nothing there except the taiga.

It can't be too hard, Dashi told herself, climbing aboard one boat. She untied it and pushed off from the piling. Since she wasn't going upriver, she wouldn't have to fight the current with a pole; the river would do the work. A tendril of current caught the stern, swinging the boat toward the center of the river, and Dashi straightened cautiously, feeling the movement of the water through her legs.

The riverboats were, by necessity, narrow things, with sides that only reached halfway up her thigh. There was a tiny, canvas-sided shelter in the center, just big enough for a few people to retreat from bad weather. She'd glanced inside once already, to make there were no inadvertent passengers, but now she took a longer look. There was a battered lantern, a worn pair of gloves and a pair of bedrolls.

She put the gloves on and picked up one of the long poles from the side of the boat, stabbing it down into the water, the way she'd seen the boatmen do. The vessel made an awkward lurch to the side, and pain slashed through her left forearm each time she lifted the pole, but she kept trying, working her way toward the center of the river

Near Karak City the river was wide, wrapping around the capital's shoulders like a relaxed arm, but it was deeper here and, Dashi realized, its placid appearance was deceptive. She no longer needed the pole. Faster and faster the river pushed until, almost too late, she looked over her shoulder and saw that the lights of New Osb were nearly out of sight. She let out a whoop of exhilaration, the way she often did while riding. It felt similar: the speed, the wind, the inebriating rush of freedom and adventure.

The near-taiga was dark around her, black hills against black sky. Though the clouds presaged a storm, at the moment the air was calm, the river moving silkily beneath the boat. An owl hooted from the shore. Dashi's thoughts flicked back to the thiefmark. Could it track over open water? Would the Yassaris be crazy enough to follow her into the taiga? She strongly suspected that the answer to at least one of those questions was no. The thought made her settle back against the stern with a pleased sigh, gently massaging her throbbing forearm.

Her first hint that the boat might be more dangerous than she'd anticipated came when she tried to stop. As much as she enjoyed the feeling of rushing into the night, the fear of running into a log or other debris was one she couldn't ignore. Once New Osb was out of sight, she decided to tie up on shore. She would start again at dawn, she thought, which should still put her ahead of any pursuers. When she attempted to pole to shore, however, the river whisked her forward so quickly that her push did nothing. Ignoring the pain that flared in her left arm, she made a second attempt, positioning the pole so that it pointed far in front of her. The boat's nose quivered in the direction of the shore, before returning resolutely downriver. She tried again, faster and stronger with each attempt, but she was no match for the river and she saw, with clarity if not timeliness, why each boat had a three-person crew.

The river became rougher without bothering to warn her, sloshing the boat from side to side, then dropping out from under her as it plunged into a series of rapids. A fine mist coated her face and hair, turning her skin clammy. The water chattered louder, but Dashi still heard the unmistakable sound of waves breaking against something hard and immutable.

Stomach lurching, she probed the darkness. The moon snuck a glance too, breaking through the clouds to shed light on what lay ahead: another plunge, straight toward a chute of looming gray boulders. Dashi swore, but the wind whipped the words away before she could hear them. The river had carved a deep passage here, and the banks loomed high on either side. She had a fleeting recollection of the taiga, of the feeling that the trees watched her.

The boat careened from side to side, following the current as it dashed through the chute. A boulder whizzed by on the left, close enough to touch if Dashi had been willing to unclench her fingers from the gunwale. Another boulder passed on the right. The boat dipped toward it, pulled by the eddy on the downriver side, and there was an ominous splintering sound. Water poured onto the deck and the boat dove again, narrowly threading more rocks.

Almost as suddenly as they'd begun, the rapids were over. The river cooled its pace. The riverbanks gentled and shrank. Her injured arm was cramped from the ferocity with which she'd clung to the side, but she retrieved her pole and plunged it downward, finding the river bottom easily now that the water was slow and shallow. Haltingly, one uneven shove at a time, Dashi edged toward the shore. She wasn't in the taiga yet, merely paralleling its border, but she could see its dark mass looming closer, waiting.

The boat butted its nose against the land, not much different than Spit at that moment. Dashi leaped out, legs wobbling, and sank gratefully to the ground. It was firm beneath her, a feeling which was both welcome and disconcerting after so long on the boat. *After so long on the boat?* Dashi glanced at the sky. It was not yet light; she hadn't been on the river for more than a few hours.

The boat seemed none the worse for its meeting with the boulder. There was a concave dent along one side, where the wood had been bashed inward, but the wound was high, where the water would be unlikely to take advantage.

Despite the perfectly good shelter onboard, Dashi couldn't bring herself to stay on the boat. Instead, after tying the bowline to a tree and fetching one of the bedrolls, she fell asleep on the solid, rocky shore.

Dashi woke with her forearm throbbing hotly and the rest of her body stiff and cold. The sky growled and she pushed herself upright, feeling every bruise from her ordeal with the Yassaris.

Towers of cloud filled the dawn sky and the air had an ominous feel to it: too still and too warm for autumn. The morning birds called maniacally, trying to complete their business before the weather broke. Even the fish felt the tension, darting to the surface in slides of silver.

Between one peal of thunder and the next, she heard the sound that had woken her.

Shifting gravel.

Footsteps.

Chapter 25

Dashi eased away from the boat—it would be the obvious focus for whoever had found her—and slid into the bushes that crowded the shore. Although the sun had risen, it was hidden by storm clouds, leaving the land sullen and dark. She stilled her mind, feeling the heaviness of the air, trying to distill the sound of danger from the sounds of nature. A shadow trembled, its outline separating from those around it: a figure, prowling closer to the boat.

No sign of accomplices. Dashi frowned. No one would come alone. Had they split up to cover more ground? Or were they, even now, flanking her position, closing on her like pincers?

The figure leaped onboard, ripping open the canvas flap of the cabin. He reached inside to touch something and then stood up, his head turning slowly as he searched his surroundings. There was a familiarity about the way the man moved, about the contradiction between the broad shoulders and the light placement of feet. Just to be sure, she waited until she'd gotten a glimpse of the harsh line carved into his cheek, then let her grip on the Yassari thorn relax.

"Sevlin."

His shoulders twisted toward the sound of her voice, his sword arm rising smoothly. "Where are you?"

She stayed where she was, naked branches scratching against her back, pulse still pounding in her throat. "How did you find me?" *And, more importantly, how far away are the other pursuers?*

"I'll tell you," he said, squinting at the shadows in the vicinity of her voice, "*and* give you the food I brought, if you sit down and talk to me."

"I'm not so desperate that I can be bought off with a few bites to eat," she protested, but it sounded half-hearted even to her. She took a step forward and his eyes caught the movement immediately.

He jutted his chin toward the boat's low cabin. "Inside?"

"I'd rather eat on the deck."

"We probably don't have long until the storm comes."

She shrugged.

Sevlin regarded her from the height of the boat. Finally, he said, "I can't tell if you're disagreeable merely out of habit or if you are intentionally goading me."

The truth was more complicated. The sight of Sevlin had set an implacable impatience humming inside Dashi, an on-edge, let's-get-on-with-it feeling that sometimes came when she was about to do something dangerous. She'd felt the contours of it in his room, with the dressing screens hemming her in and Sevlin lounging in front of her like a big cat, lazily contemplating the width of her neck. She felt it now. She didn't know what it meant—if Sevlin was a danger or if she was merely keyed up by the last few days—but she *did* know that she might explode if she was stuck in a small space with him again.

Sevlin stood silently as she pulled herself onto the boat. He seemed to be waiting for her to say something but, when she didn't, he reached into his bag and handed her a round bun the size of her hand. Dashi sank against the side of the boat and took a bite, savoring the plump raisins and spices.

"Dessert bread! You must want something," she said since it was obvious that he did.

He sat opposite her, one arm slung over the edge. "Maybe I came just to deliver bread and conversation."

Dashi snorted and kept chewing, trying to tamp down her restlessness. Sevlin would say what he wanted eventually.

"You left Spit behind," he said. "To answer the question of how I found you. A dozen of the khan's horses went missing and the guards went after them, figuring you'd taken one and released the others as a distraction. But I saw Spit in the corral. You wouldn't have left him if you'd intended to travel by horseback."

"So you checked the boats," she said, processing what he'd told her. Ese must have opened the stall doors after she'd gone. That was...unexpectedly helpful.

"One was missing. The man who'd tied it up had a reputation for being sloppy, but I wasn't convinced."

"Thin justification to start heading this way."

"I had a suspicion you'd be making for the taiga."

Here it is, Dashi thought, *the reason he came.*

"I'm going after the seamripper too," he said. "I think we should look for it together."

Dashi finished chewing, buying herself time. She wasn't surprised that Sevlin had figured out her goal.

"We worked together last time," she said. "I got the impression you regretted the experience."

He held her gaze. "Not all of it."

She thought of them stumbling out of the oven room and falling to the stone floor together, of landing on his chest and just laying there, listening to his heart hammer. She thought of him in a spore-induced lust, one hand grinding against the back of her neck like he wanted to consume her.

"Still," she said.

"If we go against each other this time, I'll win." Sevlin tilted his head back against the railing so that he was looking at her through slitted eyes. "You've never been to this part of the taiga—"

"Neither have you." Her eyes dipped to the column of his neck.

"—and, unless I miss my guess, you didn't bring much in the way of provisions. Nor were you able to grab any weapons. If you had, they would be sitting next to you right now."

"Maybe I didn't bother with provisions because I knew you'd bring me dessert bread." A fat raindrop hit her cheekbone and ran down to her jaw before she could wipe it away.

Sevlin made a dismissive motion with his mouth, pursing the right side while the left side stayed still. "You didn't know I would come."

"I thought you might." *Lie. I thought I was all alone.* "It makes it easier now that you have." *I'm glad I'm not.*

"That's it?" The right side of Sevlin's mouth tightened further. "We can work together? You're not going to argue or threaten to use me for shooting practice?"

"First of all," she said, pointing at him with the piece of dessert bread, "I don't need any practice. And, I'd love to threaten you, Sevlin, but you did bring me this bread. On top of that, my bow is locked up in New Osb."

Sevlin studied her for a moment. The sporadic splat of raindrops against the deck filled the silence. "You are being very easy about this."

"Now who's being habitually disagreeable? I agree to let you help me and—"

"I did not say I would be your *helper*. I said we could find it together."

Dashi waved a hand, still affecting an unconcerned air. "What's the difference? After we find the seamripper, I'll take it back to New Osb and we can see if it will free Idree from the needle's connection."

"*I* will be carrying the magical artifact this time, if it's all the same, and the seamripper cannot go to New Osb until we know more about it. All we have is guesswork and the fact that it's important to the khan; we don't know what a 'counterbalance of the needle' actually does. We cannot risk taking it into the khan's stronghold and then losing it to him."

"*We* can't risk it?" Dashi repeated, letting some of the breeziness leach from her voice. Finally, they'd come to the crux of what Sevlin wanted and Dashi was unsurprised to find that freeing Idree was not his top priority. "It doesn't seem like you're risking a lot either way, *Prince* Sevlin. It's not your sister who's trapped in an underground prison, so of course you don't mind leaving her there while you tinker with some artifact."

He raised his head, looking at her straight on. "I *do* mind leaving Idree there and you have no idea what I'm risking, but that is beside the point. The point is you need me."

"I don't need anything from you. I would—I will find the seamripper just fine on my own."

Sevlin stood abruptly. "Good luck without any weapons or supplies." He wasn't yelling, but Dashi could hear the tenuousness in his tone, how his usual polite calm was threatening to give way.

"Good luck without a map." Uncomfortable with him towering over her, she got to her own feet.

His eyes narrowed like she'd just confirmed something for him. "At best, you *saw* a map. That's not the same as having one."

"You say you brought weapons and food, but all I see is a single sword and a piece of bread. For all I know you ran out of there as hastily as I did."

"*No one* could be hastier than you. The weapons are with my horse."

She bristled. "So my hastiness is a liability now and you, what, want to help me out of pity? Out of the overflow of your noble ideals? That's what you tried to claim last time too, Sevlin. I didn't buy it then and I don't—"

"For the last time, I don't want to *help* you, I want to work *with* you, *despite* your hastiness." He ran a hand over his close-cropped hair and let it fall to his side.

Dashi rolled her eyes. "Don't pretend at magnanimity. You brought a horse. That just shows how much you need a map."

Sevlin's gaze sharpened. "So it's off the river, then?"

"Why do you think I brought a boat?"

"I *thought* you were too hasty to have planned anything else," he said, his voice growing more clipped with each word. "Just like everything else. Stealing from the ancestors-cursed Yassaris, hiding Idree in Thracedon."

"Thracedon wasn't hasty. We had a good life there."

"Thracedon is overrun with bandits and in the midst of a civil war! And you took the seamstress *and* the golden needle there!"

Just like that, any control Dashi had was gone, evaporated like a puddle on the steppe.

"Where was I supposed to take her, Sevlin?" She was shouting now, her face suddenly closer to his. One hand was fisted in the front of his deel, ready to transfer some of the blame from herself to him. "We couldn't stay in Karakal and you'd banned us from Tyvalar. Thracedon was the only place where we had a chance of disappearing."

"I did not," he said, his voice finally rising, "*ban* you from Tyvalar." His hands curled around each of her biceps, just below the shoulder. She could feel his fingers digging into her, imprinting themselves on her skin, vibrating with the impulse to either pull her closer or fling her away.

"Right." Dashi rolled her eyes. "Because when a prince tells you that you're not welcome—"

"You didn't know I was a prince then!"

"Because you didn't tell me! Yet you expect me to have told you everything about the needle."

His eyes flashed for a moment, reflecting the lightning that split the clouds above them. "If I had known about the needle, I could have protected Idree."

"She doesn't need *you* to protect her. She has me." Dashi plowed ahead before he could respond, afraid of what he'd say next. Afraid that it would be the truth: that she couldn't protect Idree. That she hadn't. "Don't you dare second guess me, Sevlin. I spent the last year waking up at the slightest noise, stalking around our yard with my bow drawn, ready to ambush the pursuers I was *sure* I'd heard, and then getting back under my blankets before the sun rose, just so Idree could wake before me and never know that anything was amiss. You probably spent the year in a fancy palace, being spoon-fed by servants. So you don't get to tell me how you could have done a better job if you'd been in my place."

"I didn't say that. Stop twisting—"

"I'm not—"

"You—"

A gigantic clap of thunder smothered their words, vibrating the boat with its anger and ripping a hole in the clouds. Rain tipped out, pounding so hard that the drops hit the deck and bounced back into the air. Dashi made a dive for the canvas flap that covered the entrance to the cabin, tangling with Sevlin as he tried to fit through the small opening at the same time. Her forehead collided with his chin. Her fingers were mashed beneath his knee. They both took a step back, eyes narrowed against the sheeting rain, and then Sevlin motioned for Dashi to go first.

It was a courtly gesture, but annoyance was drawn in every line of his body.

The 'cabin' was really a canvas tent stretched over a wooden frame and secured to the deck, with enough room to sit upright but not much more. It was far from weatherproof, though someone had thought to nail a lip of wood around the perimeter so that the rain didn't run beneath the canvas and into the bedrolls.

Sevlin settled cross-legged across from Dashi, the top of his head brushing the canvas ceiling. He rubbed his jaw where her head had butted him.

"I don't think we can work together," Dashi said, eying him. He looked incongruous in the small space, all still, solid lines against the flimsy canvas walls, which pulsed with each breath of wind.

"We don't have a choice, Dashi, and you know it. Do you think I'd choose—" Sevlin cut himself off, his left hand moving restlessly over his head again. Inhaling deeply, he said in a calmer voice, "Our odds of success increase if we work together. Even someone who enjoys being disagreeable should be able to see that." He shifted, trying to get comfortable, before settling on his side, propped up on one elbow. It only made him seem longer somehow.

"I don't *enjoy being disagreeable*. I get along fine with other people."

Sevlin snorted. "You don't even get along with *Idree*."

"We do now. We never fought in Thracedon."

Dashi's mind flew to their cottage: summer roses growing in splashes of color against white walls; the iridescent gleam of Idree's black hair as she knelt to fuss over that stupid goat.

"Anyway, that's unfair," she continued. "I have no idea how you get along with *your* siblings, Prince Sevlin. Perhaps you feud over who will have which throne at mealtime."

"We get along fine," was all he said, but his lips gave that little twitch that told Dashi he was amused.

"Well, I get along with everyone who's not you." She thought of Negan and his brother, both dead by her hand. She thought of Ese. "Well, mostly everyone. But when I don't it's because they have it coming."

Sevlin raised his arm to mop raindrops from his face. A few evaded capture, clinging to the short, dark hair at his temples. He glanced at her. "Do you know I never lose my temper? Ever. Except with you."

"That's the first time I've heard you raise your voice, Sevlin," Dashi said disgustedly.

"Inside my head though…"

"You thought you'd like to kill me?"

"I wasn't thinking about killing you," he said, still looking at her.

"Grievously injure, then." She waved a hand. "But you didn't. That," she said, "is the very definition of *not* losing your temper."

"Let's hope it holds," Sevlin said, looking away. His calm, level voice was fully restored now.

Dashi, meanwhile, could still feel her heart hammering in her chest. His control annoyed her. His talk of gallantry and duty annoyed her. His criticism annoyed her. Most of all, however, his perception annoyed her. It was like he had an extra pair of eyes, which specialized at seeing through all of her prevarications until he located the root of everything she did, everything she wanted. He was always watching, even when it seemed like he wasn't. He'd never looked in her direction at the banquet, she realized, and yet his appearance in Idree's cell had been timed perfectly.

And it's a good thing, her mind supplied. *If not for Sevlin, you'd be in a cell. Or worse.*

She *did* need him—his weapons, specifically—and she knew it would be foolish to pretend otherwise. In the back of her mind, she heard Baris' voice and pictured his smirk. "*All that pride is well and good, Dashi.*" *His practice sword prodded her throat, underscoring the point that, despite all her boasts and threats, he'd thoroughly beaten her. "Sometimes, though, it needs to be swallowed."*

"Is your hand okay?" Sevlin nodded at her chest, where Dashi had been unconsciously cradling her hand.

"Fine," she said, dropping it to her lap. "Got mashed against the deck by some big oaf." It wasn't a lie, exactly—he *had* ground her fingers against the boards—but the pain that spanned from her fingers to her forearm had nothing to do with that. She thought briefly of telling Sevlin about the Yassaris' plant and showing him the burns from when she'd killed it, but she felt vulnerable already, stuck in the small cabin next to him, forced to watch the raindrops suspended in his hair. Instead, she adjusted the bedroll so she could lie down and stare at the canvas ceiling.

"Idree needs to get out of there," she said to the canvas. "It's making her—the way she—"

"I saw it too," Sevlin said softly, when she didn't—*couldn't*—finish. "I still think it would be a grave strategic error to rush back to New Osb immediately."

She let out a breath, trying to marshall objectivity. "And instead...?"

"If we find the seamripper, we take it to Tyvalar." He caught her expression. "*Both* of us. Tyvalar has an extensive Purek archive, both original and copied."

Altan, Baris and Zayaa, always mapping and translating and copying, had died feeding that archive.

"We review everything we have on the seamripper," Sevlin went on. "We test it, see what it can do on its own. We try to get close to one of the khan's heralds, perhaps capture one, to measure what effect it has on their powers. Only when we have prepared as much as we possibly can, do we risk bringing it within the khan's reach." Dashi opened her mouth, but Sevlin held up a hand. "I know you want to rescue Idree, and

I hope you believe me when I say that I do too. But this is our best shot at defeating the khan before he amasses a magical army and it would be foolish to rush in without preparing to the best of our ability." He leaned toward her, eyes narrowing with the intensity. "I know you prefer not to trust anyone, but Tyvalar has resources that could aid you, resources that could aid *Idree*."

Against her better judgment, Dashi turned her head to look at him. Because of the confines of the cabin, they were quite close to each other.

"Even if you don't believe that I want Idree to be free," he continued, "you must see that it is not in Tyvalar's best interest for her to stay with the khan. We won't leave her there."

"I believe you," she said, her eyes roaming the planes of Sevlin's face, "but I need to know what happens to Idree *after* she's rescued."

"If the seamripper is the counterbalance to the needle, then maybe it can be used to break the needle's connection to Idree."

Dashi grunted, surreptitiously kneading her aching forearm. That was her hope too, and the fact that Sevlin had just voiced it made her suspect manipulation. "And if the seamripper *doesn't* work the way we hope? If Idree remains the seamstress?"

"It will depend on whether Tyvalar can acquire the needle. If the khan still has it, then Idree will stay under Tyvalaran protection. You must see that, Dashi."

Reluctantly, Dashi nodded. If the needle stayed in the khan's hands, he would use it to track Idree wherever she went. In that scenario, Idree's best hope lay in putting as much of the Tyvalaran army between her and the khan as possible.

"If *Tyvalar* can obtain the golden needle," Sevlin continued, "you and Idree would be allowed to go, but the needle would need to stay in Tyvalaran hands, where it could be protected."

His expression was closed, not a twitch of his lip or a flicker of his gaze giving away his thoughts. *Or if he's telling the truth.* Dashi pressed her lips together, trying to think through all the iterations of this plan, though she could already feel her decision pressing down on her. What choice did she have? In the long term, Tyvalar could help protect Idree from the khan. In the short term...well, she needed supplies and weapons and Sevlin was offering both.

She nodded, one tense bob of her head. The terms were as acceptable as she could make them. For now, she would have to trust that Sevlin spoke the truth, just as he had to trust that she did the same.

Chapter 26

S evlin left immediately to retrieve the rest of his weapons and supplies. His horse would be turned loose, with the hope that it would find its way back to civilization. Dashi could admit, to herself if not to Sevlin, that having him along was a relief. She'd dreamt of the taiga as she slept on the rocky shore: fingers made of mist and rats with putrid breath. The idea of traveling alone, injured and without weapons, would play in her nightmares for months to come. A breeze blew crossways from the river and Dashi shivered.

Sevlin's absence gave her a moment of privacy and slowly, almost reluctantly, Dashi folded back her sleeve. At her first glimpse of the wound, a relieved breath escaped. The swelling had gone down some—her forearm no longer strained against the fabric—and, to her practiced eye, the cut left by the Yassari's thorn had scabbed over nicely. Still, her arm throbbed, and not just from the cut itself. Gritting her teeth, Dashi tugged the sleeve up further, revealing the angry flesh, piece by piece. Her skin was a patchwork of shiny burns, the result of her handiwork with the lantern. Lines of green and black stretched from beneath the burns, winding and forking as they reached up toward her elbow. *The plant. It's still alive*, was her first thought. It took her a moment to understand that the lines were still, not writhing and growing like they had been when the plant lived. She turned her arm, eyes tracing the disturbing sight. The lines followed her blood vessels, though she couldn't discern a pattern in the black and green marbling. She pressed a finger against a particularly thick line. She'd expected a needle of pain, but it felt deadened.

She'd seen a wound turn septic before—a man she'd known in the leather circle had died from it—but this looked different. Maybe it was specific to the Yassari plant? *They* would *have their very own brand of sepsis*, Dashi thought bitterly. Wound salve, applied early and often, was a reliable cure for sepsis, and Dashi felt her worry drain away. Yet another reason to be glad Sevlin had found her when he did; he would have wound salve. Smoothing her sleeve down, she stepped up onto the boat's gunwale, doing what she always did to assuage boredom and tension: moving. Her feet slid along the thin strip of wood, eyes forward, chin level. *Look at what's ahead, not at what might pull you down.*

The boat shifted, settling under Sevlin's weight.

"Weapons?" She spun to face him, still balanced on the side of the boat.

"Hello to you, too." He wore his sword and carried a crossbow in his left hand. "I couldn't take an extra crossbow from my delegation, not when they have so far to go to reach safety. But I do have this for you."

He handed Dashi what was in his right hand: a sword, nearly as small and light as her own. Dashi pulled it from its scabbard, testing its heft against what she was used to. The image of a vine, blooming with roses and bristling with thorns, was etched into the blade.

"Where did you get it?"

He shrugged, shoulders sliding up casually. "One of the Tyvalaran soldiers offered it." He set out several knives, also for her.

"Oh?" Dashi's voice was skeptical. The weapon had been crafted with a very specific person in mind. In her experience, people didn't give up their custom-made weapons on a whim.

"She may have been bribed," Sevlin allowed.

"Or pressured by a prince?"

"It is possible." The side of his mouth moved up a fraction.

Dashi smiled slightly as she tested the blade and found it sharp. "Won't she be in danger if she's going around unarmed?"

"Don't worry about her," Sevlin said, his voice going warm with familiarity. "She's good at staying ahead of trouble."

It was no bow, but...it had been procured with her in mind. She glanced up to find Sevlin watching her.

"Thank you." The words sounded stiff even to her ears, but she couldn't help feeling caged, couldn't help seeing the invisible strings attached to that gift.

She sheathed the sword and belted it over her sash. "The storm pushed the boat up onto the shore. It'll be work to get it free."

They slid off the boat and onto the gravel shore. Their arms strained side-by-side as they rocked the bow, loosening the boat in its bed, then shoved it straight back until the water caught its weight. Sevlin leaped up, using his momentum to swing himself onboard. Dashi intended to follow, but her boots wobbled in the lapping water, slipping sideways instead of sinking into the gravel as she'd expected. The result was that she barely had enough momentum to reach the boat's side. An expletive slipped from her mouth as she clawed her way over and dropped onto the deck. *All that trouble and I got boots that slip in the slightest bit of wet.*

Sevlin was already holding a pole, his back to her. There was some relief in that, Dashi thought, standing. At least he hadn't witnessed her nearly falling into the river.

He didn't turn around, but his voice carried back to her. "I would have offered a hand, had I known you needed it."

Dashi gave him a dirty look and shoved her pole against the river bottom with a ferocity that shot the boat forward.

The shadows had grown long and the air cooler by the time they stopped. Dashi and Sevlin had barely exchanged a word since morning, other than to occasionally shout, "Watch out on your side," or, "Go left! Go left!" The river afforded little else. Dashi snuck a glance at him, watching him roll his shoulders and shift his pole to a more comfortable position. He looked every bit as tired as she felt.

The river canyon, which had been narrow and turbulent for most of the day, opened up around them, revealing a wide marsh backlit by the setting sun. The river veered east, leaving the marsh behind and disappearing into a chasm that split the steep ridge of the taiga.

"There it is," she murmured, more to herself than Sevlin. The dying sunlight highlighted each dark tree: ten thousand serrated edges, dipped in gold. She could see none of the mist that had so unnerved her on her last taiga journey.

Sevlin leaned against his pole, his arm brushing hers. "I don't relish the idea of going back in there."

"I don't know how much farther we'll be able to go by boat," Dashi said, pointing to where the river turned sharply eastward. "I remember that bend from the map. There's a waterfall just after it enters the taiga."

"We can stop here for the night and in the morning skirt the falls on foot."

"That's what I was thinking too." She watched Sevlin toss the anchor into the water and, with a practiced air, maneuver the boat into place. "Do you think we have any pursuers?

"Everyone was searching along the road when I left. More searchers might have been dispatched later, but if they did follow the river, they wouldn't have gotten this far yet."

"You caught up with me quickly enough," Dashi pointed out, but she could feel her niggling sense of worry ease.

"I rode hard and the river was slow at first. Not like the stretch we did today. We must have covered a fair distance. Speaking of which," he pulled his deel away from his chest and grimaced, "I'm going for a swim."

Without further warning, he pulled his deel and undershirt off and tossed them into a corner of the deck. Dashi blinked, taking in the stretch of scarred skin and solid muscle in the moment before he dove into the water. She made herself turn away, ducking into the cabin to apply some of Sevlin's wound salve. Even though this was her second application—she'd also done it earlier that day, during a rare lull in the river—her arm appeared unchanged. Both times she'd tended it, she'd made sure to do it away from Sevlin. The shame of being the one who'd forced them to scurry out of New Osb was still too fresh, though she would rather have cut her arm *off* before articulating that to him.

Drawn by the cool air, she went back out onto the deck. The sound of splashing water was almost musical after the roar of the river all day, but it didn't lull her as she'd hoped. Her back and hamstrings ached from holding the pole and her forearm alternated between flashes of pain and a cold, wrist-to-elbow, numbness. She closed her eyes, determined to ignore it.

The next thing Dashi knew, Sevlin was sitting down across from her, a saddle bag in one hand and a lantern in the other.

"You're sitting in the dark," he said in his carefully enunciated way. Though his dark hair looked dry already, he smelled sharply of river water and fresh air.

Dashi blinked. "I was asleep. There was little need for light."

He tossed a wad of dried meat at her and she caught it one-handed. "Now there is."

"What else did you bring?"

"Not much, unfortunately. Just what I could grab in a hurry." A sudden thought lit his eyes. "I did bring one of these." He tipped the saddle bag toward the light and Dashi glimpsed three metallic claws.

Her smile was part fond, part dismayed. "A grappling hook? I sincerely hope we don't have to use one of those again."

"I've taken to carrying one whenever I'm on a long journey."

Dashi raised an eyebrow, more at the idea of a prince making long journeys, than at the idea of him carrying a grappling hook.

"Not that I want to use it again," Sevlin said, misinterpreting her expression. "But," he shrugged, "it *did* save my life in the temple."

Dashi nodded. Her grappling hook had been left in New Osb with the rest of her belongings.

"What else?" she asked.

"Wound salve and bandages, extra bolts for the crossbow, food. Mostly food, actually." He gave her a pointed look. "I assumed you wouldn't have had time to bring anything so I thought I should bring enough for both of us."

"I took some dried meat from a tin in the stables." She thought about Ese, telling her the meat was for hunts. "There's a fair chance it was meant for the dogs."

Sevlin huffed in amusement.

Attracted by the lantern light, a beetle circled their heads before landing on the lantern globe. Oblivious to the danger, it stalked across the glass in search of an opening, casting a monstrous shadow along the deck.

Dashi's eyes went to the dark ridge of the taiga, where the real monsters lived. "What would you have done if I'd turned down your offer?"

"Eaten like a king and let you have the sword anyway." He said it in that easy way he had, which walked the line between polite and bland and didn't reveal anything.

"Followed me and tried to steal the seamripper once I found it," she countered.

The corner of his mouth lifted, but he didn't reply.

"Your disappearance will be noticed," she said slowly. "After being caught in the bushes together, the khan will assume we were allies all along."

The reality of the Tyvalaran delegation's situation—of the situation she'd put them in by being outed as an imposter—suddenly hit her. They'd brought their own soldiers, true, but they were vastly outnumbered in New Osb. If the khan jumped to the conclusion that Dashi was a spy and that Sevlin was helping her, the other Tyvalarans might be imprisoned. *Or worse*, she thought, remembering Jochi.

"He might assume that," Sevlin said. "Then again, he might not. It's not unheard of for someone to dally with a servant, for no other reason than wanting to. The fact that the servant I was dallying with turned out to be a spy? That *is* a bit of an embarrassment, both for the Tyvalarans, because it was their prince who didn't have enough sense to know he was being targeted, and for the khan, since it was his people who weren't vetted properly. The official story is that Zevi has summarily dismissed me from the delegation and that I'm on my way back to Tyvalar in disgrace."

"And you think the khan believed that?" Dashi wasn't so sanguine. If *she* were the khan, she would be suspicious of everyone.

"Well, Zevi probably did a better job of selling that story than I ever could. As I said, the khan might believe it; he might not. He's already suspicious of the Thracedonian princes, so he might suspect that one of them sent you to spy. Or one of his own nobles, making a play of some kind. The more possible culprits, the less likely it is that Tyvalar gets blamed. And the story doesn't have to be perfect, just enough to give us political cover for the present."

"I..." Dashi swallowed. "I hope they don't find themselves in trouble."

Sevlin was quiet for a moment. "There's nothing either of us can do for them, except what we're already doing," he said finally. "But if I'd thought the delegation was in imminent danger, I would have stayed. What happened," his gesture took in the two of them while also somehow recalling their supposed tryst, "will undoubtedly create tension, but nothing was going to come of that state visit anyway."

"I thought you were there as a favor to the khan, to make the Founding Day feast more...pompous or something."

"I'll tell you about the khan's political maneuvering if you tell me about the map we're following." His voice sounded amused and he nudged her leg with his. "But you can start by telling me what's so special about the boots you stole."

"Why do you think there's something special about them? They could just be boots." She pulled them off and tossed them to him.

Sevlin shook his head as he caught them, one in each hand. "There's always something remarkable about Yassari goods. Their metals are more durable. Their fabrics don't wear. Their mechanisms don't break. Their ink doesn't run. Everything they make is the top of the market and we wait breathlessly to see what they'll bring to the mainland next."

"It doesn't sound like you like them very much."

"My dealings with them have always been...complicated. In some ways, they're very open to negotiations, to commissions and alliances. In other ways...well, you heard the woman in New Osb. There are some things on which they will not budge."

Dashi tilted her head, considering. "That makes me like them more, I think."

"It would." Sevlin turned a boot over in his hand, examining the intricate birds stitched into the leather and the deep gouge left by the Yassari thorn. "Too bad the thing they feel strongest about is stealing."

"They're a little overzealous about that particular subject."

"It's an attack on their livelihood. They traffic in ideas, in inventions. It would be like someone going to a Mori clan and taking their herds. You would expect them to avenge themselves."

Dashi pursed her lips. He sounded like Idree. "Whose side are you on?"

"Yours," he said easily, "though I know you won't believe that. I'm just explaining why you'll need to avoid the Yassaris...well, forever."

A moment later he sucked in a breath as he noticed the boot's strange soles. Dashi leaned back, watching him watch the boots. His forehead was compressed in thought, his eyes nearly hidden by his eyebrows and the angle of his face. He *did* look like Prince Zevi. Now that she knew the connection was there, she could see its delineations a little clearer: the same high cheekbones, the same fine-cut lips. Zevi was more conspicuously handsome. With his scar and his deep-set eyes, Sevlin came across as watchful and cunning. Or perhaps she was only seeing what she already knew.

"These are mythological birds, characters from Yassari legends." He was looking at the stitching once more. "This one is a current strider. It chases down boats and steals young sailors." He pointed to another. "This one lays its eggs in people's dreams. When they hatch, they eat the dreamer."

Dashi smiled slightly. "I'll have to tell that to Idree. She wondered if they were real or not."

"We have similar birds in Tyvalaran mythology. One that impersonates whoever it sees. Another that turns into moonbeams." He flipped over the boot, examining the other side. "I assume climbing is easier with these?"

"It is. Though, honestly, it's not enough of a benefit that I'd risk dying for them."

"What's this?" His eyebrows rose. "Dashi expressing remorse?"

"Not remorse, exactly. I wanted to make the Yassaris pay and I did. They think they can put pyrothrite in a belt and sell it like they would a bolt of cloth. Knowing it's going to be used on someone?" She shook her head. "No, I'm glad I took something from them. I just wish it had been something a little more worth the effort and that it hadn't forced me to leave New Osb before I could free Idree. And," she met his eyes, "I wish the whole thing hadn't put your countrymen in such an awkward position."

Sevlin watched her for a long moment. "I don't know," he said finally. "That sounds like remorse to me."

"It's not," she said, rolling her eyes. "Trust me."

"Someday I'd like to hear the story of how you ransacked a Yassari caravan when I know they come prepared for opportunists like you." Despite his words, his tone had a warmth to it that conjured an answering smile from Dashi.

"Maybe someday you will." Night had closed in on them in a hurry. Driven by the steady slide in temperature, fog mushroomed on the river's surface. Despite the chill, or maybe because of it, Dashi could feel the heat from Sevlin's outstretched leg, neatly parallel to her own.

A loud slapping against the outside of the boat shattered the moment, making them both leap to their feet. Sevlin, who was closest to the noise, dropped her boots and peered over the side.

"What was that," he said, his voice low. "I don't—"

Iridescent arms shot out of the water, grabbing onto Sevlin and wrenching him from the boat.

"Sevlin!"

Dashi lunged forward, knife in hand, but the water was black and empty, with only a few ripples to mark the passage of Sevlin's body. She reached for a pole. Maybe when he surfaced—

A shout tore from her throat as something clamped onto her from above, jerking her into the air.

Chapter 27

Wings beat just above Dashi, shoving air past her face. The hand that held the knife was bent awkwardly to the side. With her free hand, Dashi ripped at the thing that held her. To her surprise, she found not the flesh and bone of some giant taiga beast but rope and wood. A talon, yes, but a manmade one. The net that held her was reinforced on the outside by thin wooden ribs. Through the weave, she glimpsed two pairs of wings above her: the first, white and translucent; the second, dark and feathered. Human legs, clad in pants and boots, dangled incongruously below.

The khan's heralds.

Far below, the bright star of the lantern glinted, marking where she'd just been sitting. She heard a shout and the sound of splashing water, but the rushing air obscured all else. The net swayed as the khan's monsters shifted direction, the heavy rope abrading the burns on her arm even through her deel. Dashi moved with it, using the momentum to flip onto her back, freeing both her arm and her knife. She began sawing viciously at the net. One strand gave way. Dashi moved on to the next. Another snapped, then another, the hole widening steadily. Putting the knife between her teeth, Dashi pulled her head and shoulders through the hole in the netting. Her hips lodged between the wooden ribs that supported the talon-like contraption. She kicked hard against them, trying to shimmy herself free.

The talon gave a sickening lurch as the moth-woman lunged at Dashi, shrieking in rage over her attempted escape. The sudden movement slid Dashi free of the hole but also ripped her hands from the rope, leaving her swinging wildly, held only by her left leg, which had become tangled in the netting. Upside down, her head whipped back and forth, offering alternating glimpses of the night sky, then the fog-shrouded river below.

With an effort, Dashi jackknifed upward, grabbing the net with both hands as the moth-woman dove again, making the talon careen wildly. The owl-woman shouted at her, though the words of the admonishment were lost in the wind. *Probably reminding her that they're supposed to bring me back alive*, Dashi thought. Or at least, she assumed they were. Else, why bother with the talon contraption at all?

Even as she thought it, she realized the two heralds had begun a hasty descent. A break in the fog showed where their trajectory would end: a rocky beach on the eastern side of the river. She remembered passing it with Sevlin. *They're going to land and then they'll subdue me for the journey back to New Osb.* Her borrowed sword was on the boat. The knife, still clenched in her teeth, wouldn't be much good against two heralds.

Dashi worked frantically on her tangled leg, finally extracting it. She clung there for a moment, completely on the outside of the net now. The wind buffeted her from all sides, cracking the severed ends of the net like a whip. They'd lost altitude rapidly, bringing the swinging net much closer to the pillows of fog that covered the river. Dashi could hear the susurrus of moving water, beckoning from beneath the blanket of white.

She sheathed her knife and took a deep, steadying breath before she let go.

Chapter 28

Dashi tumbled backward. Her back hit the river first, a smack that reverberated through her bones and stunned her lungs. When she did manage to inhale again, several long, agonizing moments later, she pulled in water instead of air. The river spun her around, shooting up her nose and flooding her mouth. She swam upward, or in the direction she *thought* was upward. Mid-stroke, her arm hit a log, a fellow passenger in the current, and she pulled her torso onto it, vomiting water and wheezing for air. When she was done, she wrapped one arm around the log and paddled doggedly toward the shore. How far away was she from the boat? From Sevlin? She called him once or twice, then decided it was too risky. She didn't want to lead the heralds back to her.

Finally, the log scraped against a gravel shoal and Dashi stumbled ashore. She wanted to rest—heaving the water out of her lungs and towing a log across the current had badly sapped her energy—but the finger of land on which she'd landed was too exposed. The heralds could spot her easily from above.

The cold river water had doused the pain and heat in her arm, which, she decided, might be worth the shivering. It had numbed her stockinged feet as well, and she stumbled forward until movement from behind a tree trunk caught her eye.

"Sevlin." The breath went out of her in a great whoosh of relief. She lowered her knife.

He stepped closer, one hand rising, but he let it fall again before he touched her. "Are you alright?"

"Half-drowned but otherwise fine." She glanced back at the river, still unsure where she'd come ashore in relation to the boat.

"We're downriver from it." Sevlin's voice was resigned. "It was too much of a target. I took what I could and started walking along the shore hoping I'd stumble upon you." He pointed to two packs resting against a tree. "Here," he said tossing her boots in front of her. "I did manage to get these."

"Thanks." She put them on while standing, stumbling backward a little as her wet sock stuck in the dry boot. "The khan's monsters scooped me up in this talon contraption. Like tongs, sort of, but made of net and wood."

Sevlin was quiet for a moment, thinking. "That sounds heavy. They must be strong."

"My thought too. I decided to jump instead of fight them. What about you?"

"A herald who was part fish."

"And?"

"And I got away."

"That is...easily the *least* exciting fight story I've ever heard, Sevlin."

"We can swap battle tales some other time," he said dryly. "Right now—" He broke off, staring at her feet, then said in a calm voice, "You're floating."

Dashi looked down at the water, silver with the moon's reflection. She had stumbled backward, into the river, when she was putting her boots on. Only she wasn't *in* it. She was *on* it. Swearing softly, Dashi stuck her hand into the water, touching her boots from the underside, certain that she must be standing on something beneath the water's surface. She wasn't.

"No wonder the Yassaris were so angry about these being stolen," she said, thinking of how she'd fallen when she tried to get on the boat. Maybe she'd slid sideways because she was floating on the water.

"Mmm." Sevlin's tone was considering.

Dashi took a wobbly step, then another, her gaze fixed on her feet. Slight indentations appeared in the moonlit water with each step, sending ripples in ever-widening circles. A glossy trout jumped next to her, seemingly undisturbed by her presence. It *should* be knee-deep here. She could see the place where the current took hold, hugging the water into its center with invisible arms. A slight tremor passed through her soles as the water picked up speed beneath her.

"*Dashi.*"

She moved without thinking, coming to crouch next to Sevlin along the riverbank. He was looking to the north, where a dark shape was circling, canting through shafts of moonlight.

"That's where the boat is," Sevlin said. "They're waiting to see if we'll come back."

Dashi grimaced. "They're much too close."

"It's lucky they didn't hear you screaming my name."

Dashi's head swiveled in his direction. "I wasn't *screaming* your name."

His eyes were still on the circling herald. "Energetically shouting, then. I heard my name quite clearly though."

"Yet I still had to drag my body out of the river on my own."

"I'll try to dispatch my opponent faster next time." He stood and pulled on his pack. "I saw a thick grouping of trees not too far back. That should shield us from anyone searching from above while we rest."

"I wish I had my bow," Dashi said, glancing back at the herald.

"Too far for a shot."

"I didn't mean for right now. I meant because..." *Because I feel weak without it.* "Just because." She cleared her throat. "I wonder how far they'll follow us."

"Where do we go from here?"

"We have to follow the river a little longer. Another day, maybe?"

"Then we'll need to parallel it from inside the trees or they'll spot us right away."

They set off for the grove Sevlin had seen. It was slow going in the dark, and more than once Dashi wished they could light a lantern. They managed not to make too much noise and before long Sevlin pointed to a grouping of trees growing taller and thicker than the rest.

"This is it."

Dashi swallowed without answering. Even in the uncertain moonlight, she could see the dark ridge that rose behind the grove. The old scar on her side wrenched suddenly.

"I'll take the first watch," Sevlin said.

Dashi tore her gaze away from the taiga. "Fine. Sure."

They were both still damp from their dunking in the river, so she undressed down to her undershirt and climbed into the bedroll Sevlin had salvaged from the boat. They had no fire, but Dashi could make out Sevlin's silhouette, leaning against a nearby tree, watchful and tense. The sight should have lulled her into sleep, but she stayed awake long into the night.

Dawn had begun to thread the horizon when Dashi felt it: a sharp pain in her left forearm, followed by the clenching of her muscles. Her fingers curled into claws. Her forearm jerked upward from the elbow, then back down, the movement sloppy and uncontrolled. When it didn't stop,

Dashi used her right hand to pin her left, holding it tight against her chest while it spasmed repeatedly. It was like watching someone else's body. After several minutes, her arm went still. Cautiously, she straightened her fingers and flexed her arm. Her muscles responded but only weakly.

She stumbled to Sevlin's pack. Her fingers shook as she reached for the wound salve. The burns were beginning to heal, helped along by the repeated applications of salve, but those green and black lines...

Had they reached above her elbow before? She tilted her arm, trying to be clinical instead of giving in to the dread circling her stomach. *Sometimes things take time to heal*, she thought, forcing herself to take deep breaths until she could apply the medicine with a steady hand. By the time she woke Sevlin, her hands no longer shook and her worries were neatly compartmentalized.

After a hasty breakfast, they retraced their steps from the night before, ending at the water's edge, though they were careful not to leave the cover of the trees. Steam rose from the river in spiraling columns as the sunlight warmed its surface. There was no sign of the heralds.

"They're probably sleeping near the boat," Sevlin said. "I doubt they would have turned back right away, not when they were so close to capturing you last night."

"They almost captured you too."

"Capture is not what the fish herald had in mind."

"Tyvalar will be implicated," Dashi said. "The heralds will report your presence to the khan."

Sevlin pursed the side of his mouth. "I don't think the two who were flying got a good look at me."

"And the fish?"

"He won't be reporting to the khan." There was a finality in Sevlin's voice that told Dashi the fish herald wouldn't be doing much of anything.

She gave him a sideways glance. "You really need to work on your storytelling."

Sevlin snorted softly, but his attention was on the river, searching for threats. Her worries about the taiga and her arm had eclipsed all else but, looking at the water, she was reminded of her discovery the previous night. *I have boots that walk on water*, she thought wonderingly.

There was a muffled flutter from above and Dashi ducked, automatically reaching for an arrow that wasn't there. Wings passed overhead and a dark shape dipped into the river near them. Dashi glimpsed a pale underbelly and a dark mask of feathers over the bird's face and then it was flying away, a fat trout in its talons. The beat of its wings was quickly lost over the rush of the river. The bird landed in a tree, deftly impaling the fish on a broken branch, before tearing into its still-wriggling prey.

"A shrike," Sevlin murmured. "I've never seen one hunt fish."

"That's because you've never seen one as big as you are."

The shrike looked up from its meal, turning its black-masked face toward them. The branch had made a dark hole in the side of the fish. Shrikes always impaled their prey; that peculiarity hadn't changed with the bird's size.

"We're not quite in the taiga," Sevlin observed. "It's ventured out."

"We're close enough."

Dashi thought of the first giant rat she'd ever seen: a snowy night long ago, a black coat as thick as a yak's. She'd thought it was a bear at first.

"That's why the Mori avoid the near-taiga," she said, "and why I couldn't believe the khan would build New Osb there." She started walking again, keeping a wary eye on the shrike. It was still watching them. "I should have guessed it had something to do with the needle's magic."

"I wish I'd had time to investigate the vein Idree spoke of."

"I don't know. That story you told us during the khan's race—about the first seamstress and how he fell into the vein—makes me think it's one of those things normal people would do better to stay away from."

"*Normal* people," Sevlin agreed, but his tone made it clear that he didn't include either of them in that category.

Chapter 29

Having practically slept on the taiga's doorstep, they crossed its threshold within the hour. Their movements were ginger, almost expecting that something would challenge the trespass. The sun had fully risen by then, showcasing what Dashi had seen in her dreams for the last year: a dense, mostly coniferous forest, painted in black and shades of green. A cloying mist, waiting in the top branches of the trees, caught the sunlight and pushed it away, remaining opalescent and inscrutable.

The scars on Dashi's side and back, legacies of the khan's race, tingled sharply and she winced, rubbing at the old wounds with the heel of her hand until the feeling abated. In the year since she'd gotten them, they'd never felt like this. A little tightness, perhaps, but that had been right after they'd healed and it had eased quickly. Of course, she would take old scars buzzing over the uncontrollable spasms that had wracked her earlier in the day. Her attention kept flicking to her left forearm, mentally cataloging how it felt and dreading what came next. Was that a spasm, or merely a cramp because she'd been gripping the straps of her pack for too long? Was that spike of pain brought on because she'd bumped the wound, or did it presage another fit?

"Are you going to tell me anything about the map?" Sevlin asked, breaking the silence.

There was a trace of impatience in his voice that Dashi couldn't help but enjoy. "That depends," she drawled. "What's it worth to you?"

Sevlin slanted a look at her pack. "You're wearing it."

"I already have the pack and I didn't have to tell you anything."

"Mmm." He ducked a branch without breaking stride. They still hugged the river, keeping just inside the trees to shield themselves from the heralds. "Maybe I should take it back."

"Then you shouldn't have given me the sword. I've gotten better in the past year."

"You sound confident. How unusual."

Dashi grinned despite the taiga. The slope had washed out in front of them and she jumped over a treacherous section, the pack banging uncomfortably when she landed.

"I think," Sevlin said, landing beside her with a grunt, "that you don't know where we're going."

"I do so."

He spread his hands in a picture of reasonableness. "Prove me wrong."

Dashi laughed. "Nice try." Her gaze tracked the landscape, looking for predators. There was nothing but mist and trees. From the corner of her eye, she saw Sevlin's almost-smile, but like her, his eyes never stopped scanning.

It wasn't that she didn't believe Sevlin when he said he wanted to free Idree from the khan. She knew that was true, despite how they might bicker about the particulars of what to do afterward. Still, her mind rebelled at the idea of voluntarily divulging information to this man. In his way, Sevlin was slipperier than Ese. Sevlin's gaze flicked to her and then forward again, but she had the sense that he was waiting.

"We've passed the bend in the river already," she said, taking a deep breath. "After that, there's a waterfall, and then the river splits, forming a finger of land between the two branches. The seamripper is somewhere on that finger.

Sevlin gave her another sideways look. "That's it?"

"There were a few other mentions of scrolls and temples."

He exhaled: one long, slow breath. "Such a paucity of information on which to base a journey. When you said you'd seen a map, I thought it was a little more definitive than that."

"The consul thinks it's definitive enough."

"Isn't that where she's been for the last few weeks, hunting for it? She could have already recovered it by now."

"I saw a message she sent ahead. She didn't find it, but she confirmed it's on the finger of land between the river branches. She said she wanted the heralds' help in retrieving it."

Sevlin was silent.

"I don't think she's wrong," Dashi said, already knowing what he was thinking. "I didn't have time to look through all the original Purek sources so I couldn't double-check her assumptions, but the notes were so meticulous, Sevlin. Even the way the scrolls were organized on the shelves: crop yields with other crop yields from the same period; Purek court histories, sorted by reign. She's been studying the Pureks for a long time and if she thinks the seamripper is there, it probably is."

He didn't answer and Dashi had to force herself not to look at him. Did he regret coming? Did he want to back out? The thought left her colder than she'd expected.

"You can turn back," she said because of course he could. "I'm keeping the sword though." *I don't need him*, she reminded herself.

Finally, Sevlin spoke. "So we'll have to cross the river."

She nodded once, still insisting that she didn't care one way or the other.

They passed the waterfall, shuddering at the glacial spray, and then the river's fork. The banks had become coated in thick undergrowth so that they had to walk single file, forcing their bodies through. Sevlin halted her with a touch on the shoulder.

"I think we should cross soon," he said.

Dashi raised an eyebrow. The river was rough here, tumbling all over itself with excitement.

"Something is following us."

"A herald?" She'd been watching the sky, waiting for them to reappear but had seen nothing.

Sevlin shook his head, his pale eyes boring into hers.

Something, not someone.

She didn't doubt Sevlin's instincts. He was nothing if not cautious and he wouldn't suggest crossing here unless he thought it necessary. Far behind them, a sapling swayed as something passed beneath it.

Dashi looked back to the river. "Too deep to wade, too fast to swim." There were the packs to consider too. They couldn't be left.

"You could use the boots to carry me." His voice held no trace of doubt.

Dashi glanced at his large form. "It would be easier if you carried me."

"Undoubtedly. But I'm not the one with Yassari boots that can walk on water."

A moment later she was sliding down the embankment. She took a few tentative steps onto the river, wanting to test it, to make sure her earlier feat hadn't been a dream or a fluke. As before, the water depressed slightly beneath her boots though it still somehow held her. Now that it was full daylight, her mind balked at the impossibility of the sight. She wobbled left, then right, the pack throwing her off balance.

"I don't know, Sevlin." She frowned down at the boots. "It feels very unsteady with the pack and it'll be worse with you." Two more steps back to shore. *Wobble, wobble.* "I know the Yassari's reputation, but I don't know if the boots will work for this."

"If only you'd asked for a demonstration to ensure the quality of merchandise." He was still standing on the embankment, his shoulders squared and ready, a contrast to his easy tone. "Try skating," he said, not taking his eyes off the forest.

"Skating?"

"You only wobble when you transfer weight from one foot to the other. Do it more gently, like you're on ice."

"Hmm." She pushed off lightly, concentrating on seamlessly transferring her weight. She slid forward, gliding on momentum. "It works," she called softly.

She held out her hand for his pack, motioning to a boulder a third of the way across. "I'll put our packs out on that rock so nothing gets them while we cross."

She practiced skating on her way to the rock, one pack slung over each shoulder. Sevlin had packed them to exactly the same weight, not sparing her any burden. Dashi smiled to herself.

"What?" Sevlin asked when she returned.

"Nothing." She faced away from him, bracing her hands on her knees. "I assume you're accustomed to being carried on the backs of commoners, Prince Sevlin."

She only heard the second part of his muttered rebuttal, but her smile widened. It disappeared, however, when he placed his hands on her shoulders. His weight was crushing. It was the sheer expanse of him that made it difficult to move. He folded his arms around her from behind, so that they crossed her chest. His torso hunched over the back of her neck, pressing forward. His legs, clenched around her waist, were so long that they dragged against her thighs, impeding her steps.

The other side isn't far, she told herself. *Keep your balance and keep moving.*

Dashi shifted her hands under his thighs, looking for purchase to keep them from pressing into her hips. Her first skating step sent her wobbling across the water's surface, cursing under her breath.

"Trust the boots," Sevlin murmured.

His breath stirred the hair at the nape of her neck and, despite the exertion of carrying him, she shivered.

"I don't trust anything Yassari."

The impressions made by the boots were deeper than before, though perhaps she should have expected that with Sevlin's added weight. She glided forward, watching the river bottom fall away. When she reached the first tendrils of current, however, her pace faltered. The river grabbed at her feet. Although the current was not at full strength this close to the shore, it was enough to spin her around. Her legs splayed as she tried to balance and her hand jerked outward, searching in vain for something to steady her. Sevlin's grip across her chest tightened. She stumbled backward into the still shallows.

"Try it again."

"Easy for you to say," she groused, but she was already skating forward, her knees bent slightly against the onslaught she knew was coming. The river clutched at her with watery hands, sending the boots in two different directions. Narrowly avoiding an upset, Dashi skated back to the shore.

"Not going to work," she panted as Sevlin slid from her back, crunching softly in the gravel.

"No." He sounded grim. "My weight is pushing the boots down too much."

She looked up at the empty bank. "You're sure there's something...?"

"Yes." He'd slung a coil of rope over one shoulder before he climbed onto her back. Now, he handed her one end.

Dashi took it and stepped back onto the river, already knowing what their next, best option would be: she would string a rope across the river and Sevlin would hang-crawl across. She would carry the packs one at a time since weight seemed to be a limiting factor for skating over the center of the river, where the current was strongest. She paused only to shoulder one of the packs. After carrying Sevlin, its weight seemed inconsequential.

Water swirled beneath her boots. She could feel it shifting against her soles, threatening to move her, but without Sevlin pressing her feet deeper she managed to resist its push-pull. The water, an innocuous green next to the shore, began to darken, becoming blue-black at the river's center. *The depth doesn't matter*, she told herself. *You're on top of the river, not in it.*

She shifted the rope in her hands, adjusting the slack. The tension from the rope was her anchor, her insurance that she wouldn't be pulled downstream. Even if she toppled, she had Sevlin on the other end to haul her back.

The current grew more turbulent at the dark center of the river, transforming the water into pulsing hillocks and frothy peaks, which Dashi bumped over and coasted down. The pack, though light compared to Sevlin, still made her top-heavy and her muscles tightened with the concentration it took to avoid a spill.

Finally, her boots touched land. Dashi scrambled up the steep bank and looped the rope around a sturdy tree. Pulling the knot tight, she squinted into the sunlight, searching for Sevlin. He'd waded to the rock where the second pack sat. Now he balanced precariously atop it, pointing his crossbow back at the bank he'd been standing on.

The tangle of brush parted, revealing a giant taiga ant. It stared directly at Dashi.

Chapter 30

The scar on her side jolted to life, but Dashi, fixated on the ant, barely noticed. Its head was oblong in shape, and walnut in color. The eyes were convex, almost bulbous, and a pair of antennae waggled like eyebrows above its head.

Before Dashi could move, Sevlin jumped onto the rope, hauling himself across the river hand-over-hand. His legs, crossed at the ankles, slid with each movement. The crossbow dangled from his back. Dashi started for the second pack, her attention darting between the ant and the current. The turbulent white water threatened to throw her off balance and she had to work to find the least treacherous path.

The ant's antennae twitched back and forth, zigging and zagging in concert with her movements. It disappeared once, only to reemerge a short distance away, next to a dead tree that had collapsed into the water. Age had stripped the tree of its bark and needles. Spiky stubs, all that was left of its limbs, stuck into the air, bleached wood against the blue sky. The ant, with its front two legs propped on the naked trunk, looked like a predator hovering over a carcass.

Closer to it, Dashi could see the differences between this ant and the ones she'd encountered before. Its body was dark brown, bordering on black. The ants that carried her into their lair and tended her wounds had been a coppery shade. This ant was larger too, though its jaws, sticking out from its face like an afterthought, were the same. She wondered if its armored exterior was hard and cool and scratchy, pottery covered with bristles.

She was so intent on the ant that, at first, she didn't notice how the birdcalls had grown louder and more numerous. A shrill whistle caught her attention. Dashi's gaze dropped to Sevlin in time to see him switch his grip on the rope and, still suspended over the river, draw his sword. A blur of black and gray launched itself from the trees, diving at his head. The giant shrike shrieked as Sevlin's blade connected. It veered away, now flapping clumsily.

No sooner had the first shrike retreated, than others took its place, circling Sevlin. Dashi drew her sword, but she was too far away to do much good. Without warning, the rope holding Sevlin broke, plunging him into the water. He disappeared for a moment then reemerged, clinging to the end of the rope that was still tied to Dashi's side of the river. The current dragged at his body, tumbling all around him. Dashi had a momentary glimpse of his face—eyes squinted, mouth tightly shut—before the river closed over his head again.

One shrike whistled and the others picked up the call, throwing it back and forth like children with a ball. When Sevlin came up again, two of them dove, one aiming for his head and the other going for his right arm, which held the rope. Sevlin ducked back under and the giant birds pulled up sharply, sending up a spray when their talons punched the water instead of flesh. The whistling started up again.

The river heaved Dashi up and down, but she had the feel for skating now. She jumped over a turbulent patch, sliding down the backside of a small wave. *Nearly there.* The shrikes circled, taking turns diving at Sevlin whenever he came up for air. Somehow, he was still holding onto the rope. It was all that kept him from being swept away.

Dashi shouted, waving her arms wildly, and six black-masked heads turned in her direction. Suddenly, the birds were wheeling toward her.

Yes, that's it, she thought grimly, angling away from Sevlin. *Look at me, not him.*

She deflected an attack aimed at her face, her sword cutting cleanly through one of the shrike's outstretched legs. Another shrike went for her right shoulder, but Dashi reversed her sword. For one frozen moment, she could see the beauty of the thing: delicate nares where beak met head; air shuddering through the soft feathers that outlined its face; her reflection in the liquid black eyes. Then her sword sank into it, scraping breastbone. The bird screamed.

A pair of talons closed around her left bicep, digging through the fabric of her deel. The wings were a powerful heartbeat, pulling her to one side, lifting her until only her toes touched the water. She turned toward her antagonist, getting off one blind swing, but the other shrikes were poised, waiting for her moment of distraction. One came from behind, latching onto her right forearm and wrist, rendering her sword useless. When she tottered, off balance, another bird wrapped its talons around her lower leg.

The shrikes began to move toward the shore, dragging Dashi between them. They were big enough that their wings should have collided, but somehow they timed the beats, angling their bodies away from one another. The sword was still in her right hand, but with talons digging into her wrist, she could do little besides wave it feebly. Dashi saw the dead tree on the approaching shore, its wood limned in sunlight, pale as naked bones. She saw the broken limbs, jutting toward the sky, and she understood, then, that they were going to impale her like they would a fish or a rodent or any other prey.

She waited for a breath, timing the wingbeats of the bird that held her leg out to the side. On the next downbeat of wings, she kicked her free leg upward, swinging onto its back. Hooking her knee around the side of its neck, she arched her body, clenching her leg with all the strength she possessed. It was a variation of the hold that Baris had shown her all those years ago. She doubted she had the strength or leverage to choke the bird, but it didn't matter: no wild animal was going to tolerate something around its neck. The bird shrieked and ducked its head, trying to free itself. The moment its grip on her ankle loosened, Dashi jerked free.

Pushing off the water with her boots, she kicked again, this time aiming at the shrike that held her sword arm, pummeling it with her boots, her shins, any part of her that could make contact. The bird's grip on her arm slackened, then disappeared. The remaining bird, sensing the inevitability of failure, tried to soar away, but Dashi grabbed a tuft of feathers with one hand and swept her sword across its neck. Its body slapped against the water, leaking blood.

She wobbled on the water, turning to see another dead shrike floating behind her. A crossbow bolt protruded from its back. Sevlin stood on the opposite shore, splay-legged and bedraggled, holding the crossbow. He looked like he wanted to shoot something else, but the remaining shrikes were little more than specks above the treetops. Breathing hard, Dashi lowered her sword. Sevlin met her eyes from across the river and shook his head incredulously.

Dashi raised one palm. *What did you expect? We're in the taiga.*

He jutted his chin at her boots. *I wasn't just talking about the shrikes.*

She glanced down at her boots, resting gently on the water's surface. She'd been sliding her feet back and forth where she stood, finding it easier to balance on the water's surface if she wasn't completely stationary. Her amusement died when she turned toward the boulder where they'd left the pack. The rock was empty. She looked in the water on either side and squinted downstream. The pack was gone.

"I don't know where—" Dashi began when she was within earshot.

"One of the shrikes flew away with it as I was pulling myself out."

Dashi stared at him, openmouthed, then whirled around to kick a rock into the river, muttering curses.

Half their food. Half their medicine. Half the crossbow bolts. One of the lanterns. Sevlin had divided the supplies equally in each pack to hedge against losing everything during just such an occurrence. Even so, the loss was harsh.

"I should've—"

"Gone to get the supplies instead of distracting the shrikes?" Sevlin hefted the remaining pack. "I couldn't have held my breath for much longer, Dashi. I'm glad you did what you did."

"I was afraid they'd clip the other end of the rope too and you'd wash up somewhere downriver."

A line by Sevlin's mouth deepened. "The ant broke the line, not the shrikes."

Dashi stared. Why would the ant sever the rope?

She let her head fall back suddenly. "My lock picks. They were in my pack."

"I thought you kept those on you."

"I usually do. After being dumped in the river by the heralds, I thought they'd be safer in my pack." She kicked another rock. "No way to shoot. No way to open locks."

Sevlin started up the embankment. "I heard you've gotten much better with a sword," he called back. "Maybe you can use it to hack through any temple doors we encounter."

Chapter 31

Dashi stood on a rocky outcropping, peering through the trees to the sliver of land beyond. She thought she'd glimpsed a Purek ruin, but now that she had a better vantage point she could see that it was only basalt pillars, fringing an adjacent cliff: undeniably majestic but entirely natural.

The shrikes had resumed their whistling soon after their attack and both Dashi and Sevlin had deemed it wise to flee deeper into the trees of the Finger peninsula. *Maybe 'flee' isn't the right word*, she thought wryly. That implied moving from danger to safety. There was the distinct possibility that they'd jumped from the stewpot only to land ass-end on the skewer, as the saying went. Yes, the trees offered protection from the shrikes and the khan's heralds, but the dark, close trunks hindered their ability to see what was in front of them. On cue, Dashi's mind conjured an image of the giant rats they'd encountered the previous year.

Sevlin stepped out from among the trees. "There is a small ruin ahead," he said. "I didn't see anything inside, but I thought you'd want to look."

"You went yourself?"

One eyebrow rose slightly. "My competence is staggering, I know."

Dashi rolled her eyes. "I meant, did you go *in* by yourself?"

"No, but it's so tiny I could see everything." He nodded in a north-westerly direction. "Just over the hill."

She skidded down the rock, touching a tree trunk as she passed. It was soft with moss. The trees grew tall and straight here, towering above her like the pillars of a dark temple. Even Sevlin was made small next to them.

He started walking, saying over his shoulder, "There is even a skeleton for you to keep company."

Dashi felt her face grow hot. She'd never been sure if he'd overheard her talking to the skeletons in the ruined library during the khan's race.

"An old habit," she said lightly.

"Keeping company with skeletons?"

"Literally, as well as figuratively." She'd outlived almost everyone she'd ever been close to. Then, so Sevlin didn't feel sorry for her, she added, "When I was little and first going to the ruins with my friend Altan, I was scared of the skeletons. He made a game of quizzing me on the names of each bone, of talking to them and inferring what they'd been like from the evidence we could see." She shrugged. "It helped."

"Mmm. I would not have predicted that."

"I think addressing fear directly always helps."

Then why are you refusing to think about your arm, her mind prompted. There'd been another spasming fit, her arm jerking up and down for a full three minutes before the sensation of muscles clenching out of control finally faded. She'd only been saved the embarrassment of Sevlin's scrutiny by the fact that she'd been walking behind him.

"I meant," Sevlin said, "that I find it hard to believe you were scared of skeletons."

He pointed to a rounded hump of a ruin, the remains of four stone walls. A creek ran nearby and a millstone, lined with moss, was partially submerged in it. Dashi stepped through the doorway, more out of curiosity than because she thought there would be anything useful inside. It was a single-room dwelling, its small size and relative lack of decoration marking it as the home of a Purek commoner. Broken dishes and cups were scattered in one corner, atop a rectangle of especially rich-looking soil, where a table had decomposed. In another corner stood a small altar, though only dust and a few beads remained on the offering shelves. Dashi held one of the beads up to the light. Painted glass, nothing precious. She tossed it back.

"This ruin is much simpler than the ones we saw during the race," Sevlin said.

"Not up to your normal standards, eh, Prince Sevlin?"

Sevlin was shifting through the rubble in one corner, picking up and discarding tools and various household detritus. He didn't so much as glance at her, let alone rise to the obvious bait.

"Here."

Dashi looked up in time to see a metallic flash as a cup flew through the air toward her. She caught it with her free hand, giving Sevlin a perplexed look.

"Yours is somewhere down the river with the rest of your pack," he said, going back to his examination.

"Thanks." It was lightweight metal but large enough for a single portion of stew. *As if we'll be eating stew any time soon.*

Sevlin was squatting next to a set of bones. No, two sets, Dashi corrected herself, noting a second, smaller, skull.

He looked up at her. "There's no logic to the cataclysm. It killed some people but passed over others. It wiped out an entire civilization but left their scrolls in pristine condition."

"One of my friends was of the opinion that the magical eruption was like a flood," Dashi said, turning the cup over in her hands. The metal was scratched and dented, but the delicate etching was still visible. "It would have bent around any topographical features in its way. So if someone was downstream of a hill, for instance, it might have protected them from the initial onslaught."

"Maybe." Sevlin's tone was skeptical. "But there are differences even within the same location. This woman's skull is cracked, while that crockery is still intact."

"Maybe she fell and then cracked it."

Sevlin grunted. "Which friend?"

"Hmm?" Her reply was distracted as she translated the words on the cup. *Ruthless...as waves...magnanimous...as rain.* Below the words was a stylized depiction of waves crashing against rocks beneath storm clouds.

Dashi frowned in thought. Hadn't Khagan Nuray said something similar? She threaded the cup onto her sash, thinking of that long-ago vision of Khagan Nuray and how the dead khagan had admonished her to protect the seamstress. Had Nuray known then that Idree was the seamstress? *Be serious, Dashi. Are you asking if your mist hallucinations knew the future?*

"Which friend had the magic flood theory?" Sevlin asked.

"Altan." She followed him outside. "He came up with all our theories."

"How did you say you met your friends?"

She gave him a sideways look, doubting that he'd forgotten. "Altan saved Idree and me from a fire and took us in after our mother died."

"The others, I meant."

"Baris and Zayaa already knew Altan when they arrived." The taiga seemed to suppress her voice so that it barely rose above a whisper. "They said they'd grown up together, but if I had to guess now, I'd say they knew each other from whatever training Tyvalar puts its spies through." Another sideways glance in his direction.

She thought about how Sevlin had once offered to find Altan's family in Tyvalar. At the time she'd thought he was merely being kind, or perhaps trying to further their tenuous alliance. She certainly hadn't thought he possessed the power to actually *do* something like that. And do it easily, with a crook of his finger and a breezy command to a servant. She kept her eyes on the tree trunks. How different their lives must have been.

"You were closest with Altan," Sevlin pressed, "not Baris or Zayaa?"

"Altan was the older brother I'd never had and always wanted." She could say it now, over a year after his death, without a starburst of emotion. The pain was still there, but it was muted now, like the howl of a wolf when she was safely indoors. Sometimes Dashi missed the vibrancy of it; without fail that pain had made her feel achingly, angrily *alive*. But mostly its dimming made things easier: easier to make decisions, easier to interact with others without tearing someone's head off in the process, easier to live.

"I've heard you talk about Baris a fair amount too." The words were innocuous enough, but she heard the undertone.

"If you want to ask, ask."

For a moment, soft footfalls were the only sounds that came from him. Then: "Were you lovers?"

His face was completely neutral, his eyes sweeping the forest. A stranger might assume his attention had wavered from their conversation.

"No. Baris and I were...too similar for that. He was my friend but the obnoxious kind."

"So you were least close with Zayaa?" His tone suggested surprise.

She gave a half laugh. "Why, you mean, since we were both females?"

He inclined his head. "Women share things that they do not confide in men."

Dashi's lip curled, remembering a conversation she'd once had with Zayaa. They'd gone to the market to purchase supplies for an upcoming trip, but Dashi had seen her at a stall that sold flattering silk garments, holding one up to her chest and contemplating her reflection in a wavy mirror.

"Did you get the silk?" Dashi had asked later. At Zayaa's sharp glance, she'd shrugged. "I saw you at the stall."

"I got one."

"I think Altan will like it."

Zayaa had laughed. "Is that why you think I got it? To impress Altan?"

"Wasn't it?"

"I got it because I miss my mother."

"What's she like?" Parents—their criticisms, their lectures, the habits they bequeathed to their children—secretly intrigued Dashi. When she caught sight of a parent and child walking in the street, she would linger, eavesdropping on their interaction and imagining herself in the child's place.

"Tall," Zayaa had said. "Dark-haired. Like me."

"Will she visit, do you think?"

"No." A huff of melancholy amusement. "She would've hated it here."

Dashi had been too taken aback by the use of past tense to notice Zayaa's clipped tone. "Is...Is she—"

"She's none of your business, is what she is," Zayaa had snapped, and the subject had never come up again.

Now, Dashi glanced at Sevlin. She wanted to ask if he thought it was possible to truly know another person, but suddenly realizing that the silence had stretched too long, she said instead, "Zayaa was a bit older than me and she...tended to remind me of that. If she had confidences, she shared them elsewhere." She paused, struggling for the right words. "That's not to say... Zayaa and Baris weren't like Altan—no one was—but they were still family to me. I would have gone anywhere, done anything, faced anyone, if they'd asked."

A pair of nutcrackers startled on her right, and Dashi almost drew her sword at the sudden onslaught of wings and noise. She stared after the birds, trying to still her pulse.

Sevlin pointed toward a spine of land running parallel to their route. A pile of boulders speared up from the top of the ridge, peering over the treetops. "That should have a view of the whole Finger."

Dashi nodded, trying not to look at the mist coalescing in the adjacent treetops.

At the top of the ridge, they didn't pause but made straight for the pile of boulders, scrambling up with few words besides grunted warnings or advice on handholds. At the top, her breath rasping in her lungs, Dashi surveyed the finger of land sloping away from them.

Twin ribbons of silver bracketed either side: the two branches of the river, slinking off into the taiga. In between was a solid green carpet. In the distance, mountains punched at the sky, snow saddling their backs in white. Dashi dug her knuckles into her thigh, then stopped when pain spread up her injured forearm. They'd been hoping for a direction, a hint of where they should search, but all that lay before them were trees.

Chapter 32

Sevlin glanced at her. "Well?"

"There should be some sign," she said, shifting the pack she carried so that the straps didn't chafe the slashes made by the shrikes. "A break in the trees, old walls, *something*."

"The consul's map didn't specify?"

"This is the area she just explored; the map I saw wouldn't have contained any of those updates since she yet hadn't returned. But she sent ahead a message telling the khan that she was sure the seamripper is on this finger of land." Dashi muttered this last part, only half speaking to Sevlin.

Sevlin didn't say anything right away. She could almost *see* his doubts, rising off of him like hazy heat waves.

"She might have been mistaken," he said finally. His tone was gentle, letting her down like a child.

"You're right," she retorted. "We should have waited until the consul was *certain* it was here—maybe when she held the seamripper in her hand? No wait, that's too soon. Too many unknowns. We should've waited until she took it back to New Osb and locked it in a vault. *Then* we'd be *sure* the seamripper was hidden here."

Sevlin crossed his arms. One side of his mouth tipped downward. "I'm pointing out the obvious, Dashi."

"And I'm telling you she's not wrong. I saw the map and the way she organized everything. I trust her."

Sevlin's eyebrow twitched.

"You know what I meant." She gestured to the land. "About *this*."

"I know you want the seamripper to be here, but that doesn't mean it is. If there was a large complex of ruins, we should be able to see it from up here. Maybe she's feeding the khan false progress to buy herself more time."

Dashi returned her attention to the land. She'd thought of that too. "Those hills are big enough to hide a temple," she said, pointing to a line at the center of the Finger.

"Maybe," he said, "but the roads should still be visible."

He was right about that too, but Dashi slid off the top boulder anyway, intent on descending the ridge. What else could she do, abort their journey *now*, when they were already here?

Sevlin caught her shoulder before she could go any farther. "I'm not here on a lark, Dashi. Be honest with yourself and be honest with me. You owe me that, at the absolute minimum." His strange, light eyes held hers for a long moment, making the subtext clear: keeping secrets about the pyrothrite belt might be in the past, but he was drawing a line about future lies and omissions.

Dashi nodded uneasily, already unsure if she could keep the tacit promise she'd just made. She was not a person given to introspection, but one of the truths she knew about herself was this: she would do whatever it took to help Idree. If that ever meant setting fire to a fledgling alliance, she wouldn't hesitate.

The ridge they'd climbed spanned the width of the peninsula, a fingernail cutting across the end of a thumb. A trickle of water fell down the ridge, gaining speed and volume as it rolled downhill to the valley below. They descended parallel to it until, halfway down, Sevlin stopped, motioning toward a sort of shelf, hewn from the rock.

"We should camp here," he said. "There's good visibility, accessible fresh water and it's nearly dark."

Dashi rocked onto her toes, then back to her heels. The unknowns about the land and the seamripper's location were an itch she couldn't scratch. She wanted to keep going until she'd fixed it, until she'd found a ruin, a road, *something* to prove they weren't on a fool's errand.

She adjusted the straps of the pack again and caught Sevlin watching. "The shrikes didn't get me that badly," she said. "I can keep going."

"I have been in wet clothes since noon. *I* would like to stop," he said and began combing the slope for wood.

Sighing, Dashi joined him.

They made a fire quickly, taking advantage of the fading light to camouflage the flame and smoke. There was no reason to advertise their whereabouts, not with the possibility of heralds in the air; the fire would need to be extinguished at true dark. Sevlin unpacked their food, while Dashi sat on the other side of the fire, examining the wounds made by the shrikes: three deep, red furrows, where her biceps met her shoulders. Dirt and shredded fabric had dried into the blood. She would have to wash the wounds before she could apply the salve.

He didn't offer to help with her wounds but he did watch her, cool eyes glittering across the flames. Scrubbing at the dried blood, she snuck a glance at him. He was barefoot, his boots steaming by the fire. His deel was laid out next to him, also drying, and she could see the dark impression of his chest through the fabric of his damp undershirt.

The wet cloth was cold, sending tingles racing up the sensitive skin of her inner arm. Dashi shrugged her deel back onto her right shoulder and set to work on the other side. She'd been careful to keep her deel on, maneuvering it to expose only her shoulders but nothing else. It wasn't her undershirt she was modest about; it was her injured forearm.

"I'm starting to miss Idree's chatter," she said. *Lie.* She wasn't *starting* to miss it; she'd been missing it for weeks.

One of Sevlin's eyebrows rose ever so slightly. "*You* could talk if the silence bothers you."

"I *am* talking."

"Well, *I* am musing."

She snorted a laugh and wrung out the bit of cloth she was using, sending bloody water hissing onto the fire. The heat of the flames licked against her bare shoulder, chasing away the dampness.

"I always got the impression you disliked idle chatter."

"I did." She thought of Idree: chattering while she milked the goat, chattering while she swept the hearth, chattering while she measured customers' feet. "But I don't think I mind it anymore."

"Life in Thracedon made you soft."

"I know. Look at me." Sliding her deel back up, she tipped her head at the trees around them. "I demand the most luxurious accommodations."

"If you and Idree end up in Tyvalar, I have just the place for you then."

"There's a vacancy in your dungeon, I take it?"

He flashed Dashi a smile, there and gone so fast that she might have imagined it, except that she couldn't stop staring.

"A room in your palace?" She pressed. "Lots of tufted pillows and rugs thicker than my leg."

"Thick rugs would only make it impossible to hear you sneaking around. I have a policy against caging wild things anyway. They scare the staff."

Now Dashi grinned. "I'm out of guesses then."

"In the summer, Lyazzat decamps to a lodge in western Tyvalar. Her mother used to make a point to take her every year, and she has many fond memories of the time they spent there." Sevlin's expression shifted subtly, becoming faraway. "It is a beautiful place. There are several streams on the land and copses of trees—not these black evergreens but wide oaks and beeches—but most of it is open, rolling hills. You can ride for a day and not go anywhere."

"An entire *lodge*?" Her voice was suffused with skepticism, but she still let the pictures unspool in her mind, let herself feel Spit galloping over those hills.

"It's actually several buildings. There is plenty of room."

"Wouldn't she...mind?"

"Not when I tell her how much it would mean to you."

Something about his tone made Dashi's eyes dart to his face, but he was expressionless as always.

"Where did you stay in Thracedon?" he asked, breaking the silence.

"A little cottage in a walled hill city."

"Ejen?"

"You know it?"

"I've never been, but its location is famous even out of Thracedon: that pinnacle of land, the valley of crevices."

"Sometimes we would go riding near the base of the pinnacle and just stare up at it. The city walls looked like they had been carved out of the living rock. Idree got comfortable enough on horseback that she would go alone if she had a day off and I didn't." Dashi paused, seeing her sister's proud smile the first time she'd gone out. "She loved making boots enough that the shop owner had to practically shoo her out. And our cottage—she loved that too. As soon as she saw it, Idree insisted we couldn't live anywhere else."

"It sounds perfect."

"High praise, from a prince."

Dashi stood abruptly and started pacing. She felt restless and morose, a consequence of reminiscing about Ejen and losing the pack and possibly, she decided, of her battle with the shrikes. Baris always said that combat was the strongest liquor there was, complete with its own hangover.

The fact that she hadn't found the ruins where she expected them wasn't helping her mood either. In her experience, plant life avoided Purek ruins, so she'd expected to see a clearing at the very least. Still, the light had been fading when they reached the top of the ridge; maybe she'd missed something. She thought, a little enviously, of the khan's heralds and how useful it would be to have a bird's eye view of where she was going instead of slogging through a maze of gloomy tree trunks.

"You never said how you came across the khan's map," Sevlin said, interrupting her reverie.

"I was looking for the needle and the map was spread out on a table."

"How did you gain access to his private rooms? His personal servants are carefully vetted."

"I climbed. Well, I climbed the first two times." Dashi looked across the flames. Through the flickering firelight, she thought she saw his gaze sharpen. "The third time, I gave his attendants something to make them sick," she said after a pause. "Then I made sure I was there when replacement assignments were being doled out."

She expected a recriminating twitch of his mouth or, since he seemed to be feeling loquacious, perhaps an admonition about loyalty to one's fellow countrymen.

"What did you give them?"

"Something called Adder's Dust."

His gaze *definitely* sharpened that time. "Where did you get that?"

She meant to tell him. Or rather, when she started talking, she hadn't seen any reason *not* to tell him. Now, with his eyes fastened on her and his voice so carefully neutral, she couldn't help but prevaricate.

"Why do you sound so surprised?" she hedged.

"It's rare. And expensive."

"I got it in Karak City after I was hired on as a servant."

He was quiet for a moment, and she couldn't tell whether he believed her or not. "You planned it."

"Not quite as thoughtless as you seem to think I am, hmm?" She couldn't help but gloat even though, in truth, she *hadn't* planned the Adder's Dust part. His earlier words—*"No one could be hastier than you"*—still stung.

"I'd never say that."

"Well, you *should*. I managed to—"

"I *meant* I would never call you thoughtless."

She narrowed her eyes. Sevlin ignored her.

"Anything else of interest in the khan's rooms?" he asked.

"He has fashioned a necklace out of the statuette. He wears it around his neck, though presumably not *all* the time because he had that safe box installed for a reason. He might take it off at night. Seems like it would be uncomfortable." Dashi sat down heavily. "Idree keeps her old deel under her pillow. There was dirt on the floor of her room."

"You were *that* close to the khan?"

"A lot of people were sick that day." She waited, again, for him to chastise her for harming innocent people.

"The dirt on the floor," he said in a thoughtful voice. "The servants must have limited access to her room."

"I thought the same thing."

"Because he worries that the servants will talk about who she is and what she does, or because he worries that she will try to escape as they come and go?"

Dashi snorted. "If he had any sense he'd be worried about her charming them into helping her."

"If he had any sense, he would be worried about the army she is creating. I'm surprised Idree is allowed to spend so much time with her stitched patients."

"The consul has been away searching for the seamripper. Maybe she hasn't seen how attached the stitched patients are to Idree." Dashi chose her next words carefully, watching the fire-lit planes of Sevlin's face. "If it was your sister who held the seamstress and the needle, that's what you'd tell her? Not to let Idree spend time with the stitched?"

Sevlin broke his meditative stare with the fire and met her eyes over the flames. "Half sister and yes. *If* Idree was in Tyvalar and *if* Queen Lyazzat wanted to create a magical army, I would advise her to limit the seamstress' contact with them. The magic clearly has some effect on their mind and their feelings toward your sister, at least initially. I would be wary of letting the bond between them grow too strong."

"Any bond they feel is irrelevant. The khan controls them, not Idree."

"I saw."

"It almost looked like he had them on leashes." Dashi's shoulders twitched at the memory.

Sevlin lay down on the only bedroll—Dashi had offered to take the first watch—and laced his hands behind his head, his arms bunching with the movement. He stared upward for a long time before he spoke again. "He may control the heralds, but *she* has their loyalty. That may end up being the key."

Dashi frowned. "I'm not trying to stage a coup, Sevlin. I want to get Idree out of there before the khan even notices she's gone."

"That would be ideal, yes."

A few minutes later the sound of deep, even breathing signaled the end of the conversation, leaving Dashi to stare at the fire and ponder the unspoken end to Sevlin's sentence: that would be ideal, was what he'd said; *but the world is not an ideal place*, was what he hadn't.

The air had become heavy and ominous, hinting at things outside of her control. Dashi looked up, almost expecting to see the taiga mist closing in on her, but the trees were somber and still. With a mental shake and one last glance at Sevlin, Dashi pulled up her sleeve. The sight of her forearm stilled her. The tangled black and green lines were higher now, rising partway up her bicep. When she prodded the skin around them, her flesh was numb.

She picked up the wound salve, not because she thought it would do much good at this point but because she didn't know what else to do. Her fingers slid over the lid, fumbling so much that, eventually, she had to set it down and wait for her hands to stop shaking.

Chapter 33

The mist was the first thing Dashi saw when she opened her eyes. It nestled in the treetops above their camp, watching her sleep. Sevlin squatted next to her. It was his hand, shaking her boot, that had woken her.

She took the ration of dried meat and stale bread that he handed her and rested it on her knee, still not awake enough to eat. The temperature had fallen overnight and her breath fled in dense white puffs, which drifted slowly upward to join the taiga mist. Sevlin had started another small fire and Dashi leaned closer to it.

"A quiet watch?" she asked.

"Nothing interesting." He cocked his head slightly. "You were dreaming."

"Was I?" Dimly, she recalled the feeling of being chased and of reaching for her sister, only to find Khagan Nuray standing there instead. Dashi couldn't remember the particulars, but she felt vaguely unsettled and foggy, like the mist had drifted out of the treetops and into her brain.

"You were muttering and twitching." Sevlin's eyes crinkled ever so slightly.

She took a bite of her breakfast. "Like a sleeping dog?"

"I would not have voiced that comparison myself, but yes, very like."

"Hmm." The stale bread was difficult to swallow and she had to reach for water before she could get it down. "I'll be sure to let you know what animal you resemble when I wake you for your shift tonight."

"Do that." He was still squatting next to her, his knee not quite touching her own. Almost as soon as she noticed, however, he rose and stepped away.

"No tracks around the camp," he said.

"Maybe it was the horses that attracted the rats last time."

"Maybe. Good that you cleaned the blood off you though."

The treetops shook and Dashi looked up. "Think the shrikes will be back?"

"I think they're opportunists, not trackers. Not like the ant that was following us."

Gulping down the rest of her meat and bread, Dashi put out the fire and rolled up the bedroll.

Sevlin hefted the pack, strapping the crossbow on the side, where he could reach it easily. For a moment, Dashi replayed the scene with the shrikes, only this time she had her bow. She would have dispatched them easily, skating and shooting, skating and shooting.

"You can carry the crossbow if you'd rather," Sevlin said, catching her staring at it. "I thought it would be better for the person bringing up the rear, just in case something was following us."

"No, you're right," she said, turning to the waiting taiga. "I have a sword."

His steps were soft behind her. "For what it's worth, I miss your bow too."

The day was overcast and oppressive. The sun never made it through the clouds and the mist never had to retreat. It threaded through the treetops, keeping pace no matter which direction Dashi took them. Her forearm remained unimproved. When she surreptitiously checked it, she found that the lines of green and black had crept even higher. Her whole arm felt cold now, although at least there had been no more spasms.

"What's wrong?" Sevlin asked.

"Just stiff."

She'd been holding her arm straight down at her side, flexing and straightening her fingers. She should have known he wouldn't miss that. Her dismissal of his question was automatic; sharing—especially sharing a vulnerability—was not a natural inclination. Still, something made her *want* to tell him, even though she'd been careful to keep it hidden thus far. Perhaps it was the inevitability of it. If her arm really *was* getting worse, Sevlin would find out sooner or later. Perhaps it was the fear that more lies and secrets would drive him away from her—and Idree's—cause.

"Well..." Dashi hesitated, then said, all in a rush, "I think it might be infected."

"It's been less than a day. Too soon for infection, and you put wound salve on it last night."

She didn't answer and had almost convinced herself that it was best to let the subject drop when she felt Sevlin's hand on her shoulder. She turned around slowly, already dreading this conversation. Why had she thought it was a good idea to confess?

There was a bare indentation between Sevlin's eyebrows—*Exaspera-tion? Worry?*—but he said only, "Tell me."

"It's not the wound from the shrikes. It's from the Yassaris. I cleaned it out as soon as I could, but I think there's something wrong—" She broke off, realizing that the expression on Sevlin's face was one she'd never seen before. His lips were parted. His eyes had widened fractionally. *Shock.*

"They *caught* you?" He ran a hand over his hair. "I thought you had gotten away cleanly."

"Almost," Dashi said bitterly. "That ancestors-cursed beast grabbed me."

He nodded gravely. "The thiefmark will never forget your scent." His head tilted toward her. "Why didn't you say anything?"

Dashi shrugged, her eyes slinking away from his. "What they did to me, and then having to leave Idree, it was all—I just wanted to put it behind me, alright?"

"Did they put anything on you?" Sevlin asked, voice sharp. "They have magnetic beads that call to one other. I've only seen them locate other Yassaris that way, but they might be used to track someone else too." She could see him working through different scenarios, trying to evaluate the possibilities.

"Oh, they put something on me," she said humorlessly. "But it was meant to kill me, not locate me." Dashi rolled up her sleeve and winced: the wound, which had scabbed over, was rimmed in black now. She had the dubious satisfaction of hearing Sevlin's sharp intake of breath. At least she wasn't a hypochondriac.

He closed the distance between them and grasped her hand, turning her arm gently. "Does it hurt?"

"Sometimes. Mostly, it's numb."

When he looked up, his eyes were narrowed with concern. *No reassurances, then.*

"What happened?" he asked.

She told him about the execution the Yassaris had planned. When she got to the part about the plant and her subsequent escape, she pulled the Yassari thorn out of her pocket.

"You *kept* it?"

"I know it seems morbid, but it was the only sharp thing I had. Until you offered me a sword in exchange for my charming company, that is."

He didn't smile. "You haven't felt the plant moving in your arm?"

"I burned it out with a lantern before I left New Osb." She pointed at the splotchy burns, some scabbing, some still an angry red-purple.

"We should try a hot compress. It might draw the infection out."

Dashi pulled her sleeve back down, wondering at Sevlin's slight hesitation before the word 'infection.'

"Tonight," she said. "We'll need to start a fire and we can't do that in the middle of the day. Not without the heralds spotting the smoke."

He didn't move out of her way, just stood there, his eyes running over her face. *It looks bad, Dashi.*

She raised her chin. *There's nothing to be done right now, Sevlin, and I can't stand being babied.*

He picked up his crossbow and dropped behind her without another word.

Dashi was so busy thinking about her arm that she nearly missed the road. She stepped over without really seeing it, dismissing the worn soil as a game trail, but her subconscious caught up in a rush. It was *too* worn for a game trail unless there was a serious migration occurring through this region on a regular basis. Yes, there was an array of animal tracks, both old and new, but it was rutted and deep. The very soil had been worn away. Animals usually only did that when they were pulling a cart.

Dashi dropped into a squat, using a stick to dig next to her. She scraped away soil, doubling, then tripling the width of the hole, before leaning back to show Sevlin what she'd uncovered.

"Paving stones?" His eyes moved back to her face.

Dashi bounced to her feet, her arm momentarily forgotten. "A road leads *somewhere*."

Sevlin peered along the road-turned-game trail. It tunneled through the trees on an east-west axis, offering no clue as to what lay at either end.

"Which way?"

"I'm not sure." She glanced at the sky. *Plenty of daylight still.*

Sevlin jerked his chin toward the east. "East will take us into the interior of the peninsula. If we don't find anything we can always backtrack."

Dashi nodded reluctantly. She hated the possibility of walking in the wrong direction—and then having to cover the same ground twice—but there was little else they could do.

"Traps?" Sevlin asked from behind her.

She'd already started walking, her gaze darting between the ground and the forest that enclosed them. "Probably not on the road. Structures are a different story." In her excitement, she'd almost forgotten the gravity of what she sought. The seamripper would have been important to the Pureks. That meant danger.

The buried road meandered beneath the trees. The wildlife had created signposts of their own every few paces: the tracks of stoat here, droppings from a deer there. Everything had been left by normal-sized animals. Twice, Dashi thought she saw a figure just ahead, but both times it proved to be a trick of foliage and light. She drained her water and had to stop and refill at a small stream. Her throat was exceptionally parched. Her pulse pounded in her ears.

They walked for another hour until two things finally brought them up short. On the left side of the road was a small circle of charred stones. On the right side was a narrow side road, which ended against a rounded hill. As one, they swung their attention to the fire's remains, to the hint of a nearby threat.

"This is at least a week old." Sevlin's hand hovered over the ashes. "Some of it has been washed away."

"Must be from the consul's searchers." Dashi's eyes moved over the road. The storm that had drenched them had probably *also* washed away most traces of where the consul had gone. *I'd like to know exactly where she searched.*

Answering her thoughts, Sevlin pointed to a blaze cut into a tree a little farther down the road. "If they marked their route like that the whole way, we won't even have to try to track them." He turned to the rounded hill on the opposite side of the road. It poked up from the forest floor like the head of a slumbering giant. "Is that...?"

"I think so," Dashi said, her voice thoughtful. She remembered something she'd seen notated on the map, about some ruins located on the wrong side of the river. The consul had described them as *earthen*.

A second mound peeked through the trees, just behind the first. Dashi started to step off the sunken road to investigate, then changed her mind. A thin fog was rising from the ground and, though it lacked the substance of the mist that dogged them from the treetops, it would make it difficult to see where she was stepping.

"Is that hole the door?" Sevlin's voice was skeptical.

"Well, I'm sure it looked better in its prime."

The "hole" was hip-height on Dashi. It would be an awkward fit for Sevlin.

"Why are you smiling?"

Dashi shook her head. "Just remembering this time my friend Baris got stuck in a ruin. The doorway had already partially collapsed and we ended up having to dig him out. He mewled the whole time."

Sevlin glanced at her. "Was that supposed to be encouraging?"

She clapped his shoulder. "Don't worry, Baris was even bigger than you are. And the hole was smaller. I'll go first."

"This doesn't look anything like the ruin where the needle was."

"It's odd," Dashi agreed. "I've seen ruins that were built into the sides of hills, but never one that *was* a hill." She looked around at the unbroken vista of leaves and black tree trunks. "Most plant life stays away from Purek things too. It's no wonder we didn't see this from the ridge. It's camouflaged from above."

She crept closer to the opening, surveying it for traps. To the right of the entrance, partially shielded by a leaf, was a footprint: the toe of a boot, half eroded by the rain. *So the consul* did *go inside.* She'd already known someone had been nearby—the charred remains of the campfire proved that much—but she felt the coil of excitement in her chest loosen anyway. This discovery had already been claimed.

"There will be fewer traps for us to stumble into if someone's gone ahead of us," Sevlin said, fishing the lantern from his pack.

"For me to stumble into, you mean."

"You won't stumble." He lit the lantern and held it out to her.

"Such faith." She took it, her fingers lifting away just before they touched his.

Dashi ducked into the low opening and was immediately assailed by the smell of damp soil. She went slowly, using a stout stick to rap methodically against the ground. Yes, the consul's searchers had been here ahead of her, but that didn't mean it was safe. Dashi halted, tapping the stick twice in the same spot. It sounded hollow, but nothing happened.

"Over there," Sevlin said. He reached past her, grabbing her hand to raise the lantern higher. She registered the feeling of his fingers, hot against the cold skin of her left hand, before she saw where he'd been pointing: to a pair of splayed legs, barely visible in the tunnel's gloom.

Chapter 34

Dashi took a step forward, her back going cold as she moved away from Sevlin. When she was level with the dead body, she stopped. It was a man, with a long mane of dark hair, tied neatly with a red leather thong, and a spear protruding from his left kidney. The air was moving into the mound, so the smell had initially been carried away from them. The stench was impossible to miss at close range, however. Dashi gulped a breath, trying to ignore the heavy odor of rotting meat.

"What is it?" Sevlin asked when she didn't move.

"There's something familiar…" Dashi said slowly, trying to figure out what was pulling at her subconscious, while also trying not to breathe through her nose.

The man had been dead for some time. Blood pooled in his face, purpling and distending his features, warping the tattoos that covered his skin.

"That tattoo," Dashi said, pointing to his neck. "It's the Tyvalaran bird you were telling me about, right? I've seen something like it before."

She used her stick to pull at the man's deel. An image of a bird looked back at them, barely visible against the blood-darkened skin. The markings on its body weren't that different from the shrikes they'd encountered, but its face was oddly human: its eyes were a little too round and long-lashed, its cheekbones too wide. Its beak resembled an aquiline nose. The rest of its face was covered by a decorative mask.

"Where did you see it?" Sevlin asked in a tone that was too even, too devoid of feeling.

"I don't know. Karak City, I guess."

He gave her a searching look. "It's a wilewing, the same bird I mentioned to you a few days ago. In Tyvalaran folklore, the wilewing can steal someone's face, impersonate them so well that even a family member or lover can't tell the difference. It causes all sorts of trouble."

"What do you think it means here?"

"In Tyvalar, the wilewing is a symbol of deception or cunning, of trickery of some sort. It's considered the patron of spies and traitors and con artists. But here?" Sevlin shook his head. "I don't know."

"Do you recognize him?"

"I don't." This time, there was a troubled undertone in his voice.

The entrance tunnel ended in a wide, round room. Sevlin straightened with a sigh of relief. The sound of water reached Dashi's ears: gentle wavelets; something, once still, now disturbed. She glanced around. The noise ended as suddenly as it had started.

"Stay where you are," Dashi murmured, staring at the ground.

The packed dirt was rippled slightly in front of the entrance: four lines bent like frozen waves. Dashi moved sideways, prowling the rest of the floor in a grid pattern, searching for—and finding—several more rippled sections. Rows of low cabinets took up the center of the room. The earthen walls had been plastered and then painted in scenes that converged seamlessly with one another. On the far side of the room, there was a second doorway and an earthen corridor leading out of the circular room. She ignored it all, turning slowly as she surveyed the room for danger. Nothing immediately stuck out, but that was how the Pureks liked it.

"Avoid the rippled patches," she said to Sevlin. "Don't touch anything besides the floor."

"I remember." He copied her path, coming to stand beside her. "What are we looking for, exactly?"

"The note that the consul sent ahead to the khan confirmed that the seamripper was on the finger of land between the branches of the river. She didn't mention what made her so sure, but I'm betting it's something she found in here."

He looked at a row of cabinets against one wall. "What if she took it back to New Osb with her?"

"If it was a scroll, she almost certainly did. But that doesn't mean there aren't more clues here, either on other scrolls or in the art." She paused, thinking. "The Pureks were extremely allegorical, so I'm not sure how they represented the seamripper. Just look for...anything that sticks out to you, I guess."

Sevlin turned to look at the walls. "Your directions haven't gotten any clearer since last time."

Dashi moved in the opposite direction, stopping in front of a painted forest scene. A doe and two fawns cavorted through a golden clearing, while storm clouds gathered on the horizon and wolves watched from the shadows of the trees. *That's what I feel like when I'm in the taiga too,* Dashi thought, giving the deer a sympathetic glance. She scraped a fingernail against the wall. It was hard, like fired clay.

"You said no touching," Sevlin said.

Dashi smirked at the painting. "That rule was for you, not me."

All of the art on her side of the room was similar in subject. A mole clawed deep into the earth. A wild pig drank from a brook. Its eyes, shiny with intelligence and gold paint, stared out at the viewer.

She turned to the cabinets, her frustration growing with each door she opened. "They're all empty. They took every last scroll back!"

"You were right though," Sevlin said slowly. "They didn't take every-thing."

He stood in front of an elaborate mural, arms crossed, leaning slightly back. It was the same stance he'd adopted when he questioned her in his room. Dashi's pulse quickened.

In the mural, a man and a woman walked along a cobblestone road, which snaked through the foreground of the painting, before appearing again among some distant hills. The sun hovered just above the horizon, painting the sky a milky gold as a flock of geese cut across it. A river, flowing beside the road, seemed to hold the couple's attention.

"You said the Pureks revered the rising sun," Sevlin said, with a note of triumph. "The road outside runs along an east-west axis and so does the road in the mural. They're walking away from the sunrise, so that means west, toward the tip of the peninsula. We're headed in the wrong direction."

"But *where* are they going?" Dashi pointed to the hills in the mural. An enormous skull sat nestled amongst them, stark in its lack of color, empty eye sockets leering. The road ended in its mouth. "We didn't see any hills like this at the tip of the peninsula and, if it's an allegorical reference, it might not have anything to do with the seamripper at all." She gestured to the skull. "It might symbolize the end of life, in general. Or marriage."

Sevlin snorted. "This is the third part of the mural. I won't prejudice your opinion, but start over there and see if you don't agree with me."

Dashi walked to the other side. The first section of the mural was an ode to destruction. A boy played in a barren field, pouring water into a shallow trench he'd dug. A girl sat next to him, scratching in the dust with a stick. Pyres, some already alight, others with waiting bodies, lined one side of the field, but the boy and girl took no notice. The gutted carcass of a yak lay nearby. An emaciated horse lipped a few blades of grass.

In the second section of the mural, a young man and woman—presumably the same boy and girl from the first mural, only grown now—followed a path into the forest, their packs and staffs ready for a long journey. Black thunderheads hung low in the sky and rain lashed the land. The skeleton of a village lay behind them, but their gazes were fixed forward, not on the past.

Dashi circled back to the first mural, staring at the tiny figures the little girl had drawn in the dust: a stylized sun; a bird; stick figures of a mare and foal. The girl's cupped hand nearly hid the last image she'd drawn, screening it from prying eyes. It was a needle, its eyelet clearly delineated even though it was supposed to be sketched in the dirt. Beside that picture was a second one: a seamripper, its sharp hooked end ready to tear out stitches. Its outline was traced in a thread of silver.

Dashi found Sevlin's eyes.

His mouth twitched, satisfied. "Are we in agreement?"

"Oh, it's definitely more than a metaphor for marriage." Very gently, she stroked the surface of the mural, where two slashes, deep enough to have cut through the painted veneer and into the earth on the other side, bracketed the seamripper symbol. "Someone thought about cutting this right out of the wall. Do you think they wanted to destroy it so no one else could see it?"

"That assumes they knew someone would follow."

"Wouldn't they guess Tyvalar might send someone?"

"Why mark the trees then?" Sevlin inclined his head, eyes narrowed in thought. "Maybe they just wanted to add to the khan's archives. Do you think the silver outline means the seamripper is made of that?"

"Maybe. It makes a certain kind of sense, with the needle being gold." Dashi pointed at the wall in front of Sevlin, where the third mural showed two mounds nestled among the trees. "Assuming those are the mounds we're standing in right now, then you're probably right about the road in the mural and the road outside being the same."

"The man and the woman in the mural are headed west, away from the rising sun, but the consul and her searchers went east from here," Sevlin said, clearing still thinking of the blazes cut into the trees. "I suppose that's why she hasn't found the seamripper yet."

Dashi looked at the travelers in the mural, their backs straight and determined, at the geese, flying assuredly across the sky, certain of their destination. Even if the khan's searchers didn't find the seamripper on this round of exploration, they would have the khan's heralds to help them in the future. What an advantage it would be to have an aerial view when looking for ruins.

"*The geese,*" she said suddenly. She pointed to tiny, almost indecipherable, buds on a bush. "It's spring. The geese would be flying north, not south, which would mean that's a sun*set,* not a sun*rise.*"

"You said the Pureks always show the rising sun." There was the barest edge of accusation in Sevlin's voice.

"They did. I mean, they worshipped it, so it factors heavily in their art. But the man and the woman in this picture aren't worshipping the sun, they're ignoring it."

"So the travelers are headed east, not west after all?"

"I think so, and the consul headed the same way."

Sevlin frowned, clearly disappointed. He gestured at the skull. "What about *that?*"

"It could just mean the journey is dangerous."

"It's difficult to tell how far the journey will be."

"The man and woman haven't visibly aged between the second and third murals," Dashi pointed out.

"So we might only be searching for months or years, not decades."

"Are you always this dour or are you just trying to offset my enthusiasm?" She elbowed his arm lightly. "This is all good news. We found a road, we know which direction to travel on it, and we know that the consul hasn't found the seamripper yet."

"Just trying to keep your feet from running ahead of you," he said, but his tone was light as they headed to the next doorway.

This passage led to the second mound they'd spotted through the trees. It was bigger than the first and, from what Dashi could tell, relatively unencumbered by traps. At first, she spotted none, which made her nervous. There was *always* a trap and if it seemed like there weren't, it only meant she was missing something.

Eventually, however, she spotted another pattern in the earthen floor: raised dots, slashing in the diagonal lines of rain. *Lots of water motifs here.* After she'd mapped the floor and pointed out the obstacles for Sevlin, she turned her attention to the rest of the room. Instead of scroll cabinets, the center of the room was taken up by four low-walled pools, clustered together like eggs in a nest. She circled them carefully, wary of all that tile and the traps it could hide. She could see the reflection of water in one of them, but Sevlin held the lantern now and, without it, she couldn't see past the shadows cast by the pool's walls.

Sevlin was examining a statue at the back of the room with such intensity, his lips silently moving, that she couldn't help but walk closer. The statue was of the same woman they'd seen in the murals, only now she was grim-faced and girded for battle, with a sword in one hand and a staff in the other. Her hair was short and braided close to her scalp. Scars crisscrossed her exposed skin: hands and forearms, shins, even her neck and face. A crown of roses was braided into her hair, resting across her brow. The artistic detail was such that Dashi could see the places where the thorny stems bit into the woman's forehead and temples. At the statue's feet was an open scroll, sculpted from the same piece of stone. Lines of Purek script had been engraved into its surface.

"A poem," Dashi said, reading over Sevlin's shoulder. She took a moment to work through the title. "'The Dance of Balance.' It's too much for me to translate all at once, but I could copy it."

Sevlin pulled a small book from his pack and handed it to her. Its leather cover was tied up with straps and a charcoal pencil was wedged against the spine. Altan had carried a similar one.

"I glanced at the murals already," she said. "Nothing as interesting as the ones from the other room, but check in case I missed anything?"

He moved off while she began scratching in the journal. The poem had several stanzas, though it wasn't as long as some she'd seen. Sevlin worked his way around the room, always careful to put the lantern where its light would reach her page.

Copying the poem was a boring, exacting slog, made worse by the swelling in her forearm. Her hand kept cramping, making her writing drool sloppily over the page. She checked her work twice when she'd finished—the Purek language was tricky and a miscopied marking, however tiny, could change the meaning substantially. Finally satisfied, she stood up, flexing her hand to make it feel normal again. Already she longed for twilight, when they could make a fire and she could indulge in the comforting warmth of a compress against her wound.

"Find anything interesting?" Dashi asked, pushing her thoughts away from her arm.

"Lots of water imagery."

Dashi nodded.

"And the skull made an appearance again."

"Hmmm, I missed that."

He pointed to the mural closest to the pools. The foreground of the picture was filled with forest life: the white and yellow splash of lichens across a boulder; a sable, black and lithe, drinking from a spring. In the background, a line of hills marched across the wall, painted in grays. It took Dashi another minute to spot the skull since it, too, was painted gray, albeit a darker shade. Sevlin held the lantern closer, illuminating the brush strokes, which curled over the top of the skull like a wave.

"They disguised it this time," Dashi said. "Like they did with the image of the seamripper under the girl's hand."

"It's almost like a game."

Dashi nodded, her brow furrowing as her eyes traced over the mural. Eventually concluding that there was nothing else of interest, she turned to ask if Sevlin was ready, but he'd gone back to examining the statue on the other side of the room.

She started in his direction, then stopped at the pools in the center of the room. Between the murals and her clumsy scribing attempt, she'd completely forgotten about them. The wall surrounding the first pool was sculpted to look like vines were growing out of the rim. *It's beautiful,* Dashi thought, even as she searched for anomalies, out of habit. Sevlin was humming something under his breath, an unhurried tune that made the muscles in her shoulders uncoil. From somewhere nearby came the sound of water rippling.

The feel of the sculpted vines beneath her fingers was hypnotizing, pulling her senses into ten points, one for each finger. Each stone leaf was exquisitely serrated, so thin she didn't see how the sculptor had done his work without breaking them. The sound of waves gently lapping reached her once more, accompanied by the plunk of water droplets succumbing to gravity. It was a slight noise, almost hidden by the sound of Sevlin's humming and the scuff of her fingers moving over stone.

Water droplets? The pool she was examining was dry. There was another barely audible splash, but Dashi heard it now that she was listening. She peered into the adjacent pool but its walls shadowed the interior and she couldn't see much besides the reflective surface of the water.

"Bring the lantern, will you?" she called softly.

Sevlin's humming ceased.

The center of the pool was dark and Dashi squinted at it, puzzled. Instead of being uniform in color, it was mottled: black in some places, lighter in others. A tile pattern? The water rippled, sloshing gently against the inside of the pool. Was water still being piped in, after all this time? Dashi leaned closer, trying to see where the pipe emerged. The shifting surface played tricks on her eyes, making the depths of the pool look mobile.

Suddenly a thick pink rope erupted from the center of the shadowed water and wrapped itself around Dashi's waist. She was yanked forward, knees banging against the pool's low wall, momentum arching her back.

There was the sensation of hurtling downward.

There was a pair of gaping jaws.

Mottled, piebald skin.

Golden eyes with elongated pupils, each bigger than her hand.

Her arms flew up, trying to brace against the edges of the mouth that stretched over her head, but the tongue dragged her inside.

Chapter 35

She was inside of it, whatever *it* was. The golden eyes and camouflaged skin had looked vaguely familiar, but she'd flown forward so quickly that she hadn't seen much else. Now, she couldn't see anything. The air around her was humid and smelled of partially digested things. A sudden rhythmic suction caught at her feet and calves, massaging the sides of her legs and pulling her downward.

Dashi drew her sword, careful to keep it free of the muscles tightening around her, and started swinging. She was nearly hip-deep in its throat now and she couldn't see what she was swinging at, but she attacked anyway. The muscles holding her lower body stuttered, then tightened even more than before. Something gurgled up from below, washing over her body and sticking there: a thick, gooey substance that smelled so foul she gagged once, then vomited all over herself. *Keep fighting*, she told herself, but she was holding her breath now, trying to keep the substance out. It was already in her nostrils. Her eyes burned.

Without warning, the beast lurched upward, and Dashi was nearly thrown free of the muscles that wrapped around her lower body. Her sword, coated in the same thick goo as the rest of her, flew from her hand. She smacked the flesh around her in a panic, searching for it. The suction began again in earnest, just as Dashi's fingers grazed metal. Only her feet were trapped now and, in the less awkward position, she was able to drive the sword straight down and drag it toward her, using both hands to force the blade through flesh.

The beast lurched again, throwing Dashi onto her side. The acidic slime was everywhere, making her gag again and again until the taste of her bile mixed with that of the beast. Somehow, her slimy fingers still held the sword. The Yassari boots were the only thing that could get a good grip in the slime. She concentrated on that, on putting the strength of her legs behind each blow, driving the sword in and out, in and out.

The brush of moving air drew her attention. She waited for it again, trying to pinpoint the exact location. A nostril? The inner tube of the ear? She'd been expecting resistance, but the sword sank to the hilt. The effect on the beast was akin to an electric shock. It gyrated wildly, and there was a sudden blast of light and cool air as the mouth opened. Dashi careened forward, arms flailing, sword lost, trying to simultaneously land on her feet and turn to face her attacker.

She got a single, horrifying look at the animal over her shoulder: a giant toad. Huge, muscular legs bent outward, while its waxen belly sagged against the floor. Its skin was a patchwork of colors, pocked with warty bumps and old scars. Though it had been hiding in the water before, it was out of the pool now, and she stumbled backward as it turned toward her. The wide, turned-down line of its mouth cracked open and Dashi flung herself sideways, rolling behind one of the walled pools. Its tongue slapped the stonework, a sharp, vicious sound next to her head. The ground vibrated as the toad shifted its enormous bulk.

It was dark in the mound, Dashi realized. She'd only seen the toad by the dull shaft of light from the entrance tunnel. Where was the lantern? Where was *Sevlin*? She drew her knife—she didn't have time to find the sword—and peeked over the edge of the pool. The toad was gone. Her gaze darted around the dark mound. Every shadow looked solid. Every breath of air was the toad's tongue, slicing toward her. There was a creak behind her. Still squatting, Dashi spun around, her back pressed against the pool's wall. She blinked her stinging eyes, wishing she had something with which to wipe them.

The ground shivered again, but she couldn't tell where the movement originated. The feeling struck her as strange this time; the ground no longer felt solid beneath her feet. It was...*bouncing*, the way a plank floor might under strain. She started to wonder if there was a subfloor below the packed earth, but a scuffing sound made her whirl leftward. She tried to quiet her breathing, straining to catch movement coalescing from the darkness.

Crack. The ground gave way with a roar and Dashi toppled sideways, hitting something solid as she fell, though it did nothing to stop her momentum. Instead, it wrapped around her, hard and inexorable. Without warning, she was flung back up into the air, bouncing several times before she came to a stop. Her immediate move, even before she'd stopped bouncing, was to fight. One hand ripped at the thing across her chest while, with the other, she slashed backward with her knife, searching for something vulnerable.

"Dashi! Stop fighting me!"

The words were half cough, half whisper, but Dashi froze. It was Sevlin's arm that was locked around her, not the toad's tongue. He was holding her against his chest.

"Don't move," he said. "There was some sort of cellar beneath the mound. The floor collapsed into it."

Light, filtered through billowing clouds of dust, came from a jagged opening above, a barely-there glow that did nothing to illuminate the hole into which they'd fallen. Splintered joists surrounded them, punching downward from the collapsed floor, like the broken weave of a basket after a fist is put through it. Darkness cloaked everything beyond that.

"Where did the toad go?" Her voice was hoarse, though she didn't think she'd been screaming.

"It fell through too."

The monster was down here. She could feel her breath coming faster at the thought of it so close, peering at them through the darkness. Her muscles tightened. *Find a better weapon*, Baris murmured. That focused her thoughts a little. She thought she'd heard her sword clatter when the toad spat her out. Maybe it had fallen into the hole too. She gulped air, trying to steady herself, and pushed away from Sevlin.

Or tried to. His arm stayed tight across her chest and, though she told them to move, her legs wouldn't budge.

"Stop moving," Sevlin hissed against the back of her neck. "We're—"

Dashi inhaled sharply as her hand found what was keeping her legs in place: sticky ropes, as thick as her wrist. *Spiderwebs.* She knew what kind of spider made those webs. Rather, she knew the *size* of the spider. She glanced behind her. A network of thick silvery lines stretched into the darkness on either side; she and Sevlin were stuck in the very center. *That would account for the way we bounced*, she thought belatedly. At least it had saved them from a painful meeting with the ground.

"Why didn't you *say* something?" she hissed.

"I told you not to move."

"I thought you were just trying to calm me down!"

"I'll be more specific next time."

She still had her knife in one hand, but she couldn't bend over to cut her boots free with Sevlin's arm encircling her. She ran the blade along his arm, slicing away the small tendrils of web that clung there. His wrist, which was fully encased in the stuff.

"They must know we're here," she said softly, trying to ignore the image of all those legs, coming closer in the dark.

"Maybe the falling floor crushed them," Sevlin said, but he sounded dubious.

"If we had that kind of luck, I wouldn't have lost my sword."

"Cut mine free and use that," he said. "Hopefully yours will turn up. I'll get run through if I don't return it."

"Yes, that's what I'm worried about right now," Dashi said, curling herself around him to examine the web that held his scabbard, "that your friend will be mad about her lost sword." Three flicks of her knife and the sword was clear, ready for her to slide it free if danger dictated.

"You don't know her."

Dashi's thoughts snagged on the familiarity in his voice. "Make it up to her in other ways," she muttered, turning back to the strands of web which entangled his wrist and hand. She began sawing her knife back and forth.

Sevlin grunted, twisting his wrist so she could get to the web on the other side. It brought his arm tighter against her, pressing hard against her breasts. "It's not like that."

"But it was."

He didn't answer, which was, she supposed, an answer in itself. Unexpectedly, the thought nettled her. Maybe because he can't have a normal conversation without lapsing into silence, she thought irritably. *Or maybe*, her mind whispered, *you're annoyed because it's true.*

"Are you inquiring for a particular reason or just idly curious?" he asked.

There was an undercurrent to his voice that made Dashi's gaze flick to his face, though not much of it was visible in the dim underground. The entire right side of his face—the unmarred side—was hidden, but the light from above fell in shadowed layers over the other half. Without really knowing she was doing it, her eyes traced the scarred line, following it along the hard planes of his face, all the way to the belabored side of his mouth. She was abruptly, excruciatingly aware of every point where his body touched hers, and every place where it didn't. He couldn't see her face, backlit as she was, but he must have noticed that she'd gone suddenly still in the circle of his arm. The edges of his lips turned up slightly.

"I'm always curious." Her voice came out even huskier than before.

In the charged pause that followed, pain lanced up her injured forearm, the suddenness of it making Dashi's shoulders jerk back. *Not right now,* she begged it, knowing that both times she'd felt this stab of pain, it had presaged convulsions in her left arm. The tense look she'd shared with Sevlin had only lasted a second, but now she redoubled her efforts in penance for her distraction, twisting his hand as she worked.

The knife blade broke through the web with an audible snap. Sevlin pulled his arm away from her and Dashi bent to cut her feet and calves free. Unable to move the lower half of her body, the movement was awkward. No matter how she twisted, her hips ground into his, but now worry consumed her mind, leaving no room for other thoughts, no matter how pleasant. If her arm started the strange dancing convulsions while she was here, in the bowels of the mound, she would be unable to grip anything to climb out. The strands of web fell from her boots in sheaves, matted together with the toad's slime.

Finally able to move freely, she turned back to Sevlin. With his free arm, he'd produced his own knife and was working to extract himself. He'd landed in the exact center of the web, where the strands converged thickly. They pillowed his head and the backs of his legs in crisscrossing lines, suspending his body exactly as it had been when he'd fallen through the floor. His feet weren't even touching the ground.

"Hold still." She put her hand on the back of his neck and carefully severed the strands that held his head, then began working to free his shoulder, concentrating on her blade and not on the feel of him beneath her hand. Hot pain stabbed through her arm again and her fingers flexed involuntarily against his deel.

There was a shift somewhere in the darkness, a rustle. Though the collapsed joists encircled them in a fortress of splintered wooden ribs, it wasn't a perfect defense. The openings were far too large. Dashi squinted, trying to see past the wood. *Rustle. Scratch.* This time she heard purpose behind the sound and imagined the multitude of legs that might be stirring the dead leaves.

"My sword," Sevlin murmured next to her ear.

She reached around him, finding his hip and then yanking his sword free. It seemed to illuminate the darkness all by itself: a glinting beacon of security. She stepped in front of Sevlin, letting him muddle through the rest of the web while she kept an eye on the darkness.

Adrenaline coursed through her. Her left hand spasmed. Another rustle, just beyond the cracked joists. There was something there, rounded and very large, but that was all she could see. Finally, she heard Sevlin step free of the strands that held his boots.

"Let's go," he grunted. She handed him his sword and immediately felt worse for it. *He's the more effective sword fighter*, she reminded herself, especially with a sword that large. She would have to make do with a tiny knife.

The mouth of the hole opened above them, just out of reach. Dirt and splintered wood littered the ground at their feet, mingling with silvery strands of spiderweb. Sevlin located his pack, which had also fallen through, and pulled out the grappling hook. It took several tries for it to catch something solid. The fingers of her left hand began another spasm, opening and closing of their own accord.

Sevlin glanced over to offer Dashi the rope, but she had already spotted her exit: a joist, somehow still intact. One end had fallen when the floor collapsed so that its unbroken length stretched between the two levels.

Even with her left hand clenching and unclenching arbitrarily, she would be able to clamber up.

When she reached the main floor of the mound she crawled toward the exit, knowing that she had to keep her weight dispersed in the unstable ruin. With her left arm clutched to her chest, her gait was ungainly and slow and she paused only once, to glance at the rounded shape just visible through the hole in the floor.

It was the toad, its milky, bulging belly leering up at her. A broken joist protruded from its stomach, a thorn in the side of the moon. Dark, leggy figures shifted over its enormous bulk: dozens of huge spiders, already feeding on the carcass.

Chapter 36

Dashi stumbled into the daylight like she was starving for it. *Water.* Her skin itched where the toad's bile had dried and her lips puckered with the taste of acid. Sevlin, coming out of the mound behind her, grabbed her by the shoulder, swinging her toward him. His fingers pressed through her deel, warm and solid. He held her sword in his other hand—he'd found it on his way out—but it was so covered in gunk that he let dangle it loosely between his thumb and forefinger.

"Are you alright?"

Dashi nodded, unable to put into words the terror of being inside the toad or her gratitude at standing in the sunshine again. She wanted to confess her fear and relief like the weakness it was, but she took a step back instead, conscious of her twitching arm, which she still clutched to her chest.

Sevlin motioned vaguely at her face. "You have…" He paused, obviously searching for a diplomatic way to tell her she was covered in a toad's stomach acid. "We can go to the stream on the other side of the road," he said finally, skipping straight to a solution.

"As long as we get away from here."

Heedless of the slime, he slid his arm around her shoulders and led her away from the mound and across the old Purek road. Dashi kept her arms crossed over her chest, pinioning her twitching left arm beneath her right. The pain came in waves, washing from her forearm down to her fingertips, and sometimes upward too, nearly to her shoulder.

"Here," Sevlin said, motioning her toward the burbling water. "I have no soap, but you can scrub with the sand and we'll see to any wounds after you're cleaned off." His eyes flicked to her clenched arms, then back to her face.

It was hard to concentrate on anything besides the pain in her arm, but when Sevlin lingered, shifting from one foot to the other with uncharacteristic indecision, she jerked her chin in a shooing motion and said, "I've got it, Sevlin."

He didn't go far—straying far from one another was questionable on a good day, but today, only minutes out from their most recent encounter with a taiga predator, it felt especially fraught—but he turned his back and leaned one shoulder against a tree, waiting. She stripped her deel off and, kneeling beside the stream, plunged her left arm into the frigid water. She'd hoped the cold would numb the pain, and it did, but it did nothing for the limb-shaking convulsions. Without her right arm holding it in place, her left lashed back and forth in the water, a writhing fish bent on escaping. White froth splashed her face and wet her undershirt, but she hardly noticed in her focus on the green and black lines that snaked up her arm. She didn't hear Sevlin until he was splashing through the water behind her, his movements purposely loud so as not to startle her. He rested a hand on her back. It was the third time he'd touched her in minutes and already it seemed normal.

"Dashi, what—" His hand shot out, instinctively trying to save her arm from its drowning movements, then stopped, afraid to touch her. "Does it hurt?"

Teeth gritted, she could only nod.

"Has this happened before?"

"Three times." She choked back a gasp as a bolt of pain shot into her fingertips. "The other times were shorter though," she added when the pain had ebbed a little.

Without answering, Sevlin straightened and started between the trees.

"What are you doing?"

"Making a fire."

Dashi glanced at the sky, surprised to find that it was only mid-afternoon. It felt like a lifetime had passed since she'd entered the mound. "You can't. A column of smoke in the middle of the day—"

"No," he said, "what I *can't* do is watch you slowly deteriorate from poison."

There was a beat of silence before she asked, "Poison?"

"I don't know what it is," he said over his shoulder. "Something naturally emitted by the Yassari's plant, I'd guess—but I recognize the characteristics of a neurotoxin."

Within minutes he squatted next to a small fire, solemn-faced as he fed it. Once it was burning steadily, he pulled clean bandages and a tiny, lightweight kettle, which they hadn't had the occasion to use yet, from his pack. The water boiled and the bandages soaked, all without them saying a word. Dashi sat down beside him, her undershirt clingy and frigid. The fit of convulsions had finally ended, but her arm hung limp and weak at her side. She'd washed her face, her hair and her injured arm with one hand, but her right arm was still sticky with grime since her left hand couldn't manage the scrubbing.

Using a stick that he'd shorn of bark, Sevlin picked up a dripping cloth strip. "Ready?"

Dashi nodded.

He laid the first strip on the incision made by the Yassaris, his eyes jumping between her wound and her face.

"It hurts," she said, "but not as bad as those spasms."

Seemingly reassured, he began working faster, until steam rose in a line from the white cloths that plastered her arm. Whenever one strip cooled, Sevlin returned it to the pot of boiling water and replaced it with another. At one point, when her entire arm was wrapped in cloth and wreathed in steam, he moved off to the stream and plucked up her deel, spreading sand over its grimy length, scrubbing and rinsing until the water ran clear, before laying it out next to the fire opposite them. He did the same with her sash and the metal cup that he'd found for her in the first, small ruin, which had been hanging from it. Then he sat down next to her again, barely rustling the grass, and began the process of replacing the cloth strips all over again.

"A prince who scrubs clothes and nurses the sick." An alien warmth was spreading in Dashi's chest at the sight of him, tending to her so carefully. She adopted a teasing tone to counter it. "Don't they have servants in Tyvalar?"

"The servants specialize in arse-wiping. I've learned to manage everything else on my own."

A laugh burst from Dashi. "That sounds like something I would say, making fun of you."

He was partly turned away from her, tending the fire, but she saw his mouth hitch upward. Her initial observation had been a floodgate; now that she was looking at him, she couldn't seem to stop. The narrow flames made his face glow bronze and her eyes roved over the jut of his cheekbones, his solid jaw, his heavy brows. The scar molded it all into something unforgettable, something stronger than it had been before, like fired clay or tempered steel. The women in Tyvalar must be blind to prefer Prince Zevi to Sevlin, she thought.

Sensing her scrutiny, he looked up, their eyes locking, light on dark. Dashi swallowed, pushing back against the want that suddenly welled up inside her. She was not of a temperament to hobble herself with inhibitions or, truth be told, deny herself much of anything, but in the circumstances, she made the attempt at least. They were in the taiga, for one thing, and she was wounded, for another, and both things dictated that she not allow any distractions. There was also the fact that this was *Sevlin*. He saw her far too clearly as it was and, she reminded herself, she resented him for it. Adding to the simmering push-pull of conflict between them would not end well and she needed his continued goodwill for Idree's sake.

Sevlin's gaze dropped back to her arm. He placed another hot strip of cloth without saying anything. Instead of taking his hand away, his index finger trailed a line up her arm, to the ball of her shoulder.

"When you showed it to me this morning, I couldn't see most of these lines because of your sleeve. But they weren't this high, were they?"

The breath shuddered out of Dashi and she turned away, staring out at the sea of tree trunks. "No."

Still not looking at the snaking green and black lines, she touched a place on her arm, halfway up her bicep. "Here, just about." After only a few hours, the lines nearly reached her shoulder now.

He traced one of the lines again. The contrast between the warmth of his fingertips and her damp skin made goosebumps rise along Dashi's arm. "These lines felt hard before we started with the hot compresses."

A dozen quips popped into her head, things about hardness and heat that would have made Baris blush, but she recognized her reaction was at least partly due to the direness of her circumstances. Altan had always joked that, in most people, fear was a curb. In Dashi, it was a goad.

She constrained her response to a bland, "Oh?"

Sevlin grabbed her fingers and placed them where his had been. The lines on her upper arm, where Sevlin had yet to place a hot compress, were hard ridges beneath her skin. A little lower, however, and the lines had a jellied consistency to them.

She pushed on them, watching the black and green slide beneath her skin. "That's...a good thing, right?"

"Yes."

"If we can draw the poison out like this, then I'll be alright?"

"I'm not a healer and I've never seen this particular poison before." Sevlin's face had become an emotionless mask again.

"Sevlin," she said, "just tell me."

"I'm not keeping things from you, I just don't know *what* to tell you, Dashi. It's possible it will work. It's also possible it won't."

"And it'll cost my life."

Sevlin blinked, which was, for him, as good as a flinch. "Or your arm."

Dashi jerked away. "*No.*"

He held up a hand. "Maybe not as dramatically as that. But the spasms mean that the nerves are being damaged and if that continues your arm may not function the way it used to."

She shuddered, gesturing at the kettle. "Put on more."

By the time he had soaked and replaced each of the strips twice more, the sun had dropped into the trees. The temperature had dropped with it and, although her undershirt was no longer damp, Dashi shivered in the dark forest.

"Since we're making camp here I'm going to get the lay of things before night," Sevlin said, glancing at the Purek mound, just visible through the black trees. He was obviously thinking of the spiders, though Dashi thought it unlikely that they would venture out of the mound when they had such a sizable feast inside. He picked up her deel, now dry, from the other side of the fire and placed it within her reach, along with some dried meat from the pack. He loaded a bolt in the crossbow and placed that within easy reach too.

Alone, she curved in on herself, using her good arm to pull her knees to her chest. Although she'd extolled Sevlin to speak plainly about her prognosis, she hadn't said much afterward. *Poisoned*. It felt circular somehow, to be poisoned as punishment for theft after she'd stolen poison to use against others. Ese would have been amused.

She prodded one of the marbled green and black lines. Still soft, it moved obligingly, and Dashi felt her spirits lift marginally. Sevlin said the hot compresses might draw the poison out and he wouldn't lie. He'd even managed to squeeze some out of her incision, once he'd reopened it. The poison had oozed forth, truculent and slow, finally letting go of her and plopping onto the ground in a black and green rain.

Dashi wrapped her deel around her shoulders, letting it drape over her arms. She could still feel the warm impressions in the cloth that marked the place Sevlin's hands had held it. As she was deciding whether to go find him, he reappeared, sliding from between a pair of tree trunks where he hadn't been a moment ago.

"Nothing unusual," he said, seating himself by the fire. His deel strained across the shoulders as he reached to help himself to some of the meat he'd laid out for her.

"What about this?" She tilted her head at the fire.

He glanced involuntarily at the mound. "I say we leave it."

Dashi nodded. After two attacks in as many days, it was the taiga's denizens that were uppermost in her worries, not the heralds. Sevlin selected a steaming bandage and reached for her arm.

"You seemed surprised that the consul's people would try to cut out a piece of the mural," he said, changing the subject. "I thought you and your friends took artwork from ruins all the time."

"*Intact* artwork. We never hacked it to pieces." The consul had removed the mound's scrolls, but that was different. It might be inconvenient for Dashi, but at least it meant the scrolls would be studied, not destroyed.

A twitch of Sevlin's eyebrow conveyed his skepticism.

"Well, Baris and I may have injured a mural during a sword fight once," she amended, "but it was an accident. Altan and Zayaa were livid, with Baris especially. Zayaa said it was worth more than the two of us put together, but Altan made her apologize later."

Sevlin's eyebrow rose further.

"She'd never have apologized on her own," Dashi clarified.

"Is that where you learned it?"

"Not liking to apologize?" Dashi made a face as he lay another hot strip of cloth against her skin. "I don't apologize because I'm always *right*."

A soft exhalation of amusement. "I thought you said you were most like Baris."

"I was, I think. Zayaa and I, we had the apology thing in common, yes, but in other ways..." Dashi shook her head. "You said something before, about my feet running ahead of me. Altan always said the same thing about me too, but Zayaa wasn't like that at all. She was astute, observant, more like him, than me. But she was quicker to anger than Altan, and mean when she did." Dashi tilted her head, considering. "Maybe that's a little like me."

"I've never known you to be mean."

Dashi rolled her eyes. "I'm not fishing for compliments, Sevlin. I know what I am."

"Quick. Ruthless. Unapologetic."

"I've killed people. I've poisoned innocent servants. I've deceived someone I'd agreed to work with." Her gaze pulled away from the fire, drawing to his without meaning to. The fingers of her right hand stilled their restless flexing. "I'm fairly certain that falls under the heading of mean."

"Quick. Ruthless. Unapologetic."

"I was going to put a sedative in your food and leave you in the taiga after I'd found the golden needle."

"For which you are still not apologizing, correct?"

She smiled a little. "No."

"I still wouldn't call that mean." His gaze was a solid force, holding her immobile, as his hands shifted a cloth on her arm.

"You may need to revisit your definition."

"Mean is cruelty, an indifference to the pain and exploitation of others. You are not those things. I would not enjoy being around you if that was the case."

Restlessness hit her all at once. Their discussions about the past usually took a different tone: accusatory, suspicious. This felt naked somehow, talking without anger to warm her.

"I don't even know if I'd call her mean, by your definition," she said, shoving the conversation away from herself. "She just...saw your weaknesses and pointed them out in little ways if she was angry. But when she was happy, it felt like you were the center of the universe, so I guess it evened out."

Sevlin was quiet long enough that Dashi changed the subject on her own.

"I was thinking about the skull in the mural: it could represent a mausoleum or a crypt."

"You've ruled out the perils of marriage as a hidden meaning, then?" A shallow dimple appeared beside his mouth.

"Not at all. It's a danger more formidable than a giant toad."

"That thing..." Sevlin's amusement faded immediately. "It barely reacted to my sword. I saw a spear hit it and it didn't flinch. Even if I'd succeeded in killing it, I was sure I'd be too late."

"I didn't hear you." Her left hand was icy. She chafed it with her right. "When I was inside the toad, I mean. I listened."

"What is it you expected to hear?"

"I don't know. Yelling. Swearing."

"Why would I yell at something that doesn't understand me?"

She shrugged. "I would've known you were out there, fighting."

"You should have known that already." His expression was inscrutable.

She dropped her gaze back to the fire. "I tried to inflict as much damage as I could. I thought maybe I could convince it to give up." The remembered sensation of those muscles clamping down on her legs was enough to make her feel sick, but she shrugged, her tone careless. "If not, at least I wouldn't go down as a pleasant meal."

"Not a happy notion," he said, then added, bracingly: "This will take your mind off of it." He tossed his journal into her lap. The charcoal pencil was wedged between the pages of the poem she'd copied.

Dashi groaned. "I'd forgotten about that."

"Unless you're too...*weakened*." He shrugged, elaborately indifferent.

"Too blatant. You're capable of better manipulation than that, Sevlin."

Amusement shone in his eyes. "The poem might be useful."

"I doubt it. It was right out in the open."

"The Pureks love tricky and obvious at the same time."

An hour later, Dashi put down the pencil, wincing inwardly. Her right hand was cramped from writing and her left arm had begun to ache steadily. It wasn't the sharp pain that presaged a fit of spasms, but coupled with her fatigue, it was enough to make concentration difficult.

Sevlin looked up from her sword. He'd sharpened and cleaned his own in the time it had taken her to translate and had since moved on to caring for hers.

"The poem is entitled *Dancing Balance*." Clearing her throat, Dashi read:

"'What is nature but a dance of balance?
What is life but kindling for death?
Watch the predator become the prey
Like night conquers day and warp counters weft.

As the wheel turns the seasons
So the scale tips to and fro.
The fields of war will yield peace.
What was famine now feeds the doe.

Like a wheel on its axle spins,
Sewn-in stitches become ripped-out seams.
One story ends as another begins,
A hero rises as a tyrant schemes.'"

Her shoulders slumped as she finished, like the responsibility of translating was all that was keeping her upright.

"What are you thinking?" Sevlin asked.

"Well, there's the obvious mention of sewn-in stitches and ripped-out seams."

"Ripped-out seams makes it sound like the seamripper only affects the people who have already been stitched," Sevlin said slowly. "It might not dismantle whatever connects Idree and the needle."

"Maybe," Dashi said stubbornly. "Or maybe the author just needed something that rhymed and didn't have time for an exhaustive list of the seamripper's attributes." She paused. "I don't think the rest of the poem is of much use."

"What about the scheming tyrant and the hero part?"

"An ancient prophesy that refers to me."

Sevlin's mouth tipped up, offering a flash of teeth on one side.

"I can't think anymore." She slid the journal toward Sevlin. "Mind if I take second watch tonight?"

He nodded absently, his eyes already glued to the translated poem, and that was all the excuse Dashi needed. She lay down on their single bedroll, barely noticing the rocky ground beneath. With one breath, she inhaled the smell of leather and sweat, metal and fresh air. *Sevlin.* With the next breath, she was asleep.

The mist was closing in on her. Dashi could feel the chill of its clammy fingers caressing her throat, tickling over her jaw. She tried to push it away, or at least turn her head, but she couldn't move.

"Dashi! Dashi, help me!"

It was Idree's voice, though Dashi couldn't see anything. The mist pressed close to her face, mingling with the cloud of her breath, beading in her hairline.

"Idree," she tried to call, but it climbed into her mouth, coating her tongue in a cool film.

She lay on her side, unable to move, while the mist ventured down her body, stopping at the healed arrow wounds between her shoulder blades, then moving to the long scar near her ribs. The scar tissue tightened, suddenly alive with feeling.

No, she told herself, *this isn't real. Sevlin woke you for watch. You added wood to the fire, then sat down next to it.* The mist ran its fingers along her neck again. *You must have fallen asleep.*

"Dashi!"

Idree...

With an effort, Dashi pried her eyes open, but the mist didn't disappear with waking. It wasn't near enough to touch her scars or to cause the strange hallucinations that had left Dashi on the ground last time. But it was close enough to make her uneasy, a white wall penning her against the rocky outcropping at the back of their campsite.

Don't panic, she told herself in a firm voice, even as the mist pulsed, piling higher with each passing second. Waiting. Watching. Should she do nothing and hope it went away on its own, or wake Sevlin up and...*what?* Stand back-to-back, ready to fight the air with swords?

Dashi glanced at Sevlin. Still sleeping. Her last clear memory had been the sound of his easy breathing and the play of the firelight over his relaxed, unguarded face. The fire was burning steadily, which meant she hadn't been out for very long.

There was a small crunch behind her, someone shifting nervously on their feet. Dashi rolled away from her blankets, coming to her feet with her sword in hand. She stared at the oblong head that loomed over her, several times the size of her own. The firelight caught and repeated in each facet of the ant's eyes: an identical view from hundreds of identical black windows.

The ant took a step toward her.

Chapter 37

The ant stopped so close that its antennae brushed Dashi's forehead, a coarse whisper across her skin. It was the same creeping sensation she'd felt when she'd been dreaming. She remained motionless, half enthralled, half terrified, while the ant swept its antennae down her body. Again, it paused at the scars on her side and back—the places she'd been healed by the other ants—brushing back and forth several times.

It was the same ant, or at least the same subspecies, that had stalked them near the river: larger than the one she'd encountered on her previous foray into the taiga, with a dark exoskeleton that shown like polished walnut. Tiny dark bristles covered its legs. Its jaws were enormous, big enough to fit around her waist with room to spare. Although Dashi eyed them warily, they remained still.

Stillness. A good strategy, she decided, her sword dangling impotently in one hand. After her initial sharp inhalation of surprise, she concentrated on calm breaths. *Don't act like prey.* Her eyes darted to its tracks, which led back to the mist, though she could see no disturbance in the white wall to mark its passage.

"What do you want?" she breathed, barely a whisper.

The ant's antennae gave an irritated twitch toward the fire, then it brushed past her, going to the rocky outcropping that towered over the back of the campsite. There it stopped, turning to stare at Dashi for a long moment, demanding her attention. Before she could decide what that meant, the ant was gone, its legs carrying it swiftly up the uneven rocks.

Dashi let out a breath. The ant had come through the mist; why had it left a different way? Were the ants hunting them, or merely curious? Her hand grazed the rock the ant had scaled, her scars tingling as she made contact.

Shaking her head, she returned to the fire, but restlessness had taken hold of her now. She wanted to move—to climb after the ant, specifically—and sitting beside the fire seemed impossible. She turned, ready to pace away her energy, and got her first glimpse of trouble. The mist was undulating, pulsing to a silent heartbeat. Then she felt it: the same tempo, so gentle that it was nearly unnoticeable, pushing up from the ground.

Sevlin woke as soon as her hand touched his arm. He pushed himself up, nearly nose-to-nose with her, although his eyes were scanning the darkness over her shoulder.

"What is it?" The low timbre of his voice was the only thing about him that seemed half awake.

"Up the rocks." She was already gathering the few possessions they had. "Something is coming."

She started climbing a moment later, Sevlin right behind. Leaving the fire going went against the grain, but the light made it easier to climb. Her left arm felt weak as she grasped for a handhold, but the Yassari boots grabbed the rock easily. In seconds she was far from the ground.

Dashi pulled herself on top of a boulder and Sevlin slid in next to her, both of them laying flat on their stomachs to peer at the camp below. The mist had finally spilled over its invisible dam, slowly sifting through their campsite. The fire hissed and sputtered at the onslaught, but it was a doomed fight. The flames died abruptly, leaving them in darkness.

Seconds later, the thundering herd passed below them, cloaked by the mist and the night. The air writhed with sounds: snorts and squeals, the staccato of labored breathing, the pound of feet. Dashi caught a glimpse of a beast in silhouette—sloped back and four squat legs, mist flowing over its shoulder in a cape of white—before it was lost from sight. Between one second and the next, it was over. The pulse that shook the boulders grew fainter and fainter.

"Giant boars," Dashi said.

Sevlin nodded. "What do you think was chasing them?"

What *had* been chasing them? Dashi peered over the lip of the boulder. The mist curled softly around a tree, but otherwise, the night was still.

"I don't know," she said, "but maybe we should stay up here for the rest of the night."

"You won't have an argument from me." Sevlin unfurled the bedroll and pulled it over himself, lifting the side closest to Dashi in invitation. She hesitated a moment, then scooted closer, arranging herself beside him so that they touched from shoulder to knee in a single unbroken line. The blanket barely covered them both.

"I've had more comfortable beds," Sevlin said, pillowing his head beneath an arm. He was looking at the stars, but she heard him hesitate, carefully preparing the words he was about to say. "Not many people would have reacted to a stampede quickly enough to live through it."

Dashi swallowed. The *ant* had reacted, prodding her while she slept, then trying to lead her up the rocks. *She'd* been so exhausted from the poison and pain that she'd fallen asleep without remembering it. What's more, she knew what Sevlin was really saying: that he thought he could rely on her, that they worked well together. But the dwindling strength and coordination in her arm would become a liability soon, if it wasn't already. For him as well as for her.

Seeming not to expect a response, Sevlin fell asleep almost immediately, leaving Dashi to shift uncomfortably against the hard rock and the undeserved compliment.

They returned to the ground in the morning, so that they could examine the palm-sized boar tracks and so that Sevlin could make a fire and tend to Dashi's arm again. He pronounced it unchanged, which he considered a good sign.

Taking its cue from the mist, the day began cold and clammy and stayed that way throughout the afternoon. The old Purek road was almost invisible in the gloom, but Dashi pushed ahead. By the time the sun finally dared to show its face, her mind felt at once tired and overactive, not at all soothed by the light. She'd woken with a headache and it worsened as the day went on. Sometimes, if she turned her head too quickly, she saw spots in her vision. They moved and shifted, a tide that no amount of blinking would remove.

Trees paraded by in a featureless succession, broken only by the occasional pile of boulders. They passed a second abandoned millstone and an attendant building, this one without any skeletal residents. When it was finally time to stop for the night, Dashi could barely make herself gather wood. Her head screamed every time she leaned over. She filled the cup Sevlin had found for her and set it close to the fire, hoping that warm water might chase away the cold that was slowly spreading up her arm. What she wouldn't give for a hot mug of *suutei tsai,* she thought, swishing the heated water around in her cup.

Sevlin sat down next to her, holding the kettle and clean bandages. Dashi shrugged her arm out of her deel. She knew—from Sevlin's silence, from the sudden tension in his shoulders, from the flash of anguish on his face, instinctually smoothed over—that the news was bad.

"Dashi," he said, voice hushed. "It's—I'm…I'm…"

It was the most emotion she'd ever heard in his voice, aside from when they'd yelled at each other on the boat. She glanced at him, then away. He was ashen, almost sick looking. She stared at the fire, not wanting to see when pity would begin to filter through Sevlin's mask. When he began to see her as weak.

"The poison has spread," she ventured.

Sevlin swallowed. "Yes."

She was feeling a little sick now too. *One arm.*

"Just…keep doing the hot bandages," she said after a breath. "It feels good and I…I need to…" To what, come to terms with an amputation? With never using her bow again? How could she ever accept that? The idea was risible.

Sevlin picked up a steaming strip of cloth, wrapping it around her forearm.

"How do you know so much about poison?" she whispered.

His fingers stilled over the kettle, then resumed their movement. "It's a consequence of having the word 'prince' before your name."

"Has anyone in your family ever been poisoned?"

He shook his head. "We have tasters."

Dashi stared, horrified enough to stop thinking about her own situation. "Do they last long?" She couldn't help but think of Cook. The khan's meals were prepared separately from everyone else's. Did Cook taste them herself?

"I've only ever seen one man die from poison and it wasn't a taster. It was a Tyvalaran nobleman and it was his wife who poisoned him. We've always been able to save the tasters. We keep the antidotes for the most common poisons on hand. But this," his eyes flickered up to hers, "I don't know this. It might occur naturally in the Yassari plant, or maybe they engineered it and dipped the thorn in it before they cut you."

Dashi gave a bitter chuckle. "Does it matter?"

"It might, if we weren't in the middle of the taiga. Someone is more likely to have discovered an antidote for a naturally occurring poison."

"If the Yassaris invented it, they're unlikely to share the cure."

Sevlin's head dipped in acknowledgment.

"So, in your expert prince opinion," she swallowed, "how long—?" She waited, letting the silence stretch out until it forced a response. It was a trick she'd learned from him.

He shifted beside her, giving in at last. "A few days."

Not enough time to return to New Osb even if I wanted to.

"How will you...?" She made a vague gesture toward her arm. She still hadn't looked at it. "We don't even have," her tongue tripped on the word *bone saw*, "the right tools to do it."

Sevlin was already shaking his head. "I'm sorry, Dashi. I thought the spread had stopped and I thought if we waited on the amputation, did more compresses maybe the arm could be saved, but now—" He looked away, then back at her and grabbed her good hand between his. "I should've done it right away. Ancestors above, I should've—I'm so sorry."

Dashi looked down then and she finally understood what Sevlin was trying to say. The green and black ropes had climbed over her shoulder, stretching across the slope of her trapezius. Her fingers probed cautiously, feeling the hard lines where she couldn't see. Up her neck, almost to her scalp.

There could be no amputation now.

Chapter 38

Their morning meal was eaten in silence and camp was broken the same way. Sevlin shouldered the pack and, though it should have been Dashi's turn, she let him. They followed the sunken road up one ridge and down another. Each step was laborious. Each step was over too quickly. *A few days,* Sevlin had said. *I'm sorry, Dashi. I'm so sorry.*

A shrike's whistle pierced the forest. Dashi and Sevlin ducked at the same time, weapons drawn, waiting for a threat that never appeared. The road wound along the edge of a bog, a boil in the middle of the forest, then up a densely thicketed hill where brush snagged at their pants and reached out to grab Dashi's braid.

"Hope there's...at least...a view," Dashi managed, trying to quell her panting.

A trickle of sweat ran down the side of her neck, disappearing into her deel. She tugged at her clothing, her fingers knocking clumsily against the Purek cup hanging from her waist before she managed to loosen her sash. Sevlin stopped, insisting he needed a drink, but she knew it was for her sake. His long stride ate up the distance, floating him along without apparent effort.

He reached the top of the ridge before she did, turning to survey the view. "Dashi..."

Pain burned in her left arm and it had begun to shake, but with the help of the Yassari boots, she was able to clamber through the scree.

She hated the sight of them now, those boots. *You weren't worth it*, she thought at the ornately stitched leather.

At the top, she clutched her spasming arm to her chest, concentrating on the view instead of Sevlin's sideways glances. The taiga stretched out below them, its towering trees and dark shadows transformed by the lens of distance into something soft and inviting. The sunken road they'd followed was invisible, completely cloaked by the forest. A valley, backed by craggy granite peaks and thick with trees spread out below them. Through the mishmash of boughs and evergreen foliage, light flashed. Dashi squinted, measuring size and distance with her eyes. It was a mound, like the one they'd already explored, only much, *much* larger. Pearly light winked at her again and she realized that the exterior of the mound must be decorated. Glass, maybe, or pieces of quartz.

She gave a low whistle, impressed. The more ornate the ruin, the more likely it was that the seamripper would be here. Sevlin nodded once, but he was looking at her arm and didn't smile.

He insisted they wait until the spasms wracking Dashi's arm tapered off before they started down the other side of the ridge. Fueled by a mixture of excitement and relief, Dashi barely registered the descent. It was only after they reached level ground that they discovered the entire valley was full of ruins, hidden beneath the trees.

"I don't understand it," she said for the third time, pausing to look into a crumbling building with an enormous tree growing through the roof. A relief sculpture decorated the walls: life-sized men and women, dressed exquisitely, queued up to enter. "Other than moss, the ruins are usually devoid of plant life. We always thought there was some sort of magical residue that kept it from taking over."

The smaller mound they'd explored a few days ago had been en-croached on by the forest too, so maybe she shouldn't have been so surprised, but this—an entire city inundated by greenery—was something else entirely.

"The needle and the seamripper are supposed to balance each other magically. Maybe their magic manifests differently too," Sevlin suggested.

"A dance of balance," Dashi murmured, quoting the poem she'd translated. "Maybe."

Wary of traps, they made their way through the valley slowly, only reaching the large mound at dusk.

"It's even taller than I thought," Sevlin muttered.

The mound was situated inside a huge, sunken amphitheater and encircled with terraced seating. Since its base was below ground level, it was taller than Dashi had thought too. She'd been correct about the exterior decorations though. The sloping sides were inlaid with light-colored rocks: quartz cut into slabs; opals, bigger than any Dashi had ever seen; a few others that she didn't have a name for. It gave the mound a restless, glittering appearance, like a large bird shifting its feathers in the sun.

She put a hand against Sevlin's chest as he started to move down the amphitheater stairs. "We need to be very careful here. It's too dark to do it right now."

Sevlin glanced down at her arm, his thoughts loud: during the khan's race, they'd entered the golden needle's temple at night.

"Last time was different," she said. "Negan and his men were on our heels." *And I am tired.*

He set his pack against the wall of a nearby building. "If we're stopping, we're going to work on your arm."

Dashi slid down the wall. "I thought we'd already decided it's not doing any good."

"Humor me." He had a small fire going in no time, with the kettle puffing merrily over it as he laid strips of hot cloth against her arm.

Dashi leaned her head back, watching the mound through slitted eyes while the heat from the bandages soaked into her arm. These ruins had a dark, damp feel. The trees leaned close, casting a sick, yellow light on the mound's exterior as dying sunlight filtered through their boughs. It felt prophetic. Unexplored ruins typically cast a spell of adventure and verve over Dashi, but this place felt ominous. Decaying.

"This *is* a temple, right?" Sevlin asked. He was toying with his knife, turning it slowly in the flames.

Dashi's attention was still fixated on the ruins. "I'd put money on it."

"Why are you so sure?"

"I'm sure it's a temple because of the way it's situated at the center of the settlement. I'm sure it's an *important* temple—the kind that might hold a significant religious or cultural artifact—because of the way it's situated at the center of all the roads." She'd noticed dozens coming from all directions, streaking out from the unknown reaches of the taiga toward the mound, rays flocking to a silvery sun. "Only a place of importance to the greater Purek empire would have that many roads leading to it."

"I wonder what kind of defenses it will have."

"Good ones." Dashi closed her eyes, shutting out the mound. "I'd put money on that too."

Sevlin sat down next to her. "Pull your undershirt back more."

"So forward," she said to hide the little thrill she got, even in her exhaustion, from those words. She tugged at the cloth, giving Sevlin access to her shoulder and neck.

A moment later, however, the thought was gone, chased away by hot metal.

"Sev—*OW!* What was that?"

Sevlin set his bloodied knife down and pulled her arm across his knee. He'd reopened the original cut made by the Yassaris and made a second incision along her shoulder. "I thought of something that might help."

"You could've—" Her words choked off in a hiss as he began to squeeze along the sides of the cut. "Cursed ancestors, are you *trying* to torture me?"

"If that's what it takes," he said, sounding grim, "to force some of the poison out."

Dashi glanced down. A few black and green droplets oozed from the reopened wound, sliding on top of her blood like oil over water. The pain was intense, ratcheting up even more when Sevlin shifted his ministrations to her shoulder.

She hadn't even realized that curse words were slipping from her mouth until Sevlin's lips twitched unexpectedly. "I've never heard that one before. You should learn Yassari for when you cross paths with them next."

"You could...teach me," she panted.

He winked. "I know all the best curse words."

Sevlin winking! Her mind reeled from the incongruity of it. She knew he was trying to distract her from the pain wending its way up her arm, but it was still a relief to go along with it.

"How is it you speak Karakalese so well?" she found herself asking.

"Many torturous hours sitting across from a Karak tutor."

"And a Yassari one?"

He nodded, lips pressed together in concentration.

"And a Thracedonian one as well, I assume." She said this last part in Thracedonian, though the pain forced her to break off with a gasp.

The right side of his mouth lifted, coming dangerously close to a smile, but he didn't look up. "But of course." He switched languages easily. "Just as I assume you *didn't* learn from tutors."

"But of course," she mimicked. "Guardsmen, gamblers and bandits, only the best of tutors for me."

"Thracedon's drunks were busy, I suppose?" He made another incision—above her elbow, this time—and Dashi clawed at the dirt with her good hand. "And whose company did you prefer: the guardsman's, the gambler's, or the bandit's?"

His Thracedonian was very good. Grammatically proper and exactingly pronounced, like his Karakalese. She had no doubt he knew more than she did. Granted, he'd stick out as a noble to anyone who heard him, but he *was* one.

"Well, a lot of the guardsmen were *also* gamblers," she said, then yelped, instinctively leaning away from him as he pressed a different spot. "It's what we did to pass the time while we waited to shoot at bandits." Dashi wiped a line of sweat from her forehead, trying to focus on the conversation, on the mound, on anything but her arm. "We did capture some bandits on occasion though, and I sat in front of their cells for hours talking to them. I was told my effort to learn Thracedonian was a punishment in and of itself."

This made Sevlin glance up. "Are you saying *you* were a guard? Was this before or after you stole the boots from the Yassari caravan?"

"During."

He stopped pressing on her arm and Dashi's shoulders went slack with relief. On the other side of the temple, the mist curled around the treetops, making the needles quiver.

"Do you think that actually helped?" Dashi asked. She eyed the tinge that seeped outward from the green and black lines, evidence of the poison dissipating into her muscle tissue.

"Some of the poison came out." His voice was even. "But there are other places where it has...solidified and no amount of pressure or heat seems to be able to dislodge it." He took Dashi's hand and positioned her fingers over a particularly dark green line on her bicep. It was hard, a splinter stuck inside her vein.

"Maybe I bought you some extra time," he said, but his hand, still covering hers, gave a little squeeze and Dashi knew that he was lying.

Dawn found them hovering at the edge of the amphitheater, while Dashi carefully tapped each of the steps. In the bright day, she could finally feel the looming adventure, starting at the crown of her head and ticking down through her bones. It pushed back, slightly, against the fatigue that dragged at her and made her forget about her icy limb. Despite Sevlin's efforts, there had been no improvement in her arm, at least as far as Dashi could tell. The green and black lines continued to climb her in subcutaneous vines, slithering over her scalp beneath the cover of her hair.

Extra time, Sevlin had said. *Will it be enough to get out of the taiga,* Dashi wondered. *If I can just see Idree again*—she squashed the thought before it got out of hand. Hope could be dangerous that way.

"Do you think they did public stitchings here?" Sevlin asked, eying the terraced steps of the amphitheater.

There was an altar in the center, directly in front of the rounded entrance to the mound, though no offerings remained. Dashi grimaced; she couldn't imagine *wanting* to watch that. Then again, if the stitching was done in public, at least everyone would know who was being stitched, and whether it was being done voluntarily.

"Maybe this is where they unveiled the survivors," she said. "The khan should have made his new city here. It already has a built-in place to showcase his spectacles."

He snorted. "He made do just fine with New Osb."

Dashi moved cautiously toward the gaping hole that was the mound's entrance.

"This ruin seems more accessible than the last one," Sevlin said from behind her.

"Might not be a good thing.

No lock. No door. No antechamber. Just a cave-like opening in the mound's resplendent facade.

She stopped just in front, studying the shadows for a hint as to what they would face. A slight breath stirred her hair: the mound exhaling. Behind her, Sevlin lit the lantern.

He held it up. "I'll—"

"No," she said. "I should go first." When he didn't respond, she pushed on. "One of us *has* to make it out with the seamripper, Sevlin, and that's more likely to be you than it is me."

Sevlin frowned, but let her take the lantern and peer inside the mound. Its light barely penetrated the darkness and what it revealed was uninspired, especially by Purek architectural standards. The floor was dirt, as were the rounded walls and the ceiling. There was no art. No tapestries. No tile work. Dashi slid an uneasy glance over her shoulder at Sevlin, but if he was bothered he didn't show it. His eyes reflected the lantern light, burning at her.

She ventured a little farther, jabbing at the ground with her staff and waiting for a response from the mound. No traps so far. Maybe this was a dummy entrance? *Steady*, she told herself. *There's no reason to think you've made a mistake...yet.*

If the mound was indeed a temple, as she'd assumed, it would have been considered a sacred area, open only to sanctioned officials and acolytes. Sacred areas always had something to keep out the curious and the rebellious: a door, at minimum. Usually *several* doors, all locked. She'd never seen one with an entrance gaping open to the world.

So either this mound wasn't a temple, or they were in a dummy entrance, or—

"Down!" she shouted, whirling to yank Sevlin toward the floor.

Chapter 39

Dashi wasn't heavy enough to pull him down, but Sevlin's instincts were good. He moved with her as a spiked ball, swinging on a sudden rush of air, swiped at their heads. Dashi landed with her back against the wall and Sevlin pressed against her front. The ball swung past twice more, a hound searching for a lost scent, before finally rising with a groan back into the ceiling where it had been hidden.

Neither of them moved. Sevlin was wrapped partially around her, his leg over hers, his arm curled over their heads. Dashi's heart thundered in her ears, every nerve in her body alert to the next danger. The chill of the wall drew goose bumps along her shoulder blades and Sevlin's deel made soft brushing sounds with each breath he drew. The lantern was still in her hand, pressed tightly between them so that heat bloomed against her stomach.

"That was…" Dashi exhaled, moving Sevlin's arm where it rested on top of her.

Her thoughts went to the night she'd escaped Negan's men, how Sevlin had been warm against her back as they'd ridden away. Silence reigned in the passage for a moment. He was watching her intently, eyes half-lidded like they had been when he'd questioned her in his rooms.

She sat up, shedding his arm like an unwanted skin. "Don't do that again," she said, her voice coming out strangled. "You can try to save me from the poison all you want, but don't try to save me in here. You're the one who needs to make it out."

"I was just trying to get as close to the wall as I could," he said, in that unfailingly neutral tone.

The lantern's adjustment knob had gotten bumped in the fracas, making the flame burn much too high, though its sturdy construction had saved it from any real harm. Dashi adjusted the wick, fiddling with the knob for a few moments longer than necessary. When she looked up, it wasn't at Sevlin but forward, at the passageway.

"Back there, with that trap," Sevlin began, "how did you know which side was safe?"

They'd been walking along the right side of the entrance, but she'd pulled them down against the opposite wall.

Dashi hitched a shoulder up. "My friend Baris used to say if a fight went well, it was because he was skilled. If it didn't, well, that was plain bad luck."

The words, originally meant as a quip, brought to mind Baris' death—of his last fight and the bad luck inherent therein. She thought of the threads of green and black working their way over her. Ese had said he thought she had a part to play in the drama unfolding around the needle. In *history*. But maybe she didn't. Maybe it was all coincidence, not connection. Luck, not fate. *Bad luck.*

The passageway transformed from black to gray and the sound of their steps changed, echoing instead of dying. They were nearing a large room. One with windows, judging by the light. *Careful*, she thought, bringing her mind back to the task at hand. *This is exactly where—*

There was a whoosh of air as her staff, angled a few steps in front of her, hit something hidden beneath the dirt. An arrow twanged into the wall.

They reached the mound's main room without further incident. Gray light filtered through the rounded ceiling, illuminating four large pools, perfectly round and inlaid with colorful tile. Statues lined the edges of the room, some free-standing, while others were displayed on pedestals. The packed earth was replaced by patterned wood on the floors and elaborate murals on the walls. At the back of the room, on a raised platform, she could make out a fifth pool, an elaborate altar, and what appeared to be a row of thrones.

Dashi glanced up. The windows were fitted with opalescent panes, perfectly disguised against the mound's elaborate exterior. Judging by the lack of deterioration in the room, the panes had remained weather-proof.

Sevlin stopped next to her. "More pools."

"Hopefully these are empty."

His arm wasn't touching hers, but her skin tingled anyway, conscious of the small space separating them. She did her best not to notice, but the scent of him—saddle and sword, sweat and the outdoors—came to her: a heady, distracting miasma.

After a careful scan of the floor, Dashi approached the closest pool, her sword in her uninjured hand as she peered over the edge. It was deeper than she was tall and several times as wide. There was nothing inside, save a thick layer of dust. She tilted her head, examining the decorative tile. Every small square was a work of art: a different design on each, all hand-painted in the same tones of green, blue, gold and white.

"There should be four pools, not five," she muttered.

Sevlin squinted, then nodded. "An even number. Balance."

"Right. Especially because these lower pools were probably used for ritual cleansing, so it would be especially important for them to be sanctified."

"So we should start at the extra pool?"

"Let's look at the walls first," she sighed. "The highest likelihood of traps is on that dais and I'd like to make sure there is nothing interesting on this level first."

"We should probably stay close to one another," Sevlin said. "Just in case there are moving walls in this temple."

"Good point."

The murals proved to be repeats of everything they'd seen in the first mound. Dashi had expected repetition—the Pureks were nothing if not predictable when it came to nature motifs—but she'd also anticipated *some* differences.

"This has to be the same artist," Sevlin said. "This woman looks identical to the traveler in the other mound."

"*Everything* looks identical. Right down to the leaves." Dashi bent low to examine the glittering veins of each bush: real gold paint.

Another part of the wall was covered in relief carvings of the ancient khagans, each posed in a way that was characteristic of their reign. She recognized more than one, including the infamous Khagan Nuray, the last khagan before the Purek empire fell. Dashi ran her fingers over every line and curve but found no hidden wire triggers.

"I can't believe there's nothing here," she muttered, staring into Khagan Nuray's stony eyes. The sculptor had managed to capture some of the khagan's haughty fire, which Dashi had glimpsed in her mist-driven hallucination. Nuray glared at Dashi down the line of her nose.

"Are you—" She looked at Sevlin and her question faltered. For a moment it looked like his lips had been moving, like he'd been reading the inscriptions in ancient Purek.

"Ready to search the dais?" He asked.

"Yes."

They turned their attention to the dais, running their hands over the wood at the front of it.

"Pay special attention to joints and irregularities," Dashi warned.

Nothing moved. Nothing clicked. Nothing sounded hollow. Deeming it safe, she pulled herself onto the edge of the dais and slowly approached the back wall, checking each footfall as she went.

Dashi gave the fifth pool a cursory look, mostly to make sure there was nothing living inside, then passed the thrones in favor of the mural on the back wall. Sevlin's footsteps followed in her wake. The image was of the same young woman from the previous series of murals, only this time she was kneeling beside a silvery body of water—a pond, Dashi thought, noting the apparent lack of current—with her hands outstretched. One arm was reddened and injured. Her hand cupped the silvery water like she'd meant to drink it, but had instead decided to let it dribble down her wrist and fingers to soothe her injuries. In her other hand, she held a small, hooked seamripper. Unlike the needle, the seamripper was silver. *Opposites*, Dashi thought.

The perspective of *this* mural was different, she noticed. The others had depicted an entire panorama, from detailed foreground to expansive, scenic background. This one was focused entirely on the woman. Other than the silvery water, everything around her was dark and shadowy.

There was another difference, too: the young woman's attire and mien had changed completely from the earlier murals. Her pack had been replaced by a sword and she wore a leather cuirass over her tunic now. A circlet of entwined roses wrapped around her head, the blooms painted in extravagant reds and yellows that drew the viewer's eye immediately. Smaller splashes of red—blood from the bite of thorns into flesh—tracked down her temples and neck.

Sevlin stopped beside Dashi. "Now she's dressed like the statue in the other mound. She's even got the same crown."

"The statue had scars all over."

"Maybe life is still waiting to mete them out."

"That's harsh."

He shrugged. "So is life, at times."

A fair point, especially coming from someone already scarred.

Dashi tipped her head back, taking in the woman's appearance. "The woman's village was burned—*years* ago, if her appearance is any guide—so she left and found the seamripper and then...got suited up for battle?" The sword looked like a masterpiece, thick and deadly with a gem-studded handle. "Maybe she's the hero from the poem, the one who 'rises as the tyrant schemes.' Maybe the sword and the cuirass come with the seamripper so whoever finds it is ready to fight."

"She looks taller than you," Sevlin observed, dry-voiced. "I'm not sure her effects would fit."

Dashi flicked him an annoyed glance. "I didn't say I wanted them."

"You didn't need to. What happened to her companion? He was in all the other paintings."

"Doesn't bode well for you."

"Now who's being harsh?"

"She doesn't look too upset about him."

"No," Sevlin said slowly. "Look at her eyes. She's sad. I think we're supposed to believe him lost."

Dashi's hands drummed her thighs. "This is all speculation. And whether she is a past wielder of the seamripper or an archetype of all wielders, none of this tells us *where* it is."

Sevlin nodded but continued his appraisal of the mural.

Dashi turned to the thrones at the front of the dais. There were four of them, big wooden affairs with armrests carved like animals and backs decorated with different celestial bodies: a sun, a moon, a star, a comet. She bent over, examining them without touching. The wooden seats were smooth from use, almost begging to be sat in and tried for size, but Dashi knew better than to play the usurper. One of them was surely rigged with a trap.

"When you're done looking at the mural, bring the lantern over so we can examine these carvings," she said. *Maybe there's a clue in the carvings or*—but the thought broke off as her left hand spasmed, sending the staff she carried clattering to the ground. Sevlin spun around, alarm etched in his shoulders, but she waved him away.

"I just dropped it."

She turned her back to him, massaging her hand. *Not now.* The fifth pool waited in front of her, noticeably plainer than the ones on the lower level. Those were all intricate affairs, with hand-painted tiles and small statuettes adorning their low walls. There were no statues around the fifth pool, and no hand-painted designs on the outside. There was, however, water inside: so still and clear that she could see straight to the bottom. *No giant beasts, at least.*

Sevlin came over, holding the lantern high so that its light encompassed her. "Which throne should we look at first?"

Dashi didn't answer. She was staring hard at the bottom of the pool. The water turned the light back at her, trying to cover its tracks, but she wasn't deterred. She leaned to one side, searching for another glimpse. There it was: a trace of silver paint along the bottom, invisible unless the lantern light caught it just so.

"Like a wheel," Dashi murmured.

"What?" Sevlin shifted closer, also staring down.

She pointed to the iridescent writing, momentarily forgetting her suspicion that he could read Purek. "It says '*like a wheel.*'"

"It's quoting the poem you translated?"

"I think it's telling us to jump."

"Jump...into the pool?"

In answer, Dashi leaned over the edge and tapped the bottom with the stick. Even beneath the water, it sounded hollow. "'*Like a wheel on its axle spins,*' is what the poem says. What if the pool bottom spins on an axle too? The other mound had a hidden lower level. Maybe this one does as well."

"The lower level in the other mound was filled with giant spiders."

Dashi swung one leg over the side.

"Wait." Sevlin grabbed her shoulder. "You're just going to jump in?"

"That's what it's telling me to do, so…" She shrugged. The water didn't look too deep. She'd have to swim down a little, but—

Sevlin sat on the wall beside her.

"Wait, *you* can't jump in."

"That's what it's telling me to do," he said, making his voice a little higher so she'd know he was mimicking her.

"The pack will get wet."

"What's left of our food is already wrapped in oilskin. That'll keep it for a bit. The rest can dry." He opened the lantern door and blew the flame out, covering them in shadow while he stowed it in its oilskin bag. Light still filtered in through the mound's windows, but it was milky and weak by comparison. "Besides, what happens if you're right and there's—wait, what *do* you think is down there?"

"Um…"

Sevlin made an exasperated noise. "Well, whatever it is, I don't want to be separated."

She hesitated, then nodded.

The water wasn't as cold as the stream Dashi had washed in but almost. Untouched by the sun and hidden from fresh air, it had a dank taste that twisted Dashi's mouth. She kicked hard, angling downward with her arms outstretched in the liquid darkness.

Her fingers touched the smooth bottom of the pool, bumping over Sevlin's searching hands in a brief flash of warm, solid flesh. She found the writing on the bottom—a slightly rougher surface owing to the type of paint used—and traveled it like a road, running her thumb and forefinger along either side of the symbols.

She noticed nothing on the first pass, so she started over, lungs burning. Her fingers paused, then backtracked, trying to find the anomaly she'd just passed over: a hairline crack, running the length of one of the characters. She touched Sevlin's arm, bringing his attention to her, then put her hands on either side of the crack and pushed. The bottom of the pool lurched open, dropping Dashi, Sevlin, and a seemingly inexhaustible quantity of water into the darkness below.

Chapter 40

Dashi hit the ground with a thud that left her gasping for air. Flat on her back, she opened her eyes to see a dimly lit cylinder overhead: the walls of the pool, viewed from below. Then the pool's false floor rolled back into place, a rapid mechanical contortion that ended in total darkness.

"I've got it," Sevlin muttered from somewhere to her left.

Light flared, bringing to life the small stone chamber in which they'd landed. The water from the pool puddled around them, combining with dust and ancestors-only-knew-what to make a black, potent-smelling mud. A low doorway led into the dark.

"At least we know the consul and her searchers didn't make it here yet," Sevlin said, eying the carpet of dust.

"Just us and the traps." Dashi thought of the mural with the burned village and dead animals. "I don't think priests and acolytes came this way either, not like in the last temple. If the seamripper is to be used by the hero against the tyrant, then only desperate people have come this way before."

She sat up gingerly, clutching her left arm to her side. It had begun to spasm in earnest just before she jumped and now, despite her grasp, her hand jigged back and forth, limp fingers drawing lines in the black mud. Dashi kept her eyes on the other end of the chamber; it seemed like the safest place to look.

Sevlin lifted the lantern. His eyes touched her arm and then he set it back down with a clunk.

"Dashi."

The way he said her name—voice caressing the syllables, the unexpected spark in her chest—pulled Dashi's eyes to him as he scooted closer, his left arm pressing against her right. He didn't say anything else, but her name, that single time, was enough. The sound reverberated while her arm shook itself out, until she could hear all the other, unsaid things as well: *you're not alone, I'm here.*

When the fit was over and her arm hung limply from her shoulder, they stayed sitting. Sevlin raised his hand and traced a finger down the side of her neck, over the knotty lines of black and green.

"The spasms are coming closer together," he said.

Dashi nodded. Spots danced before her eyes and she couldn't tell if it was the interplay of lantern and shadow or something worse. She got to her feet, making sure she moved steadily in front of Sevlin.

"Let's go," she said briskly. "Those traps won't spring themselves."

Sevlin made a sound that was partly annoyed, partly fond as he picked up the lantern, but she could feel his gaze, assessing and concerned, as they started walking.

Despite Dashi's quip, they encountered no traps. No turns, even. The passage stayed level and was otherwise unremarkable, at least for a subterranean walk from an abandoned ruin. When they finally reached a split, it was almost startling: a set of stairs spiraled up to the right, while a second passage peeled off to the left, sloping downward. Tracks crisscrossed the floor, a dusty record of everything that had passed over it, most of which seemed to fall into the category of giant insects. Sevlin let out a low curse.

Dashi knelt beside the tracks of a giant ant, mapping its contours with her right hand—her left still carried an alien numbness from the spasms.

The scars on her back and side tingled as soon as she touched the place it had stepped.

"I vote for going up the stairs, not down into the ant lair," Sevlin said. "The ants have been stalking us since we entered the taiga. No point in making it too easy for them."

"I think stalking is a bit of an exaggeration." Dashi touched another ant track, shivering when her scars sang.

"It snapped the line and dropped me into the river."

"It saved you too. If you'd stayed on that rope, the shrikes would've plucked you like a berry from a bush."

"A lovely analogy." Sevlin glanced at her. "I know the taiga ants saved you last time, but we're far away from those ants."

"*These* ants saved us too, the night that the giant pigs stampeded through. I was so tired and I dozed off on watch," she said, keeping her eyes on the tracks. It was an inexcusable lapse, one that exposed them to all manner of dangers. "An ant woke me, then went up the rocks, but before it did, it looked at me and *waited*, like it wanted me to follow."

She straightened to find Sevlin studying her. Or, at least, he was turned in her direction. The flickering shadows made it difficult to know exactly where those pale eyes rested, though she could tell what he was thinking.

"You complimented me on shepherding us out of danger," she continued, answering the unspoken question. "I was...embarrassed to tell you that I hadn't. I'm telling you now because I don't think the ants should factor into deciding which way to go. The one that came into our camp could have easily killed us, just like the ant that was following us beside the river. It didn't ambush you. It didn't need to; it could have overpowered us outright."

"Alright," he said, after a beat. "We're back to the original question, then: which way?" He glanced at the stairs. "There were mountains on the other side of the valley, behind the mound temple. We could be beneath them by now."

"You think the stairs lead to the top?"

"In the mural, the road led the travelers to the mountains. "

"To a skull too."

Sevlin spread his hands, palms up, as if to say he'd still choose a skull over giant taiga ants.

"I don't disagree," Dashi said, considering the stairs. "It makes a sort of strange sense. The ruins we've been to have both been in earthen mounds and what is a mountain but a giant version of the same thing?"

It was interesting, she thought, as they started up the stairs, the way their collective decision-making ebbed and flowed. Sometimes they bickered over nothing. Other times, they reached a decision without much need for words at all.

"Tripwires," she murmured.

"I'm looking."

The air was close around them, compressed and tight in what was, essentially, a vertical tunnel. Her breath came harder and faster as she climbed. Her pulse thundered in her head.

They climbed until Dashi's legs became embers and her lungs burned like flames. Abruptly, Sevlin halted, swinging his pack around to extract the waterskin. He took a swig, before handing it to Dashi.

She measured her sip. "We're running low."

Low, oh, oh. Her voice ricocheted off the surrounding rock.

Sevlin tapped the lantern. "On this too."

Dashi glanced upward, though she could see nothing past the turn in the spiral staircase. "At least we're going up instead of down. The stairs will run out of mountain sooner or later."

The possibility of adventure pulled at her, the promise of a great ruin, beautifully preserved and waiting for discovery. What treasures could the Pureks have left here? But after another hour of upward toil, she lost track of everything except the fickle lantern light and the steady tramp of their boots. Her throat was a steady burn and her left arm felt distant from the rest of her. After a short eternity, they reached an arched doorway with a small, circular room on the other side. Dashi stopped beside Sevlin on the top stair, peering through the doorway without entering.

The circular room was empty. Except for a second door, formed from a single slab of stone, opposite them, it was plain. There was an inscription chiseled along the lintel, but Dashi was too far away to read it.

"The floor looks clear," Sevlin observed.

"That's—"

"What worries you. I know."

Dashi leaned forward to pound the floor with her staff. When nothing shot or stabbed at them, she glanced up at Sevlin. He shrugged.

She stepped into the room, Sevlin a shadow behind her, and made her way to the stone door. The inscription above it was, for once, a simple translation.

"'*Walk upon the air*,'" Dashi murmured. "I have no idea what that means."

Sevlin drew his sword and grasped the handle of the door. "Ready?"

She stepped aside, her nod tense.

When Sevlin lifted the latch, however, the door didn't open. Instead, the walls of the room lurched around them, whirling fluidly, a molded cylinder rotating around a spindle. The door handle jerked from Sevlin's hand. He and Dashi stumbled backward, instinctively moving to the center of the room and as far as possible from the moving walls. When everything stilled seconds later, the stone door was fifteen paces to the left of where it had been. Dashed turned to look at the arched doorway they'd come through and swore. It had moved left too, coming to rest in front of a solid wall of rock. There was no way back.

They exchanged a look. Sevlin nodded at the handle of the stone door.

"Again?" he asked.

"I don't see much choice."

This time, the door flew open, hitting the wall with a crack. Dashi tensed, but nothing came through the doorway, save a blast of icy air and blinding light.

"What is it?" she asked, squinting against the onslaught. The air was fresh, carrying the smell of new snow.

"A cliff." Sevlin's hand clung to the door frame. "You can take four, maybe five steps out the door. Then there's nothing."

"There has to be a path, a door, *something*."

The splash of colors was almost magnetic after the endless dark stairs: slate gray and white, the blue of a clear sky, and, far below, a mishmash of green, black and brown. As Sevlin had said, the ledge was short and not much wider than her feet.

"There must be something else," Dashi said again.

They couldn't have come all this way only to discover a dead end. Then, she saw it: a ledge, just out of reach. There were more after that, all so thin that they could barely be differentiated from the cliff face on which they hung. All spaced out for precarious leaps. All with nothing beneath them.

"This is insanity," Sevlin muttered, noticing it at the same time. "Sadistic."

Dashi grunted an assent. That was the Pureks, alright. She took a deep breath.

Sevlin's arm shot out, blocking her way. "What are you about to do?"

"The only thing we can do."

He shook his head. "There has to be a way to reverse the spin of the walls so that we can access the stairs again."

"There won't be," Dashi predicted. "Not from in here anyway. It'll have to be done from the outside, just like in the temple: we couldn't move the wall and get back to Idree until we'd beaten all of the Purek's obstacles."

"You can still try." Sevlin was looking through his pack, belting the grappling hook to his waist.

"I think it'll end up being—wait, what do you mean *I* can try?"

"You work on regaining access to the stairs. I'll try to make it over the ledges."

"If I *do* open the stairs back up, then you won't be able to get back to me."

The ledges dropped in height as they went. Jumping down from ledge to ledge was bad enough, but reversing course and jumping *up* would be nearly impossible. Dashi stopped speaking as Sevlin's intention settled over her. He didn't think she could reopen the stairs. And he didn't care.

"You'll have to work quickly," Sevlin was saying, still looking at his pack. "I have the grappling hook. If you can find a way back to the stairs before I've gotten too far, I can use it to climb back up."

"It would be quicker if both of us inspected the walls," she said, just to see what he'd say.

"Maybe, but if the walls can't be reversed from in here, then one of us should be working on another way out."

"Then maybe *I* should go on the ledges. I'm lighter."

"You're more familiar with Purek craftsmanship." His voice was a bit too decisive, his answer a little too quick.

Something unfolded in Dashi, slow and deliberate. There was anger, though she knew what Sevlin would say if she voiced it: that she was injured, weakened, that he had a better chance of making it over the ledges. More than anything else, however, there was determination, cool and hard as ice. She would use every minute she had left to try to help Idree. She would *never* let the Yassaris rip this final adventure from her grasp. If Sevlin thought she would stay back while he went after the seamripper, then he had gravely misestimated her.

There was another thing he was wrong about too. He'd said the cliff's edge could be reached in four or five steps, but Dashi covered it in three, her feet running out of ground before Sevlin even realized what was happening.

He yelled but the wind ripped his words away before they reached her. It ripped at her hair and clothes too, as she flew through the air toward the first rock ledge.

Chapter 41

R ock rammed into Dashi's gut, knocking the breath from her lungs. The silver cup Sevlin had salvaged for her clanged against it, announcing her arrival like a small gong. Not her most graceful landing, but it was done. Dashi stood, sliding the cup along her sash until it was at the small of her back, where it wouldn't get in the way. She did the same with her sword belt, re-fastening it across her back.

She inched forward, toes over the edge. There was no running start to be had now. Instead, she could only rock her arms, then push with every muscle in her legs. She slammed against the next sliver of rock, the impact jolting through her forearms. Bracing her feet against the cliff face, she scrambled the rest of the way onto the second ledge.

The third ledge was lower than the first two, a straight drop of nearly twice her height. Reaching it wouldn't be the difficult part; not over-shooting it would be. The ledges felt minuscule compared to the towering cliff on one side and the vast space on the other, like someone had tacked a few boards to a wall and expected them to be used in lieu of stairs. Dashi let her gaze shift to the patchwork of greens and browns far below. The sense of distance was dizzying.

No, she scolded herself, grabbing the rock to counteract her vertigo. *It's like doing a flip off Spit's back. Look up, not at the rushing ground. Never focus on the fall.* Dashi took a deep breath, ignoring the spots in her vision and the throbbing in her forearm. Then she stepped off.

Her aim was true, but the ledge arrived faster than she'd anticipated, and her legs buckled with the sooner-than-expected impact. Her right hand flailed in the air, while her left clawed at the rock, searching for a handhold that wouldn't come in time. It was her boots that stayed stubbornly rooted to the hewn stone. A fist-sized piece of rock broke off behind her heel and tumbled into the colorful abyss. Her fingers clung to a divot in the cliff face and she pressed back against the cliff, chest heaving. A glance upward confirmed that she was past the point of returning. Even with the Yassari boots, she could not slither up a sheer rock face.

No reason to go back anyway. The seamripper is in front of you.

The next ledge was higher, requiring more effort from her legs, which were already tired from climbing so many stairs. Her feet fell just short of the mark, leaving her knees and shins to take the impact of the landing. Dashi grabbed the edge to steady herself, but the fingers on her numb hand failed to close. She tilted toward the open air, her hand gaping uselessly, a listing vessel with no anchor. Gritting her teeth, she clenched every muscle in her right arm, willing herself to stay centered on the ledge. Panting, she leaned forward until her forehead touched cold granite, shaking out her left hand as if that would help her.

The scrape of metal on stone reached her ears and she looked back. Sevlin was poised on the second ledge, about to make the long drop to the third one. Dashi opened her mouth, torn between shouting a warning and encouragement. Either way, it was too late. He was already dropping through the air.

Sevlin's feet hit the ledge, his arms outstretched for balance as a thunderous crack rent the air, audible even over the howl of the wind. For a moment, time seemed to stick, preserving the scene in Dashi's mind: Sevlin's face, avid with concentration, his legs perfectly bent to absorb the impact of his fall. Only the air moved, vibrating the tail of his deel, swinging the rope coiled at his waist.

Then, a section of the ledge disintegrated and Sevlin tipped backward, disappearing along with it.

Chapter 42

"Sevlin!"

Dashi was backtracking, retracing her jump to the previous ledge before she'd thought it through. She landed hard, already pushing to her feet for the next leap before she stopped herself. There was nowhere to go. Rock dust was gusting off the broken ledge, like smoke over a building fire. Dashi squinted. Was there something solid there? Legs, kicking? A hand, gripping the rock?

Somehow, Sevlin had caught the tip of the ledge with one hand. Still rocked by momentum, his body swung over open air. The pack hung from his shoulders, weighing him down further. Dashi crouched on her ledge, fingers digging into unyielding stone. She couldn't make the jump onto his ledge. She'd land practically on top of him and she doubted the remaining piece of rock could support them both anyway.

She couldn't save him; she could only watch to see if he saved himself. A blast of wind caught his pack, rocking him hard, and Dashi saw Sevlin drop a notch.

"Cut the pack!" The wind spit the words back in her face, but Sevlin must have had the same thought because a moment later the pack plunged toward the quilt of colors below.

Dashi watched it go: their food and medical supplies; water; extra clothes; the remaining bedroll. When she looked back, Sevlin was pulling himself onto the crumbling ledge. Dashi didn't hesitate; having retraced her jump onto the ledge just in front of his, she was now blocking his escape. She leaped forward, urgency lending strength to her flagging muscles.

They continued in this manner until Dashi lost count: a series of leaps, performed first by one, then the other; some easy, some managed only by luck and tenacity. Dashi's jumps were getting worse, her landings more bone-jarring. It wasn't just tired muscles and her weakened arm, though those were both factors. The ledges were spaced farther apart. The change was incremental, so slight she hardly noticed at first, but after another landing in which she barely pulled herself onto the ledge, she could ignore it no longer. Pain shot through her ribs from where she'd slammed onto her chest. A smear of red marked the place where her fingertips, worn bloody, touched the rock.

"*Pureks.*" She muttered it like a curse.

The next ledge looked to be no further than the others, but Dashi wasn't fooled. The cliff was angled here, meaning she would be jumping into the wind. It also meant that she couldn't see past the next ledge. How many more leaps could she make? Her skin was pulled tight from the wind. She licked her lips, trying to moisten them with a tongue that was already dry. The thought of Sevlin's waterskin, gone forever, taunted her.

Toeing the end of the ledge, she rocked onto the balls of her feet, keeping her eyes on her destination. The rush of wind that came when she finally thrust herself forward was strong, twisting her shoulders and pushing her to one side. Her left arm rubbed against the rock face as she flew, pulling her backward like granite fingers on her sleeve.

She started dropping too soon. The ledge was too far away, a distant target when she hadn't drawn her bowstring back enough. Her arms stretched out, searching for something to stop her downward trajectory.

Cold rock banged into her fingertips and she clenched, barely managing to keep it from slipping away.

She hung from the ledge for a long moment, just as Sevlin had done, trying to pull herself up with muscles that were too tired to respond. She could feel herself slipping. Her left hand flopped open, too weak to grasp the ledge. Bracing her left foot against the rock wall, Dashi took a deep breath, searching for one last spark of strength. She swung her left arm up, grinding her elbow down onto the rock while simultaneously pushing with her left leg against the cliff. Her injured arm screamed at the pressure and bright blotches swam in her vision, but she managed to leverage herself high enough to adjust the grip of her right hand. She paused for a moment, her breath coming in hard rasps, then heaved herself the rest of the way up, flopping awkwardly onto her belly.

This ledge was much larger than the others, and Dashi could locate no place to jump next. She crawled forward, making room for Sevlin. He landed behind her a few minutes later, not making it all the way onto the ledge either, though his landing was a far surer thing than hers had been. Dashi could feel the anger rolling off him, the way the rock dust had billowed from the broken ledge. She'd been searching for clues while she caught her breath and now she used her index finger to trace a small crack in the rock face. It ran vertically from the ledge to a height just above her head. The side of a door? She pressed around the crack, her fingers searching for some kind of trigger point. Her face was so close to the rock that she could smell it, a slightly metallic tang mingled with fresh air. Without warning, a door opened, leaning forward on a bottom hinge, drawbridge-style. Dashi scooted back, wary.

There were symbols etched into the side of the doorway. Dashi mouthed the words to herself, sorting through the meanings before she said them aloud.

"Walk upon the stone," she said. "I wonder if that will be as perilous as walking upon the air."

"Throw yourself in and find out," Sevlin suggested in a flat voice. "That seems to be your preferred method of doing things."

"Whereas *your* preferred method is that I stay out of your way."

"Those are your words, not mine."

The wind howled past, buffeting Dashi angrily. She got to her feet, nearly under his nose. "What *are* your words, Sevlin? That you wanted me to stay behind so you could be the one to get the seamripper?" She knew it was an unfair accusation even as she made it.

"What I *wanted*, since you brought it up, is to not watch you jump off a cliff when I know you've been poisoned. What good would it have done Idree if you'd missed a ledge?" His light eyes flashed with some emotion, but his tone, like always, was even. "What would I have told her, Dashi? That I let you jump off a ledge when I knew you weren't at your strongest?"

"You don't *let* me do anything, Sevlin. I'm not your subject to command." She didn't deny his accusation of weakness, though she couldn't resist adding, "Lot of good your strength did. You came closer to falling than I did."

"A ledge collapsing beneath me doesn't negate the absurdity of what you did. There's brash and there's stupid, Dashi. Don't be the latter."

The word 'brash' stung her skin, working its way inside until it lodged in her bones, right beside the last time she'd heard it used: Ese's voice, threaded with sarcasm, quoting an intercepted missive from Altan. A coincidence or a connection?

The waterskin hadn't been lost with the pack after all; Sevlin had belted it to his waist along with the grappling hook before he'd leaped. He took a drink, then handed it to Dashi, his crisp movements conveying his annoyance without words.

She took a swig. The water was so cold it hurt her teeth. "Tell me, possessor of perfect strength, when you're ready to examine this room."

He looked at her for a long moment, then turned toward the doorway without saying anything.

The room was an empty square, hollowed out of solid stone. There was nothing overtly threatening about the space. She could see the silhouette of a door on the other side. It was closed, with no discernible handle or latch.

Narrow slits in the rock walls and ceiling kept the room from being too dark. *Almost as if the Pureks anticipated the difficulty of bringing a lantern across a series of ledges*, Dashi thought, studying the slits. Taken en masse, they made a pattern: rolling waves, which began at the top of the wall and stopped at about knee height.

"I have an idea," she said.

"Ah."

There was a bite to Sevlin's tone, but after Dashi explained her reasoning, he lay flat on his stomach and inched into the room beside her. As soon as their feet slid off the drawbridge-door, it snapped shut. The light coming from the patterned holes was suddenly blotted out, leaving them in complete darkness. Then Dashi heard what she'd been expecting: the hiss of projectiles overhead. Although she was well below the arrow holes, she pressed her face against the floor anyway. Sevlin's breath kissed her cheekbone.

The light returned as abruptly as it had fled.

Sevlin raised his head slightly. "Where did the arrows go?"

"They're perfectly lined up with the holes on the other side. No evidence to tip off the next intruder."

This close, Dashi could make out the individual hairs shading his jaw, could see the way the scar pulled at his cheek, making it gnarled and dark, a knot in an otherwise smooth piece of wood.

"What about the bodies?"

"Ah, that." Dashi pushed herself onto her elbows, still unable to pry her eyes from his face. "We should get going. A sweeper will be along to move anyone left behind."

"That sounds like an inspired invention," Sevlin said, getting to his feet. "The Pureks could teach the Yassaris a thing or two."

The door on the other side of the room chose that moment to crack open invitingly. Sevlin's expression would hardly have been called concerned on anyone else, but Dashi recognized the tilt to his lips.

"I agree," she said, putting the crook of her arm over her nose and mouth. The last time she and Sevlin had walked through an unlocked door, the room had been filled with treasure—and madness-inducing spores.

"Ready?" Sevlin asked, voice muffled. When she nodded, he shoved the door open, stepping to one side. Light blazed from the open doorway. After a moment, Dashi peeked around the corner.

The scene in front of them was scaled all wrong. Enormous, jagged walls towered on either side, creating a corridor that continued for a distance before eventually turning. No seams or joints marred the walls; it was solid, natural-looking rock, interrupted only by a border of carvings along the ground and a deep, chest-height groove that ran the length of both walls. The ground underfoot was covered in massive squares of stone, not the ornamental tile or small pavers that Dashi was accustomed to seeing in ruins. It looked like a hallway built for giants, albeit one with a ceiling of frigid blue sky.

Dashi lowered her arm from her face. They were standing in the doorway, perfectly poised between one danger and the next, when the door swept closed behind them, shoving them forward into the enormous corridor. From the other side of the door, a faint grating sound began.

Sevlin glanced at her. "The sweeper?"

Dashi nodded. "One time Baris and I had to shimmy up to a railing and hang there while it went below us." She tapped the toe of her boot on the first giant stone and, when nothing happened, transferred her full weight onto it.

Sevlin jerked his chin toward the two deeply-etched grooves that stretched the length of each wall. "Are we supposed to follow those?"

"That seems too obvious."

He narrowed his eyes at her.

She grinned. "Just telling you what my gut says."

Dashi moved to examine the scenes carved along the bottom of the walls: people, both important and mundane, and daily life, both rustic and urban, all with an overarching nature motif.

"What does your gut say about this?"

Dashi turned around to look at the doorway they'd just been standing in. The two deep grooves veered upward, continuing on a parallel but vertical trajectory until they blended with the towering walls. Sevlin, however, was examining a small section of writing etched in the stone beside the door.

Dashi translated slowly:

Walk upon the air; walk upon the stone
Follow nature's essence, toward the face of bone
Stride the invisible bridges; gaze the inscrutable pool
In three hours' time, the jaw descends; only lingers the fool

"The face of bone," Sevlin said. "Is that the skull from the mural?"

"I would think so." She grimaced. "That last line makes this poem a lot more ominous than the last—"

Sevlin's gaze locked on something overhead and his eyes widened, shattering his normally calm demeanor.

Dashi's gaze jerked upward. An enormous cylinder was hurtling down at them. It stretched from wall to wall, the entire width of the corridor, suspended on rods that fit neatly into the mysterious grooves Sevlin had puzzled over. In the split second before she turned to run, Dashi noticed something else: the glint of sunlight along the spikes that covered the cylinder's surface.

Chapter 43

The pound of Dashi's feet was lost beneath the thunder of the spiked cylinder. Sevlin was just ahead, his long legs eating up the distance. Desperate for a refuge, Dashi's eyes went past him to the end of the corridor, but it was long and escape seemed far away.

Part of the lefthand wall shifted, exposing a square of blackness.

"Sevlin!"

A spear, its barbed tip shining, flew through the air. Sevlin plunged to one side, almost falling to his knees to avoid the projectile. He was up and running again immediately, plunging toward the place where the corridor bent at a right angle. *Safety.* The grooves etched in both walls veered straight up before they reached the corner; the cylinder would follow the lines, unable to navigate the turn. She stole a glance over one shoulder. It was closer now, spikes glinting faster and faster with each revolution.

"Quickly, Dashi!" Sevlin shouted over his shoulder as he disappeared around the corner.

Almost there.

Her legs surged with desperation. Air brushed against her back as the cylinder closed in for the kill.

Five strides.

A spike snagged the end of her sash, ripping off a chunk of fabric.

Two.

Dashi hurled herself around the corner, almost bowling Sevlin over. She sagged against him, both of them falling against the rock wall. Pressing a hand against her side, she gasped for air, each exhalation reverberating down her spine. The growl of the cylinder grew muffled as the grooved track curved upward. Dashi peered around the corner. It looked even bigger now that she had the chance to properly study it. The cylinder slowed, pausing while momentum and gravity warred for control, then began to roll backward, gathering speed with its descent.

Dashi's breathing turned into coughing. She shot a panicked glance at the new corridor they'd entered, then relaxed: the walls were free of grooves. This corridor was shorter, ending in an intersection not far away. Red was spattered on her palm when she took it away from her mouth. She swiped it on the hem of her deel.

"It's a maze," Sevlin said, his eyes on the intersection. "I think."

"The Yassaris have these, don't they?" Dashi asked, her breathing restored.

"They make them out of bushes, I believe."

"Bushes?"

She eyed the towering stone walls. The tops were craggy and broken, like a giant had looked down and used his finger to scratch the maze into the surface of the mountain before wandering off. The job was technically complete but unpolished.

"That hardly sounds difficult," she said. "You could push your way through a wall whenever you wanted to change directions."

"Then you should find this maze to your liking. I doubt we'll be pushing through any walls here." Sevlin straightened. "In any case, the Yassaris use poisonous bushes."

She gave him a sharp look.

"I don't think it's the same thing. The plant you described was a vine."

There was a gash on his shoulder blade, where the spear had brushed past him. Twin ribbons of blood traced down the exposed patch of skin, ducking out of sight beneath his deel.

He nodded at her side, which she was still clutching. "Are you injured?"

"Landed badly on one of the ledges."

"You didn't say anything about it before."

She shrugged. "It's nothing that can be fixed. What would be the point in mentioning it?"

"Commiseration."

"*Your* ribs aren't injured. That would make it me complaining, not us commiserating. Besides," she said, "You'd just tell me it's my fault for not staying behind."

"True enough."

She exhaled a pained laugh, but her attention was on the walls. They were extraordinarily high—higher than anything she'd ever climbed—and there was a disconcerting lack of hand and footholds.

"Too high, too slick, too time-consuming," Sevlin pronounced, following her gaze. "We have a deadline."

"Three hours." She frowned up at the sun. "I remember."

They moved on, scanning for traps, and had just reached the intersection when Sevlin cried a warning.

"Move!" He dove to one side as a dark mouth opened in the wall ahead. Dashi followed, but the split second cost her. Pain lashed her side before she hit the ground.

She lay there for a moment, making sure the danger had dissipated before she sat up to inspect the damage. A cut on her thigh, showcased by a new tear in her pants, bled freely.

"Glass and shards of pottery," Sevlin said, poking through the detritus. There was a cut on his jaw and one on his tricep, where his deel had been sliced. Both oozed blood.

Dashi stared at the wall, which had closed soundlessly. "How are we triggering the traps? I haven't seen any tripwires or pressure plates. You checked where you stepped?"

He gave her a flat look without answering.

Her eyes turned toward the slabs of rock beneath their feet. "I need the water."

"There's not much," he said, but he unstrapped the waterskin and tossed it to her anyway. Squatting down, she poured a tiny puddle, no bigger than the palm of her hand. Sevlin watched from the adjacent slab, arms crossed.

Dashi took a step backward, then another. When she reached the edge of the slab, the edges of the puddle quivered and broke, running after her like a dog following its master. She shifted left, then right. The water trailed unerringly after her.

Dashi scowled at the tiny river. "The slab is so large I can't even feel it shift."

"We'll have to assume we could be stepping on a pressure plate at any moment. I'll watch one wall and you watch the other." Sevlin glanced at the sun, then back at the intersection: two corridors heading in opposite directions. "Which way?"

Each side of the intersection looked the same. Decorative borders lined each wall, but there were no grooves to indicate the presence of another spiked cylinder. Both corridors went straight for a short distance before bending out of sight. Dashi stooped to examine the intricate scenes etched near the floor: a man planting a row of crops; a family of deer grazing in a sunny glade; wolves crowded around the carcass of a stag; a fox curled in its den; birds flying over an empty field; a crowd watching the moon rise over a lake.

"The poem at the start of the maze," she said, "what did it say about following nature?"

"'Follow nature's essence, toward the face of bone.'" Sevlin was a few steps behind her, also perusing the designs. "But *all* of these scenes are about nature."

"I know. There must be something we're not thinking of."

"What if there *aren't* more clues? We followed clues to get here. Maybe we're supposed to navigate this maze like any other: by guesswork and luck."

Dashi shook her head. "That's not how the Pureks did things. They always leave clues."

Sevlin sighed. "What about this?" He pointed to the scene showing the moonrise over water. It was on the southern side of the intersection. "The poem said 'gaze the inscrutable pool.'"

"I don't—" Dashi began, then broke off in a fit of coughing.

"Do you feel short of breath when you're not coughing?" Sevlin asked when she was done.

Dashi looked away.

"I'll take that as a yes."

He tugged her deel aside with deft fingers, exposing her shoulder and collarbone to the bite of cold air. He didn't speak, just stood there looking down with a blank expression until Dashi gave in and looked too. The fingers of green and black were thicker now. She traced them with her good hand, finding hardened lines covering her shoulder blade and the curve of her breast.

"What if heating and pushing on it forced the poison deeper? Maybe..." Sevlin's voice was hushed and, for the first time, Dashi heard a trace of self-doubt there. "Maybe I made it worse."

"What if the adrenaline and exertion of the last day made it worse," she countered, pulling her deel closed. "Anyway, you *did* warn me that you weren't a healer."

Sevlin's eyebrows sank further. "Dashi…"

"We'll take the southern corridor," Dashi said with a decisiveness she did not feel. "I don't know if the scene with the moonlit lake is supposed to be the 'inscrutable pool' or not, but we need to make a decision and we don't have time to examine every carved scene in the maze. '*Only lingers the fool.*'"

Sevlin was silent as they set out and she couldn't tell if it was because he was brooding or simply being watchful. They followed the corridor for fifteen minutes without incident. This both relieved and worried Dashi. If the Pureks weren't trying to deter their progress, did that mean they'd chosen the wrong direction? The corridor turned left, then right, then left again, before spilling them out in front of a set of giant stairs, each one rising well above Dashi's head. The walls, still jagged and uneven, rose in tandem so that the stairs never seemed to approach the towering heights above them.

Sevlin unwound his grappling hook and tried it on the first stair, but the prongs didn't catch. He reeled it back without a word while Dashi eyed the high staircase with a sense of dread. Normally, such a climb would not have phased her, especially with the Yassari boots to assist, but she felt weak. She jumped anyway. Her left hand struggled to grasp what it could barely feel, but she managed to pull herself over the stair's edge. Three strides to the next stair, and then up again. And again, and again, until her breath was a saw blade, rasping against her throat on each inhale.

Hands on her knees, Dashi bent over, concentrating on feeding the hunger in her lungs. It felt like she was starving to death and, although there was food all around, she couldn't get it into her mouth.

"Do you want—"

"Don't...Sevlin."

"I was going to ask if you wanted some water," he finished in a mild voice.

"Oh." A pause while she gasped. "Yes."

He handed her the waterskin and she drank, shutting her eyes as it rushed down her throat, soothing the ache that went all the way to her chest.

"I was also going to ask if you wanted me to lift you to the next stair."

She handed him the waterskin. "You waited to ask that until I had a mouthful of water." She coughed, a hard, full-body movement that seared her chest.

"Risky, I know. You might have spit it all over me."

A dark window slid open in the wall. Dashi threw herself sideways, landing with her arms cradling her head, her legs curled up to protect her chest and stomach, as a blast rocked the corridor. She sat up, coughing because of the dust this time. Her injuries were slight, but Sevlin had been standing between her and the blast. His deel was lacerated. His side was plastered with cuts. The fabric began to darken with blood.

"How about this," Sevlin said, continuing the conversation like nothing had happened. His hand moved gingerly over a savage cut on his hip. "I boost you, then you pull me up after?"

"I know that's only a sop to my pride. *You* don't need *my* help." She stood, swiping her wrist across her mouth.

Seeing acquiescence written on her face, Sevlin bent so she could climb onto his shoulders. "Most people," he grunted, pushing her upward with a hand under each thigh, "enjoy having others to rely on, even when it's not strictly necessary."

The remaining portion of the staircase came easier with the two of them working as a team. The final step was a little higher than the others and its riser was concave, almost a cave. Even with Sevlin lifting her, it was a struggle to pull herself up, since there was nothing to brace her feet against. Dashi stood with a ragged inhalation. Her left arm felt oddly detached. Still, it seemed momentous somehow, grabbing Sevlin's hand to haul him up the final step, seeing the stairs they'd vanquished spread out over his shoulder.

Momentous, that is, until she turned around and looked at the four passageways they now had to choose from.

"I don't see any clues to differentiate one path from the next," Sevlin said. There weren't even any decorations etched into the stone.

"Maybe we overlooked something when we were running from the cylinder. Maybe one of those scrolls the consul took contained a clue that we're not privy to."

Sevlin heard the hesitation in her voice. "Or?"

She winced. "Or we're so lost in the maze that the Pureks have stopped bothering with pretense."

"We've used almost half our time."

"I know." Sunlight brushed tepidly against Dashi's face, but its apparent weakness didn't fool her. It was still the likely victor here. She considered the four paths before them. "Let's start with the right one. If it's a dead end or we can find something to eliminate it from consideration, we'll move on to the next one. If none of them work out, we'll go back to the original intersection."

The first corridor was barely wide enough for them to walk abreast. Its high sides cast deep, almost night-black shadows over the path, trailing a chill over her shoulders.

"This one is creepy," she murmured.

"Creepier than ruins with bodies?" Sevlin's voice, like hers, refused to rise above a whisper.

"The only reason there are no bodies here is that they fell off those ledges before they ever got to this point."

The drape of shadows might not have bothered her on another day, but right now...right now, she could feel the flaccidity of her arm. She could feel her heart stuttering in her chest, its beat too fast, too uneven. The shadows seemed portentous in that context, a visible manifestation of the darkness choking off her future.

"Sevlin, I..." It would be easier to say here, she thought, in the shadows. *I don't want to die. I want to see Idree again. I want to see* you *again.*

He stopped.

"What you said before, about how you care what happens to Idree. I hope..." Dashi cleared her throat. "If I'm not there to do it, you better have meant what you said." The last sentence came out fierce and low, part threat, part plea.

Sevlin's hand clasped her shoulder and, when she didn't move, he pulled her gently forward, until she was flush against him and his arms were around her. Still, she kept looking away, not wanting her face to be visible, not wanting to see his.

"I meant what I said, Dashi. I would have looked out for her had you died in the temple with Negan, before I even knew Idree was the seamstress. I would do the same for her now."

Dashi swallowed. "Thank you."

His breath stirred her hair. It was an invitation, she knew, unspoken but there nonetheless: an invitation to look up, to stare at this intimacy full in the face. She couldn't bring herself to do it. Instead, she thought of her mother, face pale with illness, waving frantically as she urged Dashi and Idree to leave her in the burning building. To look at Sevlin now, when she could feel death's stare between her shoulder blades, would be like that. She had no desire to gaze upon something that was about to be taken from her.

His warmth felt good, a balm applied to a gaping wound. It might not be enough to fix the extent of the injury, but in an immediate and visceral way, it was still a relief. That was why she distrusted it so much. The balm was a lie. Even without the time constraint set by the Purek's maze, she could not linger and enjoy the feeling of his arms. She could feel her body changing with each passing hour—disintegrating, weakening—and her remaining time needed to be spent helping Idree, not mooning over Sevlin.

Dashi stepped back, face still turned away, already missing the warmth and strength of him. Motioning vaguely at the featureless corridor, she said, "I don't like this. There are no scenes carved into the walls and no traps since the one on the stairs. If we don't see anything after this next turn, we should turn back."

If Sevlin thought the change of subject was awkward, he didn't show it. His face remained as inscrutable as ever as he nodded and started walking again.

The corridor bent hard to the right, then ended in a narrow cleft, its walls stretching toward the sky on all sides. There wasn't much light here, just enough to see three arched doorways in the stone walls.

Sevlin looked up at the narrow patch of sky, muttered something, then looked behind them. "I'm even not sure which way we're facing."

To a stranger, his voice would have been unemotional, but Dashi caught the strains just below the surface: offended, surprised, worried. Her gaze fixed on the wall directly in front of them. Where the other walls were craggy, this one had a scalloped, almost wave-like appearance.

She wasn't sure exactly what set her nerves humming, but the feeling of unease was there suddenly, a discordant tune that had her looking over her shoulder in search of the player. Perhaps it was a stirring in the air or a trembling of rock, so slight her conscious mind didn't even recognize it. Or maybe it was just an inkling that the Pureks wouldn't let them travel the maze so easily. The skin on the back of her neck tingled. *Breath of the ancestors.*

She edged back a step and her boot slid slightly, the way it had when she'd been skating on the water. Dashi dropped to her heels, touching the ground to confirm what her eyes couldn't see in the shadows. *Water.*

"Sevlin." Even now, with danger threading the air, the place seemed to suppress her normal voice. "Back down the stairs."

He was turning in a slow circle, matching her unease. "Why not one of these doorways?"

"Because..." Dashi took a step backward as the ground began to tremble. It was light at first, like the echo of galloping hooves, but the tremors grew quickly, reaching up through her legs. "Because all the passages at the top of the giant stairs lead here. And these doorways lead back to the stairs. This is all one gigantic dead end."

Her eyes finally caught the glint of water, tracing a path between her feet and the scalloped wall in front of them. A line had appeared in the center of the wall as it transformed itself into two gigantic doors, an egg slowly cracking open. Nothing living emerged from the crack, however, only water.

Chapter 44

The tremors became quakes, the ground jumping under Dashi's feet as she ran. Pain lanced through her knees as she stumbled and fell. Sevlin jerked her upward by one arm.

"Move!"

Her legs strained to keep up with him, each footfall harder and faster than the last. A boom sounded from behind them: the gate that held back the water had opened. The sound reverberated along the corridor walls and rattled in Dashi's teeth. Gravel and dust, suddenly freed from centuries of stasis, rained down on her.

Dashi dared a backward glance. The towering mass of water looked almost solid, bearing down on her from a height as tall as the corridor itself. It was only a moment's look, but it was still enough time for her to know, with absolute surety, that if the water caught her she would not survive. Swimming would be impossible. Skating with the Yassari boots was equally unlikely. She'd barely managed to stay afloat on the river; she didn't hold out much hope that she would be able to ride the roiling wave she'd just glimpsed. She could see the giant staircase. If she could reach it....

Sevlin was there already, bounding over the edge like a stag. Dashi burst out of the corridor at a dead run, just as water spewed from the other three corridors atop the giant staircase. She'd been right—the doorways in the cleft canyon *did* connect to the corridors at the top of the staircase—but there was no time for triumph.

She jumped.

Before her feet could land, Sevlin yanked her into the hollowed-out space beneath the top step. He pressed them against the inner corner and she knew he was hoping the angle of the wave would cause it to overshoot them.

There's too much water. We'll still be washed away.

The rock trembled as the full force of the wave broke over the top step. Suddenly, water was everywhere: filling the space between Dashi's fingers, pushing away the air she hadn't quite finished grabbing into her lungs. The undertow buffeted her body, threatening to lift her. Sevlin, pushed and pulled by the same forces, jostled against her.

She had noticed, before, that the Yassari boots seemed to respond to how she moved her feet. When her toes curled, the soles of the boots mimicked the motion, clinging to whatever she was climbing. When her feet flexed, pushing against the boots' innards, the soles released their grip, letting her move freely. Now, Dashi channeled all of her concentration into communicating with the boots, if that's what it could be called. Her toes splayed and curled against the inside of the boot, clenching so hard that her feet cramped.

No, she said to her feet—to the boots—when they tried to skate to the water's surface. *Hold on.* She'd been clutching the stone wall of the staircase, but her weakened hand lost its grip almost immediately. She ground her right hand tighter, but the current ripped it loose. There was a spear of pain as something—Skin? A fingernail?—ripped away with it.

Hold on. Dashi swayed with the water's movement, anchored only by her boots, an aquatic weed caught in a current that was trying to uproot it. Sevlin was unmoored next to her; she could feel the water trying to drag him away. She wrapped her arms around him and squeezed.

Her lungs were a conflagration, burning hot despite the lack of oxygen. Dashi choked down the urge to breathe.

Hold on. Hold on.

Abruptly, the water receded. Dashi dragged in something that was half breath, half cough, leaning against the wall as her lungs convulsed. She shook the hair from her eyes just in time to see the frothy tail of the wave disappearing into a chasm that had opened at the bottom of the staircase. The floor closed silently, leaving only the stone, gleaming dully in front of her, and her wet clothes, to bear witness to what had happened.

Sevlin, half reclined against her side, said something, but her ears were still too full of the roaring wave to hear.

She tilted her head toward him. "What did you say?"

"I said, you can let go of me now."

She hadn't known what, exactly, she was grabbing as the water pulled Sevlin past, only that she needed to grab *something* to keep him from washing away. Now, she realized that one of her arms was snaked around his waist while the other crooked over his throat.

"Oh." She let him go. They both flopped to the ground.

Sevlin rubbed his reddened neck. "If the water didn't kill me, I think you were about to."

"Is that your way of thanking me for keeping you from washing away?"

"No. My way is this: thank you for keeping me from washing away."

Dashi smiled wanly. "No dry sarcasm? Just a straightforward thank you?"

He gave a bemused shake of his head. "The boots anchored you to the rock instead of skating on the water?"

"I noticed before that the soles seem to...understand if I want them to grab a surface or release it. So I just concentrated on gripping with my feet, just like I was climbing."

"Perhaps I'll thank the Yassaris someday as well."

"That's assuming we ever find our way out of here. Half-drowned and nothing to show for it but a dead end." Dashi tipped her head back and drew a deep breath.

"You could look at it this way: we no longer have to eliminate the other three corridors at the top of the staircase from consideration."

"Ah yes, so much time saved."

"Not nearly enough," Sevlin said, cocking his head at the sun. "We need to backtrack, and fast."

Sevlin ended up carrying her on his back until they reached the intersection where they'd taken the wrong turn. Sevlin could jog. After her dash from the wave, Dashi could not. They were running out of time. In the end, accepting the indignity of being carried was as simple as that.

"A little over an hour," Sevlin said, stopping so Dashi could slide from his back in the middle of the intersection. Even after moving at a run and carrying added weight, his breath came easier than Dashi's did.

She glanced once more at the scenes that decorated both sides of the intersection, but it was only cursory. She didn't need clues to know they needed to go in the opposite direction.

"I don't understand," she grumbled. "Why go to the trouble of chiseling a poem at the beginning if it isn't going to be any more instructive than that?"

"It doesn't matter." For once, Sevlin was the impatient one. "We need to move."

Only lingers the fool.

They went forward cautiously, waiting for the walls to open and hurl something at them. Dashi kept an eye on the decorative border as they went, but it proved unenlightening. They halted at the next intersection. It was circular and had eight different corridors branching from it.

Sevlin muttered a curse. "Now what? We don't have time to try *eight* paths."

"Take the four on the right and I'll take the four on the left. Study the art at the beginning of each. If they've left a clue to guide us, that's where it's most likely to be." Sevlin was already moving toward his assigned corridors. "It's also where traps are most likely to be," she called after him.

She went to her side, studying the pictures at the beginning of each corridor. At the first corridor, the scenes showed a pair of saiga on the steppe and a child playing beside a waterfall. The next corridor's scenes were of hunters cornering a boar and a field of crops below a cloudless sky. The sunlight hammered Dashi from above, making her head feel too light. She put out a hand, steadying herself against the wall. *Breathe,* she told herself sternly, *then keep going.*

The beginning of the third corridor was no more elucidating than the others had been, though a scene at the entrance to the fourth corridor did make her pause. In it, a wolf pack cornered a bull elk against a cliff edge. At first, she thought what attracted her attention was a pang of sympathy for the elk. A pair of dead wolves lay at his feet, but his great head was lowered in exhaustion and there were still many wolves left to fight. Then it hit her.

"*Balance,*" Dashi said suddenly, slapping her forehead. "Ancestors above, it's right in the title of the poem!"

From the other side of the intersection, Sevlin gave her a confused look. "There wasn't a title."

"Not the maze poem, the other one. The one from the mound. 'What is nature but a dance of balance?' The maze poem is referring to the mound poem. That's what it—the maze poem—means when it says 'follow nature's essence.' Follow balance."

Sevlin was still looking at her blankly.

"This whole thing is about balance. Idree told us that from the beginning. That's what the seamripper is: something to balance the golden needle. That's why the ruins have been so strange: built below ground when other Purek ruins were above, fertile and green while all the others I've seen are bare. It's all the opposite of what it's supposed to be. Even the mural of the travelers: they went toward the setting sun, not the rising sun. And it was right in the title of the poem the whole time! To follow nature's essence we have to look for things that represent balance." A sudden thought sidetracked her. "You don't still have your journal, do you?"

Sevlin gave a regretful shake of his head.

"That's alright." Dashi waved her hand distractedly. "It was...'What is nature but a dance of balance? What is life but a campaign against death?' Then the poem listed a series of opposites. Or maybe complements is a better word. That's how the Pureks thought of them, anyway."

"It mentioned predator and prey," Sevlin supplied, catching on, "and night and day."

"There was a line about war and peace too."

"Did we miss a scene at the last intersection?"

"Yes. I didn't realize it until this scene with the elk reminded me, but there were two scenes like it at the other intersection: one with deer grazing and another with a deer being eaten by wolves."

"Consuming, then being consumed." Sevlin tilted his head, considering.

"Both were next to the correct side of the intersection."

"So we're looking for a pair of complementary scenes. Do you think it has to be directly mentioned in the mound poem or will any pairing work?"

"I think any pairing will work, as long as it shows balance."

"Good, because I think I've already found it."

He pointed at the corridor in front of him. On one side, the decorative scene showed an old woman, clearly dying. Her hands were folded peacefully over her chest. Her family crowded around, their faces turned toward the rising sun as they commended her spirit to the ancestors. The scene adorning the opposite side of the corridor showed a pregnant woman cradling her belly as a smiling man embraced her.

"A life beginning and a life ending," Dashi murmured, approving.

Sevlin gestured in front of them. "This corridor, then?"

Dashi grinned, her fatigue momentarily pushed aside. "I'd put money on it."

Their first steps were wary, reinforced by a wall-launched arrow that narrowly missed Dashi's boot. But the sun was sinking lower and they couldn't afford to waste time when they didn't know how much of the maze was left. They pressed on, doing their best to mitigate dangers with careful, quick scrutiny.

This corridor was narrow, offering a dizzying number of turns. Twenty paces, turn right. Fifteen paces, turn left. Forty more paces, right. Dashi gave up counting.

Finally, they turned a corner to find a filmy, seething mass of steam. Dashi's nose wrinkled: the smell was unmistakably rotten.

"Sulfur," she said, recalling an ointment her mother had once applied to her ailing father's chest to help his breathing. It hadn't worked.

"Sulfuric springs," Sevlin corrected.

"There are hot springs near Karak City. They don't smell like this though." Dashi eyed the shrouded corridor. She could make out the edge of a pool—impossibly blue next to a gray stone path—but little else.

"Not all hot springs do. It depends on which minerals are present in the water."

A gust of wind made the steam ripple, thinning it out in spots.

"On the wall," Dashi said, pointing. "What is that?"

Before she'd finished speaking, the steam had billowed once more, shielding its contents. Dashi shifted uneasily. *This is just steam. Nothing like the taiga mist.*

"I don't see anything," Sevlin said.

"There was something there: large and dark but high up on the wall." When the steam didn't move again, she tore her eyes away. "Maybe it was just an outcropping rock. Let's go."

The steam hugged Dashi as she moved, a hot, close breath on her skin. Light-headedness hit her, accompanied by the spots in her vision. On her right, a spring appeared out of the steam. Large bubbles rose slowly, unfurling and dying like a species of particularly ephemeral flower. Sulfuric crystals ringed the pool: white, orange, and yellow.

"Stride the invisible bridge," Sevlin said from beside her, quoting the maze poem.

"I see it." Dashi eyed the place where the path crossed the spring. The last time she'd crossed a Purek-constructed bridge, she'd ended up with two arrows in her back. This bridge didn't arch gracefully as that one had. Instead, it stayed close to the hot water, crossing the spring in a straight line. Not that its shape had any bearing on how dangerous it was, Dashi thought, but the dissimilarity made her feel better.

Sevlin crouched, inspecting the bridge. "I don't see anything."

There was a grinding sound as he stepped forward. He froze, limbs loose. When nothing happened, he took two more rapid steps, disappearing into the cloud of steam.

Dashi waited tensely, swiping at the hair that clung to her cheeks, limp with steam.

"I'm over." Sevlin's voice sounded close, though she couldn't see him. "It's about ten strides."

She kept her steps light and quick, wanting to cross quickly in case Sevlin had triggered any traps, but she reached him without incident.

"Cursed ancestors, it's hot." Dashi wiped her forehead.

Sevlin nodded. His forehead and cheekbones gleamed and she could see droplets suspended in his stubbled chin. He didn't look nearly as hot as Dashi felt, however. Her heart was pounding uncontrollably. She plucked her deel away from her collarbone, but it made no difference.

She peered around him for the path but saw only a narrow rim of stone, colonized by minerals and crumbling at points until it was only as wide as her hand. It cut straight through the steam, dividing the springs. There was no other place to cross.

Sevlin gave the crumbling strip a skeptical look. "You should cross first. My weight might finish it off."

"Switch with me then."

The spit of rock on which they stood turned this maneuver into a strange dance: chests pressed together, arms touching, her feet between his as she tried to step around him.

Dashi stared down at the water. It was a shocking, electric blue—a color she'd only seen in paint or fabric dye, not in nature—but so clear that she could see down to an immense depth. For a moment, she wondered what it would feel like to skate over that surface, able to observe the depths without fear of sinking. Another draft of oppressive air corrected any daydreams she was entertaining. The hot spring would scald her through her boots.

Half-crazed with heat, she started across the rim of stone before she could change her mind. The crystallized minerals grew in the same bands of white, orange and yellow she'd noticed earlier. Rather than improve her traction, however, the crust came off in a single sheaf, dipping silently into the blue water and dissolving instantly. Dashi wobbled for a second but steadied herself—arms out, knees bent. The Yassari boots gripped the newly exposed stone as if nothing had happened.

"Careful," she called. "The path is loose." She glanced over her shoulder, but Sevlin was already lost from sight.

Steam pushed softly against Dashi's face. The stink of sulfur was thicker here, practically made solid by its strength. Her eyes teared, dripping onto her cheeks. Rock walls loomed over her on both sides, but there was no sign of the dark shape she'd seen earlier. A hum reached her ears, multiplying and expanding so that, after a few moments, the noise held several competing tones within itself. Dashi froze, balanced on the blade of rock. From somewhere deep in the steam, there was a flash: metal catching the light.

When it reached her, the blade was knee height, but it swung in an upward curve, like a pendulum. She jumped, clearing the initial level of the blade, but not the upswing. There was a swish and, as she landed, she saw the tail end of her braid land gently on the spring's surface. It floated for a moment, then sank into the blue water.

"Sevlin," she called, not taking her eyes off the white wall of steam as she fumbled to retie her braid, now slightly shorter. "There are blades. The first one is knee height, but it swings upward."

There was a muffled noise behind her. She hoped it was Sevlin making a sound in the affirmative and not, say, a grunt of pain as he fell into the scalding water.

"Sevlin?"

No answer.

The steam thickened, churning slowly above the hot pools. Her shoulders twitched, uneasy at being isolated, at the similarity to the taiga mist.

The springs are hot. The air is cold. It's nothing but steam.

The mineral-encrusted stone narrowed further, becoming finger-width. She doubted it would hold her weight. Her left arm clutched her side, trying to appease the ripping sensation in her lungs. *Quiet,* she told her body. *There's no place to rest here.* Dashi paused, gathering herself. Then, in an explosion of movement, she went skipping across the thin section. Once, twice, her feet landed, only to push away again before the stone could crumble. As soon as the stone widened she stopped, hands on her knees, gulping oxygen.

She straightened slowly, the disconnected feeling between her head and her body somewhat improved. As she did, she glimpsed the dark shape again, high above her. It was more or less rectangular, except for two—*Are those arms?* She'd originally assumed the dark mass was a feature of the maze, a new trap waiting to injure them. Now, as she silently examined it from below, she changed her mind: if it wasn't alive now, it had been at some point. She could see the arms, bent upward at right angles from the body, clutching the wall. As she crept forward, other dark shapes began to emerge from the steam: two hanging close together here; a whole group of them over there, clumped together in uneven rows and stacked four and five high.

Sweat slid from her hairline in steady beads, but whatever the dark shapes were, they didn't seem to mind the heat. Ancestors above, what if they were only sleeping? She'd been shouting warnings over her shoulder to Sevlin when she should have known better. Perhaps it was wariness and not incapacity that had kept Sevlin from shouting in reply. She hoped so.

She left the dark, unmoving figures behind and followed the stone rim to another low bridge. There were no visible tripwires or other indications of a trap, but her heart kept racing. *Ancestors damned heat.* A glance over her shoulder revealed no sign of Sevlin, only white steam and hot, blue water edged by a rainbow crust of minerals. She didn't dare call him but neither could she wait. The heat was a live thing, breathing down her neck.

Dashi started forward, her feet touching lightly on the bridge's surface. She was no more than halfway across when the first trap moved. It came from below: spikes that shot upward through the patina of dried sulfur in an unpredictable pattern. Dashi swung herself up onto the railing. The steam was thicker at this height, obscuring her vision as she minced forward, balanced on the narrow railing.

A mechanical hum reached her, as twin blades swung across the center of the bridge. Dashi curled her body sideways, pulling her left side out of harm's way just as the blades brushed past. A third blade followed before she had time to steady herself. She jumped, avoiding the blade, but even with the Yassari boots, her landing was too hard, too off-center. One foot slid sideways, pitching her toward the boiling water below. She twisted as she fell, trying to turn the motion into a flip and instead catching the rail full in the stomach. She sagged over it, bent in half with no oxygen in her lungs, feet dangling over the hot spring. For a moment, she clung there, trying not to fall backward while her lungs heaved uselessly.

When she could breathe again, she swung herself back onto the bridge and hobbled the last few steps, finally stepping onto solid ground in a crunch of minerals. The steam still wrapped around her, but there was a chill to it now, a hint that the end of the oppressive springs was near.

The scrape of a footstep had Dashi spinning around, but the shape that appeared out of the steam was familiar. *Sevlin.* She felt something in her chest unclench.

Sweat dripped from his face and his deel was plastered to the planes of his chest. His right sleeve had been torn off and tied around a new wound in his arm, which was already leaking blood through the makeshift bandage. He turned his face in the direction of the cool air, sensing the same change that Dashi had.

"Are you—"

"Fine," he said, running a hand over his glistening hair, "but we need to hurry. There's something—"

A huge dark shape dropped onto the end of the bridge behind him. Dashi danced backward, her sword practically drawing itself. Sevlin wheeled around, raising his sword and sliding toward Dashi until they stood side by side.

The thing shambled forward, low and ungainly, and through the whorls of steam, Dashi saw why: it was made for swooping through shadows, not walking on land. The bat opened a saliva-strung mouth and emitted such a high-pitched scream that Dashi nearly dropped her sword trying to cover her ears. It lurched toward them, the thin skin that stretched over its limbs billowing with the same rhythm as the steam.

Cool, dry air brushed against Dashi's left side, turning her perspiration frigid. She shifted in that direction, away from the bat. Better to move toward a place with decent visibility if it came to a fight.

The bat, sensing her escape, lunged forward, covering the distance in a single bound. Dashi parried the move, slicing into the bat's shoulder, but she was a touch too slow to avoid its swiping foreleg. She flew through the air, landing in a spray of sulfur crystals at the edge of the spring. Staggering to her feet, she found Sevlin standing over her, facing the bat. His sword was wet with blood, but the steam was so thick that the bat was only a gauzy silhouette and Dashi couldn't see how badly it had been wounded. Dizziness threatened to topple her, but she ignored it as best she could, stepping away from Sevlin so that the bat was forced to divide its attention. Its mouth opened in a silent snarl.

"Alright?" Sevlin murmured without looking at her.

Her breath was ragged and her left arm was almost entirely numb but neither was the fault of the bat, so she said, shortly, "As good as I was before."

"On three."

One...two...

They blurred into motion at the same moment, Dashi's sword sliding between the animal's ribs in a spray of blood. Sevlin's arced toward its head, gouging a hole in its cheekbone. The bat screamed and snapped at the air beside Dashi, narrowly missing her arm. It turned faint and gray as it retreated into the swirling steam, then abruptly grew dark again as it jumped at them. Droplets clung to the skin of its wings, luminescent gems of moisture. Dashi's hand tightened on her sword. *Through the wings and into the spine.*

The steam on the other side of the bat convulsed without warning and Dashi turned her swing into a somersault, shouting an inarticulate warning to Sevlin as she went down. She came up just in time to see a Purek trap, a spiked pendulum-like object, swing into the bat—and Sevlin, on the bat's other side. Both were swept off their feet, lost in the swirling steam. An instant later, Dashi heard the sickening thud of a soft, breakable body meeting unforgiving stone.

Chapter 45

Dashi heard the harsh rasp of Sevlin's breath before she saw him. The sound pulled at her like scent does a hound and she pushed her way through the steam until it became tattered and thin, no longer playing games with her eyes.

The Purek trap was flush against the wall of the maze. Now that she could see it better, she realized it wasn't a solid pendulum as she'd first thought but was made of bronze bars and crosspieces. It was taller than she was and spikes glinted at every possible angle. The bat lay in a dark crumpled heap, its head pinned by one of the pendulum's bars, its neck contorted unnaturally. Sevlin was also pinned, stuck between the bars and the rock wall. His head was bowed, his hands braced against his thigh.

Dashi's steps jolted to a stop. The center of the pendulum was slightly concave, a fruit with its pit already removed. Sevlin was nestled in the exact center. The logical part of her mind knew that this had probably saved him from slamming into the rock wall, but her eyes told her that he was too still. His face was too pallid.

"Sevlin?"

She'd only managed a whisper, but his head jolted up.

"Dashi." His voice was wrong: hushed, as if he was in the midst of some endurance test and had to conserve energy any way he could.

"What...?" She faltered.

His hands shifted incrementally, just enough to reveal a blood-slicked pant leg. Dashi hissed out a breath. A bronze spike protruded from his thigh, poking from the front of his leg all the way through.

"Missed the artery," Sevlin said.

His movements were methodical as he pulled his sash tighter around his thigh, but he never quite looked the wound in the eye, instead staring to the left of where metal married flesh.

Dashi approached the pendulum carefully. The openings between the crisscrossed metal bars were big enough to frame her face but too small for almost anything else. Spikes of varying lengths covered the side that faced Sevlin. The spikes that lined the perimeter of the pendulum were the longest, making a sort of cage where they embedded into the rock, hemming him inside.

He's lucky only one spike—

The thought died as she took in the fresh blood on Sevlin's calf and side and shoulders. He had other wounds; they just paled in comparison to his leg.

He took a steadying breath and Dashi grasped the metal bars with both hands, clenching in anticipation. He gave a single, quick jerk of his leg, sliding his thigh off the spike like meat from a skewer. He said nothing—not even a curse, though Dashi had been muttering them steadily—but leaned back with his eyes closed.

Do something, Dashi told herself, but Sevlin's pale-lipped grimace had turned her brain into a mire. She had to swallow several times before she could force her hands to release the bars. The arm of the pendulum angled up into the steam so that Dashi couldn't see where it began. She repositioned her hands and pulled at the bars, trying to tip the pendulum from side to side, but it never budged.

"Those barbs on the wall are holding it." Sevlin jerked his chin upward without opening his eyes.

Looking up, Dashi located the hooks that protruded from the wall, latching around the top of the pendulum.

"They snapped into place around the frame as soon the pendulum hit," Sevlin said.

Moving carefully to avoid the spikes, she scrambled up the outside of the pendulum. Steam swam past her face the higher she climbed, momentarily hiding Sevlin from her again. The hooks were immovable, refusing to twist or push back into the wall.

"I can't get them to release," she panted, climbing down.

Sevlin, still not putting any weight on his leg, didn't answer. Dashi examined the pendulum with a critical eye. The grid of metal bars along one side was hinged, as if to form a side door, but when she pulled at them, there was no movement. She got her knife out and lined the blade up against a hinge: metal on metal, painful and shrill. She'd need to sharpen her knife after this, if she didn't end up breaking the blade completely.

Sevlin hobbled over, contorting himself to avoid the spikes along the inside of the pendulum. He produced his own knife and set to work on another hinge.

"How's the leg?" Dashi bit her lip in concentration.

"It's had better days."

Her eyes flicked up to his, insistent.

"It's bad," he said quietly, "but survivable as long as I can keep it clean."

She had the angle of the blade right: perfectly aligned between pin and hinge, if she could just wedge it a little deeper. She gave the back of the knife a solid tap. The point skidded sideways, scraping loudly.

Dashi unleashed a string of curses. "I almost had it."

"There can't be much time left, Dashi."

She looked to the sky out of habit, but it was invisible behind the blanket of steam that floated overhead. Dashi realigned her knife blade against the hinge without answering.

"You have to go."

"I'll get this hinge off and we'll go together."

Sevlin's hand closed over her wrist, stopping her. "Get the seamripper."

"I'm not leaving you wounded and trapped in the middle of a Purek ruin, Sevlin."

"I'll free myself and come after you in a few minutes."

"We both know it'll take more than a few minutes to get out of this."

"Not for me." His face was completely serious, his voice determined. "I'll be out of here and arguing with you before you know it."

"If I didn't already know you're lying, I'd believe you." Dashi's lips twisted humorlessly. "You're that convincing."

Sevlin gave her an almost-smile. "It's a gift."

She looked down, where Sevlin's grip had shifted from her wrist to her hand. "I can't leave you like this."

Sevlin reached through the bars with his other hand and nudged her jaw up so that she was looking at him. Staring at his annoying commitment to duty, his tedious selflessness, and his eternal, unfathomable control of his emotions.

"I'm not asking you to stay, Dashi. I'm asking you to go."

Moisture draped his forehead and nose, channeling droplets along the stream bed that was his scar. His face was right above hers through the bars, close enough that she could see the tiny lines mapping his lower lip and bracketing the corners of his eyes.

Close enough to know exactly what she wanted.

Dashi snaked her hand through the bars and caught the back of Sevlin's neck. His lips were smooth, fitting against her mouth, a piece she hadn't known was missing. He pulled her forward into the cool metal, one hand reaching through to grip her hip. Bumping against the bars, she ran a hand down his shoulder and over his collarbone, feeling the blood on his deel, the heat through his clothes. Feeling *him*: strong, seasoned, always restrained. She wanted the bars out of the way, wanted her body pushed up against his, laying over him or under him, as close as two separate things could get. The bars remained unyielding intercessors, impossible to circumvent and impossible to ignore.

Dashi pulled back suddenly, expecting to see something—she wasn't sure what—in his face. But Sevlin's expression was already arranged: shuttered and neutral.

"Go," was all he said, pushing the coiled grappling hook and the nearly empty waterskin through the bars to her.

Dashi slung the coil over her shoulder and slipped the waterskin through her sash, next to the cup he'd given her.

She hesitated, then handed him her knife. Her last one. "In case yours breaks against the hinge."

Sevlin nodded, but he left it resting on his open palm, more like a wounded bird than a weapon. She took a step backward, then another, giving one or both of them a chance to speak, but neither of them said anything before the curtain of steam dropped between them.

Chapter 46

Away from the steam, she saw how much time was left: almost none. Fifteen minutes? Twenty, if she was lucky. The sun couldn't tell her the exact minute, but whatever the number was, Dashi knew it wasn't good.

She jogged weakly through the maze, hoping there were no more traps or that, if there were, her speed, such as it was, would disrupt their accuracy. She had to stop twice: once, because her breath was hiccuping so hard she thought she might pass out; and once more to search the carvings at a third intersection. She located the right path—marked by twin carvings showing autumn and spring—and then she was off again. One turn, then another, and another.

Dashi careened around a corner and skidded to a stop, pain shooting through her ribs and oxygen turning to fire in her lungs. There was no more corridor, no more maze. The entire space in front of her was taken up by an enormous skull, its teeth parted in a macabre smile.

Follow nature's essence, toward the face of bone.

The skull wasn't bone. It was pale granite, an outcropping of the larger rock face which reared up behind it. Two short, slanted fissures were the nostrils. The eyes were caves, slightly unequal in size and asymmetrical in position, which spoke to their natural origins.

In three hours' time, the jaw descends.

The jaws, on the other hand, were completely manmade. Although the teeth gleamed bone-white in the sun, it was only a facade; Dashi could see the metal backing them. How the jaws were attached to the granite skull, ancestors only knew. The important part—the part that had necessitated her leaving Sevlin injured and trapped—was that, when the jaws shut, the top and bottom teeth would fit together perfectly, closing off whatever lay on the other side.

It was nearly closed now.

Each tooth was as long as her arm and perfectly triangular, making the skull a strange amalgamation of human and animal. Sunlight slid against the surface of the teeth, highlighting their otherwise imperceptible movement. Dashi extended a hand, approaching like it was a wild thing that might very well bite.

The tooth was icy against her fingertip. *Marble*, Dashi thought, *the purest I've ever seen.* In Karak City, this would have been used for the khan's rooms, or perhaps a royal fountain or ostentatious altar. The Pureks had cast it into the wilderness, an offering to the natural world, perhaps, or to the magic on which they'd based their civilization.

Despite the maze's high walls, the wind still found its way to her. It tugged at Dashi's braid and ran frozen fingers down her neck. It rushed into the skull's dark mouth, becoming a multitude of voices as it pushed between the marble teeth.

Come inside, the voices whispered. *Come inside, little one.*

Sweat slicked the hair at her temples, but Dashi shivered. The jaws continued their downward slide, taunting her.

Do you dare to enter? The whispering voices seemed to come from deeper in the mouth this time. *In failing strength? With no light? By yourself? Little one, little one, little one one one one.*

She swayed for a moment, the wind buffeting her back while a gale of indecision did the same to her mind. A gust of wind pushed her forward, and she braced a hand against one of the teeth to catch herself.

It was the marble that did it: cold but solid, remarkable but real. *This is a Purek creation. Nothing more, nothing less*, she told herself. Altan agreed, whispering, "*Superstition is that which your mind fears; a fact just is.*"

It's just the wind howling among the rocks and my jumpy imagination. Dashi glared at the skull. *And this is just another ruin that needs to be explored and an artifact that needs to be retrieved*

She ducked between the upper and lower teeth and stepped into the skull's mouth.

Chapter 47

The inside of the skull was cold. *Were you expecting the warmth of a living body*, Dashi chided herself. She stood for a moment, shivering, while her eyes adjusted. There was stone underfoot and stone overhead and she could make out pearly shadows lining the sides of the cavern, top and bottom. Back teeth? There was also a circle of unmitigated darkness at the rear, which Dashi eyed dubiously. *A throat.* Exactly how far were the Pureks going to take this?

Having no light, she advanced carefully, knowing that her left arm wasn't up to the task of catching her if she stumbled. The sound of her footsteps echoed strangely as she walked down the throat, making it sound like someone was following her. She turned once, giving into her superstition, but no one was there. *It's the echo of your own feet, you brainless wonder*, she scoffed and, when self-derision didn't calm her pulse, she told herself it was Sevlin at her back, his sword at the ready.

Her feet shuffled forward in the uncertain light. Broad ridges had been hewn into the wall, which seemed to undulate rhythmically if she watched from the corner of her eye. The air moved against her face, loosening the hair that was plastered to her cheeks. Its scent was strange—part acid, part metal—but her pace quickened anyway. The echo of her steps increased too, bouncing around her. *Little one one one.*

There was light ahead, a silvery film drawn in front of the tunnel. Dashi paused, the strange smell finally pushing its way to the forefront of her thoughts. She'd been in enough dangerous situations to heed her own sense of foreboding, no matter how vague. Drawing her sword, she stepped out of the throat and into the shimmery air.

A cavern opened before her: high-ceilinged and deep, with shadows clinging to the corners. Dashi squinted, first at the shafts that had been cut into the rock ceiling to let in air and light, and then at the sight before her: an enormous subterranean lake. It was silver in color: not the silver of a frozen pond or the silver of reflected moonlight, but a color rich and pure, like molten metal. A layer of mist lay atop the surface, flashing with iridescence wherever the sunlight came through the ceiling.

The effect was so surreal, so transfixing, that for a breath Dashi didn't move. After a moment she noticed a low island in the middle of the lake. It lay flat, nearly indistinguishable from the lake's surface, with only a slight bump in the center to give any indication that something was there. She squinted at the raised section, noting the slight differentiation in color. An altar? A statue? The strange lighting made it difficult to determine.

The graveled shore on which she stood was narrow—in most places, the lake abutted the cavern's walls directly—and there was nothing to help her cross to the island. The lake was completely and utterly still. Its edges didn't lap gently at the shore but clutched possessively at the rocks. The liquid, whatever it was, looked thick. Dashi tossed a pebble. It disappeared with a hiss and a curious lack of ripples. She looked around until she found a piece of dried grass that must have been carried inside by the wind and dipped one end into the lake. The liquid was thick, almost gooey, and a plume of metallic odor rose from the place where she'd punctured the lake's surface. Dashi started coughing. For several long seconds, she couldn't stop, not until she backed away from the lake and pulled her arm up to shield her nose and mouth. Face still buried in the crook of her elbow, she studied the piece of grass: it had been cut neatly in half. The portion that had been below the lake's surface was gone, burned away to nothing.

She tested the Yassari boots too, but there was an immediate hissing sound and she jerked her foot back. A glance revealed a thumb-sized black mark on the sole. Dashi sighed, kneading her temples, where a headache was strengthening. She didn't think the boots would make it to the island and back, but she couldn't think of another way across and she didn't have much time to spare. *Only lingers the fool.*

Movement flicked over the lake's surface, as something crossed in front of a sunlight shaft. A bat? Some other taiga-dweller, after an easy meal? Eyes searching the stone ceiling, Dashi backed slowly toward the tunnel opening, her sword up.

She saw the movement dart over the silver liquid again and this time caught the source: not an animal but light, glancing off a bronze bar. The bar was anchored into the ceiling and passed directly over the island. Dashi started climbing immediately, scrambling up the rocks beneath one end of the bar, knowing that if it looked sturdy—and probably even if it didn't—she would try to cross to the lake. The jaws were almost closed and she was out of options.

The climb was not difficult, but her left hand lacked its usual strength and twice her grip simply relaxed, her hand opening of its own accord. She flexed it a few times, trying not to picture the green and black vines beneath her sleeve, before continuing, relying more and more on the grip of her boots with each step.

At the top, she reached out and grabbed the bar. It was green with verdigris but solid. Dashi felt hope tentatively raise its head inside her. She crooked her legs over the bar and, hanging beneath it, began pulling herself over the lake. The bar swayed with her movements. The struts anchoring it to the rocky ceiling groaned.

The silver lake and the dark cavern slid by, but Dashi barely registered it. Her lips pressed in concentration as she tried to compensate for her clumsy hand. She passed beneath one of the air shafts, sunlight washing over her body, distant and cool. The air seemed to thrum around her and she wasn't sure if it was her imagination or if it was simply the effect of hanging upside down.

Finally, she hovered above the island. It was a farther drop than she'd realized—the featureless silver lake made it difficult to judge distance—but not so high that she couldn't reach the bar again with Sevlin's grappling hook. Dashi slid forward incrementally, positioning herself carefully. Too far to one side or the other, and she would miss the tiny circle of land entirely and fall into the flesh-eating lake instead. She also had to ensure she missed the black object which sat at the island's center: a plinth, she saw now, though there didn't appear to be anything atop it. Dashi unhooked her feet and hung, holding herself perfectly still, before letting go.

It was a clumsy fall, quite unlike the stunts she was used to performing. Her feet hit and then suddenly she was looking at the world sideways. There was a strange numbness along the left side of her torso—not just her arm but her chest and side too. Groaning, she pushed herself upright and stumbled to the plinth. It was waist-high with vertical fluting that ended in elaborately scrolled volutes just beneath the platform. Her instinct was to circle it again and again, checking and rechecking for traps, but time was against her.

Dashi leaned close, staring at the plinth. The platform was as flat and smooth as black glass, except for a pair of cylinders, tipped on their sides and rising finger-height from the center. They were partially embedded in the black surface, as if someone had taken several large spools, emptied them of thread, and then somehow half-buried them in the stone.

Each cylinder had a scene carved into it. As quickly as she could, Dashi translated the lines of ancient Purek beneath them:

Pit the balance
Turn the wheels
One to see
Two to seal.

She dropped to her knees, surveying the rest of the plinth. There were four pairs of cylinders—*wheels*, in the language of the poem—in total, each decorated with pictures. *An even number. Balanced.*

Still squatting, she stretched out a tentative finger and turned one of the wheels. As it rotated, the scene of a hare bounding through tall grass was replaced by one showing snowcapped mountains. Dashi turned the wheel once more and saw a worm writhing in the dirt. The adjacent wheel also showed three different scenes: a pond covered in lily pads; a litter of rabbit kits flopped over one another; the wide reaches of the steppe, its grass bending in the wind.

Pit the balance on the wheels.

Which were complements: the adult hare and the litter of babies? Or the mountains and the steppe? The adult hare wasn't old or dying, so she decided that it wasn't a balance for new life. She selected the mountains on one wheel and the steppe on the other. Out of curiosity, she tried to turn the wheels a third time. They didn't budge.

Two turns to seal.

"No changing your mind, I suppose," she murmured.

The next pair of wheels was easier. Dashi selected two scenes, one depicting a wintertime Purek festival and another showing a celebration at midsummer. For the third pair of wheels, she chose a sword and a shield.

Only one left. Dashi leaned over the recessed wheels on the top of the plinth. The pictures on this last set were the most elaborate, which was why she'd saved them for last. She rotated both wheels once, then cursed aloud. The scenes on the left wheel *all* had a counterpart on the right wheel. Each pair depicted balance in one form or another.

She could pair the coronation of a new khagan with a scene showing the death vigil for the same khagan. Or, there was a scene showing an ancient seamstress, his hands raised over the prone body of one of his patients. Its complement was a miniaturization of the mural she'd seen only a few hours ago in the giant mound: the woman traveler holding the seamripper beside a pool. The final possible pairing was familiar to Dashi as well. She'd seen them in the murals of the smaller mound, before her encounter with the toad. One scene showed the devastated village, with its burned homes and dead livestock. The second scene was the young man and the young woman journeying through the woods. Dashi wasn't sure if these two scenes were complementary, but with the other scenes paired off so nicely, she supposed they must go together.

How much time did she have left? The maze poem had been un-specific as to the consequences of lingering, but given all the dangers they'd already encountered, Dashi hated to think what might await those deemed 'fools.'

Which is the right answer? She wanted to select the seamstress holding the golden needle and the woman holding the seamripper, but years of experience stayed her hand. The Pureks' puzzles always had a slightly deceptive quality to them and matching the golden needle with the seamripper seemed...too obvious. Her lips twitched. She could imagine Sevlin's frustration if she'd told him that.

It must be one of the other pairs.

The pair of khagan scenes seemed like the next best guess. What could be more balanced that the first and last day of the khagan's reign? But

Dashi's mind kept coming back to the pictures she'd originally seen in the smaller mound. The ravaged village and the young refugee travelers weren't complements, exactly; they were part of a story. They'd fled their burned village and, if the murals were to be believed, the woman traveler eventually found the seamripper at—Dashi raised her head, startled—*at a silvery lake exactly like this one*. She remembered something else from the temple mural: the woman held the seamripper in one hand; in the other, she'd cupped the silvery liquid, which dribbled down her arm, leaving red burns. The similarity was too much to ignore. Had the woman traveler been a real person? Had she, like Dashi, risked her life to find the seamripper in order to save a loved one, to stop a vicious ruler from raising a magical army?

A hero rises as a tyrant schemes. The last line of the mound poem came to her unbidden, but suddenly Dashi understood. The last two scenes, the ones she'd originally seen in the mound, *were* complementary. The burned village showed loss and pain, the utter annihilation of a way of life. The travelers, who'd survived an event that had killed everyone else they knew, were the incarnation of optimism, of the audacity to dream and plan and execute.

Devastation and hope.

The fruits of a scheming tyrant and the goals of a rising hero.

The status quo and the coming revision.

That was the true relationship between the golden needle and the seamripper. *Complements. Balance.* Dashi turned the final set of wheels and waited.

The top of the plinth began to slide silently, separating from the base. Dashi stepped back, immediately wary. When nothing shot at her or tried to divest her of important body parts, however, she grew curious and bent over to get a better look. A shallow niche had appeared. Fitted neatly inside was a small box, only as long as her hand. Dashi lifted the box from its recessed hiding place. It was made of dark, well-oiled wood, with inlaid silver filigree sprawling over the lid and two narrow handles on each end. The top sprang open as soon as her fingertips grazed the lid.

The silk lining of the box could have been made yesterday, not centuries ago. It was a deep, midnight blue, a startling contrast against the bright silver...*cup?* Dashi picked the cup up, looking for the seamripper. There was nothing under it. There was nothing inside. She pulled up the fabric lining, but there was solid wood beneath, hollowed out just enough to cradle the cup. Where was the seamripper? She didn't even *need* a cup; the waterskin was almost empty and anyway, she had the cup Sevlin had found in the ruin.

Dashi turned the box over in her hands. It was relatively light, despite how solid the wood felt. She thought of her saddle, with its hidden space. Perhaps the box had a similar secret compartment. *Or...*she narrowed her eyes at the cup. Its base was thick; did *it* have a secret compartment, the same way the statue of Khagan Nuray hid the golden needle? She held the cup up to the light. If you discounted the gleam of polished silver, it was relatively plain, not much larger than the one Sevlin had found a few days ago. It had a simple half-moon handle and a single silver braid encircling its base.

She was trying to fit a fingernail beneath the silver braid when a pebble bounced off her head. Wincing, she looked upward. All along the cavern ceiling, slabs of rock were moving, quietly sliding to one side or the other. Dashi shielded her head with one arm, while bits of rock and dust pelted her. The lake hissed wherever they sank.

The island lurched suddenly beneath her, knocking Dashi to her knees. The box hit the ground, hopping up and down like a bead of water caught in hot oil. Even the lake was shaking, oozing over the borders of the island.

No, she thought in alarm. *Not shaking. Rising.*

The jaws must have closed.

Only lingers the fool.

Dashi grabbed the box before it could skid into the lake and stuffed the cup back inside. Everything seemed to be happening in slow motion: the gravel at her feet, bouncing and hanging in the air before falling back to earth; bubbles, rising languidly from the once-still lake; her hands, trying to thread one end of her sash through the handles of the box, frustratingly slow despite the simpleness of the task. The box would bang into the cup Sevlin had salvaged for her, but there was no call for stealth, nor was there any time to correct the situation. She'd need both hands to hold onto the rope.

Stumbling away from the plinth, the grappling hook in one hand, Dashi looked up in horror. The bar was no longer there. The shifting slabs of rock on the cavern's ceiling had moved it well out of her reach. There was no way back. Dashi's head whipped back and forth, searching for some alternative, something she'd missed in her eagerness to examine the plinth. All she saw was the lake, bubbles rising faster and faster as it swallowed more of the little island.

Stupid, stupid, stupid.

Dashi took a single, skating step onto the lake, just as the ceiling shifted above her, opening up another window to the sky. Pebbles and rock dust rained down, sending up a spray of silvery liquid. She pushed as fast as she dared, but the lake grabbed at her boots, threatening to topple her. *Speed is only as good as the skill that controls it,* said Baris in her head. *Better to slow down than to make a mistake.* Falling into the lake meant a sure death. If she could keep upright, she had a chance at least. The Purek box swung on her sash, clacking against Sevlin's cup as she'd known it would. *Two Purek cups and zero Purek seamrippers.* How could she have let Idree down so badly?

The lake rumbled beneath her, sending up dozens of bubbles. Shadows swooped in the upper corner of her vision as more slabs shifted overhead, opening up the cavern and turning the lake luminous with the sunlight. Dashi glanced over her shoulder. The lake had covered the island now, greedy fingers extending up the side of the plinth. Would it fill the tunnel she needed to exit? The skull? The entire maze?

Pain curled suddenly around the bottoms of her feet. Dashi looked down to see blackened leather. The boots were peeling where the lake had splashed. Even Yassari inventions, it seemed, were no match for the Pureks.

Halfway there. She tried to ignore the pain wrapping her feet, but each time the lake sent a wave lapping over her boots it felt like a flame against her skin. She thought she could *feel* each place her flesh reddened. Then she could feel it bubbling. Then she could feel it pulling away from her bones as it burned. Her screams circled the cavern and came back to her, transformed into someone else's voice. Unrecognizable. Deranged.

Faster.

A bubble rose from the depths of the lake and popped next to her, splattering her hand with fiery droplets, but her attention was on her feet, for the pain that was smothering them, soles to tops, toes to heels, working its way toward her ankles. When Dashi glanced down this time, she could see flesh through the rapidly expanding holes in her boots, and what she saw bore little resemblance to a human foot. The skin was black and crusted with ash. Dashi forced her gaze toward the shore, vowing not to look again.

Faster.

She was three-quarters of the way across when it happened: the leather gave way as the lake consumed what was left of her boots. Without the boots to keep her afloat, she began to sink into the thick liquid. Then all she could feel was fire, reaching up her leg, eating her alive. All she could hear was her own voice, screaming itself hoarse.

Shadows were still swooping from above, coming closer, weaving in and out of Dashi's peripheral vision. Once, she might have ducked, trying to avoid whatever was falling toward her. Now, she barely noticed.

A shard of rock hit Dashi squarely in the cheek. Dust clogged her nose and throat. She had a feeling of floating, of trying to rise past the pain, but it caught her before she could outdistance it. Then there was a blast of fresh air and light, almost stunning in its suddenness.

She blinked at the ground far below, sure she was dreaming. Or dying. It was the only explanation her mind could conjure to make sense of such a rapid change of circumstances.

There were arms around her: strong ones, refusing to let her move. Craning her neck to see behind her, Dashi came face to face with the sharp-toothed smile of the moth herald.

Chapter 48

D ashi jerked backward, but the moth-woman's arms were steel bands around her. Her wings beat stolidly against the air, seemingly unmindful of the extra weight they carried. The craggy walls of the maze uncoiled below them, a tight tangle of stone, as Dashi was lifted above the cavern, above everything.

"Don't struggle too hard," the herald said, giving Dashi that sharp-tipped smile again. "I don't want to drop you."

Dashi's head flopped to one side, the pain in her legs obscuring all thought. The giant skull leered up at her, its jaws firmly clamped shut. She had a glimpse of silver, as the lake oozed between its marble teeth.

"Don't you want to know what my orders are?" the moth-woman asked.

I hope they're to kill me.

Dashi glanced involuntarily at her legs, detailed in lurid red and black. Her feet were smaller than they should be, the calves much too thin. The lake had eaten both into an unrecognizable shape.

"I'm to return you and the artifact to New Osb. You're to be kept alive."

Dashi shuddered. She'd seen enough bad injuries to know that her blackened feet and whittled legs would never carry her again. How was she still conscious? Darkness flared at the corners of her vision, before shrinking again, taunting her with the prospect of relief but never actually providing it.

The herald was still talking, but Dashi had lost track of what she was saying. Instead, she stared, transfixed by those perfect, dainty features, those unforgivingly sharp teeth. The moth-woman's lips moved in slow motion, carefully pronouncing each word.

Khan.

Artifact.

Prisoner.

Dashi's mind processed the words slowly, finally stumbling to a conclusion. She'd wondered why she wasn't unconscious from the pain and now she knew: she had something left to do. She'd only held the Purek box and cup for a moment, but she'd been so sure something was hidden there, so sure it was the answer she'd sought. The time for puzzling over murals and poems was behind her, however.

Her fingers wriggled toward her sash. She couldn't feel her sword. Either it had fallen, or the herald had taken it without Dashi noticing. The Purek box, however, was wedged between their bodies, still threaded on Dashi's sash.

The herald's gaze dipped. Had she felt Dashi's hand moving?

Make conversation. Distract her.

"You came...all this way...at the twitch of...your master's... finger?" Dashi tried to make her voice drip with disdain, but her panting undercut the effort.

One end of her sash slipped free. Dashi edged it away with a twitch of her fingers. *Almost there.*

"You think that's bad?" The moth-woman shifted her so that Dashi was staring at her own bloodied extremities. "You know nothing of pain. By tomorrow your screams will echo through New Osb."

Now. Dashi jerked at the sash, at the same time pushing herself away from the moth-woman to create a window of space. Both the Purek box and the cup Sevlin had given her fell between them. Her sash floated free, rippling outward like a banner. The moth-woman shouted something at the air above them and a second winged herald, previously unnoticed by Dashi, swooped after the plummeting box.

It was too late. The box spun wildly through the air. The owl herald was too far behind. The hot springs peeked up at Dashi through shrouds of steam, their blue faces serene. She glimpsed the outline of a bridge and, just beyond it, a shadowy figure wreathed in white. *Sevlin?* There was a tiny puff of dust, silent and distant, as the box hit the craggy side of the maze and shattered.

Shoot me, Dashi screamed, or thought she screamed. She thought she saw the figure swivel in her direction, in the direction of where the box had landed. *Shoot, Sevlin!* Her throat ached. *Please end this.* Then she remembered: Sevlin's crossbow had fallen from the ledges along with his pack. There would be no relief for her agony, other than the possibility that Sevlin—if indeed that had been him—might find the remains of the Purek box and cup and anything that might be hidden inside.

A moment later the figure was gone, lost from sight like everything else that passed beneath the herald's wings. Dashi let her head fall against the moth-woman, lulled by the knowledge that, if she had lost her chance to get the seamripper, then at least the khan had too.

Chapter 49

Dashi roused when the moth-woman landed on a balcony in New Osb. The herald who was part owl touched down a moment later. Her head swiveled, golden eyes surveying Dashi before moving away again.

Clutching Dashi tightly in her arms, the moth-woman strode toward the balcony door. No one opposed her. The guards who'd been standing beside the balcony doors backed away.

"One of you get the door," the moth-woman said. "My hands are full and my companion lacks thumbs." She bared her pointy teeth, taking obvious pleasure in the reaction they caused.

Dashi raised her head, pulled from her stupor long enough to look around. The sun was just peeking over New Osb's walls, turning the stone tawny. The courtyard was empty, except for a figure in green and gold, striding across it. Even from the height of the balcony, Dashi recognized the sinuous gait. Ese paused, somehow sensing her stare.

Dashi ducked her head as the moth-woman passed inside. The thought of being seen by someone familiar—someone who knew she'd once had a plan and hope, two working legs and two working arms—was unbearable. But Ese's gaze, cool and unsympathetic, was the last thing she saw before the palace walls blotted out the dawn.

New Osb was different as a prisoner. This was mostly, Dashi decided, due to a lack of light. The servants' areas had been kept bright; Marzhan believed that to perform well, one needed to see well.

Outside Dashi's cell, there were no torches or lanterns. She slouched in the dark, chained to the wall by both wrists. The ankle shackles lay, unused, beside her. Jaded though the guards might be, even they had not wanted to touch her melted, skinless ankles and feet.

Her cell was one of the barred doors that she and Sevlin had passed on their way to the lift box. Her mind, feverish and only loosely under her control, strayed to Sevlin, to his mouth: the long groove his lips made when he disagreed with something she'd said; the quick upward flip when she'd amused him. Her thoughts had a fragile, fever dream quality to them, soap bubbles floating blithely toward a thorn bush and, when the pain in her legs inevitably worsened, the bubbles burst spectacularly, leaving her with nothing to distract herself.

Escape. Think about that. But her body was shaking so badly that escape seemed like the remotest of possibilities. The biggest obstacle was her feet. Even if she could escape her cell and the guards, she couldn't walk.

Dashi wondered if Idree had heard about her capture. She hoped not. She could tell—both from the fever and the tears of pus oozing from her legs—that her wounds were already infected. If she was lucky, she'd succumb before the torture commenced. The moth-woman's words haunted her waking minutes. *Your screams will echo through New Osb.*

Dashi's fingers knocked into something solid: a chicken bone, leftover from a meal eaten by the cell's previous resident. Even cowed by fever, Dashi snorted. *A chicken dinner?* This was a different kind of prison than the one in Karak City, to be sure. Despite Ese's claims of oversight, she'd subsisted on half-rotten gruel sporadically flung through the bars. Then again, the khan had a special use for most of the prisoners here. He would want to keep them strong for the stitching.

Her fingers shifted down the length of the chicken bone, finding a leg joint on one end and the beginnings of a sharpened point on the other. She thought of the mural of the two travelers, of how they'd kept hoping, kept struggling, despite what they'd lost. Whoever had been in this cell before had not given up. They'd been preparing to escape, either by committing a murder or by committing suicide. *Escape*. Either method was better than waiting to be tortured to death.

Dashi gripped the bone in her right hand—her left arm could no longer move—and began sharpening it against the cell wall, slipping in and out of consciousness as she worked.

The cell door flew open with a crack as the guards entered. They pulled Dashi to her feet and she screamed, falling back to the floor.

"You knew she was injured," one of them admonished the other. He freed Dashi's wrists momentarily, before locking them into a different set of shackles.

"Who cares?"

"Put her over your shoulder...no, the other way."

"I don't want those disgusting things in my face."

"The consul said she's a tricky one. Less chance she can escape if you hold her like that."

"Pshh. Get a look at those feet. She's not going anywhere."

Dashi was thrown over a shoulder, her head flopping near the man's buttocks, her feet throbbing with each jostling step.

"She's small," said the man holding her. "I don't care what they said. I give her two days."

Someone scoffed. "Two days? Look at her. She won't get through one."

Hands grabbed her. "The consul said it was you who broke into the cellar. This is from Kanrik," someone said close to Dashi's ear, just before her feet smacked into a wall. Dashi screamed again, the sound bounding off the walls.

There was an argument behind her, but she couldn't tell what was being said. Finally, after an interminable amount of time, they continued moving again.

"Who's," Dashi coughed wetly, "Kanrik?"

"One of the guards you knocked out. He was turned out of the palace. No horse. No supplies. No clothes. Because he didn't catch you."

Dashi threw up down the back of the guard.

An exclamation of disgust. A snort of laughter.

"Not so mighty and fearsome without a sword, is she?" someone said, giving Dashi's chains another jangle.

The antagonism kept up from there, but Dashi drew inward, hardly hearing it. She could feel the half-sharpened chicken bone—such a sorry excuse for a weapon that she couldn't describe it as such even in her own mind—biting against her palm. Somehow, she'd held on to it.

Use your assets. Your goal is to defeat your opponent, but how will you get there? He'll be bigger than you. Possibly better armed. What's your strategy? It was Baris' voice she heard in her head. Altan, she heard when she was sifting through Purek ruins and artifacts, when she needed reason and logic. Baris' advice always came when she needed to fight.

My assets, she thought. *Surprise. A sharpened chicken bone. My strategy...* Here, she drew a blank. All the normal answers she would have given Baris during their practice sessions—*Gain a better weapon, use the terrain, hide*—didn't seem possible here.

Before the slow churn of her thoughts came up with an answer, the guards brought her into a bright room and, without warning, Dashi was flipped onto her back on a cold slab. Pain shot up her legs and she squeezed her eyes shut. Heavy metal cuffs clicked around her wrists, locking them next to her sides.

There were new voices in this room.

"She's in the worst shape I've seen so far," said a voice, raspy and thoughtful. "The consul won't be happy."

"She was like this when she was brought in."

"What did this to your feet, girl?" the raspy voice asked.

Dashi's eyes slit open. A middle-aged woman with short hair stared down at her, mouth set in a frown. A small pin at her shoulder identified her as a healer.

"Burned," Dashi croaked.

"Not by fire," the healer said. "Something acidic?"

Dashi turned her face to one side, coughing so hard that her back arched against the slab.

The healer's frown lines deepened. "Look at me."

Dashi let her eyelids flutter closed. She owed this woman no explanations and she certainly didn't expect any relief in return. Her pin might say she was a healer, but she still answered to the khan.

The healer placed a hand on Dashi's forehead and then one on her chest, holding them there for the span of several breaths. Then she poked at Dashi's neck and pinched her left arm.

"An unknown toxin," the healer said over her shoulder. Dashi could hear the *scritch* of someone taking notes. "Tissue necrosis."

There was a distinctive wet-earth smell and, even stranger, a purplish glow coming from somewhere behind Dashi's head. She was sure it hadn't been there before, but now it was so bright that she could see it through her closed eyelids.

The healer continued to talk, briskly prodding Dashi at intervals. "Odds of survival are not very high, despite any familial proclivity. Her physical state is severely compromised."

Dashi sighed as a cool cloth was laid across her forehead. She was thinking how she'd done the same thing for her plague-sick mother, pressing wet cloths to her face and neck to break the fever, when suddenly Dashi felt the cloth on her forehead twitch. It wasn't a cloth at all but a hand.

Slowly, she opened her eyes. The guards had stepped back, congregating near the room's door, a scared herd about to bolt. The healer had backed up as well. She stood against the wall, murmuring to her scribe, who continued to scribble furiously.

Dashi raised her gaze, stopping when she found wide, dark eyes and a thick fringe of hair.

Idree. Her lips formed her sister's name, but no sound came out.

Idree shook her head once. Tears streamed down her face.

"If I don't stitch you, she said she'll kill you, Dashi." Idree leaned close, her forehead nearly touching Dashi's. "The healer says you're dying anyway..." Idree swallowed and Dashi could feel her sister trying not to stare at her melted feet. "But relatives of the seamstress have a better chance than others...and...and you're strong, Dashi, I know you are. This," she waved at Dashi's feet, "this can't stop *you*."

"If I—" Dashi broke off in a cough.

"If you survive, you'll be healed. You'll belong to the khan and they'll use you to wind my leash tighter," Idree said calmly. "But..." A tear fell from Idree's face onto Dashi's face. "But at least we'll still have a chance."

"Idree...I don't think..."

"Physical strength is only one aspect," Idree whispered, squeezing Dashi's hand. Her fingers paused over the chicken bone, before gently prying it away. "You'll live. I know you will. You never give up."

Dashi nodded, though in truth she *wanted* to give up. But how could she leave Idree, tear-stained and struggling for composure, doomed to do this for the rest of her life?

There was something she wanted to ask Idree, something about what she'd said that didn't make sense, but analytical thought required too much energy. Dashi settled for staring at her sister's face instead.

Idree held out a hand and one of the guards stepped forward, holding a silver tray. On it, the statuette of Khagan Nuray glared disappointedly down her small golden nose, seeming to stare right through Dashi. Idree picked it up, deftly unscrewed the statuette's head, and dumped its contents into her hand. The golden needle swung around, gliding over Idree's palm until it pointed at her chest. The guard who'd brought the tray took a hasty step backward. Idree's eyes became unfocused, her face slightly slack, as if she hovered on the edge of sleep.

"Try to relax." Her sister's tone was dreamy but impersonal. "It often helps to think of a peaceful time in your life. Can you do that?"

Dashi nodded, though it was a lie. Her mind was fixed on Idree, on this strange turn of events: her arms strapped to a slab, her legs melted into unrecognizable shapes; her sister, towering over her, with magic in hand.

"Good." Idree closed her eyes.

The purple light flared around them, becoming so strong that Dashi had to squint. Still, she kept her eyes open, fixed on her sister's face.

Her sister, who said Dashi could do this.

Her sister, who said they still had a chance.

Her sister, the seamstress.

The needle rose slowly on its own, hovering above Idree's palm, cascading purple sparks. Idree plucked it from the air and, without any ado, pushed the point deep into Dashi's bicep.

It felt as though the needle came with lightning attached. Every nerve in Dashi's body sizzled, each enflaming at the same moment. Her legs and arms jerked. Her throat constricted. A blood vessel burst in her left eye, another in her cheek. Dashi screamed: a long, inhuman wail that didn't stop until she ran out of air.

"Think of a peaceful time in your life and picture yourself there," Idree intoned, while Dashi dragged in oxygen.

This time, Dashi did try. *Really* tried. For a moment she was on Spit's back, his mane snapping in her face, as they raced over the steppe. But the pain was too much, jerking her out of her peaceful world and back into the real one. The needle rose and dove again, its golden tip biting into her flesh without mercy. Dashi's back arched. Her fingernails tried to bite into the slab beneath her, breaking off instead. Again and again, the needle climbed and fell in neat, unflinching strokes.

Each time it felt like a thunderbolt had clawed its way beneath her skin.

As if her body was being turned inside out.

Her skin torn to shreds and stuffed into her chest cavity.

Her organs splayed in disarray.

As if the silver lake from the cavern was being pumped into her veins.

Dashi kept waiting for unconsciousness to pull her into its blissful folds, but it never did.

Chapter 50

Dashi's first clear memory after the stitching was warmth and light and a dull throbbing in her forehead. The headache felt like the aftereffects of too much mead, though she could not recall drinking anything. The light flickering across her closed eyelids lacked the warmth and sound of fire. Sunlight then, probably through a window.

She blinked twice and the room came into focus. She was alone, snuggled into a soft bed. There was a small table, which held a basin and a hand mirror, and two chairs situated in front of a cold fireplace. Tapestries covered the walls, nothing too ornate, but the fact that there were decorations at all was a surprise.

Where was she? The room seemed familiar, but it was difficult to know for sure. She turned her head slowly until her eyes found the confirmation they sought. On the other side of the room hung a triptych of painted wooden panels depicting a crowd of people at a spring. She recognized the piece; she and her friends had brought it back from some ruins along Karakal's northern border.

She was still in New Osb.

Dashi stared at the triptych. The light hit the panels at an angle, highlighting the wood grain beneath the layer of paint, the reason under-girding everything. Ese's words came back to her: *If you have not thought about your sister's historical importance—of your own—it might behoove you to start. I do not believe in coincidences, only connections.* She thought of her sister's face, calm and tear-streaked, as she raised the needle. Did Idree know she was alive, or had they taken Dashi away before she could be sure? And why would they move her at all, away from Idree's other patients? Being singled out, for any reason, made the fine hairs at the back of her neck flame with sensation.

Dashi's eyes, which had been roving in much the same way as her mind, halted again on the single window, alight with the winter sunshine that had woken her in the first place. Dashi sat up fast. *Too fast.* Her headache ratcheted up a notch—or four—and the room teetered precariously on its axis. When it had settled once more, she swung her legs carefully over the side of the bed. She froze there for a moment, looking down at herself. She wore only a thin shift and, below the sleeve, she could see that her left arm was no longer green and black with venom. Her legs, once burned and twisted from the silver lake, were full and familiar again.

She paused, tilting her leg in the sunlight. Her skin had—she considered the right word—a *sheen*. It wasn't a scar; her skin was shiny up the whole length of her leg, not just where she'd been burned. She raised her hand. It, too, gleamed subtly. On a hunch, she banged the side of her leg against the bed frame. Although she'd winced in anticipation, the impact was oddly muted, more pressure than it was pain.

The stitching. She couldn't remember much.

Hot, electrical pain.

The *pop, pop* of blood vessels bursting all over her body.

Virulent purple light, infusing everything from the back of her eyelids to the ends of Idree's hair.

Her sister's steady voice telling her to imagine a peaceful place.

There had been another voice too, both familiar and impossible, asking if Dashi would pull through, demanding to know what she'd done with the seamripper. She'd screamed at that voice, she thought, but she couldn't remember what she'd said. Couldn't remember if she'd admitted that the only thing at the end of the maze was another Purek riddle—a cup, a box and now no one would know what they did or did not contain.

Dashi flexed her hand again, her eyes falling on the hand mirror that lay on the table.

Despite all the changes in her body, walking felt natural, though it did exacerbate her headache. Wonderment over her healed legs warred with dread as she stopped before the table. For a moment, she considered climbing back into the bed and not looking. Then, annoyed at her indecisiveness, she snatched up the mirror and thrust it in front of her face.

Most of her features looked the same: healthy and rested but familiar. Only her eyes were strange. They were black now. *Fully* black. Hundreds of tiny facets glittered like cut gems across their surface.

And her head...*No wonder I have a headache,* Dashi thought, staring at the pair of brown antennae protruding from the crown of her head. Each antenna was segmented—ten segments on each—and covered in bristles. She raised her hand slowly and ran her fingers up the length of one. The bristles were softer than she'd expected. The sensation sent a shiver through her, and the antenna wobbled backward like a frightened colt. Her eyes narrowed in concentration as she tried to move them. They obliged her, sweeping sideways through the air.

Another sensation pulsed around the antennae. Dashi squeezed her eyes shut. She knew someone was there before the door opened. *Had been there earlier,* while she slept off the effects of the stitching. Unexpectedly, she thought of Spit nosing around in search of treats. He never nipped or butted—she'd cured him of those bad habits early on—but even at his most polite, she could always feel the press of his muzzle, concrete despite the fabric between them. The knowledge lay over her like that: a tickling pressure inside her head, indirect but solid.

The door to the room opened. The skin on the back of Dashi's neck tightened.

Breath of the ancestors, Altan said with a chuckle. *If you believe in superstition.*

Breath of the ancestors, Baris said. *Never ignore your instincts.*

Slowly, somehow already knowing who she'd find, Dashi turned and looked at the person standing behind her. The person whose voice she'd heard during the stitching. The person who was supposed to be dead.

As if from another life, she heard Sevlin's voice too. *The wilewing can steal someone's face,* he'd said, *impersonate them so well that even a family member or lover can't tell the difference.* Now she remembered where she'd seen the image of the wilewing, the bird with human features: woven into rich fabric. Her friends had chuckled about it all those years ago, the night Dashi had retrieved the amethyst pendant for Zayaa.

If only the wilewing was real, Dashi thought dazedly. *That would explain this. That would explain how I could have spent years with someone without ever knowing them.*

"The khan ordered that you be moved upstairs where it's warmer. You weren't waking up and he was worried that he was about to lose another herald. I selected the room myself. You were never one for finer things, but I thought you'd appreciate the art if nothing else."

Dashi wanted to scream, to fight, to run. She wanted to demand answers. How? Why? To *Altan*? But when her lips opened, all that came out was a name.

"*Zayaa.*"

Zayaa's smile was perfect white teeth and dimples. An amethyst pendant glittered on a chain around her neck, dazzling and sharp-faceted.

"Dashi," Zayaa said, in the same silky voice Dashi remembered. "You may call me Consul now."

To My Readers...

Thank you so much for reading! Reviews really help drive sales for indie authors like me. If you enjoyed *The Silver Seamripper*, please consider leaving a review so other readers can connect with my work.

Want more Dashi? Get a FREE copy of *Treasure Chest*, a stand-alone short story that bridges books 1 and 2 of The Taiga series. Go to https://BookHip.com/TSJFKXD

Acknowledgements

A heartfelt thank you to everyone who made this writing journey possible. Clare, you have probably read and reread this book as many times as I have. Thank you for your critiques, encouragement and commiseration. To Kdub, Nick, Piper, Katie & Sarah: I am beyond grateful to have you in my corner. Arial & Matt, thank you for reading and for talking shop. Susan, the typos fall beneath your onslaught. Thank you for the extra set of eyes. Peggy, no one reads like you do! I appreciate your excellent (and unbelievably speedy) work.

To my family—Mom, Dad, Dan, Clay, Ty, Ross, C, G & R—I am so fortunate to have you in my life. Thank you for asking after the book. Thank you for proofreading. Thank you for bouncing ideas with me. Thank you for babysitting. Thank you for the countless ways you have supported, formed and empowered me.

Brad, you are, and always have been, my rock. A million times, thank you.

ALSO BY T.J. CARROLL

THE WELLSPRING--ORDER THE THRILLING CONCLUSION TO THE TAIGA SERIES NOW!

After being forced into the khan's deadly race across the taiga, Dashi swore she'd never be anyone's pawn again.

Yet she finds herself imprisoned in a dank cell beneath the khan's fortress, forced once more into the dangerous dance of doing the khan's bidding while trying to save herself and her sister, Idree.

The khan is hellbent on finding the Wellspring, a sacred site from Purek lore thought to hold immense power. Now, Dashi is tasked with

leading the khan safely past the denizens of the taiga and into the grave-
yard of an ancient civilization. And they won't be traveling alone. The
khan will be surrounded by his monstrous heralds—human-animal hor-
rors created by the golden needle's magic—and his new consul, who also
happens to be Dashi's oldest enemy.

Dashi is certain there's more to the Wellspring than the khan's consul
is letting on, but with her own life and her sister's hanging in the balance,
she'll have to tread carefully. If she can unravel the mysteries of the
Wellspring and the consul's true motives fast enough, she might just earn
her freedom. If she can't, the world will never be the same.

About the Author

T.J. Carroll has lived all over but now calls Earth home. When she's not writing, she enjoys hiking, saying she's going to establish a family game night, and lurking in bookstores. The Silver Seamripper is a follow-up to her debut novel, The Golden Needle. She avoids social media but you can find her on Amazon's Author Central.

www.ingramcontent.com/pod-product-compliance
Lightning Source LLC
Chambersburg PA
CBHW020331010826
48973CB00005B/1221